TELL ME YOU LOVE ME

Boys of Riverside

Gracie Graham

For all the ladies looking for their next book boyfriend.

I got you.

CHAPTER 1

BRYNN

I DON'T OFTEN GET my way, but when I do, victory is so much sweeter. Especially when said victory is in spite of enemy number one.

I smile as my mother pulls into the parking lot of Hyde Hall. The tall brick building towers above us, a symbol of new beginnings, fresh starts, and the promise of an amazing four years that will inevitably kick-start my future. I have a whole plan mapped out for myself. Win my roommate over, make a ton of friends, go out, socialize, date, and hopefully find a nice boy to call mine. High school might not have gone as planned, but I'm determined to make college my bitch, and nothing is going to dull my burning optimism. *Nothing.*

Not even Jace Taggart.

I've come to terms with the fact I'm attending the same college as my brother's best friend, but there is zero reason I ever have to see him. Ann Arbor University is a large, sprawling campus with a bustling student life, and nearly forty thousand in attendance. As long as I stay away from the football field, I should be fine. AU is my oyster, and I'm ready to crack it open and find a pearl.

I practically vibrate with excitement as my mother finds a spot in the visitors' lot and turns off the ignition. "Ready?" She glances my way, beaming.

I inhale a steadying breath through my nose and smooth a hand over my blonde hair before I agree. "Ready. I'll just go sign in and tell them I'm here while you text Dad, and then we can unload everything."

"Sounds good." She reaches out and squeezes my hand. "Good luck."

I swing the door open and step out onto the pavement with my sandaled feet and straighten, ignoring the swoop of birds' wings inside my chest. This is it. My chance at independence, a normal life without the fear I've lived with for more than two years.

I cross the pavement, taking in my surroundings as a sense of peace washes over me. The sun is bright in the blue sky. Somewhere in the distance, I hear the faint hum of music. Trees dot the sidewalk and parking lot, their large clusters of white blooms a stark contrast to their dark leaves, while birds sing from their branches.

When I enter Hyde Hall, I find a girl at the desk. She's older than me, probably in her early twenties, and pleasant, but not very chatty. Once she finds my name in the computer and confirms my room assignment, she slides over a key. I take it, along with a list of rules and a flyer about the events going on this weekend for students reporting for the summer semester. When asked if I need help with my stuff, I tell her no and thank her before I spin around, almost running into another girl with dark, chin-length hair and a friendly smile.

"I'm so sorry." I reach out and steady her, only to find a genuine smile in return.

"No, it was my bad," she says, waving off my concern. "Are you a freshman, too?" She eyes the stuff in my hands.

"Yep. Brynn Nichols." I extend a hand for her to shake, and with a grin, she accepts it.

"I'm Charlotte. What room are you in?" she asks, peering down at the slip of paper I'm clutching.

"One-twenty."

"Oh, cool!" Her expression brightens. "That's right across from me and my roommate, Samantha." Then, as if something else occurs to her, her eyes darken like a cloak dropping and she shifts on her feet, her voice noticeably more subdued as she asks, "Have you met your roommate yet?"

"No. Actually, I don't even know if she's here yet."

But if her expression is any indication, maybe I should be worried.

Charlotte nods. "Right. Well, if you need anything or want to go to dinner with us, come knock on our door. I met Samantha in freshman orientation, and we hit it off, so even though

I wasn't friends with her before college, I already know she's pretty cool."

"That'd be great. Thanks," I say, wishing I had made it to freshman orientation, but my father and mother each run their own business and being in the wedding industry means spring and summer are their busiest time of year. Pulling either one of them away in May for orientation would have proved impossible, so unless I wanted to hitch a ride with Jace—I'd rather pluck my eyes out with a dull blade, thank you very much—it meant going into this blindly. Even being here today took preparation and string-pulling on my mother's behalf, and still, her time is limited.

After I wave goodbye, I push any negative thoughts I have aside, and head for the exit with a smile on my face. I've only been here five minutes, and already I can tell Charlotte and I will be fast friends.

Off to a good start.

The balmy morning air kisses my skin as I step back outside and turn for the car. I can hear my mother's voice carrying on the breeze and assume she's on the phone with my father. When I clear the cars on the corner, I fully expect to see her with an ear pressed to her phone. Instead, I freeze.

There is no phone pressed to her ear. She is not talking to my father, or even one of my siblings or an employee. Instead, she's with *him.*

How?

Why?

None other than Jace Taggart is standing in the parking lot of *my* dormitory, schmoozing my mother.

A prickling sensation claws up my spine as I take in my opponent. Armed in a backward baseball cap, a black AU football T-shirt, and athletic shorts that ride low on his hips, he somehow looks fitter than he did the last time I saw him strutting around our house with my brother, like a virus with no cure. It's like he made it his life's mission to gain ten pounds of muscle in my absence so he could show up on move-in day and rub it in my face.

Look at me, I'm all buff and muscular. Whoo!

I grind my molars to dust, watching as he says something to make my mother laugh. A moment later, like the traitor she is, she reaches out and pulls him into a motherly hug, which he reciprocates like he's the prodigal son who's returned home.

Steam erupts from my ears with my rising temperature.

Even my own mother isn't immune to his charms. Then again, she never has been. Of all of my brother's friends, she's always had a soft spot for Jace.

I'm about to combust when Mom pulls away, wiping the moisture from her eyes. Apparently, Jace made her laugh so hard she cried, and I'm not sure what's more annoying: the fact that he is here right now in the first place, or that my mom loves him like her own.

"Oh, there you are, honey," Mom says once she finally stops kissing Jace's ass to notice me standing here. "Look who came to help you move in your things. Isn't that sweet?"

I turn my prickly gaze to Jace, who grins with the knowledge his presence annoys me. "So sweet," I grind out.

"Cupcake," Jace drawls in a way he knows gets under my skin, and it takes everything in me not to chuck my key at his face.

If I hit him square in the eye hard enough, he'd be forced to live out his days like a pirate.

The visual brings me joy.

Unfortunately, all the nicknames I have for him, I can't say in front of my mother, so I just smile with murder in my eyes and press on. "Don't you have somewhere to be? A party? Football practice? Your own apartment? A free clinic on venereal diseases?"

Jace just snorts and steps forward while my mother ignores us, as if our sparring is par for the course. And I guess it kind of is; we've been doing it for the past three years.

A waft of citrus and pine hits me all at once as he steps closer and reaches out to ruffle my long blonde hair like I'm a toddler. I swat him away, which only makes him laugh harder. "You're so cute when you're angry."

I grunt and knife-hand his funny bone before I dance away from him, afraid of retaliation when Mom, who is completely oblivious to our feuding, smiles like this is the cutest interaction she's ever seen. "You ready to get your stuff?"

I nod, knowing she's on a time crunch, and make a beeline for the trunk, but Jace is quicker. He's like Houdini as he swoops in and whips both suitcases out.

"We've got it," I say, motioning for him to hand me the bags. "Mom and I can unload all of this in two trips."

"Nope. I'm nothing if not a gentleman." He winks at my mother who swoons predictably, then grabs my overnight bag and adds it to the mix. "Besides, I promised Teagan I'd look after you while we're here, so that's what I intend to do."

Ah, yes. My ex-twin brother. I remember him well.

The moment Teagan discovered Jace was accepting a scholarship from AU to play football and still allowed me to accept early enrollment, knowing he's my sworn enemy, he became dead to me. Okay, not literally. But I'm still pretty pissed at him, and I take every single opportunity to remind him just how much. But apparently, Jace's presence on campus isn't enough of a punishment. To add fuel to the fire, Teagan made Jace promise he'd watch over me.

Great!

"I'm so glad you're here," my mother says to Jace as I grab a plastic bin from the trunk, then slam it shut. "It's such a comfort knowing Brynn will have a good man here like you to call on if she needs anything."

I scoff, realizing a moment too late I did so out loud. But, seriously, Jace's reputation in high school preceded him. Not only was he well known for his epic parties on his family's property at Crow's Creek, he was also known as one of the biggest players to walk the halls of Riverside High. The boy can't even spell the word monogamous without having a good laugh. Life is one giant joke to him. He doesn't take anything seriously. The closest he comes to commitment is football. So the idea that this man-child is the best candidate to watch out for me is laughable.

My mother shoots me a dirty look while Jace smirks and cocks a brow. Everything I do and say amuses him, apparently.

"It's my pleasure to help your daughter," Jace says with a straight face, like he's a freaking Boy Scout. "I know how wild Brynn can be," he adds, winking at me over her shoulder before the two of them break out into a fit of laughter.

Ha ha. Yeah, laugh it up.

"Yes, my dear Brynn is about as wild as a rake."

My jaw drops as I gape at her. *Roasted by my own mother.*

"Hilarious," I say dryly, as I swing open the doors to the dorms without bothering to hold them open for him. Still, he somehow manages to juggle both suitcases, my overnight bag, and still allow my mother to walk in before him. "I'll have you know, I met my roommate briefly when I was in here, and we've already hit it off, we're so much alike," I lie. "In fact, we got on *so* well, we even made plans to go to a party tonight. It's going to be lit. Totally wild."

Don't oversell!

Jace eyes me like he knows I'm full of shit, but my mom beams like I just told her I've won a Pulitzer. "Really? Oh, that's wonderful, sweetie," she says, giving my arm a little squeeze. She looks as if she's about to say something else when her phone begins to ring, and she checks the screen. "Crap, that's Betty. I have to get this."

I nod for her to take the call and pause at the entrance to the first-floor hallway. Betty is her assistant, which means it's about work.

My hip makes contact with the wall as I lean against it, Jace standing across from me, and we enter into a staring war.

His aqua eyes settle on mine as he focuses on me. When I narrow my eyes, his turn to slits. When I arch a brow, he raises both.

Laughter swims in his irises as if our little battle is the most hilarious thing in the world, and I want to ask him what the hell's so funny when my mother's frantic voice pierces my thoughts.

"Brynn, honey, there's been an emergency with the appetizers for the Pierce wedding." Mom's gaze is slightly wild as she rejoins us. "Apparently, Jay, the summer hire, took the charcuterie cups with him to the shower and they're halfway to Cleveland."

"Mom," I say, reaching a hand out to calm her. "Just go. It's okay."

"Are you sure?" she asks, glancing at the time on her phone. "But I was supposed to have another hour. I wanted to help move you in and get your room set up and meet your roommate and—"

"It's fine. Honestly. Please, go ahead and fix it. You got me here, and that's all that matters. Besides, I've already met my roommate, remember?" I lie again. "It's all good. I can unpack a couple of suitcases and set up a bed on my own."

She chews her lip, and I can sense she's torn between me and her duties, so I smile, doing my best to reassure her. "Seriously, go."

"You're sure?" she asks, eyes searching mine.

"Positive."

"I can help her get settled, Nikki," Jace chimes in, and it takes everything in me to keep the smile on my face.

"That would be wonderful," Mom says, glancing between us. With a sigh, she stretches her arms out and pulls me in for a hug.

Behind her back, I flip Jace the bird.

"Thank you so much for understanding. You call if you need anything. Check in with us tonight, all right? And we'll see you soon?"

I nod and pull away, knowing she won't leave unless I do.

Once she's out of sight, I turn to Jace and drop the smile. "Great. You can go now."

"And break my promise to your mother? Never."

"Oh, yes. I forgot," I say, lugging the plastic bin in my arms down the hallway. "You're so noble."

I pause in front of room 120, suddenly unsure of what the protocol is for entering my dorm for the first time. If my roommate is already here, surely she's expecting me, and it's my room as much as it is hers. But it feels kind of weird to go barging right in. What if she's in the middle of changing, praying, or saying goodbye to family of her own? I don't want to be rude and ruin the moment.

In my peripheral, I can see the pinched set of Jace's mouth at my internal struggle, so I quickly make a decision and stick my key in, waiting until the lock gives before lightly knocking as I push the door open.

I step inside, and my gaze immediately falls on the girl seated on the bed across from me. My eyes widen as I struggle to compose myself and keep the shock I'm feeling from my face. But in truth, what I see is nothing short of terrifying.

She's wearing ripped, black tights under cutoff shorts and a black top with a giant pentagram on the front. A shaved head reveals a tattoo on her skull, but my eyes have no idea what to focus on between that and the multiple piercings in her brow, which appear to be ordinary safety pins. Clutched in her white-knuckled hands, I'm almost certain is some kind of spell book.

I swallow as my gaze darts to the wall behind her, trying to find something positive to focus on, but all I see is a poster with weird symbols taped to the wall I'm not sure I want to know the meaning of. Glass bottles line the top of her dresser, each containing a liquid in varying colors of the rainbow.

I take a single step across the threshold, noting a weird smell permeating the air. Cigarette smoke? Weed? Burning flesh? I have no idea.

I offer her what I think passes for a smile, because underneath it all, I'm sure she's a very nice person.

Her black lipsticked mouth curls into a sneer. "You must be Brynn," she says, and it sounds more like an accusation than a greeting.

I swallow while my heart stutters inside my chest. "Yep, that's me," I say with a half laugh. "And you're Cate?"

She says nothing, just continues to stare.

Behind me, the heat of Jace's breath tickles my neck as he leans into me from behind, whispering, "Mmm-hmm, you're right. I totally see the similarities."

I scowl as I glance at him over my shoulder, then turn and yank my suitcases out of his grubby paws, more than a little irritated he's caught me in a lie.

Looks like there will be no partying with my roommate. Something tells me I wouldn't be able to keep up with whatever shit she's into.

"You did your good deed for the day," I say, my tone dismissive. "You can go now."

Jace cranes his neck so he can see around me. "You sure about that? You sure you don't want me to stay and help with Marilyn Manson here?"

"Nope. I'm good," I say, ignoring the jab as I place my hands on his chest and give him a healthy shove.

It's a testament to how much I loathe him that I'd rather be alone with Satan's love child than spend another minute in his presence. That, and I'm too proud to admit the girl inside petrifies me.

"See you never," I say, then close the door to the sound of his laughter.

Turning around, I take a deep breath and decide to give her the benefit of the doubt. Don't judge a book by its cover and all that.

"So . . ." I say, stepping forward. "You like to read." I motion to the book in her hands. "Cool." When she says nothing, I try again because that wasn't really a question, was it? It was more of an observation. "I actually love to read, too. In fact, I brought a bunch of books I haven't read yet if you ever want to borrow one."

She cocks her head to stare at me some more. She'd do well in a stand-off with Jace.

I clear my throat, trying not to squirm. "They're mostly romance. Do you read romance?"

"Is there death in them?" she asks without blinking.

How is she not blinking?!

"Um, no. Not usually."

She grimaces, as if my answer disappoints her, then turns away from me to lie back on her bed.

I'll take that as a no.

With shaking hands, I turn back to my luggage and place one of the bags on the bed and unzip it. So, maybe I won't hit it off with my roommate and we won't be best buds. So, what?

My phone buzzes in my pocket, so I slide it out and glance at the screen with a frown.

JACE: Still alive? Just wanted to make sure you haven't been sacrificed at the altar.

My grip tightens on the phone as I curse all things Jace Taggart.

CHAPTER 2

JACE

MY NON-RELATIONSHIP WITH BRYNN Nichols can be summed up in two short sentences:

1. She hates my guts.

2. I think she's a hot pain in the ass.

When I found out we'd be attending the same university, I was nothing short of ecstatic. Another four years of getting under her peachy-smooth skin? Sign me up!

Brynn, on the other hand, wasn't so pleased but that didn't stop her twin, Teagan, who also happens to be my best friend, from asking me to look after her in his absence. It's a lot of pressure to put on a man who's supposed to be focusing on football. Brynn is gorgeous, with curves in all the right places, long blonde hair, violet-blue eyes, and a smattering of freckles over her sun-kissed cheeks. I have no doubt douchebags, nerds, and jocks alike will flock to her. Ensuring she's safe and smart will be a full-time job. As if I'm not already under enough pressure to perform on the field, I have to do my due diligence for Teagan, as well.

In high school, he'd been particularly protective of her, bordering on overprotective, and somehow this torch has been passed on to me. But I can't help but wonder if I'm the best man for the job as I try and erase the image of her perfect ass from my head.

Still, Teagan's parting words when I spoke to him on the phone just this morning jangle inside my brain like a creaky wind chime. *I'm counting on you, brother.*

So of course, I showed up to make sure she got in okay. But what I didn't expect was for me to worry about her afterward.

Emotions where women are concerned aren't really my thing.

I glance behind me as I dial Teagan's number, half expecting Brynn to come running down the hall any second and beg me not to go, before I snort at the image because Brynn would rather drown in her own spit than admit she needs my help.

"Yo! Spoke to my mom briefly," Teagan answers without preamble. "She said Brynn got there okay, but she had to leave you to move her in. Thanks for that, man."

"Yeah, about that," I drawl. "Her roommate's a freak," I say, eyeing the hot brunette at the front desk. I briefly wonder if she's a student.

"Fuck. Seriously?" Teagan's voice brings me back to the matter at hand.

"Seriously."

"How bad we talking?"

I exhale as I rake a hand through my hair. "I'm talking, Marilyn Manson roadie kind of shit. Quite frankly, I didn't even talk to the girl, and she scares the crap out of me."

"Damn." Teagan sighs. "I know how excited Brynn was to meet her and was really hoping for the best. How did Brynn react?"

"How Brynn always reacts." I shrug even though he can't see me. "Her stubborn ass acted like she was bunking with Pollyanna, then sent me on my way."

"You left her?" he asks, sounding upset, and while I don't blame him, what the hell does he want me to do about it?

"Yeah, I left her," I say, hearing my defensive tone. "She practically pushed me out the door. What was I supposed to do? Handcuff myself to the bed?"

Fuck, now there's a visual.

Head out of gutter, dickhead. She's your best friend's sister. Even if she is hot.

"Don't be so dramatic. I just worry about her. She really wants this to go well. I hate to think she's off to a bumpy start already. Listen, I don't wanna get into it, but she . . . went through some stuff in high school. Something other people don't know about, so she needs this to go well. And I just hate to think something might happen when I'm not around to help her."

I frown.

I have no idea what he's talking about, but because I can hear the concern in his voice, and because I'm the best fucking friend in the world, I decide to throw him a bone and ease his suffering. "Listen, no need to worry, okay? I'll have some people at Hyde Hall keep an eye and ear out for me. If there's any problems or weird shit with the roommate, or any dudes are hounding her, I'll be the first to know."

"You can do that?"

I scoff. "Who do you think you're talking to? Of course I fucking can."

Teagan laughs. "Shouldn't have doubted you for a second. Thanks, man."

"Any time. Get your shit unpacked and don't worry about your sister," I say, knowing today is moving day for him, too. Cumberland University is a Big Ten school, same as AU, so he'll have his work cut out for him.

I hang up and push off the wall, heading to the front desk, and plaster a charming smile on my face as I approach the hot brunette.

"Can I help you?" she asks.

"Maybe." I grin and lift my chin. "Tell me your name."

"Demanding, aren't we?"

"Always."

She quirks a brow, but smiles and says, "It's Andrea."

"Andrea, give me your number."

She laughs. "Are you new?"

I lean over the counter, invading her personal space. "How'd you know?"

"Because I'm a resident adviser. I recognize most of the kids from this dorm."

"Still didn't answer my question, though." I smile, turning up the charm.

"Do you form all your questions as commands? Because I'm not sure how my boyfriend would feel about me giving another boy my number."

"Damn." I snap my fingers. "The good ones are always taken."

"*Please*," her eyes glitter with amusement, "I saw you talking with that pretty blonde when you came in."

I arch a brow. "So, you admit you noticed me?"

Her cheeks pinken, but she plays it off with a roll of her eyes. "Hard not to notice."

"You flatter me," I say, pressing a hand to my chest. "Speaking of people who are hard not to notice, you know the girl in room one-twenty? She's a little different . . . alternative?"

"Oh, you mean Creepy Cate?" Her eyes widen like the moon.

"That'd be the one. You see, my friend is rooming with her"—Andrea winces—"and she's about as straitlaced and innocent as they come, so I'm a little worried about her since she's practically like a sister to me." I lie just in case this chick decides to give me her digits after all. "Do you think you could keep your eyes and ears open for any trouble? Let me know if you hear of anything concerning, or if you find out she's causing problems?"

"Sure, I could do that."

"You're a doll," I say, pleased to see her cheeks flushed.

Sliding the visitor sign-in sheet out from in front of her, I scribble my name and number on it, then slide it back.

"You know, I think it's kinda sweet, you looking out for her."

"Well, I try, Andrea." I tap the clipboard. "Here's my number, in case you hear anything." Then I take a step back. "And also, in case you change your mind, or something happens to your boyfriend," I say with a wink, and then I turn and leave.

Problem solved.

CHAPTER 3

JACE

THE BREATH HEAVES IN and out of my lungs like the rhythmic lashing of a whip.

"We are proud," Coach Greene barks. "We are not just a team. We are bound by a common goal, excellence on and off the field." Coach pauses on the sidelines, watching as we shift from skaters to squat thrust jumps. "What is our goal?" he shouts.

"Excellence, sir!" I yell along with everyone else.

Sweat drips in my eyes. I'm convinced somewhere in a third-world country, squat thrust jumps must be used as a torture device for gathering intel.

"Training is the heartbeat of our success. It's not just about physical strength; it's about mental resilience, discipline, and the relentless pursuit of greatness," Coach continues. "Every drill, every sprint, every moment of sweat and effort is an investment in yourself. Your teammates. And your dreams."

The blow of the whistle pierces through the thumping heart in my chest. If it beats any harder, it might break my rib cage.

A collective groan moves through the field.

Several guys collapse into the fetal position on the turf while others moan and stand, stumbling into one giant congealed mass in front of Coach.

I straighten on rubbery legs, only bending forward at the waist for a moment to catch my breath. In front of us, Coach watches on like a sentinel, ready to lead his army to battle. Only there's no war to be fought. Not yet.

It's only summer conditioning and our first week, but apparently, instead of easing us into things, the coaches at AU prefer to throw you into the fire. The beginning of the week, we trained mostly in the weight room, but today is our first day on the field.

Coach's gaze slowly slides over each one of us as he stands in front of us, his hands on his hips. "Football is a game of inches, but it's also a reflection of character. It's about pushing our limits, supporting our teammates, and learning from every victory and defeat. In the weight room, on the practice field, and in the classroom, we cultivate not just athletes but leaders who carry the spirit of our institution with them."

He starts to move again, pacing the turf in front of us while sweat drips in my eyes. "Now is not the time to settle for mediocrity. Success is not given; it is earned through dedication, sacrifice, and a relentless work ethic. The pain of training is temporary, but the pride of accomplishment lasts a lifetime, which is why we're not going to take it easy on you. It's not our job to baby you. If you want someone to wipe your ass, ask your mother or your girlfriend. Otherwise, we're here to create winners. Athletes. Men who don't quit."

He pauses, his gaze landing on me, and I swallow. "Let this season be your commitment to excellence. Let our actions on and off the field speak louder than words. And together, as a united front, we will overcome challenges, celebrate victories, and leave a legacy that future generations will look up to."

Coach grins, and the expression is so startling on his stern, old face, it makes me stand taller, straighter. "You had a damn good first week, boys. Welcome to Griffins football."

He waves his clipboard out in front of us and says, "Now get your smelly asses in the shower, and I'll see you bright and early on Monday."

Thirty minutes later, I sling my duffle bag over my shoulder and step out from under the cover of the stadium into the mid-day sun and run a hand through my damp hair. My roommate, Chris, one of our running backs, walks beside me. He's headed to a family function off campus, while I have plans to sleep for a month.

My phone buzzes in the pocket of my athletic shorts, so I slide it out to see a FaceTime call from Teagan. Accepting the call with a swipe of the finger, I nod to Chris. "Catch ya later, man," I say, then focus on the small screen as Teagan comes into view. "What's up?"

I make my way to a nearby bench and sink down onto the wooden slats with a groan as my muscles protest. If I feel like this now, I can only imagine what I'll feel like tomorrow. "Fuck. I thought Graham used to kick our asses with the conditioning he made us do in the summer," I say referring to our high school team captain and good friend back home. "But that's nothing compared to this. It's only been one week, and I'm spent."

Teagan grunts. "Tell me about it. Today was brutal here, too."

"I've never been happier for the weekend in my life. Normally we train on Saturdays, but he's giving us tomorrow off as a welcome gift."

Between weight lifting three to four days a week, conditioning runs, speed and skill training, and player-sanctioned practices, my summer is going to be anything but relaxing. Not to mention the humanities class I'm taking to lighten my load in the fall.

"I feel you," Teagan says. "But I don't care how tired I am. It's Friday, and I'm going out. There's this chick in my women's studies class—"

"Bro, what? You're taking women's studies?"

Teagan's smirk spreads over the screen. "I'm surrounded by a classful of hot chicks. Trust me, I'm no dummy."

"Leave it to you to pick girls up in a women's lib class."

"Hey, I'm all about women's rights. Including their right to ask me out and explore their sexuality."

I snort. "Nice. I see the appeal. But doesn't playing college ball alone help you pick up chicks? I swear, every girl I've met here who finds out I play football is immediately interested. Not that they weren't before."

Teagan snickers. "You've always been a cocky bastard."

I spread my arm over the top of the bench as a soft trill of laughter drifts toward me.

I'd know that sound anywhere.

Sure enough, when I glance to my right, I find Brynn standing outside the liberal arts building. Despite being rather modest, the white sundress she wears showcases her curves. It ties at the shoulders and cuts just above her knees, revealing slender, tan legs, and sandaled feet.

My gaze shifts to the person on the receiving end of the conversation and I scowl. The dude—whoever he is—is smiling like a dope, and I don't miss the way his gaze falls to Brynn's breasts before meeting her eyes again.

My hand grips the phone tighter when he says something else to make her laugh, and this time, she tips her head back, her long blonde locks spilling over her shoulders. My frown deepens, and I have half a mind to storm over there and ask her what the hell is so funny and who this guy is.

Tearing my gaze away from her, I glance back down at the phone in my hand, but find it difficult to keep my gaze focused because everything about Brynn begs for my attention.

Why the fuck am I so territorial?

"Sorry. What were you saying?" I ask Teagan, aware I'd totally zoned out.

"I asked how Brynn was."

My traitorous gaze slides back to her, and the sharp stab in my loins feels anything but brotherly.

Get a hold of yourself, Taggart.

"Oh, uh . . ." I clear my throat, fighting the urge to run a hand down my face. "She's good, I guess. I haven't heard anything more about her roommate Cate, so that's a good sign. Haven't you talked to her? Is she still icing you out?"

Ever since Brynn found out I accepted a deal at AU, she's been pissed at Teagan for not telling her.

"She's slightly frigid, but thawing." Teagan shrugs with a grin. "She'll get over it. How about you? Has she poisoned the water supply at the athlete apartments yet?"

I bark out a laugh. "It's only been a week. Give it time. I thought she was going to claw my eyes out when she saw me standing by your mom's car on moving day."

And I haven't seen her since until today. I'm starting to think that's a good thing, considering her reaction. "Eh, she'll get over it. I'm just glad you're there with her. Makes it a lot easier to focus on school and football knowing you're there if she needs anything."

"I've got your back," I say, feeling the sticky remnants of guilt about the fact that I haven't bothered to personally check on her all week. Another glance to my right and she's still talking to the douchebag with the wandering eyes. "Actually, I see her now, so I'm going to check in."

Teagan chuckles. "Want me to stay on the line for backup?"

I shake my head, a smirk curling the corners of my mouth. "Nah. I got this bro. Talk to you later."

"Later."

I hang up and shove the phone in my pocket as I stand and make my way over to where they're standing, sliding an arm around Brynn's shoulders, and appreciating the flicker of surprise in the douche's eyes when he sees me. "Hey, Brynn." I nod toward the guy. "Who's your friend?"

She stiffens beneath my arm, and I can feel her gaze hot on the side of my face as her eyes bore into me. The guy shuffles on his feet, glancing up at me with a nervous gleam in his eyes while I stare at him like a psycho without blinking.

Good. He should be nervous.

"Uh, I'm Stanley?" he says, more like a question than a statement. Then he stretches a hand out for me to shake. "I'm in Brynn's Intro to Psych class."

I stare down at the outstretched hand, my smile tight, until he drops it and shifts his gaze back to Brynn with a frown. "I thought you said you don't have a boyfriend?"

"I don't," she snaps, trying to shove me off her, but I'm a concrete pillar: made of stone, unmovable.

"And you were just discussing . . .?" I ask.

Stanley clears his throat. "Uh, a couple of my buddies from Psi Delta are going to Bradd's tonight. It's a nightclub just off campus."

Interesting.

I glance down at Brynn with an expression that says, *Really, Brynn, a frat guy?*

Stepping to the side, she shrugs out from under my arm.

"You're not going," I say and immediately see I've said the wrong thing.

Her eyes round, and I know without asking that if she never had any intentions of going to Bradd's before, she's now planning on it. "I'm sorry, but last I checked, you've got no say in my social life."

"Um, who are you?" Stanley flicks a finger between us.

"This overbearing ogre is my brother's best friend," Brynn says between clenched teeth.

"Your brother's best friend?" My brows lift, and I turn to face her fully now. "Brynn . . ." I grip my chest. "I've known you for years, spent more time at your house than my own, and *that's* the introduction I get? That's cold, even for you."

"Don't you have somewhere to be? Like practice or class?"

I rock back on my heels. "Just came from there, so I've got all day."

Brynn narrows her eyes, but rather than argue further, she huffs and turns back around to face *Stanley,* but his gaze is focused solely on me.

I have to say, not a great sign for Brynn.

"You're on the football team?" Stan asks.

"I'm a wide receiver." I tip my chin to him. "You a football fan?"

"Hell, yeah. Are you the new guy we got from Ohio? Taggart?"

I smirk, finding it fucking hilarious he knows who I am, especially because I know it'll annoy the shit out of Brynn. "The one and only."

Brynn scoffs.

"I've heard you're damn good. We're supposed to have the best team we've had in years."

"Hell yes, we are," I confirm, slapping his offered hand.

Stan beams. "Well, hey, if you're not busy, we'll be at Bradd's around ten. It's right off Alma Drive. It's a good time if you wanna come."

"Did Brynn say she was going?"

Stan shrugs and winks at her. "She's supposed to make it, yeah."

I want to rip his eyeballs out.

Instead, I cross my arms over my chest, my face a mask of cool indifference. "Then I'd love to join you."

"Great." Stanley starts to back away, pointing. "See you tonight?"

I'm pretty sure he's directing his question to Brynn, but his gaze flickers between us and whatever gesture Brynn makes must be confirmation because he nods and turns, leaving me alone with her.

Several seconds pass before she spins around to face me, arms crossed over her chest, ready for battle. I meet her combative expression with an arched brow as I hook a thumb in his direction. "That guy? Really, Brynn?"

"Oh, I'm sorry. Is he not jock enough for you?" she says in a mocking tone, then pokes a spindly finger in my chest. "You are *not* going to that club."

My smile tightens as I wonder why the hell she doesn't want me there, other than her obvious hatred. "Well, if I'm not going, then neither are you."

She scoffs. "I'm sorry, but I don't think that's how this works. Just because you made some misguided promise to Teagan, doesn't mean you get to tell me what to do." Her eyes slide up and down my body from head to toe and I wonder if it's supposed to intimidate me or turn me on. The former is hilarious, the latter is trouble. "You're not my brother, Jace, and I don't need you watching after me."

I shrug. "Maybe I just wanna go and dance. Have some fun."

"Whatever." She rolls her eyes so hard I fear for her eyesight. She makes a move to brush past me, but I grab her elbow, noting how soft her skin is, like silk.

The hell?

I drop my hand like it's on fire. "You don't even know that guy." I point in the direction Stan left.

She huffs out a breath, half incredulity, half laugh. "Girls go out at college all the time, Jace. I'm not the first."

"Maybe. But you never went to any of our parties in high school. You're inexperienced and naive—"

"Stop talking to me like I'm a child!"

I bite my tongue, staring into her violet eyes. The truth is, even though she and Teagan are really close, she didn't hang out with us much. Maybe a few times freshman year, and then some time during our sophomore year, she became sort of a recluse, either hanging with different people or not at all. I never understood the change. But I do know she didn't party in high school, which has me worried that she'll make poor choices because she doesn't know better. I don't want her going buck wild and doing something she regrets.

I sigh and step forward, forcing her to tip her head back so she can look me in the eyes. "I'm sorry, but it's only been a week and I don't like the idea of you going to some club alone with a guy named fucking Stan, who you barely know. Especially when there will be alcohol."

"His name is Stanley," she seethes.

"Whatever." I wave her away like his name is inconsequential. "I know what drunk guys at parties want."

"Oh, I have no doubt you do. Better than most, in fact."

I ignore her statement, refusing to acknowledge the insinuation behind her words. "You need supervision."

Her jaw tightens, the muscle flickering in her cheek. "And who said I was going alone? Not that it's any of your business, but Charlotte's going with me."

My brows rise. I have no idea who Charlotte is, but I'm glad it's not Creepy Cate. Now that would be a reason to worry.

"Well, then you won't mind if I go, too. I mean, what's one more friend? All I've done is train all week and I could use a break. My social life is feeling a little *dry*."

"What you really mean to say is that your bed is empty." She makes a gagging sound.

I grin. "That, too."

"Whatever." She holds a hand up. "Spare me the details." Adjusting the bag on her shoulder, she takes a step back. "Just stay out of my way Taggart, and I'll stay out of yours."

CHAPTER 4

BRYNN

I T'S BEEN A WEEK since summer classes at Ann Arbor started, and one week since the cute boy, Stanley, in my Psychology class worked up the courage to finally talk to me. So of
course—*of-freaking-course*—the day he finally asks me out, Jace
is here to witness it.

At least, I *think* he asked me out. I don't know. Does asking
a girl to meet him at a nightclub constitute a date?

Hell if I know. It's not like I have much experience to draw
from. My social life in high school was virtually nonexistent.
Either way, Stanley wants to spend time with me outside of
class, which feels like a win. Or at least it did. Until Jace reared
his creepily symmetrical face.

I groan at the thought of him actually showing up tonight.
It would be just my luck to find a boy I'm finally interested in,

only for Jace to helicopter like some kind of pseudo brother and ruin it.

When I found out a few months ago that we'd be attending the same college—both starting in the summer, no less—I wanted to absolutely throttle Teagan for not telling me. My brother is well aware of how I feel about his best friend. No way he didn't know Jace was planning to sign with the Griffins when I decided on Ann Arbor University. In fact, I'm willing to bet money on the fact that he not only knew, but he *liked* that he'd have someone to watch over me while I'm here, so he deliberately kept quiet.

Jace and I have an especially volatile relationship. Everything is always a joke to him. Particularly me. He's a womanizer, a certified player who treats girls like a new pair of shoes he can try on for size and discard when they don't quite fit. Or worse, breaking them in only to get rid of them because he finds a new pair he likes better. He's entertained more girls than I can count, yet he's never, not once, even come close to having a relationship with any of them.

I loathe him, yet he seems to be everywhere, always in my face.

During the last four years of high school, if Jace wasn't hanging with Teagan and their group of friends, he was coming over to our place. He infiltrated family dinners, holidays, birthdays, long weekends, and Sundays in the fall; his massive body sprawled out on our couch, watching football with my brother and father.

And through all of it, he continually found a way to get under my skin, latching on like a gnarly burr. It's as if he must fuel some constant desire to ensure I'm keenly aware of his presence.

Just like now.

Surely, he has better things to do with his time than to police his best friend's twin sister. He certainly did in high school.

I cut through the Language Arts building, taking the short-cut to my dormitory, since I'm done with my only class for the day. The walk is short. It only takes five minutes, and I find myself thanking God for small miracles that the athletes live in a separate building. The only thing worse than attending the same university as Jace Taggart would be living in the same dormitory.

Once I reach my door, I try the knob to find it unlocked, and when I step inside, Cate is there, watching some sort of slasher film. Rather than try and make small talk or act like she doesn't creep me the hell out, I drop my bag and make a three-sixty out of there. Crossing the hall, I knock on Charlotte's door, then pop my head in to find her sitting at her desk, a pair of noise-canceling headphones over her ears. It's not until I step inside, and she catches the movement out of the corner of her eye, that she turns my way and slides them down so they encircle her neck like a wreath.

I may not have won the roommate lottery, but what I lack in Creepy Cate, I gained when I met Charlotte and her roommate, Samantha.

She smiles at me, brown hair bobbing when she turns to fully face me as I move further inside the room. "Hey, chica." She smiles. "How was your morning? Did you talk to Stan the Man?" She waggles her brows and pulls her legs up onto her chair, tucking them underneath herself.

All week, I'd been regaling the girls about the hot boy in Psychology.

"He actually asked me out."

Charlotte squeals and kicks her legs out from under her. "Yaaasss, girl! Of course he did." She motions up and down my body. "What's not to like?"

I can't help but grin at her enthusiasm as I plop down on her bed.

This is what having real girlfriends feels like. Not the stand-ins I had in high school.

"Well, before you get too excited. It's not really a *date* date. He invited me to Bradd's with his friends."

Charlotte's eyes widen. "The nightclub just off campus?"

"Yep. I mean"—I screw up my face—"it's close enough to a date, right?"

"Absolutely. It's the college version of dating."

"Regardless, no way am I going to a club alone, so you better not have plans because you're 100 percent coming with me."

Charlotte beams. "You think he has any cute friends?"

"I'm certain he has cute friends. His frat brothers are going to be there, and I've seen him talking to them on campus."

"I love me some hot sophomore frat boys," she croons, which makes me laugh. "Now that we have our plans for the evening settled, I'm going to grab an early lunch." She slaps her hands on her thighs and gets to her feet. "You in?"

"Nah. I'm good. I ate a bagel right before class. I think I'm just going to hang out for a bit. Mind if I stay here instead of my room?"

"Is Cate being creepy?" I flash her a look that says, *What do you think?* "Want me to bring you anything back?"

I shake my head no as she grabs her meal card and room key, then heads out, saying hello to some of the girls down the hall on her way.

With a sigh, I settle down on her bed and slide my phone out of my pocket, scrolling through a string of unanswered texts. One of them is from one of the girls back home asking for an update, and I can't help but feel a small pang of guilt at the absence of emotion. It's not that I don't miss any of my friends from Riverside, I do, but I'd be lying if I said I hadn't kept them at arm's length. I never really got close to any of them, not in the way I wish I could have. Not like other girls. I didn't have sleepovers on the weekends or FaceTime to pick out our outfits for school. I didn't go shopping at the mall with girlfriends or order pizza and hang out at parties. It's hard to let loose and get close to someone when you're harboring what feels like a massive secret—when you feel more like a stranger to them than a friend.

And now that I'm gone, well . . . leaving Riverside felt a lot like closing a chapter on my life, one I knew I wouldn't exactly miss. It was like the moment I left, a door closed and another one opened. One I actually wanted to step through.

Ann Arbor is my chance at a new life, a fresh start. Leaving Riverside meant putting everything that happened there in the rearview mirror. It was the last bit of closure I needed to fully and finally move on. No more living in fear. No more hiding. No more pretending that nothing ever happened while everyone around me thrived.

Though that long-ago night during sophomore year seems like a lifetime ago, as long as I stayed in Riverside it would forever haunt me. It would always be in the back of my mind like a nightmare I can't shake. I've relived those moments in my dreams more times than I can count. And I was tired of wondering who *he* was. The fear that followed me left me exhausted, a shell of the person I used to be. For a long time, I was always looking over my shoulder. I jumped at the slightest touch. And the only way around it was to withdraw and slowly build armor around myself.

But it's not like that here. I can do anything, be anyone.

I can make friends and date without anxiety. When I meet a boy who shows an interest, I won't have that crippling doubt it could secretly be *him*. I can finally breathe again, truly *live*.

I may not have had the high school experience I wanted for myself, but I can have the college experience I've always dreamed of. And I'll be damned if I let Jace ruin it for me.

I laugh as I pull yet another garment out of my wardrobe and Charlotte grimaces. It's rare Cate leaves our room, but when she does, I totally take advantage. "What's wrong with this one?" I ask, staring at the yellow sundress.

"I mean, it's super cute," Charlotte says, giving me side-eye, "for a Sunday church dress."

I narrow my eyes at her before I turn my attention back to the dress. Okay, so maybe the hem is a little long for clubbing. But it's flowy and loose and comfortable . . .

My shoulders slump as I toss it on the bed with the other rejects. "Okay, you're right. Do I have nothing suitable to wear?"

"I mean, nothing that's club-worthy. Don't you have any cute tank tops or anything?"

I turn back to my wardrobe and stare into the black pit of clothes, already knowing the answer to her question. My garments aren't completely hopeless. I have plenty of cute things: tons of super cute sweaters and leggings, jeans, and flowy summer dresses, but none of them show much in the way of skin or are what most would consider conventionally sexy. Instead, they're feminine and modest, a product of not wanting to draw attention to myself.

When I went shopping to prepare for the summer semester here, I only bought a few new things, focusing on fun items for my dorm room instead. But now, I regret not taking the time to pick out more clothes.

How can I have a clean slate when I'm working with the same material? Clothes are a reflection of one's person, and if I want to date and flirt and have fun and act like a *normal* eighteen-year-old, dressing like a schoolteacher isn't doing me any favors.

"How about this?" Charlotte jumps up from her chair and darts across the hall. After a few seconds, she returns from her own wardrobe holding a silk purple bodysuit with thin straps and a plunging neckline. "And you can pair it with these," she says, crossing the room and snagging my dark skinny jeans—the tightest ones I own—off the hanger. "Add those black strappy sandals you have with the heels, and Stan the Man isn't going to know what hit him."

I cock my head, eyeing the outfit Charlotte holds out in front of herself. My gut reaction is to say no way. Charlotte is shorter than me with a smaller chest, which means the stretchy fabric will fit like a second skin, with a neckline that'll show far more boob than I'm comfortable with. I hate drawing attention to myself, particularly attention to my body, but I also know this is a hurdle I need to get over. I'm done hiding myself away like the fine china my mother only ever dusts off for holiday meals. I want to be bold. Comfortable in my skin. I want to feel free to wear whatever the hell I want just because I can, even if it's only to make myself feel good.

I want Stanley's jaw to drop when he sees me.

So, I snatch the outfit from Charlotte's grip and grin. "It's perfect."

Thirty minutes later, we walk through the doors of Bradd's, and I want to turn right back around. I'm so intimidated. Music blasts through the small club. It's crowded, and from the looks of it, the demographic is fairly young, spanning from college-aged to mid-twenties. Other than the crowded dance floor, everyone is dispersed around the club with the majority of people at the bar or standing in groups. A small sprinkle of patrons are seated at the tables flanking the perimeter.

I take a step further inside, trying to ignore the ball of nerves fisting in my gut as my eyes scan the room in search of Stanley. The bar is closest to us with the dance floor on the opposite end, but I see no sign of him when I check my phone and read his text. "He says they're standing off to the left at the far end of the bar."

"Is that them?" Charlotte points.

I turn, glancing to where she's pointing at the same time I slide my phone back into my pocket, and freeze. "You've got to be freaking kidding me."

I see red. My vision blurs with fire pumping through my veins, because Jace is already here, and by the looks of it, he's somehow become BFFs with Stanley and his friends in the short amount of time they've likely been here.

From the corner of my eye, I see Charlotte's frown. I'm sure she's wondering why I look like I could skin a cat, but I don't address her dubious expression because I'm too busy trying to burn holes through the side of Jace's face with my eyes.

Of all the ways I thought about starting my night off, having to face Jace the moment I walked through the doors was not one of them.

"Okay, did I miss something?" Charlotte says from beside me, breaking our silence. "Because you look furious. Is he talking to another girl?" she asks, craning her neck as though she's missing something.

"Nope. No girl," I say between clenched teeth. "He's just consorting with the enemy, that's all."

"Oh." Her eyes brighten and she takes a closer look. "Is your brother's friend here, the one you told me about? Which one is he?"

I'd already filled both Charlotte and Samantha in on my drama with Jace, but they have yet to meet him, so I point. "The really tall one with dark hair. He's wearing black."

Charlotte's eyes round. "The hot one with the muscles?" When I merely nod, my jaw tight, she continues, "Holy, cheese on rice, you didn't tell me he was *that* good-looking."

I shrug, annoyed with her fawning. "I mean, some girls might consider him attractive, but let's not get carried away."

"He's one of the hottest men I've ever seen."

I shoot her a glare, then motion to the corner of her mouth. "You have a bit of drool."

She smacks me, then inhales, chest puffing. "Okay, I'm good. Sorry. I just wasn't prepared for"—she waves a hand in his direction—"*all that.* But now that I've acclimated, why is he talking to Stanley?"

"Apparently, Jace thinks just because I had zero social life in high school, I should be a nun at college, too." My mouth flattens into a grim line. "But if he thinks I'm going to let him ruin my good time by policing me, he's got another think coming. Come on." I grab her arm and yank her toward them, reminding myself why I'm here. I'm Brynn Nichols, and this is my chance at a fresh start, to be the girl I want to be.

Several heads lift as we approach. Stanley's eyes meet mine and he smiles at the same time his gaze sweeps appreciatively over me from head to foot. If the glimmer in his eyes means anything, he likes what he sees. While I bask in the attention, I note the widening of Jace's eyes as he takes me in. And while I shouldn't care what he thinks—only Stanley's opinion matters, since he's the one I'm trying to impress—I can't help but feel a little stab of victory at his reaction. Anyone else might miss the way his nostrils flare slightly as he homes in on the swell of cleavage above my neckline, or the way his blue eyes heat like liquid sapphire as his gaze drifts down the length of my legs in the skintight jeans, all the way to the strappy sandals on my feet.

But I do.

I notice everything.

Whether I like it or not, I'm finely tuned to the emotional responses of Jace Taggart.

"Brynn." Stanley steps in and wraps me in a hug, crushing my chest to his, and I'm immediately engulfed in the cloying scent of his cologne.

After he releases me, he steps back, holding my hands at arm's length. "You look . . ." He shakes his head, his eyes flickering over me once more. "Amazing."

I smile, feeling the heat of a blush rise to my cheeks as someone I'm almost positive is Jace scoffs to my left. "Thanks. You, too," I say, meaning it. His thick blond hair is combed to the side, and he's wearing a polo and jeans that I'm almost certain hug his ass to perfection. If only he'd turn around.

I motion to my right where Charlotte waits. "Um, everyone this is Charlotte. Charlotte, this is Stanley."

I watch as Stanley gives a little wave, then begins to introduce his friends at the same time a deep baritone rumbles through my chest from behind. "Can I speak with you for a moment?"

I shiver. I don't need to turn to see it's Jace hovering over my shoulder. "Nope. I'm good."

"Excuse us." Jace's hand clamps down on my arm as he flashes Stanley a smile and pulls me to the side, away from everyone else.

I yank my arm from his grip. "What the hell do you think you're doing?" I hiss.

"*Me?* I can ask the same thing of you." He waves a hand toward me, his aqua eyes deepening to a sapphire color. "For starters, I'd like to know what the hell you're wearing."

"It's a top and jeans, Jace, not a micro mini and thigh-high boots." I roll my eyes and cross my arms over my chest, which is a mistake. It's meant to be a move of defiance—annoyance—but I'm not sure the message is properly conveyed when my boobs practically burst from the top, drawing Jace's gaze like a bullseye.

Twin flames of blue heat flare to life in his eyes. "Nice," he snarls. "Your tits are practically on display."

My cheeks burn, but I won't let him get to me. I have nothing to be ashamed of for wearing a sexy top, so I keep my arms crossed, though a quick glance south confirms I'm practically spilling out of it.

Swallowing, I force myself to remain as I am, refusing to validate him by readjusting myself or uncrossing my arms. "My boobs look amazing. And if you don't like it, why don't you stop staring at them?" I quirk a brow, enjoying the way his jaw clenches. The muscle in his cheek flickers with the movement as he shifts his gaze and meets my eyes while I try to find something of his to critique.

He's wearing a black shirt that hugs a firm chest I'm all too familiar with from the countless times I've seen him shirtless around our house. The soft cloth strains at the biceps and cuts at his tapered waist, and it pisses me off how good he looks in a simple T-shirt and jeans. How effortless it seems.

"You shouldn't be wearing that," he says, drawing my gaze back to his. "It's only going to draw the kind of attention you don't need. Stan might get the wrong fucking idea."

I step closer, closing the distance between us, forcing Jace to look down at me while I allow my gaze to fall to his mouth. "Maybe I *want* him to get the wrong idea," I whisper.

His brows rise to his hairline, and I grin at his surprise, before I turn around and head back to where Stanley waits, a small frown on his lips. "Sorry about that," I say. "He clearly thinks his position as my brother's best friend gives him this completely unnecessary obligation to look out for me in his absence."

"*Ah.*" Stanley's expression immediately softens. "I totally get it. I have two sisters, and if they looked like you," he says, his eyes raking over me, "well, I'd be nervous, too."

I chuckle politely, then smile as we rejoin his group of friends, glad to see Charlotte fitting right in. Since most of them are sophomores, they fill us in on what campus life is like in the fall and regale us with stories of past frat parties, insisting we go to the one they're having in a couple weeks. I'm listening to them discuss pledging when a warm palm finds the small of my back, followed by Stanley's voice as he leans in to my ear.

"I can't take my eyes off you," he whispers.

A smile stretches across my face as my cheeks heat, and I realize how good it feels to be wanted and to allow myself to want someone back after so long.

"Promise me a dance tonight?" he asks.

"I can arrange a dance," I say, my stomach doing a little flip. The last time I danced with a boy was Sadie Hawkins sophomore year . . .

"Just watch your toes," Jace interrupts, practically stepping between us. He's so close he could be my shadow. "This one, here, has two left feet.

I scoff. "I do *not*."

"You totally do." He smirks.

I glare up at him, my mouth a thin line. "Don't you have anything better to do than troll me? Like finding a girl to add another notch to your belt."

Stanley laughs, and I'm not sure what irritates Jace more. My insult or the fact that Stanley found it amusing.

Jace waggles a finger at me as if he's saying, *Ya got me!* before a venomous grin turns his masculine features serpentine. "Do you remember that time when you were convinced you'd marry Prince Harry, so you wanted me and Teagan to teach you how to waltz? I think my toes were bruised for weeks."

My hands fist. "I was eleven," I grind out.

Jace offers me a rueful smile. "Is that the same reason you only went to *one* formal throughout all of high school?"

My cheeks flush and my chest heaves with indignation as I struggle to maintain my composure. I want to snap back with a biting remark, something to knock that cocky smirk off his stupidly handsome face, but my mind is blank.

Instead, all I can think about is that night at Sadie Hawkins when I saw Jace on my way out of the locker room.

A rush of emotions floods my veins as I struggle to push them back, keep them at bay.

I try to ignore the intrusive thoughts about all the ways in which that night shaped me and how it would go on to dictate my entire high school experience.

My chest swells, filling with lead and threatening to drown me as I fight to stomp down the burning flame of memories sparking to life inside me.

"You two have a lot of history," Stanley chimes in. It's more a statement than a question, and I'm grateful because it brings me back to earth and away from my thoughts.

"Sure do," Jace says, rocking back on his heels as a dishwater blond I recognize as another AU football player comes up beside him and claps him on the back.

"Need another?" I ask, motioning toward Stanley's beer bottle, which appears to be empty. I couldn't care less about drinking myself, but I need to get away from Jace, so heading to the bar seems as good an excuse as any.

"Sure. You want something?" he asks as I grab his arm and steer him away from the group—and Jace while he's distracted.

"Um, yeah, sure," I say, even though I haven't had so much as a drop of alcohol since that night. Drinking means losing control and lowering inhibitions, which can lead to all kinds of bad decisions. For a long time, I wondered if I didn't have that little bit of vodka, maybe I would've gotten away sooner. Maybe I wouldn't have gone at all. *Maybe. Maybe. Maybe.*

But right now, I don't seem to care. Right now, I need something to numb the memories, and a drink sounds like a solution I can't pass up.

Just one won't hurt.

Just enough to take the edge off Jace breathing down my neck.

"Beer?" Stanley asks as we sidle up to the huge bar.

It's all polished wood and sleek angles. Three bartenders scurry about the circular enclosure like honey bees, slinging beer bottles, pouring shots, and filling glasses.

I'd be impressed if I weren't so freaking annoyed.

I wrinkle my nose, trying to quell my irritation and enjoy my date. "Not a huge beer fan. How about…" I glance around me, eyeing what everybody's drinking in the hopes I see something appealing, although I don't have much experience with booze.

Out of my periphery, I see Jace making a beeline for us, so I hurry. "Whatever the bartender recommends," I say quickly. "I'll be right back."

Stanley nods and turns as I spin around, turning on Jace before he can give me a lecture on drinking.

"Thought you could sneak away without me?" he croons.

"I'll tell you what I'm gonna do," I say, my smile tight. "I'm going to have a drink with Stanley. Because he seems nice and because I'm interested in him. I might even dance with him. I know this is a hard concept for you to grasp, but sometimes, when people like each other, they want to get to know each other in ways that don't involve humping."

Jace scoffs and crosses his arms. "You drink? Since when."

"Since now."

"One." He holds a finger up in my face, and I swat it away. "One drink."

This feels like a challenge.

"I'll have as many damn drinks as I want, Taggart, and you're sure as hell not going to stop me. Now, go back to your apartment or whatever bimbo you're gonna shack up with, but please, leave me alone."

Spinning on my heel, I storm toward the bar, heading for Stanley in time to see the bartender sliding over our drinks: A beer for him and something amber in color for me.

I snag it from Stanley's grip just as he picks it up, needing to prove a point as I bring it to my lips, fully intending to down it when it's ripped right from my hands.

"Didn't anyone ever teach you not to take a drink from a guy unless you've seen it poured?" Jace growls.

I whirl on him, reaching for my cup, but come up empty while Stanley watches us with a frown. "I literally watched the bartender slide it over, you jackass." Though truth be told, Jace has a point. My eyes did leave the bar.

I place my hands on my hips, and the moment Jace drops his guard, I snatch the drink back and bring it to my lips, taking a long pull, surprised at how delicious it is.

"Ooh, this is good," I say, turning toward Stanley.

"It's an Amaretto sour," he says.

Once again, Jace's noodle arms reach over my shoulder to retrieve it and my drink disappears. "Nope."

I protest, grappling at the cup. "Do you really think I'm going to go through all of college without a drink?"

"What do you even know about this kid?" Jace motions toward Stanley, not even bothering to hide the disdain from his voice. "You need to stay clear-headed."

Stanley stiffens while I grind my back molars so hard it's a miracle they don't crack. My resolve solidifies. I don't even like drinking. After that night, I have little desire to do so, but I'll do anything at this point to contradict him.

Turning, I storm over to the bar and order two shots of tequila, slapping some cash on the sleek wood surface. Once they're poured, I grab them, one in each hand, and slam the first one back before Jace can even react. The burn of liquid hits my throat, swirling through my chest and I wrinkle my nose at the taste. Before I can down the other one, it's knocked from my hand.

On the inside, I'm secretly pleased because it tastes like jet fuel. But on the outside, I'm enraged. "I can't believe you just did that!" I gape at him.

I glance around, looking for someone to commiserate with when Stanley chimes in, "Come on, man. It's just a drink," he says to Jace. "She'll be safe with me."

Jace snorts and his gaze shoots to mine. "Sorry, but I don't trust anyone. Not with Cupcake."

Not with Cupcake? What the hell?

"It's just a couple of drinks, Jace. I can handle it. I'm just trying to have fun," I say, doubling down, even though I don't really want more than the shot I've already had.

Jace moves in front of Stanley, his large body dwarfing him and blocking him entirely, like the moon eclipsing the sun. All that's left of my date are the curses I can hear behind Jace as his eyes find mine. "You don't even know him. And you have next to zero experience with alcohol, unless I'm mistaken. Don't you think it would be prudent to keep a clear head?"

"Prudent?" I snort and take a step closer.

What I hate more than Jace sticking his nose where it doesn't belong is the fact that he's right. But I'd rather die than admit that. So, instead I move until we're standing toe-to-toe, until my chin tips so our eyes meet, and I whisper, "Well then, aren't I lucky I have you here to protect me."

Then I sidestep him and grab Stanley's hand, dragging him onto the dance floor.

CHAPTER 5

JACE

THE BEAT OF THE music ricochets through me like a gun-shot, piercing everything inside. Or maybe it's just Brynn having this effect on my insides. Normally, I'd be on the dance floor, grinding behind some nameless co-ed with a tight ass and a penchant for emotionally unavailable men. Instead, I'm standing just outside the mass of people barely moving under the strobing lights, half pissed while I risk glances at Brynn. She's currently sipping a fresh beverage to replace the one I stole, and making her way onto the dance floor for the second time with Douche Dick Stanley.

"Dude, you into her or something?"

"What?" My head snaps toward Chris who showed up a little while ago with a few of the guys from the team.

"Brynn. You said she was your best friend's sister, right?"

In other words, she's off-limits.

"Yeah, so?"

Chris quirks a brow and glances toward Brynn, then back. "I know I've only known you for a week, but the way you're eyeing her . . ."

I roll my eyes. The guy is seeing things.

"It's not like that. She's just super innocent and I'm worried she's in over her head." I shrug. "I don't want to see her get into any trouble."

Chris nods, and when his gaze shifts to something over my shoulder and his brows rise, it takes everything in me not to take a look for myself.

I can do this. I can be strong.

"I get that. So, her grinding on someone won't faze you?"

I glance over my shoulder so fast I get whiplash.

My heart pounds against my ribs as I watch Brynn move to the music. Hips swaying. Arms in the air. But she's facing him, not grinding on Stanley like Chris suggested, and it takes me a moment to realize what he did.

I turn back to find him laughing his ass off and flip him the bird, making a mental note to add laxatives to his protein shakes.

"Sorry, man. I had to." He raises his hands and takes a step back at the same time a tall blonde with long, curly hair and her redheaded friend approach us.

The blonde points at me. "Hey, aren't you in my Humanities class?"

My gaze tracks over her face, but I draw a blank. My mind is too preoccupied, too concerned with what's going on behind me in the minute since I last checked on Brynn, so I simply agree. "Yeah, sure."

"You play football, right?" The blonde smiles.

I nod, annoyed with myself because instead of being invested in this hot chick, all I want to do is turn my head to the blonde behind me. "Yep. We both do, actually," I say with a nod toward Chris. "This is my roommate, Chris, one of AU's running backs."

"Hey." Chris offers them a nod, then turns his attention solely to the redhead, and if the gleam in his eye is any indication, he's going to be preoccupied later.

"And what position do you play?" the blonde asks with a flutter of her lashes.

"Wide receiver." I angle my body so I can keep an eye on the dance floor.

"That's the guy who catches the ball, right?"

I glance at her and fight a grimace. Women who don't like sports or follow football have never bothered me before. Usually I'm content with them wanting me simply because I play and look good in a uniform, but for some reason, her ignorance irritates me.

"Best damn set of hands we've got," Chris chimes in.

"Really?" Her smile spreads, and she glances down at my hands, which are still clutching the same beer I ordered when I got here. It's now warm and likely flat. I wouldn't know because I've barely touched it, afraid to dull my senses in an effort to keep a clear head for Brynn. "Mhmm . . ." she purrs. "I'm sure those hands are very talented. Maybe you can show me." Her red lips spread into a lascivious smile.

She's gorgeous; there's no doubt about it. With curls that reach her back, bright blue eyes, a pert nose, and full lips that I fully suspect know how to work a man. I'd be a fool not to jump at the opportunity for a good time with her. But the signal in my brain which should be sending all my blood down south is the same one irritated that Douche Dick Stan's arms are now encircling Brynn from behind while she moves her perfectly round ass to the music.

What the actual fuck?

Jealousy washes over me like a tidal wave, stealing my breath, and forcing me to run a hand down my face.

Get a freaking grip, Taggart. This is Brynn, Teagan's twin sister.

Focusing back on the blonde in front of me, I tell myself Brynn will be fine. Who cares if she's now grinding on him. They're on the dance floor in a public place, not in a bathroom stall or under the bleachers where anything can happen.

"What'd you say your name was again?" I ask her, trying to feel a spark—anything to take my mind off the other blonde occupying my thoughts.

Her glossy pink lips purse, eyes glittering with interest. "Heather."

"Wanna dance, Heather?" I ask, dropping my voice an octave.

"Thought you'd never ask." She grips my arm and drags me to the edge of the dance floor, where she molds her body to mine, moving to the music.

I reciprocate, running my hands down her back, to the top of her ass while her breasts brush against my chest. Dancing like this is foreplay. There's nothing else to it. Normally, I'd already be anticipating what comes next after we leave the dance floor, but I feel nothing as she moves her body against mine. No spark or heat coursing through my veins. Not even the familiar stab of lust. It's as if my libido is Elvis and he left the fucking building.

Desperate to feel something, I lean down and take her mouth with mine. Her lips are soft and pliable, but she's a little too eager. Her tongue immediately darts into my mouth, exploring it like she's Christopher fucking Columbus intent on finding new land.

The acrid scent of her perfume burns my nose, but I ignore it and sink into her further. Trying to control the kiss, I bite at her lower lip, but her responding moan does nothing for me.

Heather is the kind of girl I normally want. The kind guys like me dream about. I wouldn't have to worry about attachments or calling her the next day. There'd be no awkward moment after when I wonder how quickly I can get her out of my bed without pissing her off.

All she wants is a good time. She made that clear from the moment she approached me.

But the silent commander in my pants stays firmly tucked away, uninterested and bored. It's like he took a fucking Ambien.

I open my eyes as her hands sink into my hair while I angle my head in my search for Brynn.

I easily spot her in the crowd, and I'm immediately blinded by rage.

Stepping out of Heather's arms, I leave her hanging as she stumbles back, blinking at the loss of contact like she's been smacked.

My jaw hardens along with my gaze as I watch Brynn suck face with Stanley.

Heather turns, a dazed look on her face as she searches for the object of my attention, but I offer no explanation as my hands curl into fists and I storm over to where Brynn is pressed up against him, her mouth on his.

"What the fuck, Brynn?" I grind out, my hands coming between them even while a part of me recognizes I've become unhinged. I have zero right to interrupt, yet I can't seem to help myself. I'm no longer in control of my body as I shove Stanley away from her.

"Hey, man!" Stanley seethes, narrowing his eyes on me, clearly pissed at the intrusion.

Too bad I don't give a flying fuck.

"What do you think you're doing?" Brynn's eyes meet mine, dark under the strobing lights.

"Uh, I could ask you the same."

"It was a kiss, Jace," she says, as my gaze darts to her plump mouth.

Her lips are slightly swollen, her gloss gone. Probably on that fucker's mouth, but I don't dare look because I'm already overreacting and the sight of it will undoubtedly fill me with even more rage.

I scoff. "First, you're grinding into him, and then you let him suck your face, so I'd say it was a little more than *just* a kiss. I know where this shit leads."

Brynn crosses her arms and her chest swells. My gaze darts to the milky flesh and my dick takes that moment to make his appearance.

Of course he fucking does. Where the hell was he five minutes ago?

"Oh, you mean like you and that bimbo over there?" She nods in Heather's direction.

I fight the urge to cover her with my body, to shield the swell of her breasts from Stanley's prying eyes as he steps closer to her side, but I don't because it'll only piss her off more, and the more I piss her off, the more she seems to want to rebel.

"Hey, man, maybe you should just leave. Go back to your chick over there," Stanley says, motioning to where I left Heather a minute ago.

"And maybe you should mind your own damned business and keep your hands to yourself before I rip them off." My jaw flexes as Stanley takes a step back.

The sound of my pulse pounds in my ears, and I can feel myself losing control—of myself, of the fucking situation. I need to rein it back in.

"Is there something going on between you two?" he asks, glancing between us.

"No!" Brynn and I yell at the same time.

She glares at me, but I ignore her laser beam gaze, focusing on Stanley instead.

He lifts his hands in the air, palms out. "Listen, I don't know what the hell's happening. I think you're a cool chick, Brynn, but I don't want any trouble."

Brynn deflates, stepping toward him, her tone a plea as she says, "He's just an overprotective jackass. You don't need to worry about him."

I lift my fists behind Brynn's turned back, making a show of cracking my knuckles.

I'm not proud of how I'm acting, but if it results in Stanley leaving like a dog with his tail between his legs, I can live with it.

"Uh, yeah," Stanley drawls, eyes wide. "Well, maybe we can hang some other time," he says. "Alone," he adds, then turns and leaves her hanging.

Coward.

Brynn watches him exit the dance floor before she spins around to face me, plants her hands against my chest, and shoves. "Thanks a lot."

I shrug. "If he really cared, he wouldn't let me scare him off like that. Tells me I was right about him."

She scowls, her lip curling in disgust. "Not all guys think like you."

"Correction, Cupcake. *All* guys think like me."

"And what if I wanted a hookup? What if I wanted his tongue down my throat? Ever think about that?"

Heat floods my veins. I'm a pressure cooker turned up high and ready to explode. "Then you're lucky I stopped you when I did. You don't know what you're doing, Brynn."

"You're unbelievable." She scoffs and shakes her head, turning to leave the dance floor, but I follow, hot on her heels.

"Where are you going?"

She says nothing, ignoring me as she finds Charlotte, who's talking to a blond dude I recognize as one of Stanley's friends. She whispers something in Charlotte's ear, then gives her a quick squeeze, and continues toward the exit.

"Hey," I yell, still behind her. "Where the hell are you going?"

She whirls around, her pretty features contorted in rage as she points a finger at me. "You have some nerve, you know that?"

"What? Because I want to protect you?" My gaze drops to the angry set of her mouth, then up to her sparkling violet eyes. An outraged Brynn Nichols is fucking hot.

"We were dancing, and we kissed. That's it! I'd hardly call that a crime. It's not like I was in the back seat of his car or headed back to his room."

My stomach churns at the picture she paints.

"Whoa." I hold my hands out, and I'm about to ask if she thought about heading to the back seat of his car when she takes a step closer, stealing my breath.

"So it's okay for you to have that blonde bimbo rub herself all over you and practically swallow your tongue, but I can't do the same? Did you even know that girl before tonight? Because I've been talking to Stanley all week. I, at least, know *something* about him."

"Yeah, well, you're better than me." I shrug, like that point should be obvious.

A disgruntled sound rumbles from the back of her throat as she shakes her head, her tone resigned as she says, "Whatever. I'm done. Congratulations, Jace. You got what you wanted. I'm leaving. Alone."

I watch her walk away from me, unable to take my eyes off the sway of her hips before common sense prevails, and I remember she came with Charlotte and doesn't have a car.

I jog to catch up with her. "How are you getting home?" I ask.

"I'm walking."

"Alone?" I arch a brow.

"It's one block, Jace. I'll be fine."

"Like hell you will. I'm driving you."

She pauses at the door, turning to stare at me, and I can practically see her thoughts churning. She wants to argue. Refuse. But she won't. I'm banking on it.

I know I'm right when she sighs and her shoulders slouch. "Do I have a choice?"

"What do you think?" I ask with a grin.

She relents, dragging her feet as I guide her to my car. I open the passenger door for her before rounding to the driver's side.

"Why'd you drive, anyway?" she asks as the engine rumbles to life, and I pull away from the curb.

"I knew I wouldn't be drinking, so I figured I might as well."

She says nothing to that, and I find myself wishing she'd talk to me. Maybe insult me or bite my head off. I'd take anything other than her answering silence.

When I can't take it anymore, I glance over at her to find she's staring out the window, seemingly lost in thought. I open my mouth to say something—I'm not sure what, maybe apologize—but at the last second, I snap it shut. Better to leave well enough alone. It's not like I'd go back and change anything. I'd do it all the same, so an apology would be disingenuous.

I focus back on the road, and when I pull up to the dorms a few minutes later, her hand is already on the handle in a rush to get away from me.

"Want me to walk you in?" I ask.

"Nope." She makes eye contact with me for a few brief seconds before she swings her door open. "I think you've done enough damage for the night."

"Sweet dreams, Nichols," I yell after her as she slams the door shut in my face, then flips me the bird.

"Hope you have fucking nightmares," she singsongs.

I tip my head back and laugh.

CHAPTER 6

BRYNN

I SIT IN THE heat of the afternoon sun, enjoying the feel of it on my skin as I wait impatiently for my brother to answer his phone. I know for a fact he's finished practice already. I know because he posted a sweaty selfie of himself on social media only an hour ago. He's lucky I didn't wake him at five this morning, since I was up, brooding over my failure of a date last night and unable to fall back asleep.

After the third try, he finally picks up, his voice smooth like silk croons, "Brynn? To what do I owe the pleasure?"

"You need to call your dogs off. And by dogs, I mean Jace," I say, wasting no time getting to the point.

"I don't know what you mean."

I can clearly hear the humor in his voice, and it makes me want to reach through the phone and the five hundred miles separating us to throttle him.

"Um, how about the fact that he's completely unhinged? I met a guy from one of my classes at a club last night, and Jace totally ran him off. Like caveman, alpha male, ran him off."

"Why?" Teagan snaps. "Did he put his hands on you?"

I rake a hand through my hair and fight the urge to scream. "As a matter of fact, he did, but I *wanted* them there."

"Brynn—"

"Don't 'Brynn' me, okay? You know for a fact I'm not that kind of girl. All we did was dance and kiss. That was it. And we were in a public place, surrounded by people. I was perfectly safe."

"Listen, I'm sure if Jace went big brother on him, there had to be a good reason."

I scoff. Of course he's taking his side.

I launch into a diatribe about what an ass Jace is as I recount the events of last night, including details about how Jace's hypocritical ass had some nameless blonde hanging all over him. All Teagan does is piss me off more when he says, "Sounds legit to me."

"Really, T?" I wrap an arm around myself, annoyed. "You need to tell him to back off."

"Listen, you haven't spoken to me at all since you left for AU, and you're my baby sister. Of course I'm gonna ask him to look after you."

I snort. "I'm younger by four minutes."

"Hey, a lot of wisdom was gained in those four minutes."

"I'm serious."

He groans. "Okay. *Fine.* If you really want me to, I'll talk to him. I just . . . I don't want to see you go through what you went through ever again, you know? It killed me to see how you went from being this fun-loving, carefree girl to shutting everyone out."

I sigh and bite my lip, finding it hard to stay mad at him when I know how good his intentions are. We've always had a strong connection. When we were kids, we leaned into the twin thing. My mom dressed us in coordinating outfits. We finished each other's sentences. Could read each other's emotions with a single glance. After the incident sophomore year, I didn't tell anyone for weeks. Teagan badgered me on and off for over a month before I finally caved and told him, scared of how he'd react.

He was there for me when I had no one.

He kept my secret after I begged him not to tell my parents or our friends.

"We both care about you," he says. "You know that, right?"

I hum in response because the thought of Jace caring about me does weird things to my insides. Which is ridiculous. Jace tolerates me at best, and the feeling of hatred is mutual. Jace Taggart has never cared about a girl a day in his life. He wouldn't know a relationship if it bit him in the ass.

"So, you really like this dude, then?" my twin asks in the answering silence.

"I mean, I'm just getting to know him, which is kind of the point. If Jace runs him off, or any other guy I show an interest in for that matter, how am I ever going to know for sure? But from what I've gleaned, he's really sweet. Not that he'll ever speak to me again. Jace has probably scared him off for good."

For all I know, Stanley really does think there's something going on between me and Jace. But I don't say that. For some reason, speaking it out loud feels like planting a seed I don't want to sprout.

"Well, if he scares that easily, then he's not good enough for you," Teagan says like it's so simple.

"T, I've been talking to him for a week. After Jace acted like a caveman, I'd hardly gauge his interest in me off the fact that he doesn't want trouble with AU's new starting wide receiver. Jace is practically wearing his title like a freaking badge of honor."

Teagan grunts, which tells me he disagrees, but he won't say it. "Everything else good? You're staying safe?" he asks, changing the subject.

I bite my lip and nod, even though he can't see it. "Of course."

"What about your roommate? Is she giving you a hard time?"

"Jace tell you about her?" I deliberately didn't say anything because I know he'd report back to Mom and Dad, and I don't want them to worry.

"Well, you sure as hell didn't, seeing as you've been ignoring my calls ever since you got there."

"I was mad at you," I say like it's a good enough reason when in reality, I miss Teagan. He's my best friend; we have a special bond no one can usurp, not even him and his sneaky secrets.

"Come on, Brynn. You know how signing day works just like I do. There was always a chance Jace would choose another school," he says, referring to the day high school athletes sign contracts to play and attend their prospective colleges. "And I would have driven you, too, if I could've."

"I know," I admit begrudgingly. And with our father being one of the most sought-after wedding photographers and our mother running her own catering company, it's a miracle if they have a weekend free come April. I was lucky Mom could drive me at all.

"Besides, is it really that bad having Jace there?"

"Do you want me to answer that?"

Teagan chuckles. "He's not *that* bad. I remember a time when you didn't fight so much."

I scoff. "My memory doesn't go back that far," I lie.

Because I do remember.

I remember running around our yard in the summer and jumping through the sprinkler. I remember bike rides to Boyd Park, and ice cream on the Ferris wheel at the summer carnival. Movie nights on the weekends with popcorn and candy, Teagen between us.

"Who knows? Maybe you two can finally find a way to bury the hatchet and actually become friends after all is said and done."

"Ha! Unlikely."

"Tell me about the other girls you've been hanging with. Jace mentioned you made a couple friends."

"What is he, a freaking spy?"

"I asked him—"

"To watch out for me. Yeah, yeah," I say, more than a little annoyed Jace has been calling Teagan and updating him on *my* life. "I've been hanging out with the girls across the hall, Charlotte, and her roommate, Samantha. They're pretty cool. They're talking about pledging a sorority in the fall." I wrinkle my nose. I still haven't decided if it's the route I want to go, but it might be kind of cool to have a built-in sisterhood. "I guess Char's older sister was in one, when she was here a few years ago, so I'm considering it. We'll see."

"That's great, Brynn," he says with a warmth in his voice that makes my throat constrict. "I'm proud of you."

"For what?" I croak.

"For putting yourself out there. For being so fearless, when we both know you could've gone away to school and hidden inside yourself like you did in high school. I'm glad to see you coming out of your shell. It's a relief to see you living again."

"It's nothing."

"Don't downplay it. You're pretty amazing, sis."

"Yeah, well," I say my voice thick, "it took almost three years to stop blaming myself for what happened and feeling like I had a target on my back. So, it's about time."

"Nah. All good things come in their own time, Brynn. You took the time you needed. Now I just want you to be happy."

I swallow, wiping at the moisture in my eyes. When it comes down to it, I can't blame Teagan for worrying about me. I would feel the same. But why does he have to go and make me all emotional?

"Thanks, T. That means a lot. Honestly, I'm not sure I'd be the same if it wasn't for you."

"Aw, come on now. You're as strong as they come. Brynn Nichols is made of steel but has a heart of gold. You can do anything, but I'll always be here if you need me."

"Cheeseball," I say, smiling, ridiculously glad I called. Part of me needed the reminder. "Well, I'd better let you go. Talk to you later?"

"Yep. Call me."

I hang up, then stare out at the mostly empty courtyard, feeling slightly lighter than I had before I spoke with him. It's like a weight has been lifted from my shoulders. Last night was disappointing, to say the least. I may not know Stanley all that well, but all the conversations we've had this week before and after class have been really great. We seem to have a lot in common. Both of us come from small towns in Ohio with multiple siblings, and share a lot of the same interests in movies and music. Plus, he makes me smile.

That's a start, right?

I know Teagan is concerned mostly because he's not here to suss the situation out for himself, but he has no reason to be.

My intuition tells me Stanley is the real deal. I'd be a fool to let the chance of something between us slip through my fingers simply because Jace wants to flex his muscles and play big brother in Teagan's absence.

Screw waiting until class on Monday.

I stand, my mind made up as I cut through the courtyard and back toward my dorm.

I'm going to change into something pretty, do my hair and makeup, then I'll find Stanley's fraternity house. I'll apologize on Jace's behalf and convince Stan to give me another chance. Preferably without my arch nemesis breathing down my neck.

JACE

My phone vibrates on the nightstand where I left it last night after I flopped into bed.

I groan and roll onto my side. Every muscle in my body screams in protest at the movement, a result of the self-imposed lashing I took in the gym this morning.

I only have myself to blame. Coach gave us the weekend off, but I'd needed something to take my mind off of Brynn, and I foolishly thought killing myself in the weightroom would help. I'm already sore, which means tomorrow will be hell. The only consolation is I have another day until training resumes on Monday.

Maybe this morning wouldn't have been so bad had I gotten any sleep last night. But after dropping Brynn off and returning to my apartment, I had a couple beers in an effort to unwind while I tried to watch a movie, but I couldn't focus. My mind kept churning, thinking back to the violent rage I felt seeing Brynn's lips fused to Stanley's. I can tell myself it's because she's my friend, but that's not exactly true. I can argue it's a byproduct of my allegiance to Teagan, but that doesn't sit right with me either.

I overreacted; I know it, but I can't seem to care. Not as the memory of Brynn, looking like a fucking goddess and draped all over that asshole, slammed into me again and again like rain slashing against a windowpane.

After I got tired of my wheels spinning, I called it a night, preferring sleep to my own thoughts, but I found little relief, tossing and turning for hours. Instead of finding the solace I craved, images of Brynn in her low-cut top and tight jeans danced in my head. The memory of her hips swaying to the music and the swollen curve of her lips after kissing him taunted me.

I knead the telltale pounding of a headache as my phone continues to ring. Eventually, when it won't stop, I snatch it up, glancing at the time to see it's nearly three p.m. I napped for more than two hours. I look down at the name on the screen.

Teagan.

Answering, I press the phone to my ear as I rub the sleep from my eyes with my free hand. "What's up, bro?"

"Dude, I've been trying to call you for the last hour, and I know you had today off."

"Sorry." I sit up, my voice gravelly with fatigue. "I didn't get much sleep last night, and then I hit the weightroom."

"You're a glutton for punishment, aren't you? Who gets the day off and hits the gym? At least you're dedicated, I'll give you that."

I grunt in response.

"And could the reason you didn't get much sleep be because you had a certain blonde in your bed?"

My thoughts immediately flash to Brynn and ice fills my veins. "*What?* No."

Laughter rumbles over the line. "It's okay, Brynn told me you were all over some chick at the club."

Heather.

Relief swallows me whole. Why the hell had my thoughts immediately gone to Brynn?

I'm losing my fucking mind, that's why.

"Brynn said she wouldn't be surprised if you went back to the club and brought that girl back to your place after giving her a ride home."

I frown. She thinks I went back for her? I'll have to set her straight.

Wait . . . why the fuck does it matter what she thinks? I bagged plenty of chicks in high school. It's not like her opinion ever bothered me before.

I clear my throat and let out a half laugh, trying to rein in my wildly vacillating thoughts. "Uh, yeah. She was pretty into me, but I wasn't feeling it."

"Jace Taggart passing up an opportunity?" Teagan whistles, and I grit my teeth.

"Come on. I'm not that fucking bad, man."

"Uh, okay." He chortles. "Whatever you say."

"Did Brynn tell you about last night?" I ask, raking a hand through my hair, annoyed with him for assuming I'd hooked up with someone.

"You mean about how you acted like a caveman? Her words, not mine."

I tuck my arm behind my head and grin. "She was so pissed."

"I can imagine. She practically jumped down my throat when I suggested it was probably for the best, and you were just doing what I asked by looking out for her. Thanks for that, by the way. I knew I could count on you."

"No problem. I won't let anything happen to her under my watch."

"Which is why I trust you implicitly. So, what are your thoughts on this Stanley dude, anyway? She seems to like him, but in my opinion, if he really gave a shit, he wouldn't have just ditched her because you were playing big brother."

My skin itches at the suggestion Brynn really likes him, so I focus on my answer. "I get a major douche-bro vibe from him. I mean, I don't know the guy well enough to know for sure, but I'm gonna ask around, make sure he's on the up and up."

I'm smart enough to know Brynn won't stay away from him just because I tell her to, so a little reconnaissance won't hurt.

"Yeah. The last thing I want is for her to fall for someone who just wants to get into her pants." I grind my teeth at the thought. "But I also know Brynn is really hoping for a relationship. She didn't really get that in high school, ya know? She's banking on a different experience in college, the kind where she puts herself out there more, makes friends, dates, gets a boyfriend or two. And I want that for her, but only with the right guy."

It's true Brynn didn't date much in high school, and I'd be lying if I said I never wondered why. Regardless, if Teagan wants that for her now—if *she* wants that—then I should want that for her, too. Brynn's been a pain in my ass for years, and even though she gets on my damned nerves nearly every time we interact, she's a good person. I should want her to be happy. Which is why if Stanley turns out to be a good dude, I'll 100 percent support their coupling.

Fuck, why do I hate the sound of that?

Coupling.

My face twists with a grimace.

"So, I guess what I'm trying to say . . ." Teagan says, and I realize I spaced out, ". . . is keep up the good work, but maybe let her breathe a little? We don't want to stifle her freedom too much or come down on her too hard."

An image of Brynn's tits bursting from her top flashes in my head, and I think to myself, *I'll come down on her hard all right.*

Holy hell, I need to get a grip.

Something is seriously fucked in my head.

I run a hand over the back of my neck as heat creeps over my skin, burning me up. This is Teagan's sister, we're talking about. His fucking *sister*. Brynn Nichols, the bane of my existence.

She hates me, and I hate her.

Not to mention, she's completely off-limits.

Too good for me.

Shit. Maybe it's been too long since I've had a warm body beneath me.

Is that what's happening here? Some sort of displacement of pent-up sexual energy? If so, I need to correct the situation, ASAP.

"Yeah. Got it," I say, hearing the strain in my voice. "I'll cut her some slack." And apparently, find myself a chick of my own while I'm at it.

CHAPTER 7

BRYNN

I SMOOTH THE FRONT of the purple maxi dress I'm wearing as I take a deep breath. Earlier, when I was sitting outside in the sunshine and Teagan told me how brave I was, this seemed like a good idea, but now that I'm here, I'm wondering whether I should've waited to talk to Stanley during class on Monday.

What if he's annoyed I showed up here without notice? Or thinks I'm stalking him? What if the other night at the club was enough to turn him off?

I press a hand to my stomach as another thought occurs to me.

What if he's here with another girl? It's not like he lives in a dorm where there are rules about such things.

Oh, God. How embarrassing. It's totally possible he took someone else home after I left Bradd's. But do I even want a guy who would do that?

An image of Jace flashes in my head, but I push it away.

Why the hell am I thinking about him now? He and Stanley are nothing alike. I'm being ridiculous.

I wipe my damp palms on the soft cotton of my dress, then hurry up and stab the doorbell before I can chicken out.

If he's no good, better to know now.

Footsteps echo from within, and I wait as my heart beats like a drum inside my chest. A minute later, a kid I recognize as one of Stan's friends answers. His eyes brighten with recognition as he points and says, "Brynn, right?"

I nod as nerves twist in my stomach.

"You here for Stan?"

"Yeah, um, is he home?" I ask, wringing my hands out in front of me.

"Sure. Come on." He motions me inside and the tension in my muscles immediately drains. "I'll go get him and be right back."

He disappears down the hallway, leaving me alone in the living room where I glance around at my surroundings. The house looks different than I envisioned. Nicer, maybe? Certainly cleaner, although I imagine throughout the school year, with parties and an increase in roommates, that's not always the case.

A leather couch and several worn-out chairs sit in the living room in front of an old fireplace that appears unused. Dark wooden floors contrast with the pale blue paint on the walls. A huge flat-screen TV hangs on one of the walls, which are otherwise bare. A swift look around the corner into the kitchen reveals dated walnut cabinets and a large island with an old pizza box and several empty beer and soda cans standing sentinel.

A couple minutes later, Stanley emerges, and I smile as nerves riot inside my chest. Despite the slightly wary look in his eyes, his expression lights up as he takes me in. "Brynn." He comes to stand in front of me. "Aren't you a breath of fresh air? I certainly didn't expect to see you today." His gaze flickers up and down my body. "What are you doing here?"

I swallow, reminding myself to be bold. "I came to talk to you about last night. I wanted to apologize on Jace's behalf."

Stanley shakes his head, and his gaze drops to the hardwood. "You don't have to do that."

"I know, but I wanted to," I say.

That catches his attention. His head lifts, and he watches me for a moment as if sensing there's more I want to say.

"I'd be lying if I said I knew why Jace is such an ass. He's just . . . overprotective? Feels like he needs to step in since my brother's not here? I know he enjoys getting under my skin. Combine that with his promise to watch over me, and . . ." I shrug. "Anyway, it doesn't matter. That's not why I even came here."

"It's not?" he asks, searching my eyes.

I shake my head. "I like you."

Stanley exhales, his gaze softening. "I thought maybe there was something going on between you and Taggart."

"No way. He and I would never."

"You're sure there's nothing . . .?"

"Zero. He's like a parasite I can't shake. Half the time, I think his existence is purely meant to torture me." I take a step closer, mustering my courage. "I'm hoping you'll let me make it up to you by taking you out."

Stanley chuckles. "You wanna take me out, huh?"

I grin as I scrunch my nose. "Fair warning, though, I don't have a car, so our options will be limited, but I was thinking maybe a coffee?"

"Coffee sounds good." He smiles and his gaze drops to my mouth, which I take as a good sign. From what I recall, he's a pretty good kisser. "You available now?" he asks.

I bite my lip, fighting my grin before I nod. "Now's great."

"Just give me a minute." He reaches out and touches my arm before he turns and disappears down the hallway leaving me to smile and pump my fist in victory.

Take that, nerves!

He returns a minute later, and we head outside where we take the sidewalk into town. We make small talk the entire way, chatting about school and our favorite summer activities until we come across the coffee shop just off campus. Though it's small, the warm interior is bustling with patrons.

"Have you been here yet?" he asks as we get in line.

Warm lighting spills over the cozy interior, glinting off the glass display of pastries while an espresso machine whirrs in the background.

"Not yet. I've been wanting to, but it just seems easier to go to the cafeteria during the week." I shrug, but truthfully, Charlotte and Samantha hate coffee, so I haven't really had anyone else to join me. As I stand in line, I realize I shouldn't have let that stop me. I should've come on my own.

"Do you like lattes? Or do you just get regular coffee or tea?" he asks.

"I *love* a good latte."

"Well, I'm probably going to ruin you for life then, because once you try their Snickers latte, you'll never want anything else."

I arch a brow. "Hot or frozen?"

"Either way. Doesn't matter."

"Okay, then." I grin, and Stanley glances at my mouth, matching my smile.

"What?" he asks.

"Nothing." I shake my head.

"Nope. Tell me. Come out with it."

"It's just . . . this is nice, probably way more in my element than Bradd's was, if I'm being honest."

"Yeah? Not a fan of clubs?" he asks.

I shake my head, but he doesn't say anything in response and as we wait our turn, I start to wonder if I'm completely lame. Maybe he thinks I'm boring.

When it's our turn, we both order frozen Snickers lattes, but when he digs out his wallet from his pocket and starts to retrieve his credit card, I push his hand away. "No. It's my treat, remember?"

He hesitates. "Really? Are you sure?" he asks, arching a brow.

"Positive." I hand the barista the cash and turn to him. "I said I wanted to make last night up to you."

"Okay." He shoves his wallet back in his pocket, and grabs the first drink when the barista slides it across the counter, then takes a long pull on the straw and moans. "I'm telling you . . ." he says with a smile as I wait for them to finish the second drink.

Once I have mine in hand, we find a small table in the back and take a seat. "So, other than the conversations we've had outside of class, I don't know a lot about you. Tell me about yourself."

I fill him in some more about Teagan and my family, along with what it was like to grow up in Riverside, but I can't help but notice the glazed-over look in his eyes and the way he's nodding his head like he's bored with the conversation.

"I would hate growing up in a small town." He pulls a face. "Everyone knowing everyone's business."

I frown, thinking about one of our previous conversations last week before class and how I thought we had some things in common, one of which was growing up in a small community. "I thought you said you were from a small town, too?"

"Did I?" He scratches his head. "Huh. Mainstream suburbia is probably more accurate."

I shift in my seat as I contemplate this, then chalk it up to a misunderstanding. People have different definitions of small towns.

"Well, Riverside wasn't actually that bad," I say, feeling defensive. Which is ridiculous. Who cares if he thinks he'd dislike living in a small town? "People know you, yeah, but the gossip mill wasn't too bad. Instead, whenever someone's in trouble, everyone sort of bands together to help you out. People care, which is kind of nice."

The truth is, despite what happened in high school, I love Riverside, and I'll probably return there once I graduate, assuming I can find a job. I might have one dark memory there, but it's not enough to tarnish the love I feel for my hometown or my desire to stay close to family.

But Stanley seems unconvinced as he changes the subject. "You seem super close to your family."

"Yeah, we're really tight-knit."

"I have a sister and a brother, but we're not really all that close. Not much in common with them, you know? Honestly, I was so ready to leave high school and get out from under my parents' thumb. I just wanna do my own thing for a change."

"Yeah. Same," I say, which is only partly true. While I was ready to leave high school, it was for completely different reasons. My family was one of the best parts about Riverside.

Instead, my high school experience was hampered by fear and another emotion I can't quite name . . . shame? I wanted a clean slate to reinvent myself, which seemed hard to do inside the confines of Riverside High where the memory of what happened and the threat it might happen again haunted me. But I love my family, and I can't wait to go back for a visit. I miss them already, and it's only been a little more than a week.

"Is that why you stayed here for the summer? Or did you need to take classes?" I ask, curious to hear his answer.

"I mean, I like making my load a little lighter in the fall. But, yeah, I have zero desire to go back home and . . . what? Watch my siblings? Have a curfew again? Fuck that."

His attitude prickles at me, so I change the subject and steer us toward safer ground, something we might have in common. We talk about how campus life changes in the fall and what to expect. Stanley fills me in on rush week and different events AU hosts every year, including the hubbub surrounding football games and tailgating at away games.

"You said your brother goes to Cumberland University, right?"

"Yeah. It's going to be a blast when we play them."

"Will you wear Griffins' colors, or switch sides and support the bro?"

I laugh. "Gosh. I don't know, but I'm not sure I'd feel right if I didn't cheer him on." Rooting for Teagan on the sidelines during away games was the norm for me. I only ever watched Riverside's home games from the comfort of my bedroom. My parents never understood why I'd stream them rather than go and support him on our home turf, but at the time, it seemed safer than facing the creeping anxiety that followed me around any time I neared the stadium and locker rooms at night. Flashbacks of the fear hit too hard, followed by the irrational paranoia *he'd* still be there, waiting in the shadows for the moment I let my guard down. I worked so hard to bury the memories; I didn't want them to resurface. It almost makes me wish I'd gone to Cumberland in Maryland with Teagan just so I could finally watch him play at home and cheer him on.

"AU fans can get pretty crazy, so just a piece of advice? If you're going to wear CU colors during that game, maybe don't sit in the student section."

"Unless I have someone big and strong to protect me, right?" I wink.

"*Uh*, I'm not sure there'll be any protecting that," he says, and I shrink a little inside. Clearly, my flirting skills need work.

With a sigh, I take a sip of my drink which is nearly empty and try to think of a way to get this date back on track because it feels like it's gone off the rails. Ever since we sat down to talk, it seems we've done nothing but disagree. Are we really that incompatible? Or am I just so new at this? Maybe I'm simply unfamiliar with how awkward it can be when you're trying to get to know someone.

I lift my head from my drink, staring out toward the front of the shop, and suck a sharp breath inside my lungs. Jace stands at the front of the line, a grin spreading his lips as he talks to the cute barista with long red hair. If the way she's giggling as she leans toward him to hand him his drink is any indication, he's flirting with her.

A grunt of disgust emerges from the back of my throat just as Jace turns and catches my eye. I quickly glance away from him, in the hopes he didn't realize I'd been staring. The last thing I want is for him to think I'm pleased to see him, or worse yet, that I care he's flirting with the barista.

"I'm gonna go take a leak. You good?" Stanley asks, oblivious to the way my heart is pounding rapid fire at Jace's presence a few yards away.

"Yep. Solid," I say.

Even though I don't exactly want to be left alone, I'm over this date and sort of looking forward to heading back to my dorm room and crashing in the hopes Cate isn't there. Please, God, don't let my roommate be there.

I watch Stanley turn and saunter toward the restrooms when a deep voice cascades over me like a waterfall, pelting me with icy cold water. "I didn't run him off again, did I?"

Goosebumps creep over my arms as I tip my gaze to his with a scowl. "No. Actually, he had to take a leak," I spit out, repeating Stan's words.

Jace's brows scrunch together as he cocks his head as if trying to decipher my comment, since it's not an expression I would typically use.

I don't even know why I said it. Maybe because I'm slightly disappointed our date hasn't gone better? Whatever the reason, I'm annoyed with myself. I don't want Jace to know this thing between Stanley and I is off to a rocky start. I want him to think we're hitting it off, that I'm totally smitten, because it would give him nothing but joy to tell me, *I told you so.*

"Well, he's persistent at least. I'll give him that, "Jace says, his tone flat as he sits down in an empty chair beside me and shifts his gaze to where Stanley disappeared.

"Actually, *I* asked *him* out today." I smile, enjoying the shock rounding his eyes. "It's the twenty-first century. We women can do that, you know," I say as I raise my cup to my lips only to remember it's empty and set it back down.

The muscle in his jaw flickers. "What are your plans after this?"

"I don't know," I drawl, folding my hands beneath my chin as I force a dreamy look in my eye. "We don't really have a plan." I shrug, like I don't want the date to end. "I guess we'll see where the rest of the day takes us."

Jace's teeth clench, clearly disliking my answer, which makes my heart soar.

This is what I thrive off—insults and irritation and one-upping him. If all else fails, and this thing with Stanley winds up being an epic failure, at least I can piss Jace off in the process. "How about you," I croon. "Have any more bimbos in your pocket or has the well finally run dry?

Jace snorts. "Finding women who want to be with me never runs dry."

I purse my lips, hating that he's right. In high school, girls flocked to him. He was a hot commodity at Riverside. It didn't matter that they knew full well they were getting a bit of fun and nothing more. Quite frankly, I never understood it. I can't fathom not demanding more for yourself.

"Ah, yes," I drawl, "it's getting rid of them after that's the hard part. Am I right?" I ask sweetly.

"Something like that." He studies me, and it's like staring into the aqua waters of the Caribbean.

I freaking hate it.

"Have you kissed him again?"

"What?" I blink, thrown off guard.

"I'll take that as a no." He smirks.

My glare deepens. "Some guys take their time, you know. It's not all about rounding the bases as quickly as possible or sucking face every chance they get."

"Yeah, there will be no rounding the bases with *Stan*. Let's get that shit straight right now."

"I hate to break it to you, Jace, but I don't take orders from you, and the day is young. There's no telling where it might lead," I say, even though I'm full of shit. This date is leading nowhere but with my head on my pillow, hiding under the covers from Creepy Cate.

"Brynn . . ." He narrows his eyes, his tone a warning.

"Hey, man, do we have a problem?" Stanley interrupts.

I jolt in my chair, but Jace just glares at him, unfazed by his presence.

"It depends." Jace crosses his arms over his chest, his expression transforming to an easy confidence most only dream of replicating. "What are your intentions with Brynn, here?"

"Don't you think that's between us?" Stanley asks, glancing down at me, and for a moment, I get a glimmer of hope this day will turn around, because my date sticking up to Jace is a sight to behold.

I grin as Jace's gaze hardens on the side of Stanley's face, though if I'm being honest, I'm a little concerned for him. Stanley isn't small by any means, but he's no match to Jace in build or strength, I can guarantee it. Anyone can see Jace has the upper hand with several inches and twenty pounds of muscle on him, along with the kind of cocky demeanor that makes men dangerous.

"No, actually, I don't," Jace grinds out.

I roll my eyes and decide to do Stanley a favor before he gets his limbs torn from their sockets. "You can go now, Jace. Wouldn't want your coffee to get cold before you've even had a chance to drink it," I say archly.

I know him well enough to know he drinks his coffee super hot and black. There's no other way—I've heard him say a time or two. If it so much as turns lukewarm, he tosses it.

"Whatever." Jace stands, stretching to his full height and towering above Stanley. Did he grow in the last five minutes? "I'll call and check on you later," he says pointedly. "Answer."

I huff out a breath of indignation, but before I can say any-thing, he's gone.

"You ready to get out of here?" Stan asks.

I deflate a little, both relieved and disappointed Jace has gone and this somewhat unsuccessful outing is coming to a close.

I stand, grabbing my purse and my empty cup, backtracking to the table when Stanley forgets his, and throw them both in the trash before catching up with him at the door. Once we're outside, the sun heats my skin, and I inhale the fresh air, wondering what Stanley has in store. We may have gotten off to a rough start, but if he's willing to stand up to Jace, he must like me, right?

I smile up at him, squinting against the sun as he runs a hand down my arm and asks, "Wanna come back to my place?"

And just like that, my hopes fade.

I try to keep my disappointment from showing on my face as I hedge. "Oh, uh . . ."

"I mean, it's the one place we can guarantee we won't run into Jace, right?"

Is that why he wants to go back to his place?

"Will your fraternity brothers mind?"

He shrugs. "I mean, I don't see why they'll care." His gaze dips to my chest and he licks his lips. "We'll just go to my room."

"To your room," I repeat as if I didn't hear him right.

One corner of his mouth tips up in a sly smile. "I think we can find something to entertain ourselves."

"Um, actually," I press a hand to my stomach as it does a slow roll, and not the good kind. "I'm not really feeling all that well. I think it was all that sugar from the drink, maybe. Can I get a rain check?"

I don't even wait for his reply as I start to back down the sidewalk, offering him a smile of apology before turning back toward campus as I curse myself for being such a baby.

This is what college kids do, right?

They go back to their dorms or their apartments and hook up.

It's not like I have to have sex with him.

There are other things we can do.

Hell, we've only kissed once at the club.

So, why did he ask me to go back to his place? Wasn't that a little . . . fast?

I rake my hands through my hair, frustrated with myself. *Not every boy has to turn into a relationship, Brynn.*

But the truth is, I want to date, but I also want it to go somewhere. I *want* a relationship. I'm not sure I'm built for casual hookups. And why would I want to be? What's the point? If I want to get off, I can handle that shit myself.

No. I've seen the ugly side of lust. Witnessed firsthand what it can do, the destruction it can cause.

I want someone who will court me. Someone who does nice things for me just because they care. Someone to send me flowers just because. Who thinks of me when I'm not around. Who wants to be with me every waking moment because he can't get enough of me. I want to hear a love song play on the radio and smile because the lyrics remind me of him.

Call me a sap. Call me old-fashioned or a romantic. It's probably what led me to fall for the secret admirer schtick back in high school. But I refuse to bend on what I want just because boys like Stanley—and Jace—think it's okay to use women for one thing.

I want a fresh start, to turn over a new leaf, and have the kind of social life I didn't allow myself to have in high school. But that doesn't mean it has to include hooking up.

I define my life.

I decide my needs.

I hold my head high as I cross the courtyard on campus, catching sight of the dormitories looming ahead.

I'm proud of myself for knowing what I want and not feeling the pressure to cave for any less than what I'm worth.

When I enter Hyde Hall, I head to my room on the first floor, relieved to find my roommate gone. Flopping back in my bed, I text Charlotte and Samantha, but they don't answer, so I order a pizza and decide on a night in.

A couple hours later, I'm polishing off the last of my small pepperoni and watching the end of a rom-com when Jace's name lights up the screen of my phone.

I almost swipe it away, ignoring it, but curiosity gets the best of me as I read what it says.

> **JACE:** Are you still with that douche dick?

I clench my teeth and contemplate lying, but I'd rather let him stew.

> **ME:** Sorry. Can't answer right now. Busy.

Someone bangs on my door at the same time my text goes through, and I swallow. For a moment, I imagine it's Jace, here to give me a lecture. But when I crack the door open, Charlotte's smiling face stares back at me. "Want to watch a movie with us? I have brownies."

"You had me at brownies." I smile and hold up a finger. "One sec."

I snatch my room key off the dresser, my hand hovering over my phone before I decide to leave it.

Closing the door behind me, I can't help but smile.

Let him wonder what I'm doing, and who I'm with.

CHAPTER 8

JACE

I spot Brynn from a mile away, under the dappled shade of a large oak in the courtyard beyond the Liberal Arts building, and pause as I take her in. Brynn has always stuck out in a crowd. Her long blonde waves spill over her tan shoulders like spun gold as the soft sound of her voice drifts toward me on the breeze.

At least she's talking to a chick this time. The last time I saw her, she was with Stanley.

I steer toward her under a blue sky dotted with white clouds thick like clumps of cotton candy, grateful for them subduing the afternoon heat.

My feet make quick work of the stone pathway that leads to the massive swatch of green grass, occupied by several students lounging on blankets, enjoying the temperate weather. As I draw closer, I pull the brim of my baseball cap down over my forehead before I pick up the pace. I nearly missed her thanks to practice running late, but I was determined to catch her on her way out of class, so I hauled ass out of the locker rooms so fast I fucking slipped on the wet tile floors of the shower, crashing into Chris stark naked. It was a close call. Our dicks were two short seconds away from dueling. Fuck, I'll probably have nightmares about it for weeks.

Lucky for me, Brynn's too interested in her conversation with the brunette beside her to notice my approach. I can't help but note how the rosy color in her cheeks matches the shade of her plump lips. She radiates confidence, wearing a yellow sundress that shows zero cleavage and falls to her knees. It could easily be worn to church on Sunday: a stark contrast to the outfit she wore to the club, yet equally as appealing.

Considering the rebellious thoughts I've been having about her lately, I probably should cool it and avoid her. No good will come of seeking her out. But she didn't answer my texts the other night—the day I'd found her in the coffee shop with Stanley—so I want to make sure she's okay. At least that's what I tell myself as I approach, when the truth for why it's been almost a week since I caught her on a date with Stan and I can't stop thinking about her is a little murkier.

I bump into her shoulder as I pass, pretending not to notice her and hoping to piss her off, but she has zero reaction. With a frown, I glance over my shoulder and see she's still lost in conversation. All I get is a passing, "Sorry." She doesn't so much as glance in my direction.

As I wonder what the hell is so interesting, I close the distance between us, coming up behind her as I place my hands over her eyes.

She yelps, startled before she laughs and bats at my hands, then swings around to face me. But her smile falls instantly. "What the hell, Jace?" She swats at my arms more aggressively this time, and certainly not in a fit of giggles. "I thought maybe you were Stanley."

I spear her with a look. "You thought I was fucking Stanley? Like that loser is even tall enough to put his hands over your eyes from behind. I'd probably need to grab him a step stool first."

Brynn crosses her arms over her chest and cocks her head, a scowl painting her pretty face while her friend grins, her gaze ping-ponging between us. When I mock Brynn's rigid stance, her friend chuckles.

"Very funny," Brynn says, "but I happen to think Stanley is a nice height. Not too tall, not too short."

I roll my eyes. "Okay. If you want a *small* man, suit yourself."

"You know, boys like to think all girls care about is size, but it's knowing how to use what you've got that counts," she says, and I want to ask her how the hell she fucking knows.

Instead, I say, "You *better* not have firsthand knowledge of how small Douche Dick is. I'm just going to go ahead and take it you're assuming he's small, which I think is probably accurate based on the little-man syndrome he projects. And for the record"—I step forward and reach out, running a lock of her hair between my fingers—"I've never had any complaints in that department."

Brynn scoffs, but her cheeks flush. Candy apple red is my new favorite color.

I drop the lock of hair and put some distance between us as warning bells ring in my head. If her vengeful expression is any indication, she's two steps away from clawing my eyes out. Also, my goading as of late feels different from our typical witty banter. It's charged somehow, which spells trouble.

"Anyway," I say with a smile, "who's your friend?" I turn toward the cute brunette with chin-length hair. "You were at Bradd's the other night, right? We didn't get a proper introduction." I stretch out a hand for her which she accepts with a demure smile. "I'm Jace Taggart, Brynn's good friend."

"If it's opposite day, sure," Brynn says, sweetly.

"I'm Charlotte, and I know who you are."

"Ah, my reputation precedes me." I wink at Brynn. "Discussing me with your friends, huh?"

"Only for tips on where to bury your body?"

I snort and sling an arm over Brynn's shoulders, then proceed to give her a noogie. "This one, always the jokester."

"Aargh!" Brynn tries to shove me off, but she's unsuccessful.

"Tell me, Charlotte, did Brynn spend the night at Stanley's house a few days ago? I saw them together, and when I tried to check in with her, she blew me off."

"Uh . . ." Charlotte's gaze darts to Brynn and she winces as she says, "I don't think so?"

"That's what you want?" Brynn glares so hard it's a miracle her eyes don't pop from their sockets. "You're unbelievable, but you can relax. Nothing happened. *Now,* will you leave me alone?"

I drop my arm from her shoulders and face her straight on again. "He's a terrible kisser, am I right? Is that why you didn't go back to his place? Too much tongue? He looks like the kind of man who would swallow your whole face if you let him."

Brynn rolls her eyes. "For your information, not all girls just sleep with a guy because they can. Some wait."

"Fish lips? I bet he does the fish lips thing?" I purse my lips. "I can see Douche Dick being a fucking goldfish."

Brynn growls and shoves an angry hand through her hair. I watch the movement like a man mesmerized. "He has no problem in the kissing department, okay? Gosh, why do you even care so much, anyway?"

I grin, because getting a rise out of Brynn Nichols is one of my favorite pastimes and she's getting more frustrated by the minute. I'm like a kid at Christmas and when I don't answer, she screws up her face and asks, "Did you actually need something from this encounter, or did you just want to stop and torture me?"

Fucked if I know. I'm starting to wonder myself . . .

"I just wanted to check in and make sure you're okay. If you'd answer my texts, you'd know that, and I wouldn't have to hunt you down to see for myself."

"Trust me, I won't make that mistake again." The muscle in her jaw twitches. "You came. You conquered. Now can you leave?"

"With pleasure," I say when I spot Chris and Damon, AU's quarterback. "See you ladies later. Don't be a stranger, Charlotte," I say, pointing toward her as I jog over to join my teammates.

I reach Damon first, and he offers me a fist bump before he cranes his neck to peer over my shoulder. "Bro, who are the hot chicks?"

"Nobody you need to know," I snap.

Chris snorts. "The blonde is off-limits. Trust me. You don't wanna go there."

I don't correct him, even though it's clear he's insinuating I'm into her. But he's right about one thing: Brynn *is* off-limits. Chris can think what he wants, but the last thing I need are any of the assholes on the team getting any ideas. I know what they're like. I've been playing football since I was ten. I've spent more hours in a locker room over the years than I'd care to admit, and there's one thing I know for certain: we're all a bunch of horny assholes. Despite giving her a hard time, Brynn is too good for all of us. So, I might as well be up front about the fact that she's a no-fly zone. Plenty of other runways where they can land their planes.

"So what's the plan for tonight?" I ask. It's been a hard week of practice and after fretting over Brynn ignoring my texts all week like a fucking girl, I'm ready to let loose, have a little fun.

Besides, it wouldn't hurt to get my mind on another chick for a change. All this keeping tabs on Brynn is screwing with my head.

"We were just talking about that." Chris lifts a chin toward Damon.

"There's a party at Psi Delta. It's supposed to be pretty chill, mostly brothers and some of the team. It's kind of a feeler to see who might want to rush next year. They're always trying to get athletes."

I nod. Several of the guys on the team are Psi Delta and they've tossed around the idea of freshmen checking it out. I have no interest in a fraternity, myself. My teammates have always been my brothers, and no one can replace my crew from Riverside. We're still tight despite the distance between us. But I'm not opposed to a frat party. A change of pace and free beer would be nice. "I'm game."

"Cool." Chris glances down at the leather watch strapped to his wrist. "I've gotta jet. Family thing. But I'll see you two assholes later?"

"I'll drop by your place before ten and we'll head out," Damon adds.

I slap him on the back and turn to head for the apartments. "Sounds like a plan. Later," I call out, as we all head our separate ways.

Once I reach the apartment, I unlock it and head inside. It's quiet, and I make my way to the living room where I turn on the television, preferring the background noise to silence. My legs twitch as I head into the kitchen and peer into the nearly empty fridge before grabbing a protein drink and closing it again. I pop the lid off and take a sip of the chalky liquid, antsy as I peer out the window into the empty street below, wondering what the hell to do with myself until the party tonight.

Practice this morning kicked my ass, so the gym is out. I know by now Chris will be gone for the remainder of the day. Most days, it's like I don't even have a roommate. Unlike Brynn's misfortune, I couldn't have asked for a more chill dude to live with, but he's originally from the Ann Arbor area, which means he's always traveling to and from campus, headed to see family and friends and helping out at his old high school job. He may as well commute for how much he's gone.

Most guys my age would probably welcome the privacy of having an apartment to themselves, but the truth is I resent the solitude. Though I would never admit this to anyone, prior to college, I was looking forward to having a roommate. Living alone is something I'm all too familiar with. Without any siblings at home and my parents gone all the time, too busy with work or traveling to act like they had a son, most of my time spent inside the four walls of my home was spent alone. The only adult interaction I got throughout the week was either with Harriet, our housekeeper, or the time spent at the Nichols' household, which was the complete opposite of mine.

With Teagan, Brynn, and their other little sisters, there was never a dull moment at their place. It's vibrant, full of life, and you can always find someone to talk to. It's half the reason I spent so much time there, although it didn't hurt that Teagan's parents—Nikki and Joe—were more than welcoming. They'd practically adopted me throughout the school year. I often wondered if it was part of the reason Brynn hates me so much. Maybe she was sick of sharing her family and having me around.

I take another sip of my shake, then make my way into the living room and sink down onto the leather sofa. My parents paid a lot of money to furnish and decorate the place before I moved in. It was their way of showing me their love, I guess. Or their way of stifling the guilt of never being there when it counted. Who the hell knows. To them, material things always come first. They'd rather shell out thousands of dollars for furniture and a decorator to come and set the place up for me, rather than actually help move me in themselves and make the place a home.

I scrub a hand over my face, then pull out my phone, needing a little levity to counter the serious direction my thoughts are headed in, so I start a group chat with the guys. It's only been two weeks since my friends and I all left Riverside, going in different directions to different schools, and I miss those assholes like I'd miss a fucking hand.

ME: College football is no joke. I want a refund.

I wait as the little dots bounce on my screen before my phone pings.

ATLAS: Not sure it works like that, bro.

GRAHAM: Retirement is nice.

I snort. Atlas has always been the hard-ass while Graham took title of the golden. Not surprising considering Graham's father played for the NFL and practically coached Riverside from the sidelines. For as long as I could remember, he was planning Graham's future in football, until Graham shocked us all by declaring he was done and leaving the sport behind. Truthfully, I can't blame him, though. His father was a total dick. He and Atlas are cousins, and when Atlas transferred to Riverside our senior year, his father practically dropped him like a hot stone to foster Atlas' talent. Then some crazy shit went down between them, and let's just say it's amazing Atlas and Graham have managed to make amends and strengthen their friendship.

ME: Lucky bastard.

TEAGAN: Yeah, but college chicks really dig the football thing, even more than in high school.

ME: I wouldn't know. I've been too busy patrolling your sister to pick up chicks.

GRAHAM: Brynn giving you a run for your money?

ME: She's like a full-time job.

Though I kinda like it. But they don't need to know that.

KNOX: Sorry, I'm late to the party. Never thought I'd see Jace Taggart hit a dry spell. You're practically a virgin again.

I snort and text him the middle finger emoji, then:

ME: I intend to change that tonight.

ATLAS: Big plans?

ME: Just headed to a frat party. What are you all up to?

My stomach tightens. Of course they're hanging out with their girls. They're both nauseatingly happy and in love, something I've never once found appealing. The idea of giving everything to one person and loving them unconditionally makes me squirm. So why does the chokehold on my gut feel a lot like envy?

ME: You and Carrie broke up? Duuuude.

Out of all of us, Knox has always been the solid one. He's a friendly giant, a reliable constant in our lives. You know exactly what to expect with him, and shit, Knox had been with his girlfriend since sophomore year. If I'd have put money on any of us getting married just after college it was those two.

KNOX: Said I should have the full college experience. That long distance was too hard.

GRAHAM: Dang, that . . .

. . . only validates my negative feelings toward commitment. Why bother if they're just going to fucking leave?

ATLAS: Cold.

TEAGAN: Sorry, bro. We're here if you need us.

Could this conversation be more depressing?

ME: Welcome to the singles club where there are plenty of fish. Feel free to dive right in. The water's warm.

TEAGAN: Only you . . .

KNOX: It's been so long, I'm not sure I even remember how to flirt.

ME: Uh oh. Do I sense a lack of self-esteem here? Maybe some self-doubt? Bruh, you can bounce a quarter off your abs. And you're a motherfucking Riverside Rebel. Don't be so modest.

KNOX: Maybe. Your biceps are better, though.

I grin and type.

ME: True, but you have that crooked smile chicks go crazy for.

KNOX: Nah. You have all that thick, dark messy hair girls like to run their hands through.

ME: Your buzz cut has its own appeal. And don't forget your big puppy dog eyes.

KNOX: Thanks. I do like my eyes.

ME: As you should. Shit, maybe we should just get married?

KNOX: I mean, it depends. Who's the dominant one in this situation?

TEAGAN: Aaaaannnd now it's getting weird.

ATLAS: Yeah, I was done with this conversation five minutes ago.

GRAHAM: I puked in my mouth a little.

> **ME**: Pffft. I'm comfortable with my sexuality, okay? Anyone would be lucky to have me.

> **TEAGAN**: If you could stay interested long enough.

I grimace.

> **ME**: That's fair.

Music pumps through the back of the house, spilling out onto the patio. There's a good-sized crowd, but nothing outrageous. Most of the partygoers seem to be hanging in the backyard where there's a keg stationed.

I accept a plastic cup full of the frothy liquid from the dude manning the keg as I take in my surroundings. To our right, a game of beer pong is underway. A few yards down, several people surround a small fire pit that reminds me of a subpar version of our bonfires at Crow's Creek, and I'm suddenly hit with a pang of longing for Riverside.

Shrugging it off, my gaze scans the groups of people standing around and chatting, landing on a figure lounging on a folding chair, hand tucked behind his head, a girl on his lap.

Fucking Stanley.

He has the same smarmy grin on his face, and is wearing a pink polo shirt, the collar flipped up. "What's he doing here?" I ask, glaring in his direction.

Chris and Damon both follow my gaze to where he's grinning at the girl now leaning toward him for a kiss. A girl who is definitely *not* Brynn.

I feel a moment of relief as I make the assumption she ditched his sorry ass before I remember the way she spoke about him today. I most definitely got the impression they're at least still talking, if not dating.

"Stanley?" Damon asks, a hint of surprise in his tone. "He's Psi Delta."

My gaze snaps to Damon and I curse under my breath. How did I forget? I remember him mentioning it the first time I caught him flirting with Brynn on campus. It strikes me as odd that Brynn isn't here, but then maybe he didn't invite her. Or maybe he finds her easily replaceable. Who the hell knows? All I know is his demeanor as the brunette bombshell on his lap crushes her mouth to his lends itself to every preconceived notion I have of him.

"What do you know about him?" I ask as I drill holes in his skull with my eyes.

Damon shrugs. "Not much. Dave, the fraternity prez, is my boy, and I remember him mentioning him. I don't think he cares for him. The two butted heads a lot last year when Stanley rushed. But that's all I know."

I grunt, eyeing Stanley once more as their make-out session turns X-rated. My temperature rises because I'm almost positive if Brynn knew about the girl on his lap, she wouldn't be cool with it.

Fucking asshole.

He has someone as amazing as Brynn and he's messing around with another chick, when he should be taking her out and trying like hell to prove he's worthy. I don't care if he and Brynn are exclusive or not. She deserves better than some douchebag who's going to take her out one minute and tell her all the things she wants to hear, then hook up with someone else the next.

"You got beef with him or something?"

I blink, realizing I'm still glaring when I turn back to Damon. Chris snorts and I shoot him a look, then shrug. "Brynn's been seeing him, so based on the way he's inhaling that chick right now, I might have a problem."

"Riiiight." Chris takes a sip of his beer, talking into his plastic cup. I can hear his smile, even if I can't see it. "Brynn, the same chick you have zero interest in."

I arch a brow. "I don't have a thing for Brynn. I promised my buddy I'd watch out for her, so I fully intend to follow through. And now I see this douchebag sucking face with another girl right after I saw them cozying up in the coffee shop over the weekend? Naw." I shake my head. "That shit doesn't sit right with me."

"Seriously?" Damon asked.

"Seriously. And Brynn isn't the type of chick to play around. There's no way she'd be cool with this." I motion toward him. "She's pure and innocent and good. Loyal, too. Everything this fucker isn't, apparently."

Damon grimaces. "Damn."

"I'm gonna say something." I tip back my beer, downing the rest of it, then crush the cup in my hand.

"You sure that's a good idea, dude? Maybe you should just leave it alone. Let her deal with it," Chris says.

"Let him get his rocks off as I sit by and watch?" I grind my teeth until they ache. "Hell, no. Can't do that." I toss my cup in the grass as if to punctuate my words, hoping Stanley will have to clean it up once the party's over, then stalk over to where he's lying back on the lounge chair, the brunette straddling his lap.

I wait approximately two seconds for them to come up for air, and when they don't, I clear my throat.

The girl leans back, and blinks up at me, a glazed look in her eyes that tells me she's wasted. Stanley, on the other hand, seems to have his wits about him as his gaze focuses. Surprise flickers in his eyes before he plasters a cocky grin on his face and offers me a hand to bro slap, which I ignore. "Jace. What's up, my man. Welcome to Psi Delta."

"Cut the shit," I snap.

The chick shifts on his lap, then slides off. "Um, I think I'll get a drink."

Stanley watches her ass as she saunters toward the keg, and I have half a mind to rip his eyes out, the fucker.

"I assume you're done with Brynn, then?"

His gaze snaps back to mine. "Not that it's your business, but Brynn and I are in a good place."

My brows rise as anger smothers my insides like molten lava. This guy is a real piece of work.

"*This* is what you consider a good place?" I motion to the girl whose ass currently holds Stanley's attention. "You hooking up with other chicks when she's not around?" I laugh, the sound incredulous. I might be a player, but at least I'm upfront about it. I've never once entertained a chick without her knowing the stakes. "Wow, what a catch you are. Brynn sure won the lottery."

He shrugs. "We're not exclusive."

"So she knows you're fucking around with other girls?" When he says nothing, I have to fight the urge to implant my fist in his face. It would be worth the bruised knuckles and five seconds of gratification. "She deserves better," I grind out as I lean toward him. "And I think you know damn well how she'd feel about this."

"Let me guess . . ." Stanley flicks a piece of lint from his shirt with a grin. "You're going to tell her."

"Damn straight."

When Stanley laughs, the sound grates on me. "You're so obvious, bro."

"I'm not your bro," I say between clenched teeth. "Just doing my duty as a friend."

"A friend?" Stanley cocks his head. "She doesn't even like you."

"I have a loyalty to her family. And, unlike some people, I know what that means."

"Right," he drawls. "Whatever you tell yourself so you can sleep at night."

"What the fuck is that supposed to mean?" I snap. This guy is getting on my damn nerves.

"It means you want to dip your pen in that inkwell, but just don't want to admit it."

I snort because he's so off base, it's comical.

I might find Brynn attractive. And okay, lately, I've had some . . . less than friendly thoughts about her. But I would never.

Hell, Teagan would kill me if I even thought about it.

But it's clear I'm getting nowhere with this conversation.

"You can deflect all you want, but it doesn't change what you're doing, and it's not going to stop me from letting her know about it," I say.

"She hates you, so she'll ignore it because she thinks you're just trying to sabotage her. A notion I'm inclined to agree with." He grins. "Don't worry, though, when she comes to me to vent about it, I'll make sure I'm *very* reassuring."

I inhale through my nose, my nostrils flaring as I try to get a rein on my anger. This guy is an even bigger prick than I originally thought, which is saying a lot because I hated him the moment I saw him talking to Brynn. He must be one hell of an actor to have her fooled, but whatever she sees in him, I'll be sure to squash it.

I know Stanley's trying to goad me. Just like I know when to take a step back, so I raise my hands in surrender, satisfied at the slight frown pulling at his lips. "Whatever, man. You do your thing, and I'll do mine."

Turning, I head back to Chris and Damon, my limbs vibrating with restraint as I angle myself so I can keep tabs on him. Stanley swipes at a plastic cup on a table in front of him, upending the others and sloshing beer all over the place. Clearly, he's unhappy with our exchange, which suits me just fine.

"How'd that go?" Chris asks, arching a brow.

"Went well," I say, my tone smug. "He tried to get the upper hand, but clearly he doesn't know who he's talking to."

"Clearly," Damon says, then offers me a beer.

We tap our cups together then take a drink, but I can still feel the remnants of adrenaline from the confrontation with Stan swirling in my veins. All this pent-up anger isn't good for me. I need an escape, but my plans of finding a girl to take back to my apartment seem to have gone up in smoke. I can't focus. I'm antsy and irritable.

Across from me a cute chick catches my eye, but I quickly shift my gaze.

Even if I tried to get lost in someone, I'm not sure I could. I'm too distracted, and though I came to this party with the intention of forgetting about Brynn, it seems to have had the opposite effect. She's not even here, yet somehow, she's stolen the spotlight on my evening yet again. If this is an indication of how my first year at AU is going to go, it'll be the longest year of my life. I might as well be a fucking martyr. Maybe I should join the priesthood or maybe instead of finding a chick, I should just get wasted.

Because it sounds like as good a plan as any, I tip my cup back and chug the rest of my beer, then turn around and accept another from the kid manning the keg, and take a sip of the hoppy liquid.

"So, what's the deal, bro?" Chris tips his head and I follow the direction of his gaze to find Stanley, surrounded by a few of his frat brothers. "At first, I thought you were just totally overreacting with Brynn at that club, but he really does seem—"

"Like an asshole? Yeah. Never liked him, but he certainly has Brynn fooled."

Chris shoots me a knowing look. "And what exactly are you planning to do about it?"

I shrug. "Tell Brynn the truth. I'm sure she won't shed any tears over it. You've seen her. She's way too good for him."

"She's hot, I'll give her that." When I narrow my eyes at him, he chuckles. "Down, Cujo."

A burst of laughter comes from behind us. I turn and glare in the direction of Stanley and his friends lounging by the fire pit. Everything about his presence pisses me the hell off, which makes him damn hard to ignore when his voice carries like he's using a freaking megaphone. The kid is getting on my last nerve.

I tip my beer back and take another healthy swallow, when their conversation drifts toward me. "Whatever happened to that other chick you were talking to?"

"Brynn?" Stanley answers.

My grip tightens on the cup in my hand as Chris shoots me a warning with his eyes which I answer with a tight smile. I take another drink as Stanley continues, "We're still on," he says. "I'm supposed to take her out tomorrow, actually."

I scoff. "Not if I have anything to do with it," I mutter.

"Damn, she's fine," his friend says.

I turn now, so I'm fully staring.

"She's got that innocent, small-town-girl vibe. You hit that yet?"

I remind myself to breathe as my grip on the cup in my hands tightens.

"Hell yeah, I did."

I freeze and my hand crushes the plastic cup in my grip.

What. The. Actual. Fuck.

I blink as my vision turns hazy, sure I've misheard.

"How was she?" the punk asks.

My vision darkens, along with my gaze. I'm no longer in control of my body as I take a quick step forward. "I'm gonna kill him," I grind out as I cross the distance between us in four long strides.

"Come on, man," Chris says, a panicked edge to his voice as he follows behind me. "Be smart. Let's think about this."

I stop beside Stanley, but he's so absorbed in bragging, he hasn't noticed me yet.

"I mean, damn, man," he continues, "she's one of those chicks I could probably get to do anything I ask. Flexible as shit, too."

Fuck thinking.

I see red as I picture this asshole's dirty paws on Brynn.

My muscles coil as I inhale through my nose, out through my mouth, like I'm running a marathon and need to pace myself. I only wait to beat his ass because I want to see the fear in Stanley's eyes before I punch his lights out. "You better shut your mouth. Right. Fucking. Now."

My voice is cold and hard as steel, and Stanley blanches at the sound. I have no idea how he can be so clueless, but apparently, he had no idea I was standing so close or that his voice carries.

"Hey, man," he says with a sheepish grin I want to wipe from his face. "Just telling it like it is."

"Well, stop."

Stanley chokes on a laugh. "Sorry, but since when is my sex life your business?"

"Here we go," Chris mutters.

I step closer, ignoring Chris as I fist Stanley's shirt in my hands. "Since you're fucking around with my best friend's sister, asshole."

"Too bad she got a taste of something she liked." Stanley smirks.

I shake him so hard I rattle his bones, and I'm about to deliver a right hook when two arms wrap around me in a vice grip.

I shove against Chris's restraints, glancing around me wildly as a string of obscenities falls from my lips. "Let it go, man," Damon hisses, his voice strained as I fight to break free of their hold on me.

"You keep your fucking hands off her." I point.

"Don't worry. I'll save you my sloppy seconds," Stanley says with a grin, and I go absolutely feral.

I thrash in Damon's arms, spittle flying from my mouth as I growl at him to let me go.

"One of you want to shut your boy the fuck up before he gets himself killed?" Chris snaps, shifting his body and blocking Stanley from view as he and Damon haul me through the backyard toward the front of the house.

"What the hell are you doing?" I shout.

"Stopping you from making a mistake and getting your ass booted from the team by committing assault, dumbass." Damon releases me with a shove at the same time Chris blocks my path so I can't finish what I started.

"Get out of my way."

Chris shakes his head. "We're not letting you do this man."

"You heard what he said," I growl, waving a hand toward the backyard. "He has it coming."

"So what if he does? You need to take a minute and let the dust settle. At least talk to Brynn first before you do anything rash. Maybe I'm wrong, but the little I've seen of her tells me she's not the type of person who allows other people to fight her battles. The best way to get back at that asshole is to ruin whatever he has with her because he couldn't shut his mouth."

My gaze flickers behind them, toward the backyard where I know he's likely running his mouth, and the muscle in my jaw twitches.

They're wrong. He deserves to eat my fist.

"Look, if you rest on it and you still wanna kick his ass, I'll personally accompany you," Damon says.

I inhale, holding the breath in my lungs until it burns before I release it.

I hate it when I'm wrong, but I'm usually able to admit it, and now is no exception. Kicking Stanley's ass, though gratifying, will accomplish nothing. It'll only jeopardize my spot on the team, and if anything, it'll piss Brynn off and make her hate me even more than she already does.

With a sigh, I place my hands on my hips and nod as I stare at my new friends—my teammates—grateful as hell they have my back. Because they're right. Stanley isn't worth screwing up my future.

Regardless, I need to talk to Brynn.

CHAPTER 9

BRYNN

I LOUNGE BACK ON Charlotte's bed, wedged between her and the wall as I sip from my vodka seltzer. Several girls from down the hall have joined us, and at the moment, Samantha is regaling us with stories about her boyfriend. Now her ex.

". . . so I finally dumped his ass, and I'm not sorry for it."

"Ugh. Why are good guys so hard to find?" Charlotte complains.

"You got me. I wasted a year on Bryce."

"Screw boys," Charlotte says, raising her seltzer in the air. "Here's to a new year, new school, and being single until we find someone worth our fucking time."

"I'll second that." I clink my can to hers.

"Things not going well with Stanley?" she asks, taking a sip of her drink. "I thought you two were hitting it off?"

I pull a face. "Eh, I don't know. I mean, he's super cute, and he seems interested enough, but . . . something about him rubbed me the wrong way last week when we had coffee. He's still flirting with me before class, but something's telling me to keep my distance. Then again, maybe I'm nitpicking? I don't know what to think."

"Girl, if you see red flags now, run. Don't walk," Samantha says, taking another slice of pepperoni from the box resting on the end of Charlotte's bed.

The others chorus their agreement when Samantha perks up and holds a finger in the air. "Unless . . ." She finishes chewing and swallows, then adds, "Stanley is the smoking hot guy I've seen come to your room a couple times."

I frown and shake my head because Stanley's never been to my room. The only boy who's been to my room is . . . My eyes widen at the same time Charlotte snorts out a laugh and asks, "You mean the ripped one with messy dark hair and aqua eyes?"

"And a jaw that could cut glass?" Samantha's eyes twinkle, and I swear I see hearts in her eyes. "If you're talking about him, then all bets are off. Some things can be sacrificed. Exceptions can be made."

I roll my eyes. "That is *not* Stanley. That would be Jace Taggart, my twin brother's arrogant, pretentious, playboy best friend. Trust me, he's *not* boyfriend material."

"But he's hookup material, am I right?" Samantha wiggled her brows, a mischievous glint in her eyes.

I start to choke on the fizzy watermelon liquid in my mouth when I hear a familiar baritone, along with a pounding sound from across the hall. "Brynn! Open up. We need to talk."

I cough, whacking my chest with a fist.

"Speak of the devil." Charlotte grins like the cat that got the canary as I suck in a lungful of air and jab her in the ribs, while the racket next door continues.

"Brynn?!" *Bang, bang, bang, bang.* "I'm fucking serious, Brynn. Open the damn door."

"Wait. That's him? Right now?" Samantha asks, mouth gaping. "Oh, and he sounds angry. That's sexy."

I cross my arms over my chest and quirk a brow at her as I hiss, "Seriously? Don't be fooled by his—" I shut my mouth as another voice joins Jace's in the hallway.

I picture him talking to Creepy Cate and it brings me joy because I know how poorly it'll go.

"Well, where the hell is she?" he bellows on the heels of a door slamming.

My roommate might be an absolute bitch, but the idea of her shutting the door in Jace's face somehow makes my heart soar.

I start to smile. I'm like the Grinch who stole Christmas, only it's destroying Jace that makes me happy. But then my gaze falls to Samantha in time to catch a look I can't read as she glances at Charlotte. My stomach twists, but before I have a chance to even process it, she jumps to her feet.

"Oh, no you don't!" I shout, stumbling over Charlotte's legs as I try to scramble over her and off the bed to the sound of her manic laughter.

"This is for your own good!" Samantha yells.

My stomach sinks as I realize I'm at a disadvantage. Samantha's bed is closer to the door. I have no chance. "Don't you dare—"

Samantha swings the door open so fast it hits the wall with a *whack* at the same time my feet meet the floor and my right foot catches in Charlotte's comforter. I begin to fall, and I'd like to say it's graceful, but I'm sure it's anything but as my arms helicopter in the air and I face-plant on the scuffed linoleum.

I lie on the hard floor, body aching from the impact as two shoes appear in my line of vision. As if that's not embarrassing enough, Jace's smug face dips down to mine, only inches from the floor, eyes twinkling with amusement. It's like staring into the deep end of a pool on a hot summer day.

"Hey, there. Whatcha doin'?"

"Uh, er . . . Jace?" Samantha says, her tone meek from above me. I groan as I press my forehead to the cold, hard ground.

Luckily, I'd been able to stop the brunt of the fall with my hands at the last minute, though it's little consolation for the dull sting of humiliation coursing through me. I peel myself off the scuffed linoleum and stand.

Straightening, I stare at his shoes a moment before clearing my throat and slowly raising my gaze to find him looking hotter than he has a right to. Here I am, eating dust bunnies off the dormitory floor in leggings and a baggy tee while he looks like he just stepped off the cover of GQ with a dark-blue button down rolled at the sleeves and jeans.

He's now casually leaning against the doorframe of their room, crossing his arms over his chest. "Hey, there, Cupcake. I knew you'd be excited to see me, but I didn't know you'd be *this* excited. You could've just waited for me to come to the door, you know."

I purse my lips, trying to come up with a snarky comeback, but I'm unusually bereft. Beside me, Samantha mouths, "Sorry," and winces.

I sigh. "What do you want? Haven't you tortured me already once today?"

His gaze shifts to my friends, then back. "Can we have a minute?"

"No—"

"Yes—" Charlotte says at the same time before she winces and glances over at me with a shrug. "Er, I mean . . ."

"Don't worry about us." Samantha waves for the girls to get to their feet and head for the door as Jace takes a step inside. "We'll just be right down the hall in Laura's room," Samantha says, then proceeds to fan her face behind Jace's back. "So hot," she mouths.

I roll my eyes and lift a hand. "Bye!" I say, a little too loudly to let her know she's going to hear about this later.

Jace's gaze never leaves mine as Samantha shoves everyone out the door, and once they're gone, he wastes no time getting to the point as he asks, "Did you sleep with him?"

I flinch. "Excuse me?"

"Stanley. Did you?"

My jaw drops at the same time my cheeks flush, from anger or embarrassment I'm not sure. Likely a combination of both.

"Are you freaking kidding me? You've got some nerve barging in here and asking me that."

His mouth twists. "Technically, I was invited in, and if you haven't noticed, I'm still standing in the doorway.

Fire burns through my veins. "After you banged on my door like a maniac, demanding to speak with me."

"Answer the damn question, Brynn," Jace snaps.

"Go to hell." I cross my arms over my chest as his normally aqua eyes darken to midnight, and something inside me clicks. A small laugh escapes my lips. "Wait. Are you . . . *jealous*?"

"Jealous?" He nearly chokes on the word, then covers it with a scoff. "Stanley's not really my type. I mean, I wouldn't ever go for a dude because I don't swing that way. But I'm secure enough in my masculinity to play along. If I were to be jealous of your relationship with a dude, he would definitely have to be effeminate." He taps his chin like a thought just occurred to him. "Actually, I guess Stanley does match that description."

I pin him with a glare. "Stanley is *not* feminine."

"If you say so . . ." He shrugs.

"Whatever," I grumble, annoyed that he's somehow been able to goad me and gain the upper hand when he's the asshole in this scenario. "If you're done making jokes at my expense, you can go."

He arches a brow, then braces his hands on the top of the door frame while he leans toward me. The gesture makes my heart race, and I take a step back, needing the distance between us. "I'm not leaving until you tell me if you fucked him."

I suck in a breath. "Screw you, Jace."

"You offering?" Jace's mouth quirks, something dark glittering in his eyes while I stand there, gaping.

"So, it's okay for *you* to say things like that, but Stanley can't put his hands on me?"

One corner of Jace's mouth curves into a half grin as he takes a step closer, closing in on me until I'm pressed up against the side of Charlotte's dresser.

His gaze drops to my mouth while he lays a hand on the piece of furniture behind me, caging me in. I swallow, heart galloping, and for one insane moment, I think he might kiss me.

My back beads with sweat at the thought.

I need to get control of the situation.

I need to remember who I'm talking to.

The enemy.

Mr. Playboy himself.

Teagan's best friend, and the boy I've grown to hate.

But as his scorching gaze flickers over my face, homing in on my lips, I'm finding it hard to remember why I dislike him so much because my body didn't seem to get the memo.

I inhale, filling my lungs with a cleansing breath. "Not that it's any of your business," I say, desperate to break the tension pulling tight between us like a rubber band, "but all we did was kiss."

His brows pull together and his eyes search mine, as if trying to determine the truth in my words.

I cock a brow, challenging him to contradict me.

"That's it? You're not lying because you're afraid I'll freak out?"

"Gee. Whyever would I think that?" I ask coyly, and when he steps away from me, taking his citrus-pine scent with him, I huff out a relieved breath. "Despite what you might think," I say with more confidence than I feel, "I'm not afraid of you. And I'm pretty positive that's all we did because I was there."

His throat bobs and he runs a hand across his jaw.

I watch mesmerized as it makes a soft scratching sound over his stubble. Part of me wants to reach out and touch it too.

"That son of a bitch," he hisses under his breath, pulling my gaze away from his jawline.

He takes another step back, out into the hallway, putting more distance between us. A second ago, it was as if he couldn't get close enough. Now I'm the plague and he's terrified of catching it. What surprises me most is how I resent it.

"Why? Did he do something?" I ask, suddenly unsure whether the worst part about this encounter are the weird thoughts clanking around the edges of my brain.

"It's nothing for you to worry about. But I, uh . . ." He scratches his head. "I have to go."

"Oh, no you don't." I storm toward him and wrench his arm back before he can get very far. "You came here for a reason, and now I wanna know what it was."

He hesitates, the muscle working in his jaw. I can tell whatever it is, he's afraid to say it, which only makes me want to know more.

"Tell me. *Now*."

He nods and shoves his hands in the pockets of his jeans. "I went to a party tonight with a few of my teammates, and Stanley was there." He shifts his gaze, unable to look at me, which I take as a bad sign. "After I caught him sucking face with some chick, I also overheard him bragging to a bunch of his friends about having sex with you."

I blanch, and my limbs go numb as the blood leaves my body, but all of it must rise to my ears, because I can barely speak through the rush of blood pounding in my eardrums. "He, what?"

"I believe his exact words were something along the lines of: you're really flexible and willing to do about damn near anything he wants."

I stumble back, stricken, before my shock slowly morphs into anger. The blood boils in my veins. I'm a pot spilling over as

I imagine him, laughing and telling his friends all about our fictional escapades in the bedroom. "That son of a bitch," I grind out, repeating Jace's curse. "We kissed twice! He's not even that good of a kisser. And he has the nerve to go around spreading rumors about me?"

"I'm sorry, but I just thought you should know in case you were thinking of—"

"No, I'm glad you told me."

Jace nods, his expression stone. "Just say the word and I'll take care of him. That asshole won't so much as mutter your name again."

"No." I shake my head, my mouth a grim line as I lift my eyes to his. "No. I'll handle him myself. If you think for one minute I'm not going to confront him about this, you've got another think coming." I brush past Jace, heading for the door.

"You're going *now*?"

"Is there a better time?" I ask, pausing to peer over my shoulder.

"I'm going with you," he says, as I swipe my room key off Charlotte's desk.

"I don't need an escort. I can do this myself."

"I know you can, but if you think for one second I'm letting you go to a frat party alone, late at night with a bunch of drunk dudes—including one who lied to his friends about having sex with you—you're wrong." He cuts me off, turning to block my path. "No arguing, Brynn. You can do this your way. But I go with you, or you don't go at all."

I tighten my grip on the keys in my hand as I purse my lips, trying to act annoyed when really, I'm grateful. In truth, after what Stanley said about me, I don't want to go alone either. But he doesn't need to know that. It might go to his head and he'll get a savior complex, then he'll be unbearable. So, I try to act annoyed as I groan. "*Fine.*"

I step onto the porch of Psi Delta, and I'm hit with a wave of déjà vu. It was only a week ago I showed up here after Jace ruined our night at the club together in the hopes Stanley would give me another chance. Ever since our date at the coffee shop, I've been unsure of what to think about him. Sure, he looks good on paper and seemed to have all the qualities I wanted, but it turns out, my radar was right. Now I'm glad I kept my guard up, and even more thankful I didn't go to the party tonight, because if I had, I might still be with him, and I would have missed the opportunity to discover what a colossal tool he is.

Looks like I no longer have to straddle the fence with him. My feet are firmly planted on the side of the ground meant for moving on.

"Want me to find him and yank his ass out here?" Jace asks from behind me, obviously taking my hesitation for nerves.

I shake my head. "I texted him on the way here. He's supposed to meet me on the porch." *Probably thinks I came for a booty call.*

When the front door opens, music spills outside from within as Stanley steps out onto the porch, his smile wide as he takes me in. "Brynn . . ." he starts before he catches movement behind me, and his gaze falls to Jace and lands like a stone.

His expression sobers, which makes me question what Jace said to him before he came to find me. The air between us thickens in the silence, Stanley's posture grows more rigid by the second until he finally steps closer. "Listen," he says, hands out like he might spook me.

He's going to explain this away; he's going to lie. But he underestimates me.

My hand fists by my side, curling like Teagan taught me.

"Brynn, I don't know what he—"

I pull my arm back and let it fly. My knuckles smash into his face, and I feel a satisfying pop before Stanley screams and bends over at the waist, cupping his nose. "You bitch!"

"That's for lying about me." I shake out my hand as he glances down at the blood covering his palm, recoiling at the sight of it.

"You're fucking crazy."

My lips pull into a sneer as I lean closer, my voice hard as I say, "I'd rather be crazy *and* a bitch than your whore."

A laugh splutters behind me, followed by clapping.

I turn on my heel, past a beaming, applauding Jace, and march down the porch with his approval trailing after me.

JACE

I'm still laughing my ass off by the time Brynn pulls my truck up to the curb of my apartment. It only took minimal prodding to convince her to drive us since I had too much to drink at the party, and I'm glad. This way, I won't have to worry about her walking back to the dorms.

It's late, so the night is quiet and the roads empty. Above us, the sky is a dark bed of stars. It almost reminds me of our nights back in Riverside, if not for the girl beside me. Brynn never joined us. Maybe once or twice as a freshman before she stepped back from our circle of friends entirely. One day she was hanging out with Teagan, me, and the boys like everything was normal and then she just . . . didn't.

"I'm so glad you find my situation funny," she says, her tone dry.

"You know it's not the situation I find funny, clearly." I roll my eyes because she's so dramatic.

She turns to me. "Is this the part where you tell me, 'I told you so'?"

"Of course not." My lips twitch. "I mean, even if I *was* right, which I clearly was, I would never say that. I think it's now obvious he's the biggest douchebag on the face of the planet."

Brynn groans and leans her head back against the car seat. "The first guy I have an interest in at college and he's a dud.

I really thought he was different. Aren't there any good guys anymore?"

My mouth twists. "I hang out with dudes 99 percent of the time, except for when I seek female companionship"—Brynn snorts—"and I will tell you that no, there aren't. It's slim pickings. We're all dogs. You might as well become a nun and join a convent. I say cut your losses now."

"Oh, you and Teagan would love that. I'll just become celibate and join a convent. Thanks for the pep talk, Taggart."

"Any time." I slap a hand over her thigh in what's meant to be a friendly gesture, but my hand lingers a little longer than it should. Her skin is smooth and warm, and sends an electric jolt up my arm as her gaze drops to where my hand meets her leg.

My pulse stampedes in my chest, and my thoughts drift to dangerous places. Like the moment earlier in the dorms where I caged her in between my arms. I wanted to kiss her then. Just like I want to kiss her now.

I have no idea what the hell is happening to me or where these feelings are coming from, but the part of my brain still functioning screams at me to retreat. Bail. She's Teagan's sister—a no-go zone—so I clear my throat and extricate my hand as casually as possible, noting the pink staining Brynn's cheeks as I do. "Is it wrong that I feel like Stanley turning out to be the world's biggest dumbass was worth it just to see you deck him?"

Brynn's frown curls into a smile before a laugh splutters from her lips. "The look on his face . . ."

"So classic," I crow. "And your final burn was the most epic mic drop I've probably ever witnessed. In fact, I think we need to make T-shirts or personalized mugs."

The corners of Brynn's eyes crinkle as she laughs even harder. "It was just being honest. I *would* rather be a crazy bitch than his whore."

"Thank God for that because you being a crazy bitch makes my life a whole hell of a lot easier. After tonight, I'm not sure I have to worry about you anymore."

Brynn's laughter dies in her throat, and she rolls her eyes. "You never did. You're not my babysitter, Taggart."

And just like that, Brynn's hackles rise.

"I'll give you more space from here on out."

"Oh, why, thank you. What a gift."

I grin at her snarky tone and reach across her to turn the ignition off. "Wanna come up?" I nod toward my apartment building.

She peers up at the building through the windshield. "To your bachelor pad? No thanks. No telling what venereal disease I might catch just by breathing the same air."

"Hilarious." I huff out a half laugh.

"Why are we here, anyway?" she asks, flashing me some serious side-eye. "I thought the point was for me to have a ride back to my dorm?"

"Just need to grab something, then we'll get you home. Be right back."

I leave my truck, taking the stairs two at a time until I reach the second-story landing where I let myself into the apartment. It's quiet, so I assume Chris is still out, which is just as well. I'm sure he'd give me shit for being with Brynn right now.

I grab a plastic baggie and fill it with ice from the freezer, then return to the car and toss it to her. "Here. I know you don't have ice at the dorms. Keep this on your knuckles for a bit and it'll help with any bruising or swelling."

"I'm sure it'll be fi—"

I shoot her a look that says I'm not playing.

"Okay, geez. I'll ice them, all right?"

She starts the car and heads toward the other end of campus to the dorms. When she parks, I begin to remove my seatbelt when she eyes my movements skeptically. "What are you doing?"

"Walking you inside," I say like it should be obvious.

"Why?"

"Because I want to make sure you get in safely."

She scoffs. "What happened to giving me more space?" When I say nothing, she adds, "I live on the first floor. It's maybe a few hundred feet. What could possibly happen?"

I sigh and drag a hand down my face. "Do you have to argue with everything I say?"

She crosses her arms. "When it makes zero sense, yes."

I groan as I get out of the car and walk around to her side, then fling the door open. She makes no move to get out. Instead, she glares at me, and I wonder if we'll stay like this all night, shooting barbs at each other with our eyes until the sun rises.

Finally, she sighs like I'm the most ridiculous person on the planet for wanting to walk her to her room, and steps out.

I almost laugh at the brisk pace she sets in an effort to out-walk me because my legs are nearly a foot longer than hers. I could do my best impression of a sloth and still beat her.

She wrenches open the door to the first floor and I follow behind until she reaches her room and fumbles for her key. I don't know if my presence is making her nervous, or if it's the heavy metal rock blasting through the door causing her to flounder, but I frown and jerk my head toward the sound. "Your roommate is . . ."

"The devil incarnate? Yeah, I know."

"How are you going to sleep in there?" I ask as Brynn shifts the bag of ice on her hand, so she can stick the key in the lock with the other.

"Let's see. I'll probably ask her to turn the music off a couple of times and she'll ignore me. Then, once she finally does acknowledge my presence, she'll stare at me with dead eyes for about five awkward minutes before silently flicking it off, all while muttering black-magic witch chants under her breath."

I laugh, but quickly sober when Brynn doesn't so much as crack a smile. "You're joking."

"I wish I were," she says with a tight smile, "but welcome to my current state of life." As if to punctuate her words, she pushes the door open and the music grows louder. It's dark inside, save for a blacklight illuminating the room where, in plain view, her roommate is holding a small paper straw against one nostril while she snorts a line of something white and powdery. I'm pretty sure it isn't the Pixy Stix we used to experiment with in middle school.

"What the actual fuck?" I bark out.

Beside me Brynn gasps, mouth gaping as her roommate's head whips up, eyes glazed over. "Don't you know how to fucking knock?"

"It's my room!" Brynn screeches, waving an arm. "And that's *my* desk."

At the sound of her distress, a boy pops up from the bed behind her roommate. Like a zombie coming to life, something nonsensical spills from his lips. His eyes are bloodshot, his skin pale, and if I'm not mistaken, he's completely naked.

Without another word, I yank Brynn back out into the hall, slamming the door shut behind me. "You're not staying in there, at least not tonight."

"But . . ." She blinks, clearly shell-shocked, but I see the moment the situation sinks in, and she nods. "Yeah, you're right. I'm sure Charlotte won't mind if I crash in her room tonight."

I place my hands on either side of her face, forcing her to meet my eyes. I want to make sure she's okay before I leave her. "You sure?"

She nods. "Yeah."

I eye her skeptically before she offers me what I think is meant to be a reassuring smile but is wobbly at best. Exhaling, I glance at the closed door to her room and exhale. "I'm going to tell the front desk and get campus police up here."

"What? No!" Brynn grabs my arms, her eyes wide. "You can't do that. She'll curse me. Put a hex on me. Poison me in my sleep. You *cannot* go to the authorities."

"If we tell someone now, they'll bust her and get her booted from housing."

"Jace," her throat bobs, "she has a little doll that looks strikingly similar to me, with a two-inch lock of real blonde hair pinned to it which I suspect is from my head!" She whips a lock of her own from the side of her face and waves it in front of me; it appears to be slightly shorter. "I know what people like her do to those dolls. You *cannot* call anyone."

I eye her with a frown. I'm dead set on reporting her, but it appears Brynn is adamant we don't. Once again we're at odds, and I have no idea what the hell to do with this mess. Brynn's night has already been complete shit. The last thing I want to do is make it worse. Or make her hate me more than she already does by going against her wishes.

"Fine." I sigh. "We'll talk to the housing department first thing Monday. See what they can do. It's summer. Surely, they can offer you another room."

She nods, and the color returns to her cheeks as the tension drains from her face. "Yes, good. Thank you," she says like I'm doing her a favor.

"But until then, I don't want you going in your room by yourself. Got it?"

She nods, then crosses the hall and knocks on Charlotte's door.

Her shoulders curl into herself and a wave of sympathy crashes into me as I watch her explain the situation and Charlotte take her into her arms and pull her inside. It's been one hell of a night for her, yet she's taking it like a champ. Most girls I know would've broken down after coming back to their dorm room to find their roommate snorting coke on their fucking desk.

I bid the girls goodnight, then make my way back outside with a sinking feeling inside my stomach I can't extinguish. I don't know what it is, but it reminds me of the gnawing ache I had in my gut the time I got food poisoning in ninth grade.

Brynn is fine.

I know she's fine.

She's safe and sound with her friends.

Still, I can't help but hate the situation for her and wish there were something I could do to help.

CHAPTER 10

JACE

"W HAT THE HELL DO you mean, she's gone for the summer?" I shout at the man-child behind the desk of the AU housing department.

"As I mentioned, she left on Monday for maternity leave. She won't be back until the end of summer."

"And there's no one else that can help us?"

"I'm afraid not," the man says, and I want to rip the weird knit cap he's wearing from his bald head. It's in the middle of freaking summer!

"So, you're telling me, my friend, here," I say, waving toward Brynn who already plead her case but failed to secure a suitable solution, "is stuck with a roommate who's fucking insane and who we caught doing drugs in their room last night, and there's not a damned thing anyone can do about it? Including giving her one of the *hundreds* of vacant rooms I know you must have just sitting around empty since it's summer?"

"That's right." The man purses his mouth, and I want to give him a fat lip. "Next time, I recommend calling the authorities."

I shoot Brynn a sharp look that says, *I told you,* then turn back to him. "Look at her!" I point, taking in the giant bags under her eyes. "She had to sleep on the floor of a friend's dorm room the last two nights. Does it look like she got any sleep to you?"

"I'm sorry, sir, but—"

I growl and turn my back on him as he continues to sputter nonsense, barking at Brynn, "Let's go!"

"I told you I tried," she says as she turns to follow behind me.

I palm the door to the housing department, pushing it open so hard it vibrates on its hinges. I'm too angry for words. So angry, in fact, I want to take my aggression out on someone, so I keep my mouth shut lest I take it out on her. Quite frankly, she deserves nothing short of an award for not going completely ballistic on the idiot from housing.

We step out into the sunshine, and I tip my face to the sky, letting the warmth of it heat my skin and soothe my nerves. I'm sweaty and exhausted, and all I want to do is have a shower and ice my muscles, but I wanted to accompany Brynn to housing so I could ensure she fixed her roommate situation.

I found her after practice, looking like she hadn't slept a fucking minute all weekend. When I asked her why, she explained she made it one night in Charlotte's bed before she got a massive kink in her neck. She spent last night on the hard floor, and to top it all off, apparently, Samantha snores like a bulldog in heat, and Brynn is a light sleeper.

And now that the moron in housing is claiming no one can do a damned thing about her roommate until fall, I have no idea what to do.

I place my hands on my hips, taking a minute to think.

I can't let her go back to her room, but staying with Charlotte and Samantha is obviously not the answer. She needs somewhere quiet. Somewhere I know she'll be safe.

"Listen, thanks for trying to help me, Jace, but it seems like a lost cause. I probably just need to suck it up and go back to my room with Creepy Cate. Even if I had slept well with Charlotte and Samantha, the dorm rooms are impossibly small. I can't expect them to let me live there for the next six weeks. We'll be tripping over each other, and the last thing I want to do is annoy them because they're becoming really great friends."

"You are *not* going back to rooming with her." My mind conjures the image of the naked dude in Cate's bed, blitzed out of his mind. "If she's doing drugs out in the open like that, who knows what kind of people she's also going to bring by. I don't want you wrapped up in that mess. And Teagan wouldn't either." She opens her mouth to protest, but I stop her. "Listen, just . . . go back to your room and I'll meet you there, okay? We'll figure something out."

"What are you gonna do?" she asks, eyeing me warily.

"Go back to housing and throttle that guy's neck until his eyes snap back in his head and he gives you a new room?"

Her eyes widen. *She thinks I'm serious.*

"Nothing." I sigh and place my hands on my hips. "I just need to think."

"Okay. But I don't see what you're going to be able to do to help." She starts walking backward, shifting her book bag over her shoulder. "Thanks for trying, though."

I nod, offering a small wave as I realize this is probably the first time in her life Brynn has ever thanked me for something.

Once she's out of earshot, I pull out my phone and dial Teagan's number because in truth, I'm stumped on what to do. I know Brynn doesn't want her parents to worry about her, so they have no idea her roommate's a freak, but maybe they can call and throw a fit. The housing department might be more inclined to do something about the situation if parents are involved.

"Yo, what's up, man?" Teagan answers.

"Houston, we have a problem . . ." I say, squinting up at the blue sky as I fill him in on everything I witnessed last night.

He's so silent on the other side of the line, for a minute I think he's hung up. Once I finish, I have to pull my phone away from my head to check he hasn't.

"Shit, man. Are you fucking with me right now?" he finally says.

"I wish I was, dude. Her roommate is bad, and I don't know about you, but I don't get a warm and fuzzy feeling with her anywhere near there. I see this going wrong in a million different ways."

Teagan exhales. "I'll talk to my folks. See if they can make something happen with the roommate. Why didn't Brynn call them in the first place?"

"Dude, hell if I know, but I honestly think it's because she doesn't want to worry them. She made me swear I wouldn't tell you."

"I get that. With us out of the house and the girls growing up, my parents are busier than they've ever been. They barely have time to take a piss let alone fight this, but I'm not sure what choice we have."

"I know, and she looks completely exhausted today. I can tell she got zero sleep this weekend. I'm sure she could hold on another night or two if—"

"Or she could just move into your place."

My brows rise to my hairline.

Did he say what I think he said?

"Uh, what?"

"Dude, it's perfect," Teagan says, and I can hear the relief in his voice.

"Um, exactly what about this proposal is perfect? Brynn and me living together? Sounds like a fucking death wish for both of us, if you ask me."

"Your roommate Chris is gone half the time, you said so yourself. It's like living alone all over again, so she won't be in the way, but at least you'd have some company."

Fuck. Why'd I have to run my mouth?

"Okay, but that still doesn't mean—"

"Come on, man. She can't go back to that psycho, and if the housing department doesn't budge on this, then she's going to need somewhere to stay for more than a night or two. And we wouldn't even have to involve my parents."

I pull on the back of my neck as I think about Teagan's proposal. Logistically, it makes sense. But practically, it'll never work. We'll rip each other's throats out if we're confined to a space together. Not to mention the fucked-up thoughts I've been having about her lately.

"We are literally the last people on the face of the planet that should be living together."

"It won't be that bad."

"That's easy for you to say," I mutter under my breath.

"Brynn's actually really chill and super easy to live with. She picks up after herself and helped my mom a ton growing up. She can cook and doesn't take an hour in the bathroom. You could do a hell of a lot worse. Besides, you guys were friends once, remember? Before you made it your life's mission to piss each other off?"

Yeah, I fucking remember. I remember because I also remember when it changed. At some point, early sophomore year, she became sullen and moody, and all of a sudden hated my guts.

I've been thinking about it a lot lately, actually. Mostly because I don't understand it and wonder what things would be like between us if it had never happened—if I hadn't become her nemesis. Would we be good friends? *More?*

What the fuck am I saying? This is exactly why living with her is a bad idea.

"That was a long time ago," I say, my tone flat.

"Things change. They can change again."

Fuck. He's not helping.

And he's not wrong.

Ever since we got here, my dick's been jumping to attention every time she's around. If Teagan only knew the thoughts I'd had about his sister after the night at Bradd's, he'd think twice about suggesting she live with me.

Speaking of my third arm . . . "How the hell am I supposed to bring chicks back to my place with her there, huh? I highly doubt she's gonna be comfortable with that shit."

"So you have to keep it in your pants a while longer. It's worth it."

Is it though?

Me sexually deprived with Brynn at my disposal, feels dangerous. Like playing with fire.

I groan and lean forward because this conversation isn't going the way I imagined, and I'm trying my hardest not to be a jerk. The scary truth is, the idea of Brynn living with me doesn't sound all that bad. In fact, I kind of like it, which is how I *know* it's a terrible idea.

"You said you'd look after her for me," Teagan says, his tone hard. "Or was that all bullshit?"

I massage the knot in my forehead, wondering how I got myself into this mess. Why do I have to be such a good friend?

"How do you even know she'll accept? Brynn is hardheaded and she hates me. She'd probably rather live with Ozzy Osbourne's secret love child back at the dorms."

"Because you won't take no for an answer."

Shit.

When I don't respond right away, he adds, "I know she seems like she's made of stone, but she's not. Trust me. She's a lot more fragile than she looks, and the last thing I want is for her to retreat into her shell again. She tends to expect the worst, you know? I'm not sure how much faith she has in people."

I frown. He said something similar the day I helped move her in. Why do I get the feeling there's something he's not telling me?

The last thing I want is for her to retreat into her shell again. Like something had happened once before to make her shut the world out. It's an apt description of how quickly she changed and stopped hanging out with us. But I don't say any of these things, nor do I ask Teagan about it. Not only because I know he'd take Brynn's secrets to the grave, but because Brynn is none of my damned business, and I need to keep it that way, even if I'm now wondering what it is I don't know about her.

I stare at Brynn, unblinking; I can practically see the wheels spinning in her head.

"You're joking, right?" One corner of her mouth quirks in a smirk as she peers around my shoulder, looking for someone who isn't there, as if she thinks she's being punked.

Like I would joke about this.

"I wish I was, but unless housing gets off their ass and does something, you have no choice. It's the only solution that makes sense."

"Um, forgive me, but how does the two of us sharing the same space make any sense at all? We can barely breathe the same air without strangling each other."

"While I don't disagree, you can't stay in your room. It's not safe there. Even if that psycho doesn't do anything stupid to endanger you, I don't think it's wise to stay somewhere there are drugs. If she goes down for it, she might try to take you with her."

Brynn nods like she's thought the same thing.

"And you can't keep staying in another dorm room that's already occupied. You have no bed. You're getting no sleep. It's no way to live, and I'm sure it's against the rules."

"So, the solution is living with *you*?" she asks, her tone incredulous.

"Do you have a better idea?" I arch a brow, waiting as she stares me down. After a moment, I smile. "I'll take that as a no."

I turn and grab the suitcases I told her to pack when I texted her earlier, then begin to wheel them outside and down the hall.

"But . . . you have a roommate," she says, trying to catch up. "Don't you think you should discuss this with him first?"

"Chris will be cool with it," I say, waving away her concern.

"*I'm* not even cool with it." She huffs and hurries to my side but quickly falls behind again. "How can you be so sure?"

"Because he's hardly ever there. He practically commutes. Trust me. He's not going to care."

"But where will I sleep?" she asks, winded from matching her stride to mine.

With a groan, I halt and spin around, but Brynn isn't prepared and crashes into me.

Her face hits my upper chest and when I grip her arms to hold her steady, every inch of her body presses into mine: the soft swell of her breasts, her hips, her thighs. I inhale a deep breath as I feel a stirring in my pants and quickly push her away. Shifting, I try to get a rein on my dick along with my errant thoughts as I wonder if she's wearing a push-up bra or if her breasts really are that full.

This is precisely why Brynn coming to live at my apartment is a bad idea.

Brynn, however, rubs her forehead like my chest is made of concrete and scowls, seemingly unfazed by the impromptu body contact. "What the hell, Jace?"

"Listen," I say, putting some much-needed distance between us and raking a hand through my hair. "I don't have all the answers, Brynn. To be honest, I haven't really even thought it through properly, but we'll figure it out. Hell, I spent half my time back home at your house, so it won't be all that much different."

Who am I kidding? It'll be entirely different. No Teagan. No parents or siblings. Just us. And Chris, on the rare occasion he graces us with his presence.

"But we hate each other," she says, deadpan.

No, Cupcake. I don't hate you. Far from it.

I glance down at her, studying her expression. "Do *you* hate me?"

She cocks her head as if thinking about my question.

I roll my eyes. "Never mind. Don't answer that."

We walk a few more steps before I can't take it anymore and I halt once more. For some reason, it bothers me that she thinks I feel any kind of way about her.

I reach out and place my fingers beneath her chin, tipping her face up to mine until our eyes meet and her violet gaze sinks its teeth into me. Her eyes are like a vortex, sucking me in, and I realize as I stare down at her that I'd do just about damn near anything for this girl.

It's your loyalty to Teagan talking. Nothing more.

Loyalty or not, it's one thing to tease her, but I don't want her thinking I hate her, because it's the furthest thing from the truth. Finding ways to get under Brynn Nichols's skin is one of my favorite pastimes. I've finely honed my skills over the years, and I look forward to it like a kid on Christmas.

"I don't hate you, Cupcake," I say, my voice soft as her gaze shoots hooks under my skin. "The way I see it, you only have two options. You can either carry on sleeping on the floor of your friend's dorm, getting zero sleep and risking getting on their nerves after a while. Or you can move in with me until we find a better solution. I'm not gonna force you to stay with me if you don't want to, even if I think you should. I'm not that guy."

I swallow, and I realize with frightening clarity I care more about her decision than I should. "So, what'll it be?"

CHAPTER 11

BRYNN

I TURN THE WATER as hot as it will go, hoping the heat will soothe my nerves and quiet my thoughts. I have to admit, it's kind of nice having a private bathroom, rather than a cloth curtain and the public stalls our entire floor at Hyde House share. There's no need for shower shoes, and I can probably find a spot in the closet or under the sink to store my shower caddy, so I don't have to lug it back and forth.

Apparently, college apartments are the way to go.

Still, I can't believe I agreed to live with Jace. Even if it's only temporary, the idea of the two of us sharing the same space in any capacity is a disaster waiting to happen.

He pisses me off on a good day. On a bad day, I'm two seconds away from wrapping my hands around his throat and squeezing until his eyes pop.

I thought the feeling was mutual.

Until this afternoon.

I don't hate you, Cupcake.

His words echo in my head like the sound of a guitar string long after it's been plucked.

Was he placating me?

He certainly seemed genuine.

I remember the feel of his fingers beneath my chin. How the heat of his touch seared into me as his gaze met mine. The soft rasp of his voice. Eyes as blue as the Caribbean.

I groan as I squirt a giant blob of conditioner into my hands and run it through my hair. I can't help but feel like one of his groupies when I know damn well the reason he's being so nice. The reason he's done everything he has since we arrived at AU.

My brother.

Teagan and his stupid oath with Jace to watch over me. It's ridiculous. I can take care of myself.

Then again, my options in this case are limited, and even though Jace can't make me stay here, what's the alternative? Going back to the dorms with Creepy Cate?

Jace was right when he said there's more to consider than just the fact she clearly has it out for me. If she gets caught, I could go down with her. Not to mention the kind of people she's bringing back to our room. I've already witnessed one or two unsavory characters coming and going. At best it's an uncomfortable situation to be in. At worst, I could be in danger if I stay there.

I rinse the conditioner from my hair, then turn the water off. As much as I want my problems to wash down the drain, no amount of time spent under the hot spray is going to make everything right.

I yank open the shower curtain and grab my towel, quickly drying off before I secure it around me when I catch my reflection in the mirror above the sink. These first couple of weeks have not gone how I thought they would. My roommate is a freak to the point of I've found myself displaced, and the first guy I chose to try and pursue a relationship with turned out to be a total jerk.

My shoulders slump forward at the trajectory of my thoughts while my purplish-blue gaze stares back at me in defeat. With a long sigh, I open my cosmetic case, remove my toothbrush and toothpaste, then start to brush my teeth.

Jace was right about spending tons of time at my house in high school. But he's wrong about this being no different. Teagan's not here as a buffer. My family isn't here, either. It's just him and me. As far as I know, his roommate Chris hasn't even come home yet, and I can't help but feel this awkward tension at the fact I'll be falling asleep and waking up under the same roof as him. There's something innately intimate about seeing someone first thing in the morning, before they've had time to change out of their pajamas or have their first cup of coffee. And I'm not sure it's something I'm prepared to share with him.

Once I'm finished, I zip my bag back up and take it with me. I'm already an inconvenience, so the last thing I want to do is leave my stuff lying around. The less evidence there is that I'm here, the better.

I pad my way out of the bathroom and into the living room, grateful when I see it empty. As selfish as it is, I'd rather face Chris tomorrow, once I have a fresh head and I'm feeling a little less like an inconvenience.

I pause by the sofa where I left my suitcases to see they're gone.

With a frown, I cross the living room toward the bedroom Jace said belonged to him during my five-second tour, and peek my head inside to find him at his closet, tearing everything out of it and cramming it into his dresser drawers.

"Uh, what are you doing? Did you move my things?"

His gaze darts up to me, shifting from my damp hair and bare face, down to my baggy T-shirt and little cotton shorts. His throat bobs before he turns away again and grabs the last of his things. "I figured you could have the closet," he mumbles.

"Wait. What? No." I wave a hand and step further inside. "You don't have to do that. This is just temporary. My suitcases will be fine."

He turns and eyes me with a raised brow. "Assuming housing doesn't perform a miracle, I'm not going to let you live out of suitcases for six weeks. You can have the closet."

I open my mouth to argue, but then think better of it, re-membering my mom's favorite phrase: Pick your battles. Maybe that's all I need to do with Jace—pick my battles. It certainly can't hurt, and it might make our situation easier.

So instead of arguing, I tell him, "Thanks," and he nods in reply. "Well, if it's okay with you, I think I'm just going to go to bed now," I say, feeling the weight of everything that's happened in the last few days heavy in my chest.

To say parts of my college experience thus far have been somewhat disappointing is an understatement. The only bright spots have been Charlotte and Samantha. Thank heavens for them and our budding friendship. Though I suppose things could be worse. I could have no one at all.

"Yeah, of course," he says, moving toward the doorway to his bedroom. "I'll just get out of your way."

I frown, confused. "If you have a spare blanket and sheets, I'll make up my bed on the couch."

"You mean, *I'll* make up my spot on the couch."

"Um, *no*." I place a hand on his chest, stopping him as he tries to brush past me, pillow in hand. "You're not sleeping on the couch, Jace."

"Did you seriously think I would let you take the sofa? Teagan would have my balls."

There it is again. I roll my eyes. *Boys and their promises.* Truthfully, it's getting a little old.

"I don't care about my brother," I say. "I'm the one who's crashing your place and inconveniencing you. There's no way in hell I'm sleeping in your bed while you take the couch."

"Yes," he says, gripping my shoulders and guiding me toward the queen-sized bed, gently shoving me onto it, "you are."

"*No.* I'm not." I spring up from the mattress to face him, arms crossed over my chest.

"You are," Jace grinds out. He presses on my shoulders again and forces me back down.

"Not!" I yell-hiss as I grab his arm and yank him toward the mattress, but he's too solid, and barely stumbles forward as our knees bump together.

"I'm not arguing about this, so you might as well just get your pretty ass in bed." He points.

I bark out a laugh. "Wow. What a sweet talker. Since you asked so nicely . . ."

He growls and rakes a hand through his hair. "Brynn, I swear . . ."

"You swear, what?" I grin.

"Why do you have to be so fucking obstinate? Stop arguing and just take the damn bed."

"There is zero chance of me taking your bed and letting you sleep on the couch for six weeks. You have training, practice, and there's no way am I going to be responsible when you start shitting up the field because your back hurts and you're tired." I turn around, furiously gathering up one of the blankets off the bed, along with a pillow. "I'm smaller. It only makes sense. I have the couch."

"Nice try." He blocks my path to the door and yanks the blanket from my hand. "But there's no way in hell I'm letting you crash on the couch in those booty shorts so Chris can get an eyeful first thing in the morning."

My jaw drops and I glance down at myself. Admittedly these shorts are short, but they're freaking pajamas. What does he expect? "Do you want me to wear a freaking mumu, Taggart?"

"That would be a great start," he says icily.

My eyes harden. "I'm not sleeping in your bed."

"And neither am I." His smile tightens. "Looks like we're *sharing* the couch, then. How should we do this? Do you want to spoon, or would you prefer my face at your feet? I take you for a big spoon kinda girl."

I fake gag as I grapple with the blankets once more and storm into the living room.

If he wants to be a jackass, I'll call his bluff because there's no way he'll share the couch with me. His massive body would barely fit alone without me hogging up more than half the couch myself.

Jace follows, hot on my heels, as I practically catapult myself onto the cushions with a loud thump. I wince. This couch isn't nearly as soft as it looks. In fact, it's kind of hard, a little like concrete.

Regardless, I keep a straight face as I place the pillow behind my head and pull the blanket up to my chest, content on settling in when all of a sudden, a gust of cool air hits me as Jace rips the covers down and crawls in beside me.

"Oh, this is *niiiice*. Cozy," he says, like the complete jackass he is. "A little tight," he squeaks out as he wedges himself behind me, pressing into the back of the couch and nearly pushing me off the sofa altogether. "But definitely nice."

I say nothing as my face heats. His entire body is smashed against my backside. Even the littlest of movements will put us in dangerous territory.

I'm so mad I could spit.

My breathing turns shallow as I try to tamp down my anger in the silence. Yes, anger. Nothing else. I'm definitely not turned on by his firm body smashed up against my own.

I know what he's doing. He thinks that if he inserts himself on the couch with me and I'm uncomfortable enough, he can make me crack and I'll take the bed.

Well, he better guess again if he thinks he'll win because my resolve when it comes to Jace Taggart is made of steel.

I roll over and sit up slightly to face him and tell him as much, barely stopping myself from spiraling off onto the floor. "If you want me off this couch," I say, jaw clenched, "you'll have to make me get off." I regret my choice of words the moment they leave my mouth, and based on the heat flaring in Jace's gaze, he caught the double entendre. He starts to shift, hands reaching under my legs. "And I swear to God if you try to carry me, I'll kick you in the balls before you have the chance," I add.

His eyes darken to denim in twilight and time slows. "Fine." His lips curl. "I'll make you get off another way."

I gasp, but before I can protest, he straightens and pushes me. I start to fall before I yelp and grapple with his arm. But he doesn't count on me having the dexterity of a spider monkey as I cling to him like a suction cup to prevent myself from crashing to the floor.

He tries to stand, but I'm still attached, starfishing his body like I have suction cups on my limbs, even as he tries to peel me off.

"What the fuck?" He extricates one arm only to go for the other as I suction right back onto him.

"My limbs are glue," I say, beginning to pant from the exertion of maintaining my grip on him.

Sweat beads at the back of my neck as he takes another tactic and lowers me back onto the couch where my hold on him backfires. I'm suctioned to him so tightly, he comes with me, the weight of his body pressing me back into the cushions. I struggle harder to maintain my hold as he tries to remove himself from my grip.

After a couple minutes of my floundering, he stops fighting me. The tension in his muscles eases. Our heavy breathing fills the silence between us as we find a momentary truce to catch our breath. Our eyes meet and the hard planes of his chest press against the soft swell of my own, the heat of his breath washing over my neck as I become increasingly aware of all our points of contact. His heart beats against mine, pounding a steady rhythm while my legs tighten around his waist.

I want to unwind myself from him like a shriveling vine, but I'm afraid to move. To breathe. Especially when his gaze drops to my lips and something dark glitters in his eyes.

My stomach swoops like I'm plunging down the steep dip of a roller coaster, and before I have a chance to react, he crushes his mouth to mine.

I'm frozen in place, iced over as my mind registers the contact.

His mouth is warm and impatient as he brushes his lips against my own, then slants his mouth again to try and coax a reaction from me.

But my mind is playing catch up.

This is Jace Taggart.

His mouth is on mine.

And he's kissing me.

It's obvious he's no amateur by the way his mouth expertly parts my own, his tongue tracing the seam of my lips and cajoling me into action as I begin to kiss him back.

The ice around my heart thaws at the taste of mint on his tongue. It figures he'd taste as good as he looks. Everything about him is dangerous. Even his tongue is weaponized. But I'm onto him. The war he's started is not lost on me. He's pulled out the big guns. He thinks this will scare me off. That I'll retreat like some delicate flower. That by kissing me, I'll be repulsed or pissed—he's probably banking on both—and retreat to his room like a coward.

Boy is he wrong.

Two can play this game.

My mouth parts and I angle my head, brushing my tongue against his as my hands sink into his thick locks, yanking slightly at the roots and smiling when he sucks in a breath, clearly surprised I'm so fervently reciprocating. His shock fades quickly, though, as he slides one hand up my side, leaving a trail of goosebumps in his wake. His hand stops at my jaw, angling my face so he can gain better access to my mouth.

He's experienced, I know this. Jace Taggart has been with his fair share of girls. He *should* be good at this. Yet his kiss still exceeds my already high expectations. In fact, he's so skilled, it's not hard to understand why girls drop their panties at his feet.

Fireworks burst behind my eyelids. The burning heat of arousal claws up my spine, awakening places in my body that have long since gone into hibernation.

He tries to dominate the kiss as the delicious weight of him pushes me further into the cushions, hips pressing into mine, hands everywhere as I try to keep pace.

My hands slide underneath his shirt, tracing the hard ridges of his muscles, mesmerized by the way they undulate under my touch. A growl vibrates in the back of his throat in response as he drags his teeth over my bottom lip, hands moving to the sliver of skin below the hem of my shirt. They leave a trail of fire, torching every inch he touches.

I moan when his mouth moves to my neck, pressing soft kisses under my jaw until he reaches my mouth again. A shift of his weight, and I can feel his arousal, hard against my stomach.

Alarm bells go off in my head, and I blink my eyes open, staring at the ceiling as reality comes crashing in.

What the hell am I doing? And how far am I willing to let this go just to prove a point—to win some weird battle of wills?

His hand dips below the waistband of my shorts and it's like a bucket of ice water has been poured over me.

I pull my mouth from his and shove at his chest. A brief trickle of fear sprouts before he lifts his head almost immediately and meets my gaze. The black of his eyes swallows the blue, and I don't know what he sees when he looks at me, but he receives the message and shifts to the side, allowing me the space to scoot off the couch as relief crashes over me.

A glimpse at his expression in my periphery tells me he's unfazed, like our heated make-out sesh didn't freak him out like it did me. I'm just another girl, and it's another day in the life of Jace Taggart.

My cheeks flame as I get to my feet and stomp toward his bedroom door without a second glance in his direction.

I'm too embarrassed. Too pissed off. Too turned on to look him in the eye.

Which is precisely the problem.

Turned on by Jace Taggart?

Nooooo.

It's like a nightmare come to life, too mortifying for words.

I slam the bedroom door behind me to the sound of Jace's chuckle, and proceed to prop myself up against the slab of wood while I wait for my racing heart to calm down.

I hate that he got the best of me.

I hate that I enjoyed it far more than I should have.

I hate that he's out there laughing, while I'm in here just trying to hold it together.

Fucking Jace Taggart.

CHAPTER 12

JACE

I GROAN WHEN MY alarm goes off and attempt to sit up, but instead roll off the couch like a sack of potatoes.

"Morning, princess," Chris's chipper voice calls out from the kitchen. I glance toward the sound with bleary eyes to see him standing by the coffee pot, a shit-eating grin on his face as he sips from a steaming mug. "Sleep well?" he asks with a chuckle, and I flip him off.

Fuck. It feels like someone threw a party on my spine last night.

I manage to stand and stretch out my back. "That fucking couch sucks. I'm throwing it in the dumpster out back," I say, my voice raspy as I cross the living room into the kitchen and pour myself a cup of coffee. You'd think for the small fortune I know my parents likely paid for it, it'd be a little more comfortable.

I take a sip, savoring the taste of the strong brew, and praying it works a miracle, because that's what I need if I'm going to get through practice like this. Otherwise, my ass is grass.

"Regretting your life choices?" Chris asks, eyeing me over the rim of his mug with a smile.

I grunt. "It'll be fine." Or it would have been, had I not fucking kissed Brynn last night.

I run a hand over my neck as I recall what she felt like pressed against me, her hot mouth on mine, tasting like forbidden fruit. All I wanted was to sink my teeth into her.

What the hell was I thinking?

I wasn't. Obviously. What started as some ridiculous competition to get the other to cave and take the bed took a turn I wasn't expecting.

It's not like I meant to kiss her.

One second, she was pissing me off because she's so damn stubborn, and the next, she's wrapping her tight little body around me, and I'm slipping my tongue in her mouth in an effort to teach her a lesson.

Well, I got what I wanted, all right. She high-tailed her ass to my bed real fast after that.

I close my eyes, reliving the memory of her panic-stricken expression as she fled from the couch.

Shit, I'm screwed.

She probably hates me even more than before.

Sleeping on the hard-ass couch is my punishment. Penance for taking what's not mine, further atoned by the memory of her lips keeping me awake all night.

"What's up with you?" Chris asks, startling me from my thoughts.

"Huh?" I focus back on him to find him staring. "Nothing," I say, a little too quickly. "Nothing happened." When he narrows his eyes, I clear my throat. "Uh, thanks for letting her stay here. I know it's probably not what you had in mind for your first college apartment, but she can't go back to her room, and there's really nowhere else for her to stay."

"It's no problem, man," he says, his tone suspicious. "Glad I could help. I'm gone half the time anyway." He pushes off the counter, still eyeing me like he can read my mind. "I'm gonna go grab my gear and get an early start. Meet you at the field?"

I nod at the same time my phone pings.

I cross the kitchen, cup of coffee in hand, and sink down onto the couch. I grab my phone from the coffee table and groan when I see a message from Graham in the group chat.

GRAHAM: Rest in peace, brother.

The blood drains from my face. For a moment I think they somehow know what happened last night.

That Teagan knows I mauled his sister.

But a quick glimpse at the conversation reveals that Teagan outed me sometime last night—probably when I was sucking Brynn's face—and Graham is simply referring to my living with Brynn, *not* the heated make-out session on the couch.

I release the air in my lungs as my fingers quickly fly over the keys on my phone, relieved enough to type back a response.

ME: What happened to taking this to the grave?

TEAGAN: Oops. It was too good not to share.

ATLAS: So, how did your first night go? Are your balls still intact?

KNOX: Twenty bucks said they argued within the first fifteen minutes.

Close. She took twenty in the shower, *then* we argued. Then kissed.

Fuck. I rake a hand through my hair. I sure as hell can't share *that.* Touching Brynn will go with me to the grave.

ME: It was more like twenty minutes.

KNOX: So, how the hell did this happen?

TEAGAN: Brynn has a psychotic room-mate who also likes to do blow in her spare time.

GRAHAM: Seriously?

ME: Seriously. The other night, I walked Brynn back to her room after an alter-cation with Douche Dick Stan, and when she opened her door, there she was. Creepy Cate in all her glory, snorting that shit right on Brynn's fucking desk.

KNOX: NFW!

ATLAS: Who's Douche Dick Stanley?

ME: Some tool she was seeing for a very brief moment before she served him a right hook.

> **TEAGAN**: Sis did me proud.

> **ME**: I haven't seen him yet, and Brynn said he wasn't in class yesterday, but I wouldn't be surprised if she broke his nose.

> **ATLAS**: LMFAO! And now she's rooming with you? Good luck with George Foreman.

I roll my eyes.

> **GRAHAM**: No offense, T, but your sister scares me.

> **ATLAS**: I'll second that.

> **KNOX**: Can you trust your roommate not to slip his dick in her?

> **GRAHAM**: Dude.

> **ATLAS**: Have some fucking decorum!

> **TEAGAN**: He better fucking trust him.

> **ME**: Of course I trust him. Do you think I'd bring her if I didn't? Fuck.

I exhale, pinching the bridge of my nose before I return back to my phone.

> **ME**: Besides, I've let it be known to my teammates that Brynn Nichols is un-touchable.

> **GRAHAM**: Ooh, bet she loved that.

> **ME**: It's caused some friction.

Poor choice of words as my subconscious conjures the image of my hips grinding into hers on the couch, and I curse under my breath.

> **ATLAS**: LOL!

TEAGAN: Apparently, Jace made a scene during her first night out at a club when Stanley started grinding on her.

ME: And hands. There were roaming hands and tongues. I'm not a total asshole.

GRAHAM: You are a total asshole.

TEAGAN: I told him to lighten up a bit.

ME: Hey, I was right about him, wasn't I? You're welcome.

GRAHAM: Hmmm… I see where this is headed.

ATLAS: The writing is on the wall.

Sweat pricks my back, beading at the nape of my neck. Clearly, they're not talking about me and Brynn and . . .

I start to type, *Nothing is gonna happen with us*, when another text comes through.

> **ATLAS**: To make it easier, tell us now who you want to speak at your eulogy.

The breath rushes from my lungs. Of course, that's what they fucking meant.

It's official, I'm losing it.

I shake my head and drag in a deep breath.

> **ME**: First of all, every single one of you fuckers better have something to say. Second, if she's gonna murder me, I'll be sure to have her do it in the middle of the week, so you have an excuse to miss a couple days of conditioning. You're welcome.

> **TEAGAN**: See, this is why you're my best friend.

> **KNOX**: Where's she gonna sleep?

Why'd he have to ask that? Doesn't he know it's a fucking sore spot?

> **ME**: I gave her my bed.

> **GRAHAM**: I'm sure you did.

> **ME**: Don't be a dick. I slept on the couch. She'd probably castrate me in my sleep.

And based on the way she stormed off last night and slammed my bedroom door, she still might.

> **TEAGAN**: True story. She'd Lorena Bobbitt your ass so fast.

> **TEAGAN**: I'm just glad I don't have to worry about any funny business since she literally hates your guts.

I swallow, staring at his text before I run a hand over my face. Guilt unspools in my gut like a ball of twine before I cut it off.

Last night was nothing. *Nothing.* I was trying to prove a point and had a lapse in judgment, that's all. If anything, all I did was solidify Brynn's loathing of me.

> **ATLAS**: Oof. You're a better man than me, Taggart. I can't imagine sleeping on the couch then train the next day.

I grimace as my back throbs in agreement.

> **TEAGAN**: The first and last girl Jace will probably ever live with.

> **GRAHAM**: Grab the popcorn, gents. This should be fun watching him fuck this all up.

> **ATLAS**: Remember. Sleep with one eye open.

I shoot them a text with the middle finger emoji and click my phone off. If I want to make it to practice on time, I'd better get my ass in gear. That, and call me a coward, but I'd prefer not to be here when Brynn wakes and risk the wrath of her this early in the morning.

Rising to my feet, I head for the shower and groan as my back protests with the movement. This is going to be a long day.

Hell, this is going to be a long summer.

BRYNN

I lie in bed as I listen to the clanging of someone in the kitchen, followed by the whine of the shower, audible through the bedroom walls. I already heard someone leave and when I risked a peek through the crack of the bedroom door, I confirmed it was Chris. So, I know it's Jace in the shower now, and I firmly intend to stay right where I am until he exits the building.

What feels like an eternity later, I hear footsteps by the bedroom door, so I yank the blankets over my head, afraid he might try and come in here.

I'm not sure what gives me more anxiety: the idea of him saying goodbye like nothing happened last night, apologizing for it, or gloating. Any one of those is a possibility, so I pull the cotton tighter like a shield. I've been reduced to toddler behavior, intent on pretending to be asleep if he tries to speak to me before leaving.

I inhale, breathing through the heavy fabric only to realize it smells like him—all musky and rugged. It's enough to make my head spin and my heart race as I relive those moments last night when his hands and mouth scorched my skin.

I hold my breath, unwilling to allow my thoughts to go there or even ponder for another second how amazing his blankets smell—how amazing *he* smells—when I hear the footsteps retreat and the front door close, a key clicking in the lock.

I lie here a minute longer, just to be sure he's gone, before I tear the cloth prison from my face and gasp like a newborn baby, greedily sucking in air for the first time.

My lungs fill with fresh, Jace-less oxygen, burning from the exertion of holding my breath. I fling the blankets to the floor entirely, needing to get up and out of this bed. It's playing with my head, hijacking my thoughts and making them wander to places they shouldn't.

Opening his bedroom door, I peek my head out of the room first, half expecting him to jump out of the kitchen, smirk firmly in place as he teases me about my reaction to his kiss last night. But the place is empty, miraculously so, allowing me to make my way into the kitchen where I find several cups worth of coffee still hot in the pot.

I open several cupboards, most of which are empty, to find a coffee mug and fill it, then begin to sip as I nose around the rest of the space. It's not hard to deduce it belongs to two college boys based on the lack of small appliances, cookware, or really anything domestic. Inside the small pantry cupboard, I find huge tubs of protein powder, both pre-workout and electrolytes. However, when I open the fridge, I'm both surprised and pleased to see actual food. My choices are simple: eggs, yogurt, deli meat, cheese, and fruit, but as I wasted too much time hiding in bed, and because the dining hall is on the other side of campus, I grab an apple and start to eat it in between sips of coffee; it's a weird but surprisingly tasty combination.

My eyes drift to the couch and my stomach clenches.

To say I'm pissed Jace kissed me is an understatement. He played dirty and won. But it's not the kiss, or even the way his hand slipped under my shirt or to the waistband of my shorts that has me angry. It's the fact that I didn't hate it. In fact, some might say I even enjoyed it. Not only did I lose myself to his mouth, but for a moment, I forgot who I was with. His taste was intoxicating, and his reaction to me even more so. There's no denying he was every bit as turned on as I was. So much so, what started as a game quickly morphed into something much more. At least for me.

But what bothers me isn't how good Jace's hard chest felt under my palms or that he's an expert with his mouth. Those things were expected, really. A given. What gets my goat is that I allowed lust to cloud my judgment at all. I gave my enemy the upper hand.

And *that* is unforgivable.

I grimace as I think about the prospect of Jace rubbing it in my face or using it against me, which is precisely why I need to act completely unfazed. There's nothing more unnerving to an egomaniac than complete and utter oblivion. So, ignorance is my game. As far as I'm concerned, our little angry make-out sesh never happened.

CHAPTER 13

BRYNN

IT'S BEEN A FEW days since the kiss that never should have happened, and despite wanting to forget about it, Jace's magic mouth is all I can think about.

His magic mouth?

Even my thoughts are pissing me off. Ugh.

I stab my chicken salad with a fork, picturing Jace's face in my mind.

"Ah, thank goodness! We were hoping to catch you here, at our usual spot."

A lunch tray appears on the table across from me, and I glance up to see Charlotte beaming beside a grinning Samantha.

"Nice to know you weren't abducted by aliens," Samantha says as she settles into the seat across from me.

"Or sacrificed by Creepy Cate." Charlotte shivers.

"Unfortunately, none of the above," I say dryly.

"Uh oh." Charlotte's brows pinch. "So, if you weren't sacrificed on an altar or abducted by soul-sucking aliens with green faces and big black eyes, where the hell were you? When you didn't show Monday night, we were worried."

"Especially when someone didn't answer their phone," Samantha adds.

I sigh. "Sorry. It all kind of happened fast, and then I got . . . distracted." *By Jace's tongue.* I grimace, taking another bite of salad to hide it while my friends wait expectantly. "I was at Jace's apartment," I finally blurt, my mouth half full.

Samantha's eyes widen as a huge smile splits her face, and Charlotte's jaw drops.

"Did you sleep with him?" Samantha asks, leaning across the table.

"What? No!" I straighten. "No, of course not."

Charlotte eyes me like she doesn't believe me. "Did you do, you know"—she motions with her hand—"other things?"

My mouth hardens, and I point between them with my fork. "See, this is exactly why I waited to tell you two."

"What?" Samantha shrugs. "Jace is sex on a stick, and you expect us to believe you stayed at his place the last two nights and *nothing* happened?" She scoffs like the concept is ludicrous.

"He went with me to the housing department on Monday, after they refused to help me and plead my case, but they wouldn't budge. Said something about the director being on maternity leave and there's basically nothing that can be done. Blah blah blah."

"That's bullshit," Samantha says.

"Exactly." I spear a piece of chicken with my fork. "Anyway, later that night, he shows up at my room, saying I'm gonna stay with him and I'm not going to argue about it."

"*Hot*," Charlotte says.

I shoot her a glare. "I tried to fight him on it, but he refused to listen. He said my brother was onboard and that he doesn't trust Cate not to drag me down with her if she gets busted, not to mention my safety being at risk while she's there doing Lord-knows-what. And staying with you guys is technically against housing rules, so I'd be putting all of us at risk of getting into trouble. Plus, there's the fact there's hardly any room for the three of us. So . . ." I shrug. "I gave in. Crashing at his place seemed easier, so that's where I've been. Hopefully, housing comes through, but if they don't, I guess I'll be there until fall semester starts and I can get a change in roommate."

"Wow. I can't even imagine living with that boy." Samantha fans her face. "Oh, the things you'll see."

Charlotte's lashes flutter. "Fresh from the shower with nothing but a towel wrapped around his waist."

I turn to her with wide eyes while Samantha groans.

"Or just after his workout, all sweaty, his muscles straining and engorged against his damp shirt," Samantha says, grinning like the Cheshire Cat while my cheeks turn crimson.

"Do not ever use the word 'engorged' in the same sentence as that boy," I threaten, fake-gagging.

"*Ooh oh!*" Charlotte practically vibrates in her seat. "Or him lounging around in gray sweats and a tight T-shirt."

Samantha bites her lip. "I think I just got a lady boner."

I chuck a crouton at them both, and they burst into a fit of giggles.

"You forget he hung out at my house all the time in high school. It was practically like having another brother around. And trust me, drinking half a gallon of milk straight from the jug and belching in my face, leaving his stinky football equipment everywhere, and him using all the hot water for a thirty-minute shower where he's doing who-knows-what, is not all that impressive."

Samantha's lips quirk, letting me know she thinks otherwise. "Wanna trade places? I'll take Jace, and you take Charlotte."

Charlotte makes a sound of offense, her mouth a round O.

"You've seen the boy," Samantha says in defense. "Don't act so shocked that I'd trade you in for a set of bulging biceps, a rock-hard chest, and washboard abs, okay?"

Charlotte shrugs. "I can't even be mad."

"Ha ha," I pantomime. "You're both unhinged."

"Whatever." Samantha takes a bite of her burger. "Ten bucks says he's in your pants by the end of the month."

"That's only two weeks," I say, my tone indignant.

Charlotte narrows her eyes on me and purses her lips as if considering. "Her hatred runs deep. I give it four."

I gasp, then recover as my resolve hardens. "Never gonna happen."

Little do they know, for one brief moment Monday night, my body was singing a different tune.

"Famous last words," Charlotte singsongs.

"So, where have you been sleeping since you've been there?" Samantha asks, her tone smug.

I purse my lips and drop my gaze back to my salad, hoping the guilt I feel inside is not written all over my face, but when I say nothing, Samantha claps her hands. "Oh, please say you're sleeping in his bed. *Please*."

My gaze darts back to hers and I scowl. "Maybe, but he's sleeping on the couch."

"Wait. Jace gave you his bed and took the couch?" Charlotte gawks at me like that kind of chivalry is unheard of. And I'll be honest, I'm surprised by it myself. I never would've taken Jace for the kind of guy who'd put a woman before him, especially me.

"He was rather insistent, actually," I say with a frown.

"Huh. I mean, that's kinda . . . sweet, right?"

"Super sweet," Samantha chimes in.

"Pah! Sweet? No." I shake my head. The last thing I want to do is think of Jace as sweet. "Trust me, we fought about it, and he was a total jackass," I say, then instantly regret it because it brings back memories of the kiss that puts all other kisses to shame, and my cheeks heat.

"Her cheeks are turning pink." Samantha points with her sandwich, like it's a loaded gun. "Aren't her cheeks pink?"

"Definitely a blush coloring those candy apples," Charlotte croons.

"It's nothing," I say a little too loudly before I cram a forkful of salad into my piehole. Maybe if my mouth is completely full and I can't speak, they'll drop it.

"Something totally happened." Samantha narrows her eyes, then says, "We'll wait," as she takes a bite of her sandwich.

Both Charlotte and Samantha stare at me, their gazes drilling into the front of my skull. Any minute, my brain will start oozing out. But my lips are sealed, an impenetrable fortress. There's no way I'm telling them what happened, especially not after the bet they just made.

Silence descends over us. The crunching of the cucumber in my salad magnifies in my ears as I focus on chewing and keeping my mouth closed.

"You know, I sometimes see Jace after he leaves practice," Charlotte says casually. "I wonder, if I asked him why you might blush when talking about your sleeping arrangements, what he'd have to say about it?"

I pause, a tomato halfway to my mouth. "You wouldn't . . ."

"Oh, I think I would."

"She totally would." Samantha smiles and offers her a fist bump.

I glance between them, eyes narrowed to call her bluff. When she doesn't so much as blink, I cave and practically melt onto the table like a popsicle. "Fiiiiine." I groan. If I don't tell her, and she does mention it to Jace, then he'll think what happened affected me, and that's worse than any amount of gloating my friends can do. "We were arguing about where I'd sleep, so I stubbornly made a bed on the couch, and he tried to stop me—"

"Like, physically stop you?" Samantha holds a hand up, and I nod.

"Ooh, I like where this is going," Charlotte says.

I roll my eyes. "Anyway, we were fighting over the blankets, and he was trying to take the couch instead, so when he tried to push me off it, I kind of . . ." I pause and swallow, thinking about the scene I made. "Clung to him like a spider monkey. Then he did some kind of WWF move and slammed me on my back and . . . kissed me. Hard."

Charlotte gasps while Samantha's brows rise so far up her hairline, they're invisible.

"He kissed you?" Charlotte asks.

"After he"—Samantha makes air quotes with her fingers as she says—"'slammed you on your back'?"

"Yes." My voice is a hiss in my ears as I close my eyes, and the scene replays in my head in wild technicolor.

"Oh, this is just too good. So, how did it end?" Samantha asks.

"We kissed—"

"So you kissed him back?" Charlotte's hazel eyes brighten.

"I had a moment of weakness, okay?" I say, exasperated. "Don't judge me."

"Hey, no judgment here." She raises her hands.

"Here neither." Samantha sighs and stares dreamily into space. "If that boy's tongue were in my mouth—"

"*Anyway . . .*" I cut her off. "We were kissing, and it turned into our usual sparring, except instead of words, it was our tongues and hands doing the fighting, and neither of us wanted to concede and admit defeat. But when his hand started to dip below my waistband, I snapped out of my lust-induced stupor and waved the white flag of surrender. I retreated immediately. That's it."

Samantha flops back in her seat. "Damn, that's hot."

I shoot her a glare.

"So, do you think it meant anything?" Charlotte asks, a sparkle in her eye.

"The kiss?" She nods as I mull it over.

There's no way Jace feels anything for me. Not only does he not do emotions where girls are concerned, but I'm also not his type. I'm too serious. Too snarky. Too sullen and stubborn. Too . . .

I shake my head. "No. No way. I mean, we were arguing, and we're always goading each other. I don't think it was anything more than that. I honestly think he thought the second he pressed his mouth to mine that I'd get pissed and leave. When that didn't happen, it went a little further."

Samantha hums under her breath like she's not buying it. "I don't know. Are you sure all that pent-up loathing isn't just a cover? Maybe under the surface is this whole layer of sexual tension just waiting to be released."

I scoff. "You've been reading way too many romance novels."

She shrugs.

"And then what happened the next day?" Charlotte asks.

"Rather than face the awkward I-sucked-my-mortal-ene-my's-and-brother's-best-friend's-face-last-night confrontation, I waited until he left to leave the bedroom to emerge. I even missed class." I grimace. Not the best move, but at least I didn't have to see Stanley. "Today, I didn't even have to try. The second I woke up, he was already gone."

"Nice." Samantha grins.

"You're going to have to face him sometime, you know," Charlotte says, stating the obvious.

"Do I? Because I was thinking I could get through the remaining summer semester hiding away in his room like a hermit and only come out after dark, like a vampire."

I'm joking.

Not really.

"Whatever. If you ask me, your confession just increased my chances of winning the bet exponentially," Samantha says, puffing her chest in pride.

Charlotte frowns. "Dammit. I should've gone with a week."

"Guys, *come on*." I knew they'd have a field day with this—it's part of the reason I hadn't texted them to let them know I'd be staying with Jace—but I didn't think they'd be *this* bad. "Nothing's happening."

"You're right," Charlotte says, her tone contrite. "I'm sorry. We'll behave and drop the whole bet thing." She bites her lip like the effort might kill her.

I turn my gaze on Samantha and she mimes zipping her lips.

"Thank you," I say, relieved.

"So, really, what are you gonna do when you see him, though? Do you think you'll bring up the kiss? Clear the air?"

I shake my head, thinking about what I'd decided earlier. "I don't know. I mean, it's clear he was trying to get under my skin, to one-up me, and he won. So in my eyes, he has no reason to mention it. So I'll be damned if I let it get to me," I say, even though it's obviously already getting to me or we wouldn't be having this conversation. "That leaves me with only one recourse. I'm just going to carry on like it's always been between us and pretend like it never happened."

"Interesting tactic," Samantha says, picking up a french fry and popping it in her mouth. "I like it, especially because if it was more than that to him, he'll eventually crack."

CHAPTER 14

JACE

I GRIP MY WATER bottle in hand and enter the weight room. Most of the team is already there stretching and I find Chris and Damon near the free weights and join them. We start with hip rolls, moving onto high knees when Damon peers over at me. "I heard you went back to the Psi Delta party after you left and clocked Stanley in the face."

Chris's gaze snaps to mine. "You didn't tell me you went back."

I frown. "Who told you that?"

"A bunch of the brothers were talking about it."

"But you didn't, right?" Chris asks.

My forehead creases as I continue high knees, the air puffing from my lungs like a steam engine. It's not a lie entirely. I did go back, just not alone. And it wasn't me that decked him.

"Fuck. You did, didn't you?" Chris asks, pausing to glare at me while he catches his breath.

"It's not like that, though. I told Brynn what happened and she wanted to confront him, so I took her."

"And that's it . . .?" Damon asks, arching a brow.

I purse my lips as we move onto shrugs, which I freaking hate.

"Awww, come on, dude." Chris groans.

"What? Brynn punched him, not me, I swear. My fist went nowhere near the dude."

"But they're saying it was Jace?" Chris asks Damon.

"That's what I heard. Probably trying to save face so he doesn't look like a pussy." Damon glances at me. "Your chick must have a brutal right hook. Dude's fucking nose is broken."

"First, she's not my chick." I run a hand over my mouth, then, "Shit. Forget the rest. Is it really broken?"

"If the gauze crammed in his nostrils and the twin bruises under his eyes are any indication, I'd say it is." Damon smirks. "Dude looks like a fucking raccoon."

"Jace, bro, you've only been here for a few weeks, and this girl is already causing you a shit-ton of trouble." Chris eyes me warily.

I know why he's saying it, what he's getting at. That I should cut my losses and stay the hell away from her. Shit, he's probably right, too. Maybe I *should* stay away from her.

But for some reason, I can't do that. And it's not just because of Teagan. Now that I've had a little time to mull things over, I realize maybe there was more to our impromptu make-out session than I originally thought. Part of me wonders if I've been denying what is becoming glaringly obvious since summer school started.

Maybe I've always had a thing for Brynn; it was just easy to ignore with her hatred and Teagan standing between us.

I exhale and shift my gaze to the ceiling.

When I say nothing, Chris tells Damon. "She's fucking living with us now."

"Come again?" Damon blinks, his gaze bouncing between us.

"It's a long story that starts and ends with her crazy roommate and the housing department being worthless," I say as we move to one of the benches where I start to prepare the bar for our upper body routine.

Damon takes the bench first, lying on his back and bracing his hands on the cold steel bar. "You sure she's worth all the trouble?" he asks before he lowers it to his chest, then pushes it back up as he releases his breath. "From what I've heard, she can't stand you."

I shoot Chris a meaningful look, and he shrugs. "She might be hot, but from the little I've seen and what you've told me, she's fucking feral with you."

The muscle in my jaw flickers as the urge to put Chris in his place strikes me like an iron fist, but I shove it down. He's not wrong, and I know he's just looking out for me and going based off what he's seen. I can't fault him for that.

"She's my best friend's sister," I say. "They're like family to me. I've known her for years, so yeah, I'm not gonna just turn my back on her. And she doesn't really hate me," I say, even though after the other night, I'm not sure how true that is. "It's just . . . sort of a game we play."

Was the kiss a game, too?

My mind wanders to everything Chris said, and I decide he's not wrong. So far, conditioning is going well, I've met some pretty cool people, and I'm managing my summer class. The only blip on the radar has been my preoccupation with keeping tabs on Brynn and the resulting drama. Which is precisely why kissing her the other night was one giant mistake. A mistake that can't happen again.

Football is my focus. Classes. Casual flings and having a good time.

None of those things include Brynn.

I'm not this guy. I don't do messy. I don't go anywhere near chicks I already have some sort of emotional connection with, good, bad, or otherwise. So, what the hell am I doing?

CHAPTER 15

JACE

I PAUSE OUTSIDE OF Bradd's when my phone rings, and glance down to see Teagan's name flash across the screen. After my epiphany in the locker room earlier, I decided I'd better steer clear of the apartment. I need to get my head on straight and remember who I am. I'm Jace *fucking* Taggart. I can charm the pants off damn near any chick I set my sights on. When I set my sights on something, I get it. I'm a no-strings, low complications kind of guy, with zero struggle at finding female companionship when I want it. So, when I mentioned rounding up a few chicks and heading to the club, Chris and Damon were all in.

This is exactly what I need. Clearly, my dry streak is fucking with my head and once I get whatever the hell this is out of my system, I'll be able to keep my hands off Brynn and life will return to normal.

"Shit," I hiss under my breath.

"Problem?" Chris asks.

I shake my head, glancing from my phone to him. "No, but I should probably take this."

"You want us to wait?"

"Nah, go ahead. I'll be right there."

He nods and escorts the ladies into the club while I take a deep breath and prepare myself for whatever the conversation with Teagan brings. I'd be lying if I said I didn't feel a little stab of fear that Brynn might have told him about our close encounter the other night.

"Dude, where have you been?" Teagan asks when I answer, sounding more curious than annoyed, which I take as a good sign. "I've been trying to call you the last two days."

I pull on the back of my neck and stare out into the parking lot of the club, trying to ignore the guilt churning inside me like butter. "Oh, yeah, sorry. Kind of a crazy couple of days," I say. "What's up?"

"Nothing. Just got off the phone with Brynn."

I tense, rigid as a steel beam. "Why'd you talk to Brynn?"

"I just wanted to check in on her, make sure she moved into your place okay and was coping well with this little roadblock."

I swallow, sliding a hand down my face. So, she didn't tell him?

"Oh, yeah. That makes sense. What else did she have to say?" I ask, digging.

"Just that she hasn't seen you since Monday night and that you're probably out whoring it up." Teagan laughs. "You know, the typical."

"Hilarious," I deadpan.

Is that what she thinks I'm fucking doing?

I glance toward the entrance of the club and grimace because she's not wrong. I came here on a mission to look for a careless hookup.

Teagan, oblivious to my quickly shifting mood continues, "Yeah. I think her exact words were, 'he's probably out spreading crabs all over campus.'"

"She sure has a sense of humor, doesn't she?" I fake a laugh, but it falls flat. Brynn thinking I'm sleeping around doesn't sit well with me, and I have to ask myself why.

"Can you blame her for assuming?" he asks with a chuckle.

"I guess I can't." My cheeks heat with indignation, but I can't argue, so I don't. He knows as well as I do, I had a reputation in high school, and I'm a lot of things, but a liar isn't one of them. I fully intend on going inside and losing myself in the lips and curves of the girl I came here with.

"Anyway, I just wanted to call and thank you again. You have no idea how much better I feel knowing she's away from her roommate and at your place where you can look after her."

My guilt from earlier returns, doing the freaking backstroke in my veins. "Yeah, anything for you, bro." I clear my throat and rub the tension knotting in my forehead. "Anyway, I better go. I have a tall brunette waiting for me inside."

Teagan barks out a laugh. "Right. Good to know some things never change."

I hang up and angrily shove my phone in my back pocket, staring at the doors to the club as a cluster of college students head inside.

My conversation with Teagan eats at my resolve to stay clear of Brynn when it should have the exact opposite effect. Her opinion of me has never mattered before, so why should it matter now?

I'm doing the right thing by taking a step back. I need to cool my heels and focus on something else—someone else—which is exactly what I intend to do here. If Teagan had an inkling I laid hands on his sister, I'd be dead to him.

It's because of him that I push my shoulders back and step into the club, making my way through the crowd, strobing lights from the dance floor flickering off the walls. The music grows louder the closer I get to the dance floor, vibrating the floor beneath me. While the bar is crowded, the dance floor and booths lining the perimeter aren't, which makes our little group easy to spot.

They're seated in a corner booth, and from the looks of it, Damon is already cozying up to a blonde, while Chris seems to be holding a conversation with two other chicks.

The urge to bail hits me like a wrecking ball. More concerning is the desire to head back outside in search of Brynn, so I can check on her and see if she's feeling any kind of way after what happened the other night.

But those compulsions are dangerous. Which is exactly why I put one foot in front of the other and join my friends.

The brunette, Teresa, lifts her head at my approach, so I plaster on my most charming smile and slide into the booth beside her. A pitcher of beer sits in the center of the table, and I help myself, needing something to take the edge off my thoughts. By the looks of it, the girls are already halfway finished with some kind of mixed drink, so I down half the frothy liquid in a single go, then top my glass up.

"So, what did I miss?"

Beside me, Teresa licks her lips. "Not much. Just waiting for you, so I can have a dance." Her gaze drops to my mouth, a subtle hint at what she wants and an invitation I'll gladly accept as soon as I'm another beer deep, but not yet. Not with thoughts of Brynn dancing in the back of my mind.

But that doesn't stop me from grinning and eyeing her mouth. "Then let's not keep you waiting."

The next hour passes in a blur. I don't know how many beers I drink while grinding up against Teresa. Each song bleeds into the next as the alcohol works its way through my bloodstream, sufficiently numbing my thoughts. My problems fade from view, seemingly far in the distance as she tugs me by the shirt, leading me back to our booth.

We both do a shot of tequila before her mouth collides with mine. She's aggressive, her lips firm and far too eager as she nips and bites and sucks. It's so different from the soft, fevered caress of Brynn's. I can't help but compare them even through my hazy thoughts.

I growl, pissed she's found a way to emerge from my subconscious, even while drunk, but if Teresa notices, she doesn't say anything as she slides a hand up my shirt. Her breath catches as I trail a string of kisses down her neck, and when I find her bare thigh beneath the table, she doesn't move or flinch or slow down. Instead, she pulls me closer like an invitation, a sign she's willing to take this wherever I want it to go.

Somewhere in the back of my thoughts I idly wonder if Brynn would push me away again, and I imagine the sounds she would make—the little, tiny gasps and throaty moans.

I grunt as I bite Teresa's lower lip, pissed at myself for even considering it.

"Ow." She pulls away, hand to her mouth where I can see a small drop of blood forming on her lower lip.

Good. Maybe she'll push me away, too. Call me an asshole and storm out.

It's what I deserve for thinking about another chick while my hands are on her. It's what I deserve for thinking about Brynn at all.

But instead of being repulsed or angry, she grins and leans toward me. Her breath is heavy in the shell of my ear as she places one hand on my chest and whispers, "Wanna go back to your place?"

I nod, not even having to think about it, even though I don't. Not really.

So far, she's not the distraction I hoped she'd be. If anything, my traitorous thoughts are worsening.

It's out of sheer desperation I grab her hand and pull her from the booth, catching Chris's eye on the way out as I offer him a not-so-subtle nod. It crosses my mind that Brynn might be at the apartment, but it doesn't stop me. If anything, it drives my decision. I could take Teresa back to my truck or a cramped bathroom stall, and I'm sure she'd oblige my every desire, but I don't.

The dirty truth is I want to take her back to my place where Brynn might be holed away in my room.

And I'm not sure what's worse. The fact that I couldn't give two shits about the woman beside me, or that I suddenly *want* Brynn to see us together—to hear us.

These thoughts run through my head the whole way there. Bradd's isn't far from my apartment, so even on foot, it doesn't take long before we're tumbling through the front door.

The last shot of alcohol sits in my stomach like a brick. My head spins and my legs feel like Jell-O, but I'm committed to the cause. It doesn't matter that I'm so drunk my brain is numb. I'm going to be a fucking hero and see this through.

Teresa laughs as she kicks her shoes off and backs up toward the couch where she takes a seat and curls her finger, beckoning me forward.

I amble toward her, slowly unbuttoning my shirt, noting the hungry gleam in her eyes as she tracks my movements. My normal finesse is lacking as I settle myself over her and crush my mouth to hers, ignoring the stale taste of booze coating her tongue.

With a moan, I hitch her dress around her hips while she slides my shirt off me. Through the fuzzy haze of my thoughts, I remember the last time I was here, on this same couch kissing someone else.

I pull back momentarily and glance down to find a familiar pair of violet eyes staring back at me as the memory comes alive.

Teresa's mouth breaks the spell as she moves to my neck, and I remember it's not Brynn I'm with, but fuck if I don't want it to be.

Her hands find the fly of my jeans.

Maybe this is all I need to get Brynn out of my system. I can allow myself to indulge the fantasy of her. Even if it's wrong. Even if I know I shouldn't. I need to get her out of my head one way or the other.

But when Teresa murmurs my name, her voice is all wrong and I sit back with a jolt.

She leans up on her elbows, flashing me her sexiest smile while I blink down at her like an idiot. Then, before I can stop myself, before I even know what I'm doing or saying, I tell her, "You have to go."

She barks out a laugh, like this is some kind of joke.

I wish it were.

"What?" she murmurs when she realizes I'm not kidding.

"I can't do this." I shake my head. "I can't—"

The sound of a door slamming cuts me off. "What the hell?"

My head jerks, and I find Brynn hovering in the doorway, mouth open and eyes wide with surprise, as two girls I vaguely recognize as her friends hover behind her.

I recoil, jumping off the couch and nearly falling on my ass in the process. Holding my jeans up, I fight for words as Brynn's jaw hardens and her hands fist at her sides. "Real nice, Jace."

She whips around and makes a beeline for the door while I stumble after her, calling out, even though I shouldn't. "Brynn, wait—"

This is what I wanted, wasn't it?

Yet the disgust contorting her pretty features wasn't nearly as satisfying as I thought it'd be.

I reach a grasping hand outside the door, but it comes up empty and I lean outside to see she's already gone.

"You have a girlfriend?" Teresa shrieks from behind me. "That's why you said you couldn't do this?"

I turn to her, my hands raised in surrender as her pupils turn to pinpoints. "No, of course not." I shake my head. "She's not my—"

"Asshole!" she blurts before she storms out, and I want to yell after her. To kick and scream and shout. Because I'm not her fucking boyfriend. Not by a long shot.

Girls like Brynn Nichols don't date guys like me.

CHAPTER 16

BRYNN

THE NEXT FEW DAYS pass without incident, mostly because of my expert avoidance skills. My first encounter
back to class with Stanley involved a lot of glaring on his part and
a whole lot of cold shoulder on mine, but if I was worried about
him confronting me after class and what I would say, I shouldn't
have been. He exited the lecture hall so fast you'd think his
shirt was on fire. As for Jace, I've managed to align my coming
and going from the apartment to when he's conveniently not
around.

It's amazing how quickly one can learn someone else's sched-
ule when highly motivated.

Most of my time has been spent with Charlotte and Samantha during the day, studying in the library or taking long walks
around campus, then hanging out with the girls again at night.
If Jace has noticed my absence, I wouldn't know. Maybe he's

avoiding me, too. It's hard to tell. Either way, I need a distraction from my conflicting feelings where he's concerned, something to keep me busy.

This newfound motivation leads me to the student affairs building on a Friday where I meander along the hallway until I find the large cork bulletin boards outside the office. I scan the flyers for something to catch my interest.

I'm not sure what I'm looking for, but I'm confident I'll know it when I see it. I imagine in the fall, these boards are filled with active clubs and campus events, but in the dead of summer, most of the listings appear to be for jobs.

I see openings for waitresses, babysitters, and dog walkers. Requests for tutors and invites for chess club join the mix, along with a plea for resident advisers. But none of these things feel right. None of them click. Until a brightly colored pamphlet with a picture of children for a foundation called Helping Hands captures my eye, with the heading *Volunteers Wanted*.

I make quick work of the brochure, reading it out loud: *"Looking for volunteers to work with local youth ages five through eleven. Will attend sporting events, field trips, and work hand-in-hand with youth from underprivileged backgrounds throughout the summer and school year. These kids need you! Join and become a positive influence in a child's life today."*

I rip off one of the business cards pinned to the flyer with a smile and stare down at the phone number. Back in Riverside, I spent my summers working at a daycare center throughout high school, and though I know it's not the same thing, I loved every minute. Spending time with kids always puts a smile on my face, and since I have aspirations to work in pediatric nursing, any experience like this can only be seen as a bonus when it comes to my resume and landing a job after school.

I wander away from the student affairs office as I dial the number, and when a woman answers I express my interest in volunteering. A few minutes later, I hang up with an appointment for later this afternoon to meet her in person and fill out the paperwork to see if I'm a good fit.

They'll need to perform a quick background check since my clearance in Ohio doesn't apply to another state, but by the time I get off the phone with her, I feel like I accomplished something for the first time since I got here.

As much as I've grown to love Charlotte and Samantha, I need something else to focus on, and since I'm nowhere close to finding a boyfriend, helping to make a difference in the lives of children might be just the ticket. I was lucky enough to have an amazing family and childhood, but I also know what it's like to go through a dark time. Helping someone else rather than focusing on my own problems will be therapeutic.

With renewed purpose, I wander out of the building, feeling better than I have in a while. Everything that's happened between me and Jace since we started school has really messed with my head. One minute I hate him, then I'm kissing him, and the next he's bringing other girls back to the apartment for me to walk in on.

It's emotional whiplash, but I'm used to the anger and loathing. It's the attraction and desire that's wigging me out.

If I had anywhere else to stay, I'd be gone, but as it is, I'm stuck.

I guess I should look at the bright side. This happened during summer semester, rather than the fall, which is nearly double in length.

Only five weeks left.

Which reminds me, I have yet to properly thank Chris for letting me crash at their place. Even though Jace appears to be right and he's hardly ever there, I should do something nice to thank him.

Being daughter to a caterer, and sister to a brother and athlete, has instilled in me the deep faith that the way to a man's heart is through his stomach, so I make a plan. Lunch, then my interview, and afterward, I'll stop by the convenience store to buy ingredients for my favorite cupcakes.

The scent of chocolate fills the air as I lightly touch the tops of one of the cupcakes to check if they're cool. Satisfied, I pull my finger away and cut the tip off the Ziploc baggie holding the fluffy peanut butter frosting I made, then start piping it onto the cupcakes.

Not a minute later, the front door swings open, and I curse. I was hoping to be done by the time they finished practice. You know, so I could leave a lovely note of thanks with the cakes for Chris, then go back to avoiding Jace for all of eternity.

Fat chance.

But at least I won't have to face him alone. At least I'll have Chris as a buffer.

Focusing on the task at hand, I remind myself to breathe, to act cool as I continue piping frosting. When I can't take it anymore, I spare them a quick glance, then immediately wish I hadn't because my stomach does a backflip at the sight of Jace. He's wearing a backward baseball cap, and when he lifts his duffle bag over his head, his muscles flicker under a T-shirt that hugs his chest in the most delicious way. Time slows as my gaze homes in on the sliver of tanned skin and toned abdominals peeking out beneath the hem, to the thin trail of hair leading beneath the waistband of his shorts.

He lifts his head, and my cheeks burn as I jerk my gaze away, praying he didn't catch me staring. Beside him, Chris kicks off his sneakers, then calls out, "Hey, Brynn." He lifts his chin toward the cupcakes, hope glittering in his hazel eyes. "*Please* say those are for us."

I'm not sure what I expected from Chris the first time seeing him in his apartment. Maybe a rundown of the rules? Some level of awkwardness since he doesn't know me? A timeline of when he wants me out? What I didn't expect was warm indifference and a friendly smile.

"Almost. And they're for *you*, actually." I smile, glad I thought of the gesture.

Behind him, Jace meets my eyes for the first time, and the force of his gaze strikes me like a lightning bolt to the chest. I'm surprised my heart keeps beating.

Slowly, he arches a brow, his aquamarine eyes shifting between the cupcakes and me while butterflies fight to rise through my stomach into my windpipe.

I quickly drop my gaze back to my work, scolding myself for allowing him to have any effect on me at all.

One kiss and I'm turning to knots in his presence.

Okay, maybe it was more than a kiss. A reaction is expected after he laid me down on the couch, pressed his body to mine, and ravaged my mouth. The way my heart's pounding is merely the aftereffect of a traumatic experience. Like the aftershocks of an earthquake. Nothing more.

"Seriously?" Chris asks, coming closer and tearing me from thoughts of Jace. "What's the occasion?" His eyes light up as he watches me ice the last one, then begin to top each of them with a mini Reese's Cup.

I shrug. "I wanted to thank you for letting me stay here. You barely know me, and having some strange girl hanging around isn't exactly ideal. At the very least, I'm sure it's not how you imagined your first month at college going."

Jace snorts, and Chris and I both turn to him.

He heads straight to the refrigerator, avoiding my eyes as he swings the door open and pulls out the orange juice, proceeding to drink straight from the carton.

Normally I'd gag or scoff at the rude behavior. But instead, my gaze zeros in on his lips, recalling how commanding they were as a flush of heat moves up my neck.

I swallow before remembering myself and force a grimace hoping he'll turn around and see me, but he doesn't, and it leaves me wanting.

Note to self: don't drink the juice.

Chris shifts back toward me, a smirk curling his lips like he finds Jace's reaction, or lack thereof, humorous. "So, when can I have them?" he asks, and I grin.

"Have at it. I'll wrap the extras up whenever you're done."

Chris chuckles. "That's cute. You think there will be some left."

At that, Jace pauses, the carton hovering in front of him, eyes narrowed on his roommate. Oblivious, Chris peels the wrapper off one of the cupcakes and takes a huge bite, easily consuming more than half the cake at once. "Oh my God," he drawls, mouth full.

Frosting clings to his lower lip, but it doesn't deter him as he crams the second half in his mouth, then proceeds to tip his head back and groan like he's in ecstasy.

Behind him, Jace shoves the carton back into the fridge and slams the door. "Get a fucking hold on yourself, dude."

"I can't," Chris mumbles, and I stifle a laugh as crumbs fall from his lips and he reaches for another. "These are the best things I've ever eaten. Where did you even get the stuff to make these, anyway?"

I shrug, blushing at his praise. "I managed to get everything I needed at the convenience store down the road."

"You shouldn't walk there alone," Jace admonishes. "There are some shady dudes that hang around that place."

Why shouldn't I be surprised at Jace's reaction? Ever since we got to school, he's treated me like a piece of my grandma's old china, like I might break at the slightest provocation.

"You went during the day, right?" Chris asks, and I nod. "See, she's smart. There are tons of students and other people around during that time. I'm sure it was fine. But just for the record, I would 100 percent risk getting robbed at gunpoint if it meant I could have these afterward," he says, starting in on another.

I cover my mouth with a hand, drowning a chuckle. "I've never seen someone quite so enthusiastic about cupcakes before."

"That's because these are fucking amazing, and Edwardo over here," he says with a jerk of his thumb in Jace's direction, "has us on a strict diet of protein and vegetables." He pulls a face.

"Edwardo?" Jace asks dryly.

"Yeah." Chris shrugs. "You look like an Edward."

I cross my arms over my chest, having fun with this. "You know, now that you say that, he does look like an Ed."

Jace scoffs. "I don't look like a fucking Ed or Edwardo or anything starting with E-D. And you can't get jacked by eating junk all the time."

If Jace and I had any kind of an amicable relationship, I'd be inclined to agree based on his chiseled physique. But we don't. So, I stare at him like he's an ogre.

"See?" Chris turns back to me, a thumb pointed over his shoulder at an angry Jace. "This one's no fun. But just because he's a dessert prude, doesn't mean you need to be. You gotta try one, Brynn."

"Oh, no. That's okay," I say, with a little shake of the head.

"No. I insist. If you're going to work hard on something, then you should enjoy the fruits of your labor. Kinda like how Jace feels about his body and chicks, am I right?" He winks at Jace, and I wonder if he's purposely trying to piss him off when he brings the portion of his uneaten cupcake toward my lips and offers me a bite. "Come on. Just one," he says, stepping closer.

Unsure of what to do, I hesitantly take a bite as he feeds me, acutely aware of Jace's stony gaze boring a hole in the side of my face the entire time.

"Good, right?" Chris drawls, a seductive edge to his tone as he reaches out and brushes a bit of frosting off my lips.

"Stop fucking flirting with her," Jace snaps.

Chris grins before he turns to face his roommate. "You're just jealous she made me cupcakes and not you."

"Why would I be jealous?" Jace asks, a hint of pink creeping into his cheeks.

Holy cow. Is that anger or a blush I see? Could Jace Taggart actually be blushing?

I stare wide-eyed as he continues, "I live here. They're mine, too."

"No." Chris shakes his head. "No, they're not. Brynn specifically stated they were mine for being so sweet and generous in sharing my apartment with a virtual stranger, remember?" He grins, and I'm positive now he's goading him, which makes him my new best friend.

Jace scoffs like he doesn't care, but his white-knuckled grip on the countertop behind him tells another story. "Brynn moving in was *my* idea."

"But she's like family to you, right, Taggart? Isn't that what you said?"

He said that? My brows rise as I peer over at him in time to see his eyes harden to steel.

He shifts, either from the weight of my gaze or something else, but when he does, our eyes lock. I don't know why this knowledge disappoints me, but it does.

I turn back to the counter, busying myself with cleaning up my mess.

It shouldn't bother me. Hell, I've said the same thing about him. Over the years, he's been like a second, more annoying brother.

But for some reason, hearing he's referred to me in the same way hits different.

Or maybe it's just the remnants from our kiss still messing with my head. Because the way he touched me, the way his mouth moved with mine was anything but brotherly.

I start wiping the counter, ignoring the scowl on Jace's face and the muscle flickering in his jaw as Chris loudly licks frosting from his fingers. After downing another cupcake, Chris sighs and says, "Well, ladies, I'll just take a few of these with me and be out of your way. I'm supposed to babysit my sister's kids today," he says with a grimace. "Might as well get hopped up on sugar now." He piles several more cakes on a plate, then heads to his room, leaving me and Jace alone.

I swipe at the counter, furiously rubbing at a spot of dried frosting, acutely aware of Jace's proximity to me.

A minute passes before he pushes off the counter and closes the distance, his body hovering just behind mine, so close I can feel him in the space between us as if he were pressed to my side. He leans down, his breath tickling my ear as he says, "Are they really just for him? I find it hard to believe, all things considered."

My heart riots in my chest; it's a caged bird pounding furiously against my ribcage in an effort to escape. "What are you talking about?" I hiss.

"I call you cupcake, and the next thing I know you're in my kitchen baking them for my roommate." He squints. "Seems a little calculated.

"I thought you didn't eat junk?" I deflect.

"One won't hurt."

Like one kiss?

The thought burns my brain.

Is that what ran through his mind moments before his mouth crushed to mine?

My breathing grows shallow at the memory, and I curse myself for thinking about that night in his presence. I'm supposed to be acting like nothing happened. Pretending. Forgetting.

I shake my head as my thoughts twirl like a baton. "It's probably best if you practice some restraint, don't you think?" I scrub harder at the counter. "Once you have one, you'll want more." *Shit. What am I saying?*

I want to take the words back, to swallow my tongue.

I close my eyes and try to focus on my breathing, grateful he can't see my expression from where he's standing behind me because clearly, I'm losing my mind.

He hums in response, and the sound rumbles in my chest.

"But restricting myself will only make me crave one that much more," he says.

The butterflies from earlier erupt from hibernation, returning with a vengeance.

Are we still talking about cupcakes? Is he flirting, toying with me?

I have no idea, but I refuse to be his plaything. I can just imagine him laughing about this later. Obviously, his massive ego assumes the kiss affected me, and he's simply testing his theory to see just how much.

Anger spikes in my veins at the thought. I'll be damned if he's going to win. "Ah, I see your dilemma," I say, my voice cool. "But there's just one problem?"

He moves even closer, hands landing on the counter on either side of me, caging me in. All it would take is to turn my head and our lips would touch. "What's that?" he whispers, his breath tickling the back of my neck.

"These cupcakes are off-limits. They're too good for you," I say as I shift and start piling them into the large plastic container I found in one of the cupboards.

"Too good for me, huh?" He takes a tiny step back, and I'm both relieved and resentful.

"Yep," I say, pushing the container aside and turning toward him. "They don't belong to you. They're meant for someone else's mouth."

Meant for someone else's mouth? I inwardly roll my eyes. *Smooth, Brynn.*

"But they *could* belong to me." He makes a move for the cupcakes behind me, but I block him.

"No, they can't." His hand darts out again, but I swat it away. "You can't just claim somebody's cupcakes."

His brow furrows, and he focuses on me, his tone gruff as he says, "Brynn, give me a cupcake."

"No." I grip the counter behind me, forming a shield between me and the cupcakes like I'm a mama bear and these are my cubs. I've clearly come unhinged. "You can't have one."

"Brynn . . ." he says in a warning tone.

"Jace . . ." I mock, arching a brow.

His aqua eyes glitter like brilliant pools of water on a hot summer day when his arm darts out without warning. He reaches behind me toward the container while I squeal and grapple for a hold on it.

I should've known he'd have catlike reflexes.

He pulls the container toward him while I grab the other side, yanking it back toward me.

"You're being ridiculous," he says, tugging on it so hard I almost lose my balance.

"I am not! They're *mine.*"

"I thought they were Chris's?" he challenges, and I want to punch him.

"Mine *and* Chris's." I use all my strength to yank the container from his grip at the same time he lets go, and the next thing I know, I'm flying through the air.

With a yelp, my body torpedoes backward, crashing back into the cupboards. A sharp pain radiates through my spine before I crumple to the floor like a ragdoll. Cupcakes scatter around my prone body, one landing icing down on the bare thigh exposed by my dress which has risen so much, it's almost X-rated.

I sit there, dazed, as Jace gapes down at me.

I try to catch my bearings as his gaze wanders, taking in the cupcake massacre when he springs toward me, reaching for one, but I squash it with my hand, mushing it into the linoleum before he can grab it.

"You little . . ." Turning, he eyes another and darts for it but slips on a glob of frosting and almost faceplants right into my crotch.

I squeal as he braces his weight on his arms, stopping his trajectory and he quickly lifts his head at the last second. We lock eyes for one heated moment, and then just as quickly, his gaze flickers to the cake on my thigh, perilously close to his face, and it's like I can read his thoughts.

Before he can reach for it, I snatch it up and throw it across the kitchen where it hits a cupboard with a *whack*. It's catty and petty, and I'm sure I look completely ridiculous, surrounded by crushed cake and frosting, but I don't care, because I refuse to let him win.

He narrows his eyes up at me while my lips quirk, triumphant. He might've won with the make-out session on the couch, but I won today.

This knowledge has my grin widening into a full-blown smile as I prepare to bathe in the bliss of victory when he slowly rakes his gaze over me. Down my chest and arms, to my waist and legs, fully exposed by the skirt bunched high up my thighs.

My smile falters.

A wave of panic crashes into me as he licks his lips, and my gaze drops to whatever has him looking as though he might devour me, only to see the smear of frosting across my skin from the cupcake I hastily threw.

My eyes widen at the same time he drops his head and drags his tongue over the smooth, sugary skin of my thigh.

I gasp as my skin catches fire at the same time a shiver racks my body.

I briefly wonder if I'm feverish or maybe just losing my mind. Either would certainly explain the delirium as I sit immobile and watch him clean the frosting from my skin—slowly, languidly—with nothing but his tongue.

Once he's finished, he sits back, arms casually slung around his bent knees as he licks a bit of frosting from the corner of his mouth and hums with satisfaction. "Chris was right. Fucking amazing."

With my heart pumping and breath heaving in my chest, mortification at what he just did—what I allowed him to do—sinks in as I struggle to get to my feet.

Leaning forward, I shove at his hard chest while he smirks. "You're an asshole, Jace Taggart!" Then I spin on my heel and head toward his bedroom, slamming the door behind me.

"I've been called worse, Cupcake," I hear him call out.

But I can't form the words to respond. I don't even want to as I turn and press my forehead against the cool hard surface of the wall where I curse under my breath and mutter, "Jace two. Brynn zero."

CHAPTER 17

JACE

I'M SWEEPING UP THE massacred cake in the kitchen when Chris hurries through the room, keys in hand on his way to the door. Pausing, his brows rise. "Do I wanna know?"

I grit my teeth and shake my head.

"Okay, then." He twirls his keys in his hand with a laugh. "I'll see you later. Try not to kill each other while I'm gone."

I flip him the bird as he leaves, but once the door closes behind him, I sigh and lean on the broom, my gaze drifting to the closed bedroom door where Brynn is probably plotting my demise at this very moment. Maybe she'll consult Creepy Cate and see if she can get her a voodoo doll with my likeness. I'd deserve every prick of the needle.

I close my eyes and sigh as I think about what just happened.

What the hell is my problem?

Only a couple days ago, I decided I needed to take a step away from Brynn and focus on football. I even tried a random hookup to chase her from my thoughts and failed miserably, so the next time I see her, I decide to lick her leg like a fucking lollipop?

Fuck me, but I felt like I might die if I didn't taste her skin on my tongue.

The first night here was about pissing her off to get my way, even if I lost control and enjoyed the kiss far more than I should have.

But today . . . today, I have no excuse.

It was a lapse in judgment. And if I'm being honest, maybe a teeny bit of jealousy at the way she and Chris were flirting right in front of my face. So this is partly his fault, the fucker. He knows she's off-limits and respects it. Which tells me he also knows exactly what he was doing.

Hell, what was he thinking? One second, he's suggesting I take a step back from her, and the next, he's goading me.

I replay the audible gasp Brynn let out when my tongue made contact with her soft skin, and I groan. Her reaction made me want to lick a hell of a lot more than her thigh. I was more turned on in that moment than I've been in a long ass time.

Not helping Taggart.

The soft murmur of her voice muffled by the closed bedroom door catches my attention, and my eyes fly open. I prop the broom against the cabinets and cross the living room, drawing closer to listen. I cock my head and quickly confirm it's her voice when it hits me.

What if she tells Teagan what happened?

The thought plows into me, shuddering like the Titanic hitting a fucking iceberg. I press a hand against the pain in my chest.

Teagan's like a brother to me. His folks and sisters are more like family than my own. If anyone knows my track record with women and how I loathe the thought of anything serious, it's him.

He'd hate me for putting my hands on her.

He'd think the worst, that I'm using her, when the truth is I have no idea what the hell I'm doing. All I know is I can't seem to control myself around her anymore.

Teagan's always been especially protective of Brynn. Before we left for school, I could see the fear in his eyes when he talked about being in Maryland while she's all the way in Michigan. I could tell it bothered him being so far apart. So, when he asked me to watch over her, I gave him my word.

He trusted me.

And I betrayed that trust—not once but twice—with my mouth, my thoughts, the raging fucking hormones that tell me to ignore all the reasons touching Brynn Nichols is a bad fucking idea. I can hardly blame him for pushing us together. It's not his fault I can't seem to keep my hands to myself and my head from the gutter.

Oh, you asked me to keep her safe from creeps like Stanley? No worries. Took care of that for you. I gave her a good eye fucking, then shoved my tongue down her throat in the process.

Oh, and don't forget the time I licked her thigh like a fucking ice cream cone. You're welcome.

I scrub a hand over my face, then step away from the door as I promise myself I'm done. If she doesn't tell Teagan and I get a pass, I won't lay another finger on her. I'll leave her alone. Focus on football and school. No matter how good she looks, or how amazing she smells, or how jealous I get . . .

With a grunt, I ball my hands into fists. I can make a million promises, but deep down I know I'm in trouble.

BRYNN

Steam drifts toward me as I fill my travel mug with piping hot coffee, topping it off with sugar and cream, then grab the bagel I prepared and turn for the door. I try my best to be as quiet as possible so as not to wake Jace who's still sleeping on the couch.

It's Sunday, and while he has the day off from practice, I start my first official day with Helping Hands. Call it cowardice, but we've yet to address the cupcake incident, and I'd rather avoid a confrontation first thing in the morning. Especially when I'm tired from a night out with the girls and have yet to consume enough coffee to wake the dead.

I turn with my breakfast in hand and halt in my tracks at the sight of a bare-chested Jace standing before me. Even with bed head and bloodshot eyes, he's easily the hottest thing I've ever seen, and I hate him for it.

My mouth flattens into some semblance of a smile as I mutter a "good morning," and try to skirt past unscathed when his hand grips my arm, stopping my retreat.

Holding my breath, I glance up at him, wary of the intensity in the depths of his blue eyes. "Did you . . ." He clears his throat, but it does nothing to relieve the rasp in his voice as he asks, "You went out last night?"

I nod, wondering where he's going with this. If he thinks I'll tell him I went and hid at the coffee shop until they closed as a way to circumvent my feelings before running to my friends, he's wrong.

"Did you come home last night?"

"No. I stayed with Charlotte and Samantha."

He nods, his gaze softening. He lets go of my arm, and it takes an effort of epic proportions not to stare at his bare chest. I want to tell him to go put on a shirt, but that implies I notice and care about his half naked body. So, I don't.

"You've been avoiding me, so we haven't had a chance to talk."

"It's fine." I shake my head, wishing the floor would swallow me whole. I try to dodge him, again to make a play for the door, but his large body blocks my route for the second time.

He ruffles a hand through his already rumpled hair and sighs. "I don't even know where to start," he mumbles. "About the night I brought Teresa home, I—"

"Oh, was that her name?" I ask, hearing the bitterness in my voice. "I'm impressed you remembered." And because I'm feeling particularly stabby, I add, "Actually, I'm surprised you got a name at all.

Regret passes over his masculine features, hot and sharp.

I glance away from him, reminding myself I shouldn't care. "Listen, can we not do this? I just . . . it's fine. Everything is fine."

He says nothing for a moment, while I stare down at the cup in my hand, and the silence grows.

"It's obviously not fine or you wouldn't be avoiding me and running out of here like the room's on fire."

"I'm in a hurry, that's all." I peek up at him, noting his frown and the crease in his brow that tells me he thinks I'm lying. And because I don't want him to misconstrue how I'm feeling, I say, "I took a volunteer position working for Helping Hands and I don't want to be late."

"Oh." His gaze softens. "I didn't know. But that's . . . amazing," he breathes before he drags a hand down his face and lets out a half laugh. "Do you *have* to be so fucking perfect?"

My head jerks to his, eyes narrowed on his face. "I'm not perfect."

As if to punctuate my words, my traitorous gaze drops to his bare chest.

I'm just . . .

Trying to live my life.

Forget about our kiss.

Your hands.

Your tongue.

You.

I swallow, tearing my gaze away. "So, like I said, I'm not avoiding you. I just have somewhere to be." Both a truth and a lie, but the lie is so thin it's transparent, and I know he can see through it.

"Okay." His tone suggests he doesn't believe me, but I exhale in relief when he steps past me, glad it seems he's going to let it drop.

His arm brushes mine and the contact sends an electric jolt to my bones. Without thinking, I track his movement, watching him fill a mug and take a sip, even though I should leave. "You don't believe me?" I ask.

"I mean, you've been living here for over two weeks, and I've only seen you a few times."

I have no answer to that, because he's right.

"Look," he sets his mug down and grips the counter behind him, causing his muscles to flex in ways that should be illegal. "I just don't want things to be weird between us."

"They're not," I say a little too quickly, because if it were awkward, it would imply I care about the kiss *and* him bringing a girl home.

He arches a brow. "I owe you an apology."

I sigh. "Jace, you really don't need to do this."

"For bringing that girl home," he says, ignoring me. "And for yesterday with the cupcakes. The night on the couch." He tips his head in the direction of the living room. "All of it."

"This is your place, Jace. You owe me nothing. You can bring whomever you want here. You can bring the whole cheerleading squad here, if you like. It's none of my business. You're already sacrificing enough by letting me stay here, by giving up your bed," I say, ignoring the parts where he kissed me.

"You're wrong. Bringing her here, I knew it would make you uncomfortable. Hell, part of me thinks that's why I did it."

I file this piece of information away before I can analyze it because I have no idea what it means except that it doesn't matter, and making more of it than it is won't help my cause.

"Bottom line, I shouldn't have done it, and I want you to know it won't happen again."

"Okay, then," I say, with a curt nod, my tone tight.

"And about the other stuff—"

"Forget it." I shake my head, not wanting to hear it, mostly because I've been doing a pretty damn good job of ignoring it all together. "No explanation needed. I know you regret it. Consider it off the record. Never happened."

He stares at me for a moment as if trying to read my thoughts.

Good luck, buddy. Even I don't know what the hell I'm thinking.

"Right." Grabbing his mug, he pushes off the counter, closing the distance between us, and just when I think he's going to let it be, he pauses beside me, hovering so close I can feel the heat of his skin, hear the gravel in his voice as he says, "But for the record, I don't regret it."

I suck in a breath as my gaze slowly lifts to his.

"At least not for the reasons you think," he adds.

CHAPTER 18

BRYNN

A JET OF FREEZING cold water blasts me in the boob, then changes trajectory and shoots Charlotte square in the face. Maniacal laughter follows, then fades into the distance as our assailant heads to the water pump for a refill.

I rub the wet spot on my chest and turn to a dripping wet Charlotte. "I can't believe I let you talk me into this," she says as she shakes her body out like a Labrador, sending a spray of water droplets into the air.

"Come on. Look at how much fun they're having." I motion to the hoard of kids, ducking behind makeshift forts in the park and blasting each other with water guns.

"Hurry, let's cut off their water supply."

I snort. "I don't think that's possible."

"Always the cynic," she mutters. "But at least now I understand the desire for pediatric nursing." When I look at her in question, she adds, "You get to stab these little heathens with needles."

I laugh. "That is *so* wrong."

After I visited Helping Hands and filled out my application earlier in the week, I'd found out they were short volunteers for today, so I told Charlotte about it, and she'd agreed to help, saying it would be great for her resume as well since she's an education major. Now we're embroiled in an intense water war at the local park, which has helped her discover an inconvenient truth. She's not a fan of kids.

"Well, actually, there's one positive outcome to you roping me into volunteering today."

"What's that?" I ask, as I duck below a flying water balloon.

It hits Charlotte right between the eyes, and I gasp. Covering my mouth with my hands, I fight the laughter bubbling in the back of my throat.

"I now know I want to teach high school," she grinds out.

I bite my lip and pick a piece of red latex out of her hair as she wipes her eyes. "Come on, we're sitting ducks here. Let's go," I say as she turns to glare at me.

I nod in the direction of the bathrooms where we can find cover while scouting out a target. We run toward the small building with me in front, covering Charlotte and shooting a little redhead in the back. A spray of water nails him right between the shoulder blades and he drops his gun.

Once we reach the building, I press my back against the wood and motion for her to do the same. If we're lucky, we can hold out here until the timer goes off and it's time to head back to the community center.

Charlotte takes the opportunity to catch her breath and check the time.

"How much longer?" I ask.

"Only ten minutes, thank heavens."

I peek around the corner of the building, making sure not to give away our position, but the coast is clear. With a sigh, I relax, and take a moment to catch my breath.

"Jace apologized this morning on my way out the door."

Charlotte gasps. "He did? You've been holding out on me." She jabs me in the ribs. "That should've been the first thing you said this morning! So," she drawls, her tone impatient, "what did he say?"

"Just that he never should've brought a girl back to his apartment because I'm staying there, and he knew it would make me uncomfortable." I shrug.

"Oh."

I glance over at her and laugh. "Not what you were expecting?"

"No. It's just . . . I don't know. I guess I was hoping for something a little juicier. Like, I'm sorry I brought a girl back to my place *that wasn't you.*"

I bite my lips.

"*Oooh!*" She points at my face. "What's that look? He said something else, didn't he?"

"He might've also apologized for the cupcake incident and kissing me on the couch."

Her eyes round. "And what did you say?"

"Nothing. I mean, what could I say? I know how close he is to Teagan. Just like I know Teagan would be furious if he found out, so I'm sure he's worried about it. I mean, he asked him to keep an eye out for me, not to suck my face."

"But sucking face is so much more fun," she says, and I shoot her a look. "Sorry."

"So, anyway, I just said something about how I knew he regretted it and not to worry, that I'd keep it between us. Hell, the last thing I want is Teagan finding out, then coming out here and causing some big scene. I want to do this on my own." To prove I no longer need his protection. "And he just sort of stared at me a moment, and then he brushed by me and said, 'I don't regret it.'"

Charlotte releases a high-pitched squeal so loud, I'm sure it's alerted the entire universe to our position.

"Shhhh." I cover her mouth with my hand, glancing around me to see if any of the kids have noticed. One off in the distance turns around, searching for the source of the sound, but at his angle, he mustn't see us.

"He said that?" she mutters beneath my palm.

"Yeah." I drop my hand.

"So, what do you think it means?" she whisper-hisses.

I exhale, my mind wandering. I thought a lot about it on my way over here this morning, and I'm still unsure. "I don't know." I shrug.

"He likes you. Jace totally has the hots for you."

"No way," I say, a little too quickly. "We hate each other."

Charlotte's brow quirks. "Hate is just another form of passion. Besides, you definitely hate him more than he hates you. In fact, I don't think he hates you at all."

I fall silent for a moment, mulling over her words. Is that true? Maybe I've just been projecting my own feelings onto him.

"Why *do* you hate him so much, anyway?" she asks, unfazed by my silence.

"What?" I ask, blinking at her like I didn't hear the question.

She rolls her eyes. "Jace. Why do you hate him? Is it just because he's a player?"

I push at the memory pressing against the edges of my mind. I learned a long time ago how to control my thoughts surrounding the incident, so I'm not about to let them come crashing in now. "Yeah, exactly. I mean, he takes nothing seriously. In high school, everything was always a joke to him, and all he did was party, hang with the boys, and hook up with girls. It's gross. Guys like him should come with a warning label. Cocky, womanizer. Don't call me, I'll call you."

Charlotte slowly nods as if letting that sink in. "What if you're wrong? What if he's changed and actually likes you?"

"Char, women have been sold that lie for centuries, and I refuse to be one of them. Besides, it would be delusional. The other night when we walked in on him with that girl is proof that he's the same old dog up to the same old tricks. Boys like him don't change."

Charlotte sighs and sinks back into the building. "Too damn bad you have no interest in a fling, because that boy is—"

Before the words are even out of her mouth, a short kid with a crop of black hair rounds the corner, pointing his squirt gun at her head as he screams, "You guys! They're over here!"

My spirits soar as I head off campus toward the apartments, taking a detour to the coffee shop where I grab an iced latte and mull over my situation with Jace. Both my talk with Charlotte and my time away from the apartment have helped to clear my head. Jace and I have had a diabolical relationship for years, but there's been a shift in the dynamic between us for the second time since I've known him. Only, unlike the first, I can't pinpoint the cause. Maybe it's the absence of Teagan as a buffer. Maybe I said or did something to piss Jace off beyond moving in with him, and now he's retaliating.

I think back to a time before we were at odds, when things were amicable between us. When my family moved to Riverside in grade school, Teagan and Jace became fast friends. By the time sixth grade rolled around, Jace was a permanent fixture in the Nichols' household, but I didn't mind so much. My sisters, Trista and Sabel, were only babies, and as my father so eloquently put it, he and Teagan were outnumbered, so it was nice to have another guy around.

Even back then Jace was a charmer, quickly winning my mother's affections and a space at our table. I remember being transfixed by his aqua eyes and broad smile, and even though he was Teagan's best friend, he always made it a point to include me. We'd ride bikes, watch movies, and play video games, spending countless hours goofing off and just being kids.

But the summer before eighth grade, an awareness started creeping in. I'd always known Jace was good-looking, but his attraction became obvious in a way it hadn't previously. While I still felt awkward and a little shy around boys, he was the opposite. Outside of Jace and my brother, I barely talked to the guys in our class. Meanwhile, Jace was a shameless flirt. I remember overhearing him tell Teagan about necking with a girl behind the bleachers at school and blushing because my friends and I had yet to even kiss a boy.

One week that summer, we had a heatwave with record highs. The kind of heat that steals your breath and makes your clothes stick to your skin the second you step outside. Mom got tired of us lounging around in the air conditioning, so one morning after Jace slept over, she kicked us out of the house and handed us squirt guns.

By noon, Teagan had called it quits. Out of breath and soaked, he retreated to the house for pizza and video games. But I refused to admit defeat and Jace wasn't ready to give up, either. The rest of the day was spent one-upping each other. After Jace popped out of the bathroom shower and nailed me square in the face with an icy stream, I dumped an entire bucket on him while he flirted with our neighbors in the yard. He put ice under my sheets just before bed, so I shoved ice in the toes of his sneakers. We went on like that for two days until the heatwave broke and Jace's parents returned from their trip to Santa Monica, and my mother made us stop.

I pause on the sidewalk, wondering if that's our problem.

Jace and I have been engaged in a proverbial water fight for years.

It doesn't matter who started it because we both want to win, and neither of us will stop until we do, even if it destroys us. The only difference is somewhere along the line we traded our squirt guns in for sharp words and insults. Even more threatening as of late is the sexual warfare Jace seemed to declare. It's dangerous territory, one I'd very much like to flee from because it can't go anywhere good. The mixture of hatred and sexual tension is giving me whiplash.

We need to call a truce, but my mom's not here to stop us like she stopped the water war all those years ago. And though the last thing I want to do is wave the white flag of surrender to the enemy, if I don't, he never will. That much is clear, and someone needs to be the bigger person here.

So, why can't it be me?

CHAPTER 19

BRYNN

I PUSH THE DOOR to Jace's apartment open to find him staring out the windows. The television blares in the background, so he doesn't hear my entrance, which is further evidenced by the way his reflection in the window stares unseeingly at the street below. I wonder what he's thinking about when he notices my reflection, and his blue eyes meet mine in the glass.

He stands like that for whole seconds, taking in my watery image as if I'm a mirage and not actually standing several feet behind him while I give myself a pep talk.

I made the decision on the way here to form a truce, and it's time to implement it, but now that I'm here, face-to-face with him, a pocket of nerves bursts in my chest like an abscess filling me with doubt.

I hurry into the little kitchen where I refill my stainless water bottle at the sink and take a long drink. By the time I'm done, I turn to find he's facing me. "Hey," I say, trying to keep my tone casual as I ponder how awkward this feels.

"Hey back." He shoves his hands in his pockets, staring in a way that tells me he's trying to gauge my mood.

My stomach clenches as he closes the distance between us and joins me in the kitchen. A wave of his masculine scent washes over me, and I suddenly regret coming in here. The kitchen is too small, too confined. Not to mention, one of the only two other times we've ever been in this space, his tongue collided with my leg.

As if he can read my thoughts, his gaze slides to my legs in my cutoff shorts.

I clear my throat, and he jerks his head away, meeting my eyes guiltily. "Hungry?" I ask, wondering if I'm going to regret this. "I thought maybe if you haven't eaten, we could try that Greek place a block down."

"You want to have dinner with me?" He points at his chest, but doesn't even wait for me to respond before he says, "I figured you wouldn't come home until I was either out with the guys or in bed."

"Why would you think that?"

"Come on." He arches a brow. "Didn't we establish this morning that you've been avoiding me?"

"Okay, maybe I have a little," I mumble, staring down at my hands. "But can you blame me?"

His grin is answer enough.

"Do you remember the summer we had the water war?" I ask.

His eyes glitter and he tilts his head. "Of course. I remember we had that heatwave, record temperatures. What made you think of it?" he asks, indicating he's not gleaning the same wisdom from it I did.

I shrug. "I don't know, really. But it got me thinking. For so long, you and I have been stuck in this war. When one of us strikes, the other retaliates. Only lately did it turn . . . weird." I grimace. "But like it or not, I'm stuck here for the rest of the summer semester, and it would be nice for both of us if we didn't have to feel as though we're walking on eggshells the whole time."

Jace's eyes narrow like this is a trap. "What are you getting at?"

"Let's have a truce, a cease-fire to our personal war. From here on out, you and I are no longer at odds."

"A truce." The word rolls off his tongue like he doesn't know the meaning of it. "And you think you're capable of that?"

"I do." Mostly because I don't have a choice.

If I truly want this to work and my remaining days of summer to be devoid of conflict, then I have to put in the effort.

He pushes off the counter, coming closer, and instinctively, I take a step back. "So, if we're no longer enemies, that makes us . . . friends?" His eyes search mine, and I sense he's looking for something, but I'm not sure what. Whatever it is, I don't like it.

I swallow. "Friends might be a bit of a stretch."

He laughs under his breath. "Just roommates, then?"

I nod. For some reason, this label I can handle. Maybe because it only requires a temporary level of commitment. Roommates can be a lot of things. You can hate your roommate, love your roommate, or tolerate them. It leaves room for something in between or nothing at all.

"Roommates." I stretch a hand out to shake on it like we're forming a business deal.

Jace chuckles but humors me, his hand lingering over mine longer than necessary. His palm is slightly rough and calloused, his skin warm. It's the first time I've noticed the sheer size of them or the way the tendons in his forearms flicker with the subtle movement, and I wish I didn't know how they feel sliding under the hem of my shirt, gliding over my hot skin, or gripping my chin to kiss me.

My skin flushes, and I avoid his gaze, hoping he can't read my thoughts when he pulls away with a smirk. I exhale in relief as he brushes past me and stops by the door. "You coming?"

JACE

To say I'm more than a little surprised at Brynn's proposal to bury the hatchet over dinner would be an understatement. I'm floored. Shocked. Bewildered. But I'm also pleased. This is my chance to make up for crossing the line by putting my hands on her. All I need to do is behave and I'll call this night a victory.

Hell, maybe we can even be friends. I know she thinks it's a stretch, but I plan on proving to her it's not.

Because the restaurant is close, we opt to go by foot instead of driving.

It's a nice night, hot but not overly so, and the humidity is low. The scent of freshly mowed lawn scents the air, and the sound of shouting from a pickup basketball game in the courts outside the apartments echoes in the background.

I walk beside her, slowing my pace to match hers. "Stanley hasn't given you any crap since everything that happened, has he?" I ask.

She shakes her head. "No. He hasn't spoken a word to me. Hasn't even looked in my direction, in fact. Just comes and goes as if it never happened."

"Good." I shove my hands in my pockets. "Let me know if that changes."

I feel her gaze heavy on the side of my face. "Can I ask you something?"

I cock my head. "Shoot."

"What were you thinking about when I walked in the apartment earlier today? When you were staring out the window. You looked so deep in thought."

My throat bobs, and I wonder how long she was standing there before I noticed.

I give a little shrug, trying to keep my expression neutral. "Not much. I spoke with my parents earlier."

"Oh. Everything okay?"

I note the concern in her voice and wonder what it must be like to have the kind of parents who actually care.

"Sure, yeah." I run a hand through my hair and laugh, but the sound falls flat. "They just wanted to let me know about their travel plans. Looks like they won't be home in August during break. In fact, they'll be gone the entire time until I come back to school in the fall."

"Wait." Brynn pauses on the sidewalk, and when I glance back at her, she frowns. "You won't see them at all?"

I shake my head.

"But . . . they didn't move you in, either."

I pull on the back of my neck, avoiding her gaze.

What does she want me to say? Didn't she ever wonder why I spent so much time at her house? It wasn't just because of my friendship with Teagan. I mean, sure, that was the main reason, but I absolutely hated being alone in our big ass house all the time. I grew up loathing the silence. It's the reason I prefer background noise in the apartment to nothing at all.

But the truth is, my parents have never been there for me. Not when it counts. Sure, they've given me a roof over my head, a full belly, and everything I could possibly need. But never their time. Never their love.

"It's no biggie," I say, and for the most part, I mean it. I'm used to it by now.

"Well, what about your games in the fall? I'm sure they can't wait to watch you take the field."

I arch a brow and laugh. "Well, they won't be at any in person, that's for damn sure."

Brynn returns to my side, her pace slower than before. "But . . . you get tickets, right? For family and stuff?"

I huff. "I know you didn't go to many home games in Riverside, but if you had, you'd know that my parents never really came to watch me play. I have no illusions about the fact that just because I'm playing for the Big Ten that's going to suddenly change. Hell, if they catch a game on television, it'll be an accident."

Silence settles between us, and I can see Brynn's concern morph into a frown. The last thing I want is her pity, and I inwardly chastise myself for being so open. I don't normally talk about my folks. Not to the guys or anyone else for that matter. So, why didn't I want to sugarcoat the truth with her?

"Well, you know my mom would love to have you at our place," Brynn says, breaking the silence. "And I'm sure Teagan would be thrilled to have twenty-four seven to catch up."

I bump her lightly with my elbow. "What about you? Would *you* love to have me?"

I already know the answer. Having me back in her home after a summer semester spent in my apartment must be her worst nightmare. It's glaringly obvious, but I ask anyway because for some reason, I *want* her to want me there.

She says nothing, confirming what I already know. I don't let it faze me, though, and instead, change the subject. "Wanna race?"

"What?" She glances up at me, a question in her eyes.

"Last one to the shop at the end of the block buys dinner."

She scoffs. "Like I stand a chance. I'm exercise adverse, and you're a college athlete."

"'Exercise adverse'?" I arch a brow.

"I said what I said."

Grinning, I spin around, walking backward so I can face her. "Well, I thought you might say that, so we'll race backward."

"Um, I've seen all those drills you do, Taggart. You can run backward in your sleep."

"You been watching me, Cupcake?"

Her cheeks flush. "Hardly. I remember from high school."

I hum under my breath. "What if I give you a five-second head start?"

She purses her lips. "Ten."

"Damn, you drive a hard bargain." I place my hands on my hips as if I need a minute to consider her terms before I nod. "Okay. Ten, but not a second more.

"Deal." Brynn smiles. "Get ready to go down."

I stop as she spins around on the sidewalk and I ask her if she's ready. "Countdown starts when you go."

Brynn nods, inhaling before she takes off, running backward as fast as her feet can carry her, which isn't very fast at all. I nearly laugh as I hold my fingers up in the air, counting her head start out loud. "One. Two . . . Nine. Ten!"

And I'm off.

With my arms bent at my side, I start jogging and quickly begin to close the distance when Brynn squeals and picks up the pace. "You're going down, Cupcake!"

I dodge a fire hydrant and Brynn nearly falls on a massive crack in the sidewalk.

I pull ahead slightly despite her valiant effort. Several people curse as we nearly plow into them. Brynn misses getting her foot caught in a bicycle rack by inches, and a yappy chihuahua charges at me on his owner's leash.

By the time we both reach the stop sign in front of the restaurant, we can barely contain our hysterics. Brynn tips her head back, laughing so hard she gasps for air, and I croak out, "I'm ordering the most expensive thing on the menu."

"Ha! Lucky for me, I brought you somewhere cheap."

I chuckle as my breathing evens out. A lock of hair has fallen out of Brynn's ponytail, so I smooth it back with my hand, lingering a little longer than I should as her laughter fades. Our eyes lock; the moment feels loaded. Pressure builds inside my chest like the cork on a shaken bottle of champagne.

It wouldn't take much to set me off, so I drop my hand and clear my throat. "Ready?"

Without waiting for her response, I turn and head for the doors before I do something I'll regret. Lord knows I've done enough of that in the past two weeks, and I'd like to think I'm the kind of guy that can learn from my mistakes.

We enter the restaurant and head to the hostess booth. Since it's early yet, it's not very crowded and we don't have to wait long to be seated.

Our waitress leads us to a small table in the back. The atmosphere is casual with bright lighting, upbeat music, and eclectic patronage. Everyone from families with kids to singles and students occupy the tables, which saves us the awkwardness of feeling like this is a date.

I wonder if that's why Brynn chose this place.

Not seconds after we sit, Brynn announces she has to use the restroom and as she stands, she asks, "If the waitress comes for our drinks, will you order me a—"

"Coke with lemon? Sure."

Brynn pauses mid-rise as she stares over at me in surprise. "How did you know?"

I turn my attention to the menu. "I notice a lot of things about you."

Quite frankly, it's kind of hard not to. I've always noticed Brynn. Does she really think I pay so little attention to her?

She's still standing across from me, staring at me like she doesn't know what to make of this revelation. I admit, I'm a little confused by how dumbfounded she is. It's such a small thing to notice. But I get the sense it kind of freaks her out, so I take pity on her and joke, "It's an easy thing to remember, since it's so disgusting."

"You mean, amazing." She tips her chin, indignant, and I grin.

"If it's opposite day, sure."

She chuckles and shakes her head as she finally heads to the restroom.

Once she's gone, I inhale, trying to loosen the knot in my stomach. This whole notion of a truce wasn't even my idea, yet the pressure for it to go well sits inside my chest like a stone. I've never cared so much about making a good impression on someone. Hell, I've never had to try a day in my life with a girl before. It's disconcerting.

When the waitress stops at our table, I order Brynn's drink and get water for myself, trying to ignore her obvious attempts at flirting. By the time Brynn returns from the bathroom, the waitress delivers them, dropping the straws in front of me with a wink.

Brynn watches her go, mouth curling in disgust.

I clear my throat, hoping she doesn't think I did anything to provoke her, then wonder why the hell I care if she does.

This isn't a date, jackass.

We take another couple of minutes to go over the menu before the waitress returns for our orders. When I request the lamb kabobs, she leans toward me, her full breasts on display in her low-cut top. "Large or small? You look like a large to me," she says with a grin.

I press my lips together. *Do* not *laugh.*

Across from me Brynn snorts, and I manage a clipped, "Large will do."

"Do you like it pink?" She practically purrs.

Fucking hell.

Brynn chokes on her drink, hacking and coughing as she bangs on her chest like a gorilla.

"You all right over there, Cupcake?" I ask with a raised brow.

At her answering nod, I glance back at the waitress who's intently waiting for my answer, not the least bit fazed by Brynn's near-death experience. "Uh, well done, thanks."

Her smile fades as if disappointed at my answer before she takes Brynn's order in a monotone voice, barely offering her a second glance. Afterward, she leaves to place our orders, and when Brynn turns to me, I can't tell if she's impressed, mortified, or both. "Wow," she says, eyes wide.

"What?" I shrug like I have no idea what she's talking about.

"Does that happen to you everywhere you go?"

"Not everywhere," I mumble with a shrug.

"Must be nice to have women falling at your feet and propositioning you all the time."

"She wasn't propositioning me." I ignore her scoff and cock my head, giving her a meaningful look. "Like you don't have dudes doing the same."

She laughs. "Do you think if I did, I'd still be single?"

I roll my eyes. "You're single because you don't put yourself out there."

"No way." She shakes her head.

"Seriously. I could name about five guys on my team that have asked me about you, and would take you out in a heartbeat had I not threatened them bodily harm."

Oops. Did I say that out loud?

I wince, afraid of how she'll take this.

"Wait, seriously?"

I'm not going to lie to her, so I simply shrug.

Surprising me, she laughs and takes a sip of her soda. "Figures."

A few minutes later when our food comes, Brynn eyes my meat kabobs and veggies with growing interest. "What?" I ask.

"Nothing. Just . . . have you always eaten so clean? I don't remember you being so strict with your diet back home. In fact, I recall the time my mother made a double batch of homemade bread and you ate two loaves of it in two hours. I was so mad because I didn't even get a piece.

My lips quirk. "You fat-shaming me?"

"I would never," she says in mock offense. "But I'm genuinely curious."

Brynn being curious about me is something I can get used to.

"First of all," I say, taking a moment to shovel a forkful of vegetables in my mouth and chew, "your mom's bread is fucking amazing." Brynn snorts at this. "Second of all, you haven't noticed me being so strict before because I'm not. I mean, it's true, I have been watching what I eat a little more since starting conditioning because I want to be at my prime, and the extra protein is making a difference in the gym." I note the way her gaze flickers to my biceps and then my chest, and the attention gets me hot. "But mostly, I'm playing a joke on Chris."

Her gaze lifts to mine. "What?"

"Yeah." I smile as I explain, "He has a killer sweet tooth, so me and the guys thought it would be funny if we convinced him the team requires a restrictive high-protein diet during conditioning. He's been eating nothing but lean meat, protein shakes, and vegetables at every meal." Jace laughs. "Meanwhile, I have a stash of chocolate hiding in my can of super greens in the pantry, and based on the way he devoured your cupcakes like he was starving, I'd say he's more than a little desperate."

Brynn covers a laugh. "*No.* That's so mean!"

"It's fucking hilarious is what it is. We passed a couple of kids after practice the other day eating ice cream, and I thought he was going to cry."

"Jace Taggart!" She flings a sugar packet at me, but I block it with my right arm. "That's terrible."

"Oh, come on." I hold up my hands. "He's hardly even at our apartment half the time. I'm sure he's binging when we're not around."

"You're the worst," she says with a chuckle. But for some reason, coming from her, it sounds like the best.

"So, tell me," I start. "We've been here for about three weeks now, and you used to spend a lot of time at home in high school. Are you homesick yet?"

Brynn pauses, taking her time as if she's really thinking about the answer, and I like that about her, that she truly considers how she feels instead of just giving me a generic response. "I'm not, which is surprising. I actually thought I would be because I'm so close to my family, but . . ." She shakes her head, and I wonder if she's trying to process what she's feeling. "I don't know. I think I just really needed this, you know? The change of pace. The independence. I really wanted a fresh start, and despite the road bumps so far, that's exactly what I'm getting. I'm making friends and I'm putting myself out there. I'm trying to date, even if it's not going as well as I had hoped. I signed up for a volunteer position with kids . . ."

She trails off for a moment, bowing her head to poke some of her food around with a fork and I can tell she's not finished.

"Back in high school, it felt like I was just trying to get through, to pass the time, but here, I'm making choices for myself. For the first time in a really long time, I feel like I'm actually *living*." She offers me a shy smile. "Does that even make sense? Or does it sound stupid?"

I shake my head because she's the farthest thing from stupid. "No. It sounds pretty damn smart, actually. Like you're creating your own happiness."

Her smile spreads until it reaches her eyes, and it feels like a reward. "I like that," she says. "Creating my own happiness." She bites her lip, and my eyes follow the movement; it makes me want a taste.

I swallow, shifting my attention back to my plate.

The rest of dinner passes quickly. We talk a lot about her family and a little bit about what we want to do when we return home before fall semester. I discuss football and my hopes for the season while she fills me in on the volunteer position she took at Helping Hands.

By the time we've exhausted our stay at the table and can no longer stall, I'm sorry to see the night end. Our waitress stops by with the bill, sitting it on the edge of the table where I slap a hand on it, dragging it toward me before Brynn can get to it first.

"Jace, you are not paying."

I glance up from my wallet. "I got it."

She reaches across the table and tries to pluck the slip of paper from my hands, but I hold it just out of reach.

She huffs and grits her teeth. "We had a deal, remember? I lost the race."

I tsk and wave my finger. "I was just joking. I didn't actually expect you to buy me dinner, and if you think there's a world in which I take a girl to dinner, whether it's a date, a friend, a roommate, or otherwise, and I allow her to cover the bill or even go Dutch, you're crazy."

"This is the twenty-first century." She rolls her eyes and waves a little leather pouch attached to her key ring. "Look, I have my own wallet and everything."

"Cute. What do you carry in that thing? Monopoly money?" I flag the waitress down and hand her my card as Brynn protests.

"Jace, you cant pay. It makes it seem like a . . ."

She pauses, and my smile grows wicked. "A what?"

Her cheeks flush crimson as she opens and closes her mouth like a guppy, the words lodged in her throat. I've seen Brynn Nichols in a lot of different emotional states over the years, but flustered is a rare occurrence. I think it's my favorite.

" . . . a date," she finally finishes.

I put a hand on my chest and suck in a dramatic breath. "Brynn Nichols, first you ask me to join you for dinner, and then you try to pay. Is that what this is? Why didn't you just say so?"

She chucks her straw at my face. "Shut up."

"I didn't even wear my date shoes."

She scoffs. "You have *date* shoes?"

"Of course I have date shoes," I say, making up shit as I go. "You don't? No wonder you have no game."

Her lips twitch, eyes glittering with humor as she asks, "So, tell me. Were you wearing your date shoes the other night when you brought that girl back to the apartment? What was her name . . . Teresa?"

I wonder what it means that she remembers her name while I hiss and rub my chest. "Ouch. Way to hit a man where it hurts." I hold up a finger. "In my defense, you are currently occupying my bedroom, so it's not like I could go somewhere and close the door."

"How sad for you."

I nod. "It is sad. In fact, my back was aching from the concrete sofa, and she offered to help me out by coming to my place and rubbing out the knots. *See!* It all started as an innocent massage, due to said sofa I'm occupying because you stole my bed, so really this *is* your fault."

She laughs, then reaches out and pokes me in the chest. "*My* fault?"

"I said what I said."

"You're incorrigible," she says, with a smile.

I beam at her. A short time ago, she would've scowled and told me I was a pig or something equally as insulting. Maybe this is progress.

The waitress returns with the receipt. I sign it and set it aside when I notice my copy has a note for me to call her together with her name and number.

I risk a quick glance at Brynn, but she's sliding from the booth, her gaze elsewhere.

With a wash of relief, I cover it with my hand as I rise and follow after her, leaving the receipt behind.

CHAPTER 20

JACE

I PACE THE LENGTH of the apartment, tossing a football between my hands as I try to pass the time. Chris left more than an hour ago for a party some of his old buddies from high school are throwing. He invited me to go with him, but I wasn't in the mood. If I'm being honest, I stayed in the hopes Brynn would come back and we'd get a chance to hang out. Though we've talked more this week than we have in a long time, thanks to my apology and her impromptu truce, she's been gone most of the day—most of the week, actually—with Charlotte and Samantha occupying most of her time.

I heard her talking on the phone the other morning when she thought I was still sleeping. Apparently, the night before they'd been hanging at Bradd's and another bar downtown. Is that where they're off to every night? Is that where she'll be tonight?

Fuck. I don't like it.

In retrospect, I should've taken Chris up on his offer and gone with him. Left alone to my own devices, I have too much time on my hands. Time to sit here and wonder what Brynn and her girls do at the club and who they talk to.

Has she found someone to replace Stanley? Is she hooking up with guys?

And why the hell do I care?

As long as she's being smart and safe about it, Brynn is a grown-ass woman. She might be a little on the inexperienced side, but she's also no dummy. She can take care of herself. Stanley's broken schnoz is evidence of that.

I twirl the ball in my hands, then tuck it under my arm and swipe my phone off the kitchen counter where I text the group chat, needing something to do.

ME: What are you ladies up to tonight?

I wait, wondering if I'm the only loser hanging by his phone when a text comes through.

ATLAS: Kenzie and I are hanging out.

GRAHAM: On my way to Chicago to see Skylar.

Again with the girlfriends.

ME: Smug bastards.

I head to the couch and sink down, back aching from weeks of sleeping on the hard cushions. For the first time, I see the value in having a girlfriend rather than a hookup. It would be kind of nice to have someone you know who you can rely on for company. Someone who will always be there without even having to ask. I've been alone more than I'd like to admit, and this shit gets old after a while. The silence is deafening, even if my thoughts aren't.

TEAGAN: A group of us are going out here, so I'm getting ready now. Something up, bro?

I sigh. It's been a while since I've spoken with him, and though that's going to happen with all of us at different schools now, clearly, he senses something's up.

ME: Nah. Just thought I'd check in. Feeling restless but not in the mood to go out either. I think I might stay in tonight.

Because I'm bored as shit and going out of my mind thinking about your sister.

> **GRAHAM**: Jace stay in? The life of the party? That's a first.

> **ATLAS**: Who died?

> **ME**: Very funny, dickheads. Last time I went to the club, I got wasted and brought a chick home with Brynn here. Let's just say it didn't end well.

I think about my night with Teresa and the look on Brynn's face when she walked in on us. Despite apologizing for it, Brynn still doesn't know I told her to leave just before she walked in and saw us, and even though it feels significant, what would be the point in telling her? It's not like I have a chance with her, and even if I did, is she supposed to be impressed I couldn't follow through with someone else because my thoughts were filled with her?

Has she told Teagan about it? Shit, I hope not. But if she did, now is the time for him to mention it.

> **TEAGAN**: What's Brynn up to? We talked earlier and she seemed like she could

use a night in. Said she's been running a lot. Why don't you ask her to hang out?

GRAHAM: Um, do you want him to get murdered?

ATLAS: Even I know that's a bad idea.

KNOX: Wait a minute. I think Graham's onto something. After all, you were the one that suggested she move in with Jace in the first place. Maybe this is all a part of your master plan. WHAT DOES JACE HAVE ON YOU AND WHY DO YOU WANT HIM GONE?

Teagan texts him a middle finger emoji and I snort.

ME: I'll take it under advisement.

TEAGAN: Seriously, Taggart. Don't hang out by yourself like a sad motherfucker. Text my sister. Your fragile heart can't take the solitude.

I snort.

> **ME:** Yeah, yeah. I'll consider it.

I exit the group chat and stare at my phone. If Teagan knew the way I've acted around Brynn these last few weeks, I'm not so sure he'd be suggesting we hang out. But I'd be lying if I said the thought of spending an evening alone with her didn't sound appealing. Our dinner together last weekend was a lot of fun, and I've wanted a repeat ever since.

Opening my contacts, I stare at her name and number while I try to talk myself out of texting her.

She's busy.

I'm the last person she wants to spend a Saturday night with.

It's only going to make me think about her more.

If she says no, I'll feel like the world's biggest douchebag.

We're in a good place, and chances are I'll do something to fuck it up, and then we'll be back at square one with her hating me and me playing along because it's all I can get.

All of these things are true, yet the persistent voice in the back of my head is louder. It tells me to throw caution to the wind because the cold, hard truth is I got a taste of Brynn and all I want is more.

BRYNN

I slide into the passenger seat of Charlotte's Honda and sigh when the sweet relief of the air conditioning blasts through the vents. "Today is a scorcher," I say as I peel the sleeveless top I'm wearing away from my damp skin to try and get some air.

"I know. I'd kill for a swimming pool and a spiked lemonade." Charlotte fans her face, her cheeks pink from the heat.

"And a hot man to rub sunscreen all over us," Samantha chimes in.

I chuckle as Charlotte pulls out into traffic at the same time my phone vibrates, and I check the screen. My stomach tumbles at the sight of Jace's name. It's been a week since we had dinner together, and things between us are surprisingly good. I no longer hide away in his bedroom. Instead, I come and go like a normal person without worrying about whether I'll be seen. I eat breakfast at the little eat-in dining table, fix myself meals. And, bonus, Jace has kept his lethal lips and tongue to himself. He's even toned down the lectures, despite my having gone out the last three nights in a row with Charlotte and Samantha, hitting up both Bradd's and the new pool hall downtown.

I don't know whether this shift in dynamic is due to a change in his behavior or mine, but whatever it is, I'm relieved. Turns out the truce was the best idea I've had in a long time.

I swipe open my screen and stare down at his text.

> **JACE:** What are your plans for the night?

I think for a minute before answering. My knee-jerk instinct with him is to say something snarky, but instead, I settle on the truth and hope it doesn't somehow bite me in the ass.

> **ME**: Not sure, but I think I'm just going to stay in. I've gone out the last few nights with the girls, and I'm spent.

I hit send and fight the niggling hope he'll be there.

> **JACE**: Wanna chill and watch a movie together?

I stare at my phone, blinking. Did he just ask me to hang out with him?

Only a couple weeks ago, spending any amount of time in the same room meant we'd be at each other's throats within the hour. But things are changing, and we live together. Hanging out when neither of us have plans is inevitable. So why does the thought of watching a movie with him make my heart race? And is it weird that I actually *want* to hang out with him?

"*Hello?* Earth to Brynn," Samantha calls out from the back seat.

My head snaps up from my phone and I blink over at Charlotte, then behind me to Samantha, who's waiting expectantly. "Sorry. Did you say something?"

"We said we're gonna just chill at the dorms tonight. Charlotte asked if you're joining us, or if you wanted us to drop you off at the apartment."

"Oh, uh . . ." I should probably go with them to the dorms. Girl time is good for me, and Jace and I alone together is a bad idea considering, as of late, I never know what I'm going to get with him.

But I've been spending the majority of my free time with Charlotte, Samantha, and a couple of the other girls I've gotten to know at Hyde Hall, and it might be kind of nice to just put on some PJs and watch a movie until I fall asleep or decide to drag myself to bed. Which is why I find myself saying, "I'm beat, honestly. It's been a busy week."

"Yeah. I'm with you. Between classes, how many times we've gone out this week, as well as the heat, I feel like I could sleep for days."

"Fine, then." Samantha sighs. "I guess I won't meet James for drinks tonight."

I snort. "You make it sound like a standing date."

"That's because it is," she says, like I'm stupid.

"He's the bartender. He has to be there," I point out, though in truth it doesn't seem to deter her. She still flirts relentlessly while he only half listens as he works.

"Details." She waves me away, and I laugh.

My phone buzzes in my hand again, drawing my attention, and I realize I never answered Jace back.

> **JACE**: I promise to keep my hands to myself—lips, tongues, and all.

I grin, fighting the flush rising to my cheeks and, apparently, losing because when Charlotte comes to a red light, she leans over, peering down at my phone. "Who ya talkin' to?"

"What. No one," I say, yanking it out of sight.

"Oh, she's definitely talking to someone. Five bucks says it's lover boy."

I arch a brow. "Who the hell is lover boy?"

"Jacey-poo." Samantha dramatically flutters her lashes.

"Jacey-poo?" I repeat. "Do not *ever* call him that again."

"So, is it?" Charlotte arches a brow.

"If you must know, yes, it just so happens to be Jace." I roll my eyes, then hurry and text him back before he takes my silence as a rejection.

> **ME**: Well, that's no fun.

I hit send, and instantly regret what I said.

Shit. Shit. Shit. Shit!

I reread my text. What was meant as a joke came off as insanely flirty.

What if he thinks I'm serious?

I tap on my phone screen as if I can rescind the text by sheer will as panic claws through my chest. WHY DO PHONES NOT HAVE INSTANT DELETE BUTTONS?

I have to say something else, follow it up with a joke. But what?

Shit. I can't think as I type out and send: *Just kissing. Haha!*

My eyes widen as I see my mistake, and I try to correct myself.

ME: Kissing!

Argh!! I clutch my phone, wishing I could disappear. *Kidding, I mean kidding!!*

JACE: No touching. Just kissing, got it.

I groan as I palm my face, completely mortified.

ME: Kidding! I swear I was joking and then I meant to type "just kidding."

JACE: Right. I believe they call that a Freudian slip.

"Kill me now," I mumble.

"Problem?" Charlotte asks.

"Oh, just, you know, humiliating myself in front of my enemy, one foot in my mouth at a time," I say. *Or whatever the texting equivalent is.*

Charlotte's lips quirk while Samantha peers over my shoulder. "Ooh, let me see." When she lets out a giant guffaw, I want to choke her. "Smooth."

I exhale, ruffling the hair around my face as my phone dings once more.

> **JACE**: Or at least I'm hoping it was a Freudian slip.

And then he sends me a winking emoji, and my heart skips a beat.

He's flirting with me.

I almost can't believe it. Jace Taggart, my brother's best friend, and easily the hottest guy on campus—although I never said that and will deny it to the grave—is flirting with me.

I wonder how many times his teasing was flirting before, but my judgment was too clouded with irritation to see it? Jace must sense my stupor and saves me from myself with a benign text.

> **JACE**: So, is that a yes?

I chew the inside of my cheek, mulling it over. I wonder if Chris will be there, but I don't have the courage to ask because it might imply I hope he's not.

Wait. Do I hope he's not?

I cover my face with my hands because I'm totally overthinking this. Thank heavens this conversation is over text and not in person or I would have to drop out of AU just to save face.

I drop my hands, preparing my response. The truth is, I really, really want to say yes. So, I inhale, type out my response, then hit send.

ME: Yes.

CHAPTER 21

BRYNN

B Y THE TIME THE girls drop me off at the apartment, it's after seven.

My palms grow damp as I try the door and find it unlocked. I don't know what I expect when I step inside, but the living room is empty and the place quiet. I see no signs of Jace, and for a moment, I feel a pang of disappointment, thinking he's changed his mind in the twenty minutes it took me to get here.

I hang my purse on the hook by the door and place my shoes neatly on the rug beside it. When I straighten, it's to the sight of a bare-chested Jace sauntering into the room. My eyes make quick work of his chiseled pecs, washboard abs, and the perfect V that leads into his joggers, and I swallow.

Get a hold of yourself, Brynn.

It's not like I've never seen him without a shirt on before. Back home, I'd seen him and Teagan throwing a ball in the yard, playing basketball, and doing any number of activities outside and shirtless far too many times to count.

Yet I don't ever recall wanting to trace the ridges and groves of his abdominals like a blind person reading braille until now.

My gaze lifts, quickly noting the damp hair and realize he must've just gotten out of the shower. It serves as a reminder of my own skin, sticky with sweat.

"Hey." Jace grins as he meets my eyes. I can't tell if it's on account of my gawking or if he's just happy to see me. Maybe both. "You ready?"

"Actually, can I just jump in the shower really quick?"

"Sure." He crosses the room for the kitchen. "You want popcorn? I can make us some while you're showering."

"Uh, yeah. That'd be great," I say, thinking how weird this is, me and Jace conversing like two normal people. *Again.* Here, at our shared apartment. *Alone.* Getting ready to watch a movie. It's almost like we're . . .

I don't finish that thought as I scurry off to his bedroom where I quickly grab a pair of sleep shorts and a soft cotton T-shirt, then make a beeline for the bathroom. Once I'm under the hot spray, I sigh as I wash the sweat and grime from my skin, taking extra care to shave my legs and shampoo my hair with my favorite coconut shampoo and conditioner. By the time I turn the water off and get out of the shower, I feel refreshed and relaxed enough that I'm no longer freaked out about the prospect of hanging out with Jace alone.

I towel dry my hair the best I can, then quickly lotion my legs, which is definitely not on account of Jace, and slide on my pajamas.

When I open the door to the bathroom and step out, Jace is still in the kitchen, his back turned to me and thankfully, he's now wearing a shirt. When he hears me, he spins around. His gaze slides down my body, making a round trip back to my face.

I wonder what he thinks about me like this, with damp hair and no makeup. I'm a far cry from the girls he usually goes for. Not that I care. Of course I don't. But he and I have been at odds for so long, I realize I don't know how to read him as well as I'd like.

A flush creeps up my neck, aware of the fact that I'm standing here like a mute.

He winks at me and my stomach bottoms out.

Turning, he grabs a plastic bag and a massive bowl of buttery popcorn, then heads to the fridge. "You want a Coke?" he asks. "I have lemon."

"You do?" I fight a stab of surprise as I step closer, peeking into the depths of the fridge.

He nods. "I bought some the other day," he says like it's nothing. Meanwhile, my heart is thundering inside my chest, like Thumper from *Bambi* pounding his little furry foot.

Somehow, Jace manages to juggle everything in his arms as he turns and heads for the couch. "What movie are we watching?"

"Uh, I don't know. Do you have anything in mind?" I ask, following him.

I take a seat on the firm cushions while he sets our snacks on the coffee table, then drops down, his weight causing me to tip into him.

"There's a new thriller on Netflix, but I'm open if you'd rather watch a chick flick," he says.

I wrinkle my nose at the thought of a thriller, but then I think about the prospect of watching a budding romance on screen while sitting next to Jace after the tense weeks we've had, and think better of it.

Jace laughs. "Okay, so no thriller.

"No. A thriller is fine."

"Uh huh. Sure. You look like you want to watch a movie about a psycho murderer about as much as I want a punch to the nuts. So, chick flick it is." He lifts the remote.

"Jace, we don't have to—"

"What's that one you watched a billion times after you turned eighteen?"

I frown. "*Bridget Jones's Diary*?"

"Yeah, that's the one."

He turns back to the television, and I watch as he searches for it, somewhat shocked he thought of it. My mother is a stickler for rules and television ratings, which meant Teagan and I were stuck waiting to watch all the popular shows and movies until we were old enough. Because *Bridget Jones's Diary was* rated R, I couldn't watch it until I was eighteen, but once I did, it quickly became my favorite. I think I watched it so many times, I memorized the script. I'm shocked Jace paid enough attention to remember and hate how it means something to me that he did. My feelings are already turning in circles as it is. I'm like a freaking dog chasing its tail with him. I can't quite seem to grasp how I'm feeling, and I have no idea what's gotten into me tonight, but I'm starting to wonder if this was a bad idea because my libido seems to be in overdrive.

"Perfect." He finds the movie and clicks on it before rummaging in the plastic bag and pulling out a box of Sour Patch Kids, Goobers, and Swedish Fish. "Pick your pleasure."

My stomach clenches, and I repress a groan. *Why does everything he say have to sound so . . . sexual?*

Without answering, I grab the box of Goobers. There's nothing sexual about a Goober.

"Hmmm, interesting," Jace says, picking up the box of Sour Patch Kids.

"What's interesting?" I ask, mocking his tone.

He shrugs. "It's just that a person's candy choice says a lot about them."

I snort. "And what does my choice of chocolate-covered peanuts say about me?"

"You thrive on traditions and your tastes are classic. Comfort and predictability are your wheelhouse. You tend to be introverted, and hate surprises."

"In other words, I'm boring."

"Oh, Cupcake, you're far from boring."

His voice vibrates deep into my bones, and I frown, wondering how the hell he got that from a box of chocolate candy, because it's pretty accurate. Ever since the incident, I hate surprises, loathe them in fact, and the last three years, regardless of the reasons, proved I was as introverted as they come.

I swallow, my throat dry, before I pop a Goober in my mouth. "Fair enough," I say, wanting to change the subject.

"Can I ask you something?"

I brace myself. With Jace, I never know where he's going. "I'm not telling you the color of my underwear."

He barks out a laugh. "Damn. A man can dream." He winks and I melt into the couch. "As much as I'd love firsthand knowledge of that information"—a flush spreads to my neck—"I want to know why you always smell like a piña colada?"

"*That's* what you want to know?" I ask, grinning.

"Desperately."

"It's my shampoo and conditioner." I shrug. "The base scent of it is coconut. I also have the same brand of lotion, too."

He groans and the sound is so sensual, my stomach turns inside out. "I fucking love it," he says.

"Uh," I clear my throat, trying to keep my cool. "Good to know. If you ever wanna borrow some, let me know. It's the least I can do."

"Eh, I'd rather just smell it on you," he says like it's nothing. "Wanna hear something funny?"

"What?"

"Chris found my stash of chocolate in the greens today."

I gasp as I picture him opening the tub of super greens only to find it filled with Snickers bars. "What did he do?"

"He was pissed. Made me watch him eat the whole bag like it was food porn, the perv."

I tip my head back and laugh until it hurts. "Too funny. Poor Chris."

"Poor Chris?" He arches a brow. "Poor *Chris*? If you ask me, I was doing him a favor. He ate an entire month's supply of chocolate bars, the glutton, and you still feel bad for him?"

"Jealous?"

"Hell yeah, I'm jealous. I'd like a little Brynn Nichols's sympathy thrown my way."

He crosses his arms over his chest, and I can't help but notice how adorable he is when he's playful like this. Or maybe this is just the Taggart charm he uses on all the other girls that makes them swoon and I need to be careful.

Either way, I know I'm in trouble because I'm finding it hard to care when the movie starts and he turns his attention to the screen instead of me.

JACE

Brynn lifts the can of soda to her mouth and takes a sip.

I won't stare at her mouth.

I won't stare at her mouth.

Shit, I'm staring at her mouth.

I shift on the sofa, training my gaze back to the screen. Ever since the kiss, I think about her mouth pretty much every waking moment. I've replayed those few minutes on the couch more than I'd like to admit, along with the day in the kitchen when the heat from her skin seared my tongue. It's like the shape and feel of her lips have been branded in my brain and no amount of wishing them away will make them disappear.

I grab a handful of popcorn and cram it in my mouth, focusing back on the movie. We've been watching it for thirty minutes, but all I've gotten out of it is that Bridget has a thing for Hugh Grant, but he's a huge wanker. I don't even know his character's name because I can't focus on a damn thing with Brynn sitting beside me, smelling like fucking tropical paradise in shorts that showcase her long, tan legs, and hair still damp from a shower.

I run a hand over my face, trying to get a grip on my thoughts. Maybe this was a bad idea.

I'm used to fighting and not getting along. This newfound truce is disconcerting. Mostly because I can't stop thinking about what she'd look like naked.

Teagan's my best friend. The Nicholses are like family to me. By default, that makes Brynn my responsibility. I need to handle her with care. I can't honestly say I've done that, and I can't imagine a world in which the way I'm starting to think of her will help.

But hell if I don't want to spend time with her. With every passing week and each day that goes by, the reasons for why we were ever enemies in the first place start to grow a little fuzzy. In fact, I'm having a hard time remembering when the feuding even started.

I risk a glance at her as she shifts on the couch to set her soda can back on the coffee table. Her shirt rides up her torso as she moves, revealing a sliver of smooth skin, and fuck if I don't want to reach out and touch it.

I bite the inside of my cheek, forcing my eyes forward.

"What?" she asks, pulling my gaze back to her.

Her cheeks are flushed, and I'd like to think I'm the reason: that my eyes on her are enough to send her blood pumping in her veins.

"Nothing."

She quirks a brow but returns her attention to the screen, and I exhale. Focusing back on the movie, I try to pay more attention in an effort to redirect the blood rushing south.

Thirty minutes later, I'm watching with rapt attention. Hugh Grant's character, Daniel Cleaver, I've discovered, is a womanizer who can't or won't settle down. But he's fun and charismatic and good-looking. I'm not sure I like the parallels being drawn in my mind between me and him, but they're there. The only difference between us is I've never cheated. Then again, I've never gotten serious enough.

Then there's Marc Darcy, who seems like a giant prick at first, but really, he's just wounded and misunderstood, but secretly develops feelings for Bridget throughout the course of the movie and several chance encounters. Really, if I'm looking at similarities to my own life, Brynn and I sorta have the hate-to-love thing down.

"So even though they appear to hate each other, they both secretly like each other?" I ask, waving toward the screen.

"Right."

"Hmmm."

"What?" I can feel her eyes on me.

"Nothing." I fall silent for a moment before I add, "It's just kind of funny, isn't it?"

"What? That they hate each other?"

"No. That this is your favorite movie, and yet, the romance between the two main characters starts as them hating each other and being enemies until it slowly turns to more."

"Why is that . . .?"

Her words trail off as she glances at me, and I smirk.

She swallows, then mumbles something under her breath I can't hear and goes back to watching the movie. When Marc Darcy shows up at her apartment after Bridget's pivotal speech, I sense this is the ending.

"*What are you doing here?*" Bridget asks, and I roll my eyes. *Isn't it obvious?*

When she goes to change into her sexy underwear, I scoff. "What? So, they haven't even really dated and now suddenly, they're going to get it on?"

"Are you really slut-shaming fictional characters?" she asks, her tone incredulous.

I shrug. "Just seems a little fast to me."

Brynn chuckles and shakes her head.

But when we get to the part where Bridget chases Darcy out into the snow in only her underwear while "Ain't No Mountain High Enough" blasts in the background, I scoff and roll my eyes. "Come *on*."

"What now?" Brynn asks with a hint of irritation in her voice.

"No way she would do that. She would totally grab some pants first."

Brynn laughs and chucks a piece of popcorn at me. "She's in love and going after him because she thinks he's leaving."

"He's not?"

"No."

I groan.

"It's a romantic comedy. Did you really think it was gonna end with him reading the mean things she wrote about him in her diary, then leave? The End?"

I shrug. "Maybe," I say as I wonder if Brynn has a diary, because if she does, I'd like a peek.

Turns out Brynn was right and Marc Darcy, the amazing man that he is, was simply just popping across the street to buy her a new diary. After a rather cinematic kiss in the snow, they pull apart and Bridget says, "*Wait a minute, good guys don't kiss like that.*"

And Marc fucking Darcy, the clever bastard that he is, answers, "*Oh, yes they fucking do.*" They go back to kissing, and I hold my breath. Beside me, Brynn watches with a dreamy expression.

But I can't do it. I can't hold it in any longer, and I burst out laughing.

"Excuse me. That is a spectacular ending," she says, pushing her shoulders back, her expression one of quiet indignance.

"Whatever you say."

"You didn't like it?" she asks.

I shrug, letting her think I didn't because, even though parts of it were cheesy as hell, it was pretty funny and I kind of dug it. But most of all, I loved it because she did.

The credits roll and my smile fades, disappointed it's over already as I'm nowhere near ready for bed. Brynn's presence somehow has me wired, like I've downed several shots of espresso in a single sitting, and I know there's no way in hell I'm falling asleep anytime soon.

When she makes no move to retreat, I take it as a sign maybe she feels the same way. Maybe she's not ready for the evening to end either, so I take this as the green light to engage her in some conversation. "You seem to be getting pretty close to the girls," I say, thinking how weird it is I'm trying to strike up a conversation with Brynn that doesn't involve pissing her off.

"Yeah. Honestly, they're pretty great. My roommate might've been a dud, but in a weird way, I'm grateful I got placed where I did because, otherwise, I might not have met them. What about you? You seem to like Chris, but you haven't said a whole lot about the rest of your teammates?"

"So far, they seem to be a pretty good group of dudes. Time will tell how well we work together on the field, though. We're a pretty young team and right now, the pressure is off." I nudge her side. "Think you'll come to our games?" I ask, trying my best not to picture her in an orange and blue jersey with my number painted on her cheek. In high school, I had plenty of girls over the years cheer me on, but none that mattered.

"I might stand to make a couple of games." She grins, and it does strange things to my insides.

"I can introduce your girls to a few of the guys," I offer. Hell, maybe if I did, we could all go out together.

Fuck, why does that sound like a double date?

Brynn laughs and rolls her eyes. "I'm sure they'd love that. Although Samantha has her eyes set on one of the bartenders at Bradd's. His name is James, and it's completely ridiculous, but so far, we haven't been able to deter her."

"You've been going there a lot?" I ask, trying not to pry, even though that's exactly what I'm doing.

She shrugs. "Some. Samantha has zero chill. She'd drag us out every night if she could, and though I've been enjoying being social and making friends, sometimes I miss just staying in."

"Meet any new guys?" I ask, staring at my hands like her answer doesn't matter when the pinching inside my chest tells another story.

"Jealous twice in one night, are we?" She pokes me in the side, but I catch her hand as it makes contact with my ribs.

Carefully, I thread my fingers through hers and I tug her forward, enjoying the tiny gasp of surprise that escapes her lips. "What if I am?"

Her throat bobs, drawing my gaze to the smooth skin of her neck.

A bubble of nervous laughter pops in her chest. "I'd say that's a first."

She's not wrong. Until this summer, I've never been jealous. I never care enough. But Brynn's another story, and I'm well aware of what a catch she is. These past few weeks have only shown me exactly how much she has to offer. She's funny and smart. Gorgeous and intuitive. Not to mention, kind and reserved in a way I find far too sexy. Any man with eyes is going to scoop her up, and the second they discover she's as beautiful on the inside as she is out, they're never letting go. Anything else would be foolish.

I clear my throat in an effort to cool my blood as she stares over at me, confusion and something else I don't recognize warring in her eyes. I wish I knew exactly what she's thinking, but despite how long I've known her, Brynn has always been a mystery to me. An enigma I can't quite figure out. She chooses the people close to her wisely and doesn't open up easily, and I find I desperately want to be one of those people. I want to belong in her inner circle, to know everything about her. All her tells, and her deepest and darkest secrets.

"You never answered my question."

"I forgot what it was," she murmurs, her breath tickling my neck.

I brush my thumb over the back of her hand, and her lashes flutter. "I asked if you met anyone new?"

"No."

The band in my chest loosens, but the moment feels charged. I idly wonder if it will always be this way between us. No matter what end of the spectrum we're on between love and hate, will our interactions always be this intense?

"You have the most beautiful eyes," I say, focused on the purplish-blue. They're like a cross between an amethyst and a sapphire. If I were an artist, I'd paint them. They deserve to be memorialized. Instead, I'll have to settle with seeing them in my dreams.

"Jace . . ." Her gaze dips to my mouth. "What are you doing?"

That's a good question. One I don't have a fucking answer to. All I know is that these past few weeks have been torture. She's all I think about, despite doing everything I can to push her from my mind, and I'm not sure how much longer I can hold out. I'm not sure I even want to.

Brynn and I are a very bad idea for a lot of reasons: my inability to commit and Teagan topping the list.

I stare at her a beat longer, warring with myself over my next move. If I was smart, I'd call it a night and go to bed. I can see where this is heading, and it's likely to end in disaster. But I've always been more impulsive than I have calculated, and a bigger part of me wants to see where this goes.

Fuck it. "Do you ever think about me?" I ask.

She swallows, and I watch the movement in her throat, transfixed.

"I don't know what you mean," she whispers.

I cock my head, my lips curving into a grin as I search her eyes. "I think you do, but I'll be more specific." She's like an emotional vault, giving nothing away. I have no idea what she's thinking or feeling. All I can do is go with my gut because it's rarely wrong, and my gut is telling me she wants me every bit as much as I want her. "Do you think about the night we kissed? Because I think about it all the time."

I hear her breathy exhalation before her gaze drops to my mouth; it's the second time in the last few minutes, which I take as a good sign. I want to kiss her more than I want to breathe, but unlike the other times, I won't initiate. If Brynn wants me to kiss her, she's going to have to make the first move. I won't push. She has to want this.

"I think about it, too."

I thread my fingers tighter with hers as both of us instinctively lean closer. I want to kiss her again and again, and I have no idea what the hell that means.

I lick my lips. "Do you know how hard I've tried to forget how you taste? I've tried distractions or losing myself with other chicks, but in the end, my thoughts keep circling back to you. You're all I think about. Your lips, the curve of your jaw, the way you smell like fucking coconuts. The soft sound of your sighs. The building rumble of a moan in your chest. You're like a fucking drug I can't get out of my system, and I can't—"

"Jace," she presses a finger to my lips, "shut up already." And then her mouth slants against mine and we're kissing.

The world fades as I reach up, cupping her cheek as fire burns in my chest, a raging inferno only she can snuff out. Our breath mingles as I pull away briefly and shift position, drawing her onto my lap where she settles with a soft groan.

I may have waited for Brynn to initiate, but I won't sit back and allow her to take the reins. I need more. And what started as a soft exploration, quickly turns frantic.

Brynn's hand finds the back of my neck as her body molds against my own. Our breath becomes one. Our heartbeats synchronize.

I nip her bottom lip, relishing the breathy moan that escapes her lips, sending my pulse into a tailspin. I'm no saint, yet Brynn moaning in my lap because of me is the single most erotic experience of my life.

Her hands find my back, sliding beneath my shirt. The warm press of her fingers keeps me grounded as I pull away and press a soft kiss over her jaw, below her ear, the pulse thrumming wildly in her neck.

I groan when she shifts her hands, gripping fistfuls of the soft cotton, pulling my mouth back to hers. I tug on her lip with my teeth and gently suck, thinking of all the things I'd like to do to her as my hand slides over smooth, warm skin to find her lacy bra.

Her breath quickens, and I remind myself of who I'm with. Despite my escalating feelings for Brynn and how badly I want her, she's still Teagan's sister. I might've fucked up by crossing the line, but both of them mean a lot to me, so I need to slow down, to treat her with care. She's not a girl at the club or a meaningless hookup. She's worth a lot more than one night.

And so as delicately as I can, I remove my hands and cup her face, slowing our kisses before I pull away.

Another groan rumbles from the back of my throat as I press another kiss to the corner of her mouth, her jaw, then lean my forehead against hers, while both of us catch our breath. "Cupcake," I murmur, "I think you just might be the death of me yet."

CHAPTER 22

BRYNN

M USIC BLASTS THROUGH THE speakers of the tiny apartment. Chris, Jace, Damon, and a few other guys from the football team are currently working on crushing a case of beer and eating an obscene amount of pizza when I exit my bedroom and head for the kitchen. I briefly say hello as I pass through, trying not to make direct eye contact with Jace as I do. Though my days of avoiding him are over, after our consensual make-out session last night, I'm more confused than ever.

Jace isn't the boyfriend type, so I can't help but question his motivations and what this means to him. Is he genuinely interested in me? It certainly seems that way, but knowing him like I do, I can't be sure. It's quite possible he views last night as simply a harmless flirtation, a moment of spontaneity. Maybe he thinks we can have a friends-with-benefits situation. The problem is I just don't know, and the thought of outright asking him petrifies me.

Do you know how hard I've tried to forget how you taste? I've tried distractions or losing myself with other chicks, but in the end, my thoughts keep circling back to you. You're all I think about. Your lips, the curve of your jaw, the way you smell like fucking coconuts. The soft sound of your sighs. The building rumble of a moan in your chest. You're like a fucking drug I can't get out of my system . . .

I groan as I grab a glass from the cupboard. I can't get his words out of my head. I mean, who talks like that?

Apparently, Jace does.

I knew he was a charmer, but I've never been on the receiving end until now, and I'm not sure what to make of it.

Gnawing on my lip, I turn and fill a water glass from the dispenser in the fridge when a warm body slides in beside me. I don't need to glance at his face to know it's Jace. My body can sense him. Like a finely tuned engine, my heart thrums in his proximity.

"Hey." He leans a hip against the fridge, looking irresistible in joggers and a T-shirt that clings to his chest.

"Hey." I take a sip of water, needing something to occupy myself with and cool the heat shimmying up my spine as I relive last night in my mind.

"You're dressed up." His heated gaze slides down my body and back, and I shiver.

"Uh, yeah. I guess I am." I glance down at the little black dress I bought this morning with the girls. The hem is a little shorter than I'm used to, but the halter top style suits me well and the soft material clings to my curves in a way that's both comfortable and sexy.

In truth, I thought of Jace when I tried it on, and the way he's staring down at me like he wants me for a snack tells me I did a fabulous job.

He clears his throat, dragging a hand over the scruff of his jaw while he tears his eyes from my legs and asks, "Are you avoiding me today?"

"No," I say, somewhat surprised by the question. Although to be fair, it's Sunday and I haven't seen him much. Considering how the last few weeks have gone, it's a reasonable assumption. "What makes you say that?" I ask, unsure of what he wants and lacking experience to help me tread these murky waters.

"Well, you won't look me in the eyes, for one."

I swallow. Slowly, I lift my head and any uncertainty I had melts away as I murmur, "I'm looking at you now."

He assesses me for a moment, then reaches out and runs his fingers over a lock of my hair. "Do you regret what happened last night?"

I swallow, shaking my head. I don't need to ask if he did because the warmth of his eyes already tells me all I need to know. It's both a relief and absolutely terrifying because I don't know what he and I mean. All I know is for Jace to ask, for him to even care about how I feel after we kissed, is huge. What we did was nothing for him, but his question recognizes he knows it was a big deal for me.

I clear my throat and allow the smile tugging at the corner of my lips to surface. "Weirdly enough, I don't."

"Good. Then do you want to come hang out?" Jace's smile slices right through me as he nods in the direction of the guys.

My eyes widen. His invitation surprises me, and he must be able to tell from my reaction because he chuckles. "I promise to make them behave." When I don't say anything right away, he squeezes my hand and adds, "We have pizza."

I glance over his shoulder to the empty pizza boxes and smirk. "You *did* have pizza."

Jace's head whips in their direction and he groans at the sight of a nearly empty pizza box. "You fat asses."

"Hey," Chris says, his mouth full, "you snooze, you lose."

Jace rolls his eyes as he turns back to me, but I just laugh because in all honesty, Chris is pretty hilarious. He reminds me a lot of the dynamic between Teagan, Jace, and their friends back home.

There's a knock on the door and Chris jumps up from his seat. "I got it," he calls out.

"Um, actually. I can't stay. That's probably the girls now."

Jace glances back at me while Chris greets them at the door. "Well, hello, ladies. Brynn's in the kitchen."

I turn, needing a reprieve from the intensity of Jace's gaze at the same time Samantha and Charlotte reach the kitchen. "Ready?" Samantha asks.

Jace shoves his hands in his pockets. "Where're you ladies off to?"

"Um, just dinner," I say.

"A triple date," Charlotte blurts out at the same time as me.

I offer her a meaningful look as Jace's gaze darts between us. "I'm sorry. Did you say a *date*?"

I clear my throat. "Yeah. Samantha texted us about it this morning, actually. That guy I mentioned she's been talking to at Bradd's, James? Well, he finally asked her out."

"The bartender."

I nod, amazed he was paying enough attention to remember.

"So, why are you and Charlotte going?" He points between us.

I glance at Charlotte for help. She offers me a rueful smile before saying, "Since Samantha doesn't know him all that well, she asked him if he had any single friends, and we arranged a triple date. We figured we're all single. Why not?"

The muscle in Jace's jaw twitches. "Cool, cool. So, where *is* this date?"

Samantha narrows her eyes. "It's at Pizzuto's, that fancy Italian place downtown?" She shakes her head and grabs my arm. "Anyway, no need to worry, Daddy. We'll keep her safe and bring her home before bed."

"Daddy," Jace mumbles with a scoff.

With a smile, Samantha yanks me toward the door while Chris watches our exchange with a shit-eating grin.

"Wait—" Jace calls out, stumbling after us.

Beside me, Charlotte elbows me in the ribs and mouths, *He totally likes you*, before we turn around again to face him.

We blink at him, waiting while he stares at me with a blank look. Clearly, he has something he wants to say, but he seems to be at a loss for words as a mixture of emotions I can't read play over his face.

Part of me hopes he'll beg me to stay. Save me from the awkwardness of a blind date by crossing the distance between us, taking my face in his hands, and claiming me with his mouth.

Instead, the silence stretches, and it starts to turn awkward. Charlotte smiles at him, her eyes glinting. "You don't have a problem with Brynn dating, do you?"

I want to choke her, but I'm also oddly grateful because if Jace doesn't want me to go, here's his chance to say it.

"No," he says, recoiling as if the thought repulses him. "Of course not. I mean, if she wants to go on a date, she should go on a date. It's not like I can stop her." His eyes lock with mine. "Right?"

He's asking me if I'll stay for him without actually saying he wants me to. At least that's what it feels like.

But I *want* a man who can say the words. I want a man who has no qualms about declaring his feelings for me.

My thoughts flicker to last night and how much fun we had, how natural it was. I'd love to stay here and see where this goes. But I'm also a coward who's starting to feel things for her brother's best friend that she shouldn't. I'm a girl who wears her heart on her sleeve.

I know how quickly I'll fall if I allow myself, and with Jace's track record, I'm afraid of getting hurt. So instead of telling him I'd rather stay and hang out, I simply nod and say, "Right."

JACE

I only last a few minutes after Brynn leaves before Googling Pizzuto's on my phone, then storming into the living room like a tornado, upending Damon's beer as I make a beeline for Chris. "Come on, let's go." I wave for him to follow.

"What? Where? Dude," he glances at the mess I made while Damon curses me out and mops up the frothy liquid with some napkins. "We're watching the ball game here. It's the fucking Dodgers."

"Who cares about the Dodgers. You guys ate all the pizza, so we're going to pick up some more."

"Just order it to be delivered like a normal person," he says, dismissing me with a flick of the hand as he leans back on the couch and takes a sip from his beer.

I move, blocking the television.

"Come on, man," Chris protests, craning his neck to try to see around me. "Move!"

"They don't deliver."

"What do you mean they don't—" Chris stops abruptly and gives me a hard stare. Something in my expression must give me away because his eyes widen before they narrow to slits again. He's like a cartoon come to life. "Let me guess. We're going to Pizzuto's."

I shrug. "They're known for their homemade dough and buffalo mozzarella."

Chris snorts and picks up his phone and types something into it before he glances back up at me again. "Did you seriously Google that so you could use it as your excuse?"

I smirk and shrug.

"So, this trip has absolutely nothing to do with a cute blonde in a tight black dress who's headed there as we speak?"

"Nope."

He stares at me for a moment, and I hold his gaze. I can do this all fucking day.

"You're not going to leave me alone until I do this, are you?"

"Nope."

With a sigh, Chris sets his beer on the coffee table. "We're out, boys."

Everyone groans, and two of the guys start to rise when Damon shouts, "But it's only the bottom of the third!"

I roll my eyes. Thanks to good ole Mom and Dad, we have the biggest TV out of all our friends, and I have no doubt any and all sporting events will be watched in our apartment. "Relax," I tell them. "You guys can stay. We'll be back. We're just making a quick stop."

There's a cumulative sigh of relief as they settle back in. "Hand me the chips, will ya?" Damon asks Brandon, one of our linesmen, as he cracks open a fresh beer.

"You guys suck," Chris throws back at them. "I just want you to know that."

"Cheers!" Damon lifts his beer, a smug grin on his face.

Chris flips him off. "Tell me why I'm your wingman again?" he asks when I swipe my truck keys off the kitchen counter.

"Because I have gorgeous blue eyes," I say, batting them, "kissable lips, and washboard abs you could do your laundry on."

Chris harrumphs. "You're making assumptions. Maybe I have a thing for beer bellies and thin lips."

I nod. "You got me there, but I do have magic hands, or so I'm told. Magic hands make up for it, right?" I wiggle my fingers in front of his face, and he bats them away.

"What the fuck?" Damon mutters from his perch on the couch.

Chris gags. "Save it for your girlfriend, will ya?"

Girlfriend.

The word makes my stomach flip, and I almost correct him, but I don't.

I press my lips together, pondering this as I head out the door.

Brynn may not be my girlfriend yet, but the thought of making her mine is strangely enticing.

CHAPTER 23

BRYNN

I'M SITTING AT THE end of the table in Pizzuto's with Charlotte to my right. The dining room is dimly lit, with glittering chandeliers hanging from above. Squat vases of roses adorn each table, along with linen napkins and far more utensils than I know what to do with. Across from me, Chad smiles, revealing a row of pearly whites so blindingly bright I think I need sunglasses.

When he lowers his menu and his brown eyes meet mine, I remind myself to give him a chance. Maybe he doesn't have Caribbean-blue eyes, but he's cute and clean-cut with a short crop of sandy hair and a lean physique. Bonus: he's not a commitment-phobe. I know this because he's mentioned his ex-girlfriend, who was his high school sweetheart, at least twice since sitting down and we've only been here five minutes.

Wait. Why the hell am I comparing him to Jace?

"So, Brynn, when Samantha suggested we all meet, she said you were going to school for nursing? What made you want to go into medicine?"

It's a reasonable question, one I'd expect on a first date, but I can't help but think of how boring it is.

I give a little shrug. "I've just always liked caring for people. I have two younger sisters who both happen to be clumsy, and in high school, I was always patching them up. Plus, I want to wear scrubs every day." I laugh at my own joke, but it falls flat when Chad doesn't even so much as crack a smile.

I sober and shift in my seat. "What about you? Did I hear something about accounting?"

He nods. "I'm a numbers man."

Silence descends between us. I take a sip of water as I glance down at the table, wondering if I can fake an emergency phone call. Too bad I'm with my friends already, although I have no doubt Jace would pick me up if I called.

When the waitress comes to take our orders, it's a welcome respite from the awkward silence. Beside me, Charlotte seems to be having a better time with Kevin, and anyone with eyes can see Samantha is having the time of her life with James at the end of the table.

I could be at home with Jace.

I close my eyes and give myself a pep talk. I can do this. I can make conversation and have a good time. I haven't even given Chad a chance. He could be an amazing man, and for all I know, we might make the perfect match.

Straightening in my seat, I puff out my chest, which leaves Chad blushing as he ogles my boobs. "So, tell me about what you like to do for fun?" I ask.

"Let's see . . ." He drums his fingers on the table as if he needs time to think about it when my phone buzzes in my purse.

"Well, I love to golf. In the summer, more often than not, you'll find me out on the green. My ex-girlfriend and I actually used to golf together all the time. It's a great couple's activity." His eyes slide to my chest again, and he licks his lips. "If you're ever interested, I'd love to take you out."

I know this is my opening to accept, but I don't want to commit to anything, so I simply smile and offer him a polite nod as my phone pings, indicating I have a text.

"Oh shoot." He winces. "I mentioned my ex again, didn't I?"

I wrinkle my nose. "Yeah, I'm afraid you did."

Another notification goes off when I leave the text unanswered. First a phone call, then a text. I'm bored enough to want to check it, so I raise a finger and motion to my purse as I slide it out. "Sorry, I just need to . . ."

I bite my lip as I swipe open my phone and see a text from Jace.

What could he possibly have to say to me while I'm on a date?

JACE: You look like you're bored to tears.

How does he . . .

My head jerks up from my phone. After quickly scanning the restaurant, I spot him in a dinner jacket that's far too small for him, sitting across from a disgruntled-looking Chris.

The second our eyes meet from across the room, Jace winks and my insides melt.

Tearing my gaze from his, I quickly text him back.

> **ME:** WTH WHAT ARE YOU DOING HERE?

> **JACE:** I was hungry. And Chris ate all the pizza, remember? Also, tell nerd boy to keep his eyes above your neck or I'll re-arrange his face.

A quick glance at Chad reveals he's taking my distraction as his opportunity to freely gawk.

My cheeks flush as I quickly type: *Go away!*

Clearing my throat, I set the phone on the table beside me and Chad's gaze jerks up to meet my eyes. "Sorry about that," I tell him. "Anyway, you were saying?"

"Um, I think I was just about to say I'm sorry." He wipes his brow where a bead of sweat has formed. "When you're with someone for a long time like I was with Beth, you have so much history and it's hard not to talk about yourself without talking about them, too."

"It's okay, really," I say, meaning it. Mostly because I'm not convinced this will go anywhere. If I was really into this guy, on the other hand, I would be super disappointed.

He lets out a little laugh and when he thanks me for understanding, I instantly feel guilty for even replying to Jace's texts in the first place.

Still, that doesn't stop my eyes from flicking in his direction to find he's still staring at me. Leaning back in his chair, he grins, holds his phone up in one hand and starts to type.

"So, what about you?"

I pull my gaze away. "Huh?"

"What do you like to do in your free time?" Chad asks.

"Oh. Um, honestly, I don't really have any one single hobby. I like to go to the movies, read, and visit different coffee shops. When it's nice out, I like to go for walks and hike. I'd say I'm pretty low-key, but I'm open to trying new things, though."

My phone pings, and I struggle to keep a straight face, but when our waitress stops by to deliver our entrees, I take the opportunity to check it.

> **JACE**: What could you possibly be talking about with snooze fest over there?

> **ME**: How do you know I'm bored? Maybe he's really interesting.

<blockquote>JACE: Unlikely.</blockquote>

I set my phone down face up so I can see it, even though I absolutely will not check it again, and as soon as our waitress leaves, I tuck into my pasta, needing something to keep my gaze from wandering across the restaurant to Jace again.

"To be honest, I was really nervous about coming along on this date. These things are usually so awkward," Chad says as he cuts into his chicken.

My phone pings again, and even though I hate myself for it, my eyes slide to the text.

<blockquote>JACE: You look beautiful.</blockquote>

My heart leaps.

The bite of food in my mouth turns to paste and I swallow. Offering Chad a polite smile, I say, "Yeah, I know what you mean. To be honest, though, this is my first blind date."

"Really?"

I nod, wondering why he sounds surprised. *Am I supposed to have gone on a ton of blind dates by the time I'm eighteen?*

Ping.

<blockquote>JACE: You're too good for him.</blockquote>

A wet sort of smacking noise draws me up short. I glance up to see Chad eating his chicken parmesan with his mouth open. The food rolls around his tongue as he smacks his lips, chewing, and I quickly drop my gaze.

Okay, so he's not the politest eater.

Chomp, chomp, smack.

And he's loud. *Really* loud.

I clench my teeth as I try to ignore the mashing sound of Chad's mandibles across from me. *It doesn't matter that loud eaters are your biggest pet peeve; you can get past this. In the grand scheme of things, eating loud is a small thing.*

Chomp, chomp, smack.

I shudder. *Oh my God, I'm gonna carve my ears off with my butter knife.*

What am I thinking? I'm not freaking desperate. I don't need a man so badly I have to put up with something I hate. Why am I still here?

Because I don't want to give Jace the satisfaction of knowing he's right and I'm having a miserable time.

I flick my gaze to Jace over Chad's shoulder and catch a self-satisfied smirk.

Right. I can do this.

Chomp, chomp, smack.

Never mind. I can't do this.

I shoot up from my chair so fast, I nearly knock it over.

Startled, a speck of food falls from Chad's mouth onto his lip. I think I might barf.

Pressing a hand to my stomach, I mumble, "If you'll excuse me, I need to . . ." I trail off with a jerk of the thumb as I turn and make a beeline for the restrooms we passed on our way in.

I catch Charlotte's worried gaze as I pass, but ignore it. She'll have to assume I'm fine.

My feet fly over the polished concrete floors as I contemplate my next move. I could ask Jace to take me home and listen to him gloat. Or I could simply spend the next twenty minutes in the bathroom until it's safe to come out and Chad has finished his supper. It runs the risk of him thinking I'm in here taking a giant shit, but at this point, it feels like the safer bet.

The palms of my hands meet the thick oak door of the bathroom as I push inside. The door swings shut behind me and I don't take more than two feet before a familiar embrace swallows me up, wrapping around me like a warm scarf.

I jump as my heart claws into my throat.

In the back of my brain, I know it's Jace, but it doesn't matter. Memories flood my brain, taking me with them on the current. For one frightening moment, I'm back at Riverside, inside the high school locker room where fear clogs my throat.

It's pitch black. I'm searching to see if he's inside waiting for me. Without windows, it's so dark, I can barely see my hand in front of my face and the light switch won't work. Thick arms come around me, pinning me against the cold metal.

A gravelly hum rumbles through my chest from behind, and I blink, waiting as the image in my mind fades and the bathroom comes into view again.

I remember where I am—the restroom at Pizzuto's—submerged in the masculine scent of citrus and cedar.

The arms holding me weaken as I turn around to face a grinning Jace. "Miss me?"

I wait for my heart to settle back into my chest, then offer him a playful smack. "You scared the crap out of me." I try to laugh it off, but inside, I'm reeling.

"Sorry," his gaze softens, "but I had to see you. Touch you."

"You know, for a guy who supposedly never gets jealous, you seem to get jealous *a lot* lately." I smirk as I rake my hands in his hair and pull him closer.

Is he really here right now? Is this really happening?

"Only with you."

I swallow, and my insides melt. "You shouldn't say things like that."

"Why not?" He searches my gaze. "It's true." He dips his head, burying his face into my hair.

"Are you . . . smelling me?" I ask with a chuckle.

He grunts out a yes, then follows it up. "Your hair. It smells amazing. Coconuts are my new favorite food."

I laugh and lean into him. "You're unhinged."

"Only because of you," he says, his voice gruff.

Leaning back, he cups my face in his large hand, then lowers his mouth to mine. Our lips brush, and I chase the intensity of the kiss, pressing into him as he growls. "Do you know how crazy it makes me to see you with another guy?"

The breath in my lungs stalls, and I think, *if this is how he acts when I go out on a date, then maybe I should date more often.* "Is that so?" I manage, between gasps for breath.

Jace's hands tighten around my waist where he guides me until my back meets the wall behind me.

A throaty moan escapes my chest as his tongue parts my lips and he deepens the kiss. My hands bunch in the back of his blazer, and I pull him even closer. Until he's flush against me. Until our hearts beat in sync. Our breaths are one breath.

His mouth moves to my jaw, and I grasp the lapels of his jacket, grounding myself as a chuckle erupts from my chest.

He pulls back, amusement spreading his lips as he arches a brow in question.

"Whose jacket is this?"

"It's a loaner." Jace returns to my jaw, peppering me with kisses as his mouth slowly forms a trail back to mine where he speaks between each brush of his lips over my skin. "Apparently, I wasn't dressed well enough for Pizzuto's. I had to give Chris the good one, since I dragged him here."

My breath rasps in the back of my throat. "It looks great with your joggers."

"Doesn't it, though?" He leans in, smiling against my lips as he presses his mouth to mine once more.

Tiny fireworks erupt in my chest as he takes his time, like tasting me is a full-time job and he's putting in overtime.

His hands roam, shifting behind us to pull one of my legs up and over his hip. My dress rides up, bunching at my waist, but I'm too lost in the sensation and his touch to care.

His hand anchoring my leg to him, hip to hip. The delicious press of his hard center to mine. The tiny affirmations rolling off his tongue each time he releases my mouth to rake a kiss over my neck.

You feel incredible.

Kiss.

You smell so fucking good . . .

Kiss.

You're so sexy.

Kiss.

Your lips are like fucking velvet.

Kiss.

I'm so preoccupied with the deep rasp of his voice in my ear and the goosebumps chasing my skin that when the bathroom door bangs open, it barely registers. It's not until I hear the loud clearing of someone's throat beside us that I open my eyes and find Charlotte staring at us in wide-eyed disbelief.

"*You!*" She points.

With a grunt, Jace releases my leg and glances beside him while continuing to shield me with his body, one hand still pressed to the wall at my head.

"Um . . . found me?" I say with a feeble smile.

"To think I was worried about you when you left so abruptly and then took so long, but here you are, and . . ." She shakes her head, eyes glittering with amusement as Jace adjusts himself before fully turning around.

"Yep. I'm fine. *All* good."

"I can see that." Charlotte purses her lips as if holding back a smile. "Can I just tell you, I told you so?"

"No, you cannot," I say, my tone indignant.

Charlotte snickers while Jace glances down at me. "What did she tell you?"

"Oh, you know," Charlotte beams. "Just that I was right about you two having chemistry."

"Can we please talk about this later?" I ask with a tight smile.

"Fine. Shall I tell Chad you got sick and called an Uber?" She winks at me, and if I weren't so grateful for her taking the heat off me with Chad, I'd strangle her.

"Yes," Jace and I say in unison, which only exacerbates her gloating expression.

"Okay, then. You two kids have fun," she singsongs, then winks, and disappears back the way she came.

With a sigh, Jace plants a kiss on my forehead, then takes a step back. His gaze slides over me and he drags a hand down his face with a groan before stepping forward and smoothing the front of my dress like it pains him to do so.

Once he's finished, he takes my hand in his and tugs me toward the door. "Come on. Let's get out of here."

CHAPTER 24

BRYNN

I SIT IN THE passenger seat next to Jace who has one hand on the wheel and the other holding mine between us on the center console. A smile curls the corners of my lips as I ride the blissful wave of our earlier interaction at the restaurant.

The now familiar streets blur behind my window in the fading daylight as we drive back to campus. Soon, it'll be dark. At any moment, the moon will replace the sun, and stars will blanket the sky. I'm feeling sentimental as we near the apartments, thinking about the irony of me and Jace as something more than enemies—more than friends. Never in my wildest dreams would I have guessed Jace Taggart to be the jealous type, or that he'd be following me on a date, pinning me against bathroom walls, and telling me he wants me all to himself.

I glance over at him in the shadows. He's so much different than I thought. So much *more*.

I wonder if this is just hormones talking or if it's real.

Behind us, Chris is sprawled out in the back seat, eating breadsticks and pasta from a takeout container. "Well, you two certainly seem to be getting along now," he says between bites. "Makes me wonder why you ever hated him in the first place."

I stiffen, feeling the wave I'm on crest and break as I risk a glance at Jace, who appears oblivious to the discomfort this statement causes.

My eyes find the side mirror and I watch Chris sop up sauce with a chunk of bread, gums flapping. "What happened in high school, anyway? Did you have a crush on him or something and he rejected you? Did he bully you? Steal your boyfriend?" Chris asks with a snort. "Yeah, that's it. I can totally see that one."

Jace offers him an arched brow in the rearview mirror, but his expression remains one of quiet bliss while I swallow, shifting in my seat.

Memories press against the edges of my mind, and I know it won't take much for them to come flooding in since I already went there once this evening. Two reminders in one night are one too many.

But I really don't want to think about what happened that night in high school. The night that changed me. More than anything, I want to forget, or at the very least, ignore it.

Music trickles softly through the speakers of Jace's truck. I try to focus on the melody, letting the soft notes soothe the jagged pill of the memories lodged in my throat.

"I mean, don't you ever wonder, man?" Chris asks Jace, continuing his tirade. "Have you ever told him, Brynn? Or is it some kind of secret?"

My stomach knots, bringing with it a rush of nausea, and I know what's coming. Squeezing the door handle with one hand, I brace for the coming storm and close my eyes. I might not be able to stop the memories, but maybe I can control them. I can skip past the worst of them and fast forward to the moment Jace became my enemy, the moment his words imprinted the shame I felt into my soul like a bruise I could never heal.

I stumble from the locker room out into a moonlit sky with my heart in my throat. Stars twinkle overhead like diamonds, witness to my humiliation.

A glance behind me confirms I'm alone, thank God.

Regardless, I pick up the pace and run. My dress slides down my chest, so I clutch at it, holding it up with the busted strap. Something is caught on it, but I don't stop to check it out as I focus on moving my feet.

Hair falls from my updo, curtaining my face. I can only imagine what I look like, amazed that in my tumultuous state I even have it in me to care. Tears blur my vision, turning the passing stadium into a watery image as I head for the student parking lot.

My breath rasps in and out of my lungs, my feet pounding a steady cadence when I slam into a brick wall.

I have a moment of delirium, fearing it's him *and a scream builds in my lungs until I glance up to find Jace Taggart.*

I catch my balance while his gaze soaks me in, then quickly darts away again as my stomach bottoms out. Does he know what happened? Or does he think . . .

I don't finish that thought as I hurry to push past him, my heels clicking on the asphalt like the staccato rhythm of my heart. A smattering of students leaving the dance early trickle into the parking lot ahead. I lift my gaze in search of my car when his voice draws me up short and I freeze. "Can I get sloppy seconds?"

Ice fills my veins.

Mortification and shame wash through me.

My eyes burn with the fresh sting of tears and as I glance at him over my shoulder, a smirk curls his lips as his eyes find me.

I suck in a breath and I allow my shaking limbs to carry me the rest of the way to my car. Once I open the door, I sink inside and press my forehead to the steering wheel. A guttural moan escapes my lips as the dam bursts open. My tears flood the tight confines of the car as a keening sound rips through my chest.

"Dude, fucking leave it already."

The harsh tone of Jace's voice cleaves the memory in two, and I jerk my head to find him staring at me, his blue eyes clouded with concern. It takes me a moment to remember where I am and what was happening before I zoned out.

On our way home.

Chris and his hypothesizing.

Jace must've had enough.

His brow furrows as I swallow and casually release my hand from his, feigning an itch on the back of my neck at the same time he pulls into a parking spot outside their apartment complex.

I waste no time as I unbuckle my seatbelt and get out, climbing the steps quickly, hovering in front of the door before Chris and Jace join me. When they unlock it, we pile inside, and I'm instantly grateful it's empty. All of the guys must've left while we were at the restaurant.

Chris announces he's headed to his room, and I do the same before Jace grabs my arm, stopping me. "Hey." His voice is so soft, it tightens my throat. "What's going on? Talk to me."

"Nothing," I croak. "I just need a minute."

"Did I do something wrong?"

I shake my head, unable to speak through the chokehold of emotions gripping me.

You didn't do anything wrong.

It's not you, it's me.

I'm the problem.

I feel the tenuous hold on my tears falter as my jaw wobbles. "I just . . . I need . . ." I trail off before yanking my hand from his. "I'm sorry," I say as I turn and head inside his bedroom and close the door.

The pit in my stomach swells as I sink down on the edge of the bed. My hands play with the soft seam of the comforter while I focus on my breathing. I tell myself I don't need to go there. I don't have to think about that night any more than I already have. I've been doing so well putting myself out there. Making friends. Dating—well, sort of. I don't need to go back to that dark place and open that box. I don't need the reminder.

But as much as I'd like to think I can ignore the press of memories, I can't. The pull to the closet where the little wooden box hides is too strong to resist. So, I slide off the edge of the bed and cross the room, unzipping the front of my suitcase and sliding out the wooden jewelry box.

With trembling hands, I trace the edges of the smooth wood and the intricate pattern carved into its lid as I close my eyes.

I know what's inside, just like I know I don't need to open it to remember how strong I am. But I want to prove my resilience. I crave the reminder that I can survive hard things and come out the other side. I've moved on. And the contents of this box and the memories that accompany them no longer rule my life.

With a deep breath I flip open the latch and lift the lid.

Inside, is the small, crumpled note. I recall how excited I'd been at the prospect of a secret admirer. Moreover, I remember the thrill of a big reveal after several weeks of notes. Looking back, I see how naive I'd been. But I'd only just turned fifteen. I was practically a kid. A romantic.

Reaching into the box, I bypass the note and take the masculine leather cuff in my hand. My fingers trace the inscription etched onto the metal plate that says, "Bub." I remember how I laid awake at night for weeks, trying to figure out who it could belong to. I'd never seen it before, and I knew no one with that name or anything similar.

I should've asked around to see if I could determine who it belonged to. I should've turned it into the authorities, but I was too afraid. Too ashamed and embarrassed. I was worried what people might think of me. I worried they'd say it was my fault. That I deserved it. I worried about who *he* might be, and if he'd come back for me when I least expected it and try to finish the job.

From that day forward, I lived my life in fear, knowing what he got away with, but also what he *wanted* to do before I escaped. Would he try again? Was it only a matter of time before he cornered me?

Part of me didn't want to know his identity. What if it was a friend or a teacher? Someone I trusted, looked up to, and respected?

So I stayed silent, at least until Teagan started asking questions. He wanted to know why I was so withdrawn. He couldn't understand why I suddenly stopped hanging out with everyone. Why I no longer wanted to spend time with our circle of friends, and instead, avoided them like the plague. I could no longer stand the sight of the football field because it was the first thing I laid eyes on after I emerged from the locker rooms that night.

My silence hurt my brother, but missing his games, at least all the home ones, hurt him more. His pain is the reason I told him.

I blurted out my story through a tumult of tears, thoroughly convinced the moment I spilled my guts the walls would cave in, and the sky would fall.

But they didn't.

If anything, a weight lifted, and I could breathe again.

There was something wholly therapeutic about sharing the load of that horrible night with someone I could trust.

Teagan listened to my wishes and never told another soul about what happened, but I noticed a shift in him. He became super overprotective, cautious where I was concerned. A worrier. While I focused on my studies and poured myself into schoolwork, he sank his frustration into football. Eventually, I started hanging out with some of the nerdier kids at school. The kind of kids who studied on the weekends rather than go out. The ones who avoided school functions like the plague. And I was fine with it, even if I missed out on a lot of experiences I wished I hadn't.

That's why I'd been so excited to start college. I have no history here. AU is a chance at a clean slate, a fresh start. One where I'm not expected to be Brynn Nichols, the slightly cynical, antisocial twin.

But I hadn't planned on Jace attending AU alongside me and representing all the things I left behind in Riverside, including the person I'd once been before my world turned upside down. He's a reminder of the darkness that lurks in the shadows, the memories I've worked so hard to forget. It took years to go anywhere alone without looking over my shoulder. I only recently stopped believing *he* would find me.

I know Chris's questions about how the rift started between me and Jace are innocuous and meant in jest, but they're also a reminder I can't outrun my past, at least not fully. It's a part of me. It made me who I am, for better or worse.

Jace saw me that night. And he made an assumption based on my frazzled appearance and where I'd been about what I'd been doing.

He thought I'd had a quickie in the locker room, and though he had no way of knowing what really happened and that I'd been attacked, I put a wall up. From that day on, I turned my shame and fear into anger. Even a single glimpse of him reminded me of my walk of shame, stumbling from the locker rooms into the moonlight. It brought back the fear and loathing. The stupidity I felt at falling for *his* tricks. Making Jace my enemy had been easy.

I swallow over the lump forming in the back of my throat, set the leather cuff back inside the box, and snap the lid closed.

What happened made me stronger. I'm a fighter. I fought my way out of danger that evening, and then fought my way through the darkness that followed. I've moved on. It doesn't define me.

Jace's assumptions shouldn't define him, either. He had no idea what really happened, and somehow, over these past few weeks, the walls I resurrected between us have begun to crumble. My feelings for him have changed on their own accord, and maybe I'll get hurt. Maybe what I'm feeling isn't even real.

But maybe it's time to clear the rubble.

JACE

I drag a hand down my face as I stare at the bedroom door, debating whether I should knock. I have no idea what the hell just happened, but I saw the shift in Brynn the minute Chris started running his mouth about why she hated me.

I don't know what it means. Hell, maybe I don't want to know. But I can't go back to being enemies, so I raise my fist and rap it against the door. If the past is an indicator of what to expect, I brace for silence but it's surprise that hits me when her voice calls out, "Come in."

My eyes lift to the heavens, and I exhale before I turn the knob and step inside.

Brynn is crouched in front of the closet, sliding what looks like a jewelry box back into her bag. "What's that?"

With a shake of the head, she stands. "Nothing that matters."

I nod. Though I sense there's more to what she was doing in here, I don't press, afraid she'll shut me out. "You okay? You were quiet on the ride home, and the way you ran in here . . . I was worried I did something to upset you."

She shakes her head and offers me a smile. When it reaches her eyes, I sigh, relieved. "You didn't do anything, I swear. And I'm good. Promise."

I step forward and draw her into my arms. Her body is warm and soft, and it molds to mine. I drop a kiss to the top of her head, wondering what the hell happened to the old Jace

Taggart. This isn't me. I don't seek comfort from girls. I only offer physical affection when I know it's leading somewhere, not just because I care.

But Brynn is different. Maybe she always has been.

"Jace?" She tips her head, lifting her gaze to mine, and I swallow.

Here it is, the moment she tells you she doesn't want this—want you—because she'd rather have someone boring and normal like the schmuck back at the restaurant. Someone who's not adverse to relationships.

I straighten my shoulders, steeling myself for what's about to come out of her mouth. "Yeah?"

"I was just thinking . . ." She licks her lips, her violet eyes darting to the door. "I know how you've been complaining about your back and how hard the sofa is, and I know what a pain sleeping in the living room must be, so I just thought . . . well, I wonder if maybe you'd want to sleep in here."

My brows lift. *Not* what I was expecting.

Just to be sure, I ask, "With you?" She nods, biting her lower lip, and I grin. "Cupcake, are you trying to get me in bed?"

"What? No!" Her cheeks flush. "I just figured it wouldn't hurt anything just to sleep together."

I bark out a laugh as her mouth rounds into an O. "That's not how I meant—"

"I can't disagree with you. Sleeping together sounds like a great idea, best one you've had yet." I wiggle my brows, and she turns another shade of red.

"Jace!" She smacks my chest. "I mean just to *sleep*. Literally."

"Oh, damn." I snap my fingers as my eyes glitter with amusement. Of course I knew what she meant. Whatever is going on between us is new, and the last thing I want is to pressure Brynn into doing anything she's not ready for. Rushing her isn't even on my radar, but it's not for lack of wanting her. "If you wanted to cuddle, Cupcake, why didn't you just say so?" I give her a playful squeeze, then bow. "My body is at your service. Use me how you want." I wink, and her cheeks turn to lava.

"You're cruel," she says, crossing her arms over her chest.

"You know I'm teasing." I laugh. "I knew what you meant from the start, and I promise I'll be on my best behavior. Scouts honor," I say, raising two fingers in a Boy Scouts' salute.

Brynn snorts. "You are the furthest thing from a Boy Scout." Then she pokes me in the chest and tries to brush past me, but I yank her back, leaning down to brush a soft kiss over her lips. "Why don't we get ready for bed?" I whisper.

She stares up at me, her breathing shallow. I didn't mean for the request to sound so sensual, but considering how much she turns me on, I'm not surprised by the raspy growl of my voice.

With a silent nod, she pulls away from me and grabs her pajamas while I leave the room to give her some privacy. After we've both brushed our teeth, I return to the bedroom to see Brynn is already nestled in bed looking like a fucking dream.

I reach over my head and yank off my T-shirt, throwing it in the hamper beside the door before I turn to find her staring. Holding her gaze, I drop my pants, smirking at her valiant effort to keep her eyes waist-high but she fails and lets it dip to my boxer briefs for a split second.

I crawl under the covers beside her and when she turns on her side, I press her smaller body against my larger one, holding her close. I've never done this before—cuddled with a girl—and I wonder if it shows. I wonder if I suck at it, even as my palm flattens over her abdomen and I pull her tighter only to discover it's still not close enough. Something tells me I could be inside Brynn and still never get enough, so I slide my hand under her shirt, letting the heat of her skin burn through my palm as I close my eyes.

With a sigh, I relax into the mattress. My muscles loosen and my breathing evens out. Lying beside her like this makes it easy to imagine what it would be like to be with her—to *really* be with Brynn in every capacity.

And as I lie here, basking in her coconut-vanilla scent, I think about what it would be like if she were mine. Completely and utterly mine.

I've never pondered the merits of a relationship before. I've never thought about more than fleeting pleasure with a woman, but Brynn makes me want to change everything. She makes me think there might be more out there than I ever thought possible.

My eyes flutter closed, and as I start to drift, it feels a lot like falling when I whisper, "Goodnight, Cupcake."

CHAPTER 25

BRYNN

I CHECK THE TIME on my phone, then tuck it in my backpack as I hurry down the sidewalk toward Laughner's, the student cafeteria. Overhead, the sky rumbles, and I glance up warily, hoping the rain holds off until I'm inside. I'm already running late for my standing lunch date with the girls, and I hate to get there soaked to the bone.

After what happened at Pizzuto's, they're dying for details. Any longer and they'll send out a search party.

Bowing my head, I pick up the pace when I see someone coming and dart to my right at the same time they do, and we crash into each other. Stumbling back, I right myself as the contents in her arms scatter to the sidewalk.

"Oh my gosh. I'm so sorry," I say as I bend to retrieve her phone and a book strewn on the sidewalk.

"No worries." She bends beside me, grabbing a paper takeout bag before she straightens and my jaw drops.

Teresa. The girl Jace had on his couch not long ago. The long chestnut hair, pouty lips, high cheekbones, and perfect body—I'd remember them anywhere.

I avert my gaze as I stretch an arm out, handing her the rest of her things and trying my best not to picture her shirtless and underneath the boy I left in my bed this morning. A flush rises to my cheeks, and I make a move to leave when her words stop me.

"You're Jace's girlfriend, right?"

I pause, my gaze flickering to hers and I expect her to laugh or smirk, something to tell me she's joking. But she appears to be stone-cold sober and entirely serious. "Uh, no. Jace and I aren't . . . I'm not . . . what makes you think that?"

I have no idea what Jace and I are to each other now, but we definitely weren't anything to each other the day I walked in on them.

"Oh." She straightens with a frown. "I'm sorry, I just assumed when he told me to leave, that he couldn't—" She shakes her head and starts to brush past me. "Never mind."

I frown, reaching out to stop her. "What do you mean he told you to leave?" From what I saw, he looked pretty comfortable to me.

A nervous laugh spills from her lips. "This is kind of awkward, but we were having a good time . . . and he stopped and said he couldn't 'do this.'" She makes air quotes with her fingers.

"Then asked me to leave. The next thing I know, you walked in and, well . . ."

Butterflies riot in my stomach at this revelation. Jace stopped Teresa and asked her to leave *before* I barged in.

She tilts her head, studying me. "I'm sorry. I just assumed with the way he looked at you, along with your reaction, that you were together. You weren't?"

I shake my head, still processing what she just told me.

"Well, you know he likes you, right?"

I swallow as something tugs in my chest. That night feels like forever ago, and things have certainly evolved between us, but was he really thinking about me even back then?

It seems impossible. Romantic, even if it shouldn't be. But deep down, it feels right.

I glance up at her, my insides growing warm and fuzzy, as if I've downed a shot of whiskey.

"Anyway . . ." She trails off, and I realize I've been standing here, staring like a mute. "I guess there's no need for apologies. See you around?"

I nod, offering her a polite smile and a wave as she turns to leave with me staring after her in the rumbling thunder.

I burst inside the brightly lit cafeteria and bypass the lines and stations for food, scanning the tables for Charlotte and Samantha. I find them waiting in the back at a small round table, so I hurry toward them and slide into the seat between them.

"You're late," Charlotte points out.

I grimace. "Sorry."

"You can make it up to us only by sharing every minute detail about how good Jace is in the sack," Samantha says, then adds, "Is he packing? I bet he's packing."

I laugh. "Well, actually, we didn't sleep together."

Samantha's mouth unhinges, and for a moment, I fear for her.

"Let me rephrase." I clear my throat. "We didn't have sex. We did, on the other hand, cuddle."

"Oh my gosh. Is he a cuddler?" Charlotte asks, taking a bite of her apple.

"He makes the most amazing big spoon. He just kind of"—I open my arms as if giving the air a hug—"wraps around you with his whole body."

"Yeah, yeah." Samantha waves this information away. "As great as that is, Charlotte said when she walked in on the two of you at Pizzuto's, it looked like he was about to take you right there, so what the heck happened?"

I pause because the truth isn't something I want to share. "Um, I don't know. We got in the car with Chris, and he was asking all these questions about why we used to hate each other. Then we got back, and things felt kind of heavy and awkward for a moment."

"Nice. His wingman killed the mood." Samantha scowls.

I shrug because she's not wrong. "Kinda."

"So, he settled for cuddling. Wow." Charlotte beams. "I need me a Jace Taggart doppelgänger. Does he have any brothers, by chance?"

I scrunch my nose. "Only child. Sorry."

Samantha huffs. "I can't believe there are *no* juicy details even though you left our group date with him. So, why was he there, anyway? Did you at least get that much out of him?"

I smile. "When he found out we were going on a group date, he got jealous and followed us there."

"Ugh! I can't take it." Charlotte groans. "He is *everything*. Please tell me you're going to pursue whatever this is with him."

I bite my lip and nod, causing Charlotte to let out a loud squeal. "At first, I tried to fight it, mostly because of my adverse feelings toward him and because it's Jace, you know? I've known him for years. I've seen how he is with girls. He's never had a real girlfriend because he can't commit, and so this whole time with the kiss and the cupcake incident, I just assumed he was messing around. Jace being Jace. But I don't think I can fight it anymore. I can't deny that I feel something for him."

"But do you think he actually wants something with you and not just a hook up?" Samantha asks as she pops a fry into her mouth.

I can't blame her for questioning his intentions when I've questioned them myself, but my thoughts drift to Teresa and everything she just told me, and I smile. "I actually do," I say, biting my lip and thinking about waking up this morning to him wrapped around me.

"What about your brother?" Charlotte asks, bringing me back to reality. "Will that be a problem?"

I sigh because I have no doubt Jace is the last person Teagan would want me to be with. Not because he thinks Jace is a terrible person; my brother doesn't hang around with assholes. Teagan is as good as they come and he surrounds himself with good people in return. But when it comes to relationships and women, Jace has a reputation. If Teagan had even an inkling of what's happening between us, especially with my past, he would not be happy. It's not lost on me that Teagan will forgive me for keeping this from him because I'm his sister. But it's different for Jace. He isn't family. They might be as close as brothers, but at the end of the day, they're best friends, separated by blood.

So, will Teagan be a problem? I just don't know.

"I'm not sure," I say, my tone wary. "But I think we're probably wise to see what comes of this thing between us, if anything, before we run and tell him. It's new. A lot can happen in a short amount of time."

Samantha hums in the back of her throat as she flops back into her chair. "Well, get ready to tell him because something tells me that boy is smitten."

CHAPTER 26

JACE

WE AMBLE OFF THE football field, muscles sore and our practice gear soaked to the bone with sweat. I grip the face mask of my helmet, still slowing my heart rate after the suicides we just did. The days in the weight room are bliss compared to our training on the field, but when I step foot on the turf, it gets me excited for what's to come in the fall. Football is now less than two months away, official practices only a month out, and I can't wait to see what the season has in store. If the last month is any indication, I'll dominate the field.

When I first promised Teagan I'd watch out for Brynn, I thought she might be a distraction, that she'd pull my focus. But since things have taken a turn for us during the last couple of weeks, I've played better than ever. It's like the closer I get to her and the more we talk, the more I'm able to harness all my energy onto the field.

My thoughts drift to the time we spent together over the weekend, and I can't wipe the goofy-ass grin off my face. Showing up at Pizzuto's . . . sleeping beside her all night . . . I've never felt this way with a chick. It's like I can't get enough. Like I don't want whatever this thing is between us to end. And it feels damn good.

"What's that smile for?" Damon asks as we make our way into the tunnel that leads to the locker room. "You were particularly chipper this morning, considering all those suicides and bleach sprints."

Chris snorts. "Hmm, I wonder why that is?" He delivers a blow to my ribs and adds, "Guess who didn't sleep on the couch last night?"

Both sets of eyes swing my way, but I shrug. "Nothing happened. We literally slept. That's all."

"Right," Damon drawls. "The ole 'we just slept,'" he says, making air quotes with his hands.

I roll my eyes as we enter under the huge archways that lead into the front of the locker room. "Seriously, that's all that happened." Then I change the subject because I know they'll never let it drop. "What do you think Coach wants?"

Chris drops down on the bench across from his locker and shrugs. "No idea."

I pop mine open, then yank my jersey up over my head. We were informed at the start of practice to wait for Coach, which has us all on edge, wondering what he wants. Luckily, I don't need to wait long to find out what it's about. Coach enters the locker room not more than a minute later, and the atmosphere immediately shifts. All joking fizzles out, smiles straighten, and conversation dies.

Silence fills the cavernous space as Coach Greene stands before us, clipboard in hand. "Hello, gentleman. You can relax," he says, holding out his hands when several of the players rise to their feet. "I'm just stopping by to talk about something our team does every year." His gaze tracks the room, bouncing from face to face. "For the rookies here, the Ann Arbor Griffins have a program called Griffins' Gifts. Veterans already know about the volunteer work we do, but it's pretty simple. Here, at AU football, we believe strongly in giving back to our community, so a few years ago, we created the program for that very reason. Basically, several times a year, particularly around holidays and big events, we perform some kind of charity work or do something nice for the people of Ann Arbor. At Christmastime, we bring gifts to the kids in the oncology pediatric unit. On Labor Day, we participate with a float in the parade. Those are just two examples. Each player must volunteer at least once a year to meet their obligation to the team, and the first events of the season are this week, so, I thought I'd drop by to let you know."

He nods toward the exit to the locker room. "Sign-ups are on the door. Again, it's only mandatory to participate once a year, other than the parade, so if you can't find the time this month, there will be plenty of opportunities."

Coach turns to leave, then swivels back around. "Oh, and Damon, those drills you've been doing have really paid off.

Gabe, your footwork's lacking. Need to work on it, brother." He points his pencil at Briggs, our cornerback. "Great job containing the receiver. And Jace . . ." He grins. "Nice hands."

"Nice hands," Chris mocks beside me as Coach leaves and I whip my towel at him. I know he's just messing with me, but damn, it feels good to hear Coach verbally acknowledge my work is paying off.

"Wonder if it would be wise to get this volunteer thing over with while we have more time on our hands?" I ask.

One or two guys rise from their spots on the bleachers and head toward the sign-up sheets while Damon shrugs. "Totally up to you. I always do the Christmas gigs. It's pretty cool because if we've had an awesome season, fans are especially pumped to see us. But I'll admit, it's nuts trying to squeeze something in throughout the fall, so go for it."

"Worth at least checking it out," Chris says. "See what they have."

I'm already moving toward the door when I call out, "You coming?"

I feel Chris at my side while I stop and scan the sheet. The top of the page is for a gig reading children's books at the library, but one of the other guys who beat us to it has already snagged it. A visit to a nursing home. Meet and greet at Rainbow Babies Children's Hospital . . .

I blow out a shaky breath and wince. "Damn. Just the thought of sick kids . . . Not sure I can do it."

Chris nods, his expression stony. "I had a cousin who fought cancer growing up. It was rough for everyone." He shrugs. "I'll take it."

I place a hand on his shoulder. "You're a better man than me," I say, and then my gaze snags on an entry at the bottom of the sheet for a flag football event at Helping Hands.

Helping Hands. I repeat the name over and over until it clicks. A memory of Brynn pops in my head. She's sitting cross-legged on the couch, her hair mussed from running her hands through it, telling me about the volunteer work she signed up for to occupy her time and hopefully give her an edge on her resume.

"I'll take this one," I say, quickly scrawling my name below it.

"Flag football with the kids at Helping Hands?" Chris reads with brows drawn, before he frowns. "Damn, that sounds like fun. I should've taken that one."

"Brynn helps out there."

Chris turns to me, one brow raised with a shit-eating grin. "She does, does she?" He crosses his arms in front of his chest. "Interesting. I distinctly recall only a few weeks back you claiming that there was nothing going on between you, and now just look at you. Skipping the club to stay in with her. Sending a good lay home because you couldn't stop thinking about her—"

Shit. I knew telling Chris about that would come back to haunt me.

"Crashing dates," he continues, ticking each thing off on his fingers. "Cuddling together without sex. Volunteering at the same places . . ." He trails off with a shake of the head.

"So?" I cross my arms over my chest, feeling an odd pressure in my chest.

Chris tips his head back and lets out a loud belly laugh. "Oh fuck. You are so gone."

"Maybe I like her, so what?" I shrug, which only makes him laugh harder.

"Oh, you more than like her, dude. Just admit it." He reaches out and ruffles my hair like I'm a toddler and I swat his arm away. "You *wuv* her."

I roll my eyes at him and head back to my locker, but I don't deny it. What can I say? I've never felt this way about anyone. I don't even know how to define it. I couldn't if I tried. All I know is the more time I spend with her, the more I hate being apart.

I slide my shorts off, followed by my boxer briefs, then grab a towel and sling it around my waist. When I slam the metal door closed, Chris is there, staring at me with a rueful smile. It's times like these he really reminds me of the boys back home, which makes me wish I could talk to them about this, hash out what I'm feeling. But this is the one thing I can't share with them, and it fucking sucks. I hate keeping things from them.

Chris props his shoulder against the locker, and stares at me with shrewd eyes. "Maybe you just need to hook up. All that pent-up sexual tension isn't good for anybody. Once you do, she'll either be out of your system, or . . ."

"Or?" I grind my teeth and the muscle in my jaw pulses. Referring to Brynn as nothing more than a hookup rubs me the wrong way.

Chris's expression turns serious. "*Or* I'll be going to your wedding in a few years."

"Fuck off." I retort, causing Chris to laugh. "I might like her, but she's also my best friend's sister. I'm not sure how far this can go. He'd have my ass if he found out."

"Dude." Chris pushes off the lockers. "He goes to school in a whole other state. He doesn't even have to know."

I frown and cross my arms over my chest. "I hate lying to him." Hell, it already feels like I'm lying to him, and it doesn't sit right with me. I get indigestion just thinking about what Teagan would do if he knew. "But maybe we can keep it under wraps for now. At least until we know where this is headed."

"Damn straight." Chris nods in agreement. "That way if this thing with you and Brynn crashes and burns, he never has to know. No need to piss him off until you need to."

I grip my towel at the waist. "Yeah, you're totally right."

"Of course I am." Chris claps me on the back.

"And if things with us progress . . ." I start.

"Then you reassess. You tell him once it gets to that point, and then at least you can look him in the eyes and say, *I might be banging your hot ass sister, but at least I love her.*" He holds a straight face for all of two seconds before he bursts out laughing.

"Asshole," I mutter, flipping him off before I head for the showers.

I crank the water and step under the hot spray. The salt and grime on my skin washes away as I think about Brynn and how crazy it is we're even in this position. Had someone told me a month ago that the untouchable Brynn Nichols and I would be more than friends—hell, more than enemies—I would've told them they were crazy. And now, here I am, risking my best friend, my *brother*, because I want to claim her.

I can't imagine what it would be like without the Nichols family in my life. I'm closer to them than my own parents. Over the years, they've done more meaningful things for me than my own flesh and blood, so losing them is unthinkable.

But I can't stop this thing with Brynn even if I tried. She came barreling into my life like a freight train, and now that I've boarded the car, I'm not getting off until I make her mine.

CHAPTER 27

JACE

MY FEET SINK INTO the spongy grass. The ground is still slightly soft from rain the previous evening, but the sun is high, and it's supposed to be hot today, so I suspect it will dry out quickly. I cross the fields of the recreational park toward several groups of children who vary in age. Some are knee-high and others appear to be pre-teens. At the helm of one of the groups talking to the kids, is a hot blonde I recognize.

Her hair is tied into two braids I find so fucking endearing I can barely stand it. Tight yoga shorts show off her tan legs and she waves her arms animatedly in a loose tank and sports bra.

With a smile, I slowly head her way, trying to keep my thoughts decent considering I'm surrounded by children.

I pause a few feet behind her, grinning at her intense explanation about how there is no contact today—flags only—which is a little disappointing because I wouldn't mind an excuse to tackle Brynn. I'm not beyond bending the rules though to serve my own selfish purposes, and body contact is definitely one of them.

Once she's finished, I clear my throat and watch with bated breath as she turns around.

I wonder if she'll be excited to see me.

My heart pounds at the prospect. I've never cared much about what people thought of me. I've always done my own thing, and it's worked in my favor. But I care far more than I'd like to admit about what Brynn will think when she realizes I'm here to volunteer.

A couple of the kids point, and her head turns.

When she spots me, she freezes. There's a momentary widening of her eyes before the violet floods with warmth. She takes a step toward me, a smile crinkling the corners of her eyes. "What are you doing here?"

Her voice gives nothing away, so I'm only slightly relieved as I shrug. "I'm one of the volunteers today."

"You're . . ." She blinks. "Seriously?"

I nod, and just when I wonder if this was a huge mistake, she flings herself at me. Her arms wrap around my neck as she draws me in for a hug, her laughter filling my insides like sunshine. "That's amazing." She pulls away slightly, glancing over her shoulders as her cheeks flush. "I thought most of the recruits they got were from local high schools."

"Oh, great! You made it." A plump middle-aged woman wearing sunglasses half the size of her face approaches from the side, a clipboard in hand. "I assume you're Jace Taggart from the Griffins?"

I nod, my gaze never leaving Brynn who's biting her lip to hide a megawatt smile.

"That's me."

"Fantastic." The woman extends a hand, and I reluctantly turn to her and shake it. "I'm Maggie, the director of Helping Hands. I could tell by the way you carried yourself, along with your physique, that you had to be a Griffin. It's so nice to have you. Any time someone from the team volunteers, we're so grateful. The kids just love it and think it's really cool to have a football player from the university playing with them. Don't be surprised if a few of them ask for an autograph. You guys are celebrities around here."

I offer her a polite nod. "Not a problem. It's my pleasure to be here. Anything for the kids."

Maggie beams and motions toward the children. "I see you found a group. If you're good with staying here, this works perfectly."

"Ma'am?" I ask, squinting over at Brynn, fighting my grin. "Does this work for you?"

Her lips twitch. "He'll do, Maggie."

"Great. Brynn, this is Jace." She waves between us. "I'm sure you've gathered he's a Griffin and here to help us out today. Jace, this is Brynn Nichols. She's actually a student at AU also. She started working with us on a volunteer basis a couple weeks ago, actually."

"Yes," I say, through a small cough of polite laughter. "We actually know each other."

"Oh. You do?" the woman glances between us, the excitement in her tone evident. "Well, fabulous. It's a perfect match, then."

Brynn beams and winks at me, and while it's certainly not the first time a chick has winked at me, it's definitely the first time I've found it sexy.

"Do you need anything before you get started, Brynn?" Maggie asks.

She shakes her head. "Nope. We're good."

"Perfect. I'll let you take it from here and check on the others."

Brynn nods, watching as she disappears. The second she's out of sight, she steps forward, peering up at me with eyes glittering like jewels. "Tell me, Taggart, are you stalking me?"

I bark out a laugh. "Maybe. Does that freak you out?"

She gives me a coy little shrug. "Depends. What are you gonna do now you've found me?" Her eyes sparkle with mischief as she steps away and turns back around, and I swear if we weren't standing in a public field with more than a dozen children staring right at me, I would take her right here.

"Okay, gang, listen up!" she hollers. "Mr. Taggart is going to be helping us today," she motions toward me. "He's actually on AU's football team, so he knows his stuff."

A couple of their faces light up as their gazes turn to me at once.

"So cool," one boy drawls.

"What position do you play?" asks another.

"Wide receiver." I grin as several of them nod in unison.

"My daddy says the Griffins' passing game sucked ass last year."

I cough to cover a laugh while Brynn shoots him a glare. "Coop! Language."

"Sorry," he mutters.

"Well, it wasn't great, that's true," I chime in. "There was a lot of missed passes and stunted plays, but I'm hoping to change that."

"Do you have a girlfriend?" a tiny little brunette with pigtails in the back asks.

Brynn gasps, and I swear her cheeks turn ten shades of red. "Kiera!" she admonishes.

"What?" the girl pouts. "It was an honest question."

"It's okay," I say to Brynn, then I turn to face Kiera. "Maybe not an official girlfriend yet?" I say like a question, and I wonder if it's weird we're having a status talk in front of a bunch of nine-year-olds. "But I am seeing someone, and she's pretty special." I chance a quick glance at the blonde standing beside me to see she ducks her head a little, an adorable shade of pink crossing her cheeks.

Coop screws up his face. "Then why don't you just ask her to be your girlfriend?"

"Yeah," another boy says. "Then she has to kiss you all the time."

Brynn rolls her lips before she turns to me, eyes dancing with humor. "Yeah, Jace," she says, tossing the football back and forth between her hands, "why don't you ask her?"

"Will she kiss me all the time?" I take a step toward her, and her expression is so playful, I want to reach out and nip at her smile. But I can't and someone saves me from whatever stupid thing I was about to say with another personal question, forcing Brynn to turn and glare.

"*Ooookay.* Let's ask questions at the end, shall we?"

BRYNN

The moment I saw Jace behind me on the field, I was floored. I'm not sure what surprised me more: the fact that he's here at all, or the fact that he listened, really listened, when I told him what organization I volunteered for enough to recognize the name.

I watch as Jace gives instructions on the proper form for throwing the football, and my thoughts drift back to his answer about whether he has a girlfriend.

I am seeing someone, and she's pretty special.

Until now, I wasn't sure if Jace considered us anything at all, but clearly, he does. Though his answer leaves room for interpretation, I think it's safe to say, at the very least, he thinks we're dating. And the fact that Jace Taggart is acknowledging he's seeing someone at all, let alone specifying that she's special, is staggering. Even more mind-blowing is the thought that his "someone" is *me*.

Jace spends time with each child, correcting their posture and giving them attention, explaining the right placement of their fingers on the ball. How to throw a spiral. How to tuck and run. He also goes over the basics of the rules. By the time he's done, my crush on him—yes, I think it's safe to say I have a huge crush—has turned to full-blown infatuation.

He leans down and helps Lynn, the little brunette from earlier who seems to share my taste in boys, and helps her place her tiny fingers over the laces of the football, properly positioning her hand.

As it turns out, Jace Taggart is ridiculously good with kids. It's newfound knowledge about him I wish I didn't know because it makes my heart grow three sizes. If it swells any more, it won't fit inside my chest.

I don't know what I expected. Maybe a male version of Charlotte? For him to ignore their pleas for help, cringe and turn away from their dirty hands, and snotty noses? Snap at them for asking the same questions for the millionth time? Instead, he's beyond patient. He laughs and jokes, accepts a pass from Coop, only to have three children tackle each of his legs, clinging to him like barnacles on the side of a ship as he runs, somehow still managing to pass the goal line.

After some time, I dismiss the kids so they can get a drink before we play the big game and divide up into teams. Jace saunters over to me, a cocky smirk on his ridiculously handsome face. It's unfair for someone to be graced with such immaculate bone structure. The perfect slope of his patrician nose, the square line of his jaw, and cheekbones chiseled from stone. My heart can't take so much perfection.

I try not to look at him as he settles in beside me, instead focusing on the kids swarming the Gatorade table, because it's less scary than this growing feeling inside I'm afraid to fully acknowledge.

He yanks the hem of his shirt up to wipe the sweat from his brow, and my willpower only holds for a second before I glance at his toned abdomen, and the delicious V of his Adonis belt dipping below the waistline of his shorts.

I swallow and quickly realize he's caught me staring. "Like something you see, Cupcake?" He winks, and butterflies erupt inside my chest.

I swallow with a soft chuckle, further cursing his cutoff T-shirt when he rakes a hand through his thick hair and his biceps flex.

I swear he's doing it on purpose.

I fan my face, which I'm sure is so red Crayola could name a crayon after me, and he laughs. "Can I ask you something?" I ask, unable to help myself.

His gaze drops to my mouth, and my heart skips a beat before he lifts his chin, eyes returning to mine. "Shoot."

"You know the night I came home to find you with the girl on the couch? Teresa?"

He nods slowly now, his gaze wary.

"Why didn't you tell me you sent her home right before I barged through the door?"

His eyes search mine, a crease forming between his brow. "How did you . . .?" He clears his throat. "I figured you wouldn't believe me."

Maybe I wouldn't have.

I lean closer, tracing circles over the back of his hand, unable to meet his eyes. "And did you tell her to leave because of me or was there another reason?" I ask.

I don't know why I need confirmation from him, but I do.

"Brynn," his tone is firm as he adds, "look at me."

I bite my lip, almost afraid of his answer. Afraid he'll say no because I want him to say yes. I already feel so much more than I probably should.

But when his gaze finds mine, his smile turns the blue of his eyes liquid. "I thought I could block you out. That's why I brought her home in the first place." He shrugs. "Hell, maybe I even brought her back to the apartment because I wanted to push you away, but it was a mistake. I knew it before we even got there, and I damn well knew once I had her there."

His throat bobs, and I stare, mesmerized by the movement. "I sent her home because I couldn't stop thinking about you. The whole night, and the whole time I was kissing her, I thought of you. I *wanted* it to be you."

A shaky breath escapes my parted lips as he leans down, pressing his forehead to mine. "You've put a spell on me, Cupcake," he whispers.

My chest aches with the need to pull him closer. The warmth of his breath fans over my skin as I reach out and fist my hands in his shirt. "Taggart, what are you doing to me?" I ask, a tremble in my voice before I tip my head up to him and take his mouth with mine.

Our lips brush for only a moment in the lightest of touches. Like a secret whispered in the dark, I latch onto it, holding it close to my chest where it will stay for all of eternity.

When we pull apart, I can feel eyes on us at the same time a chorus of *ooooohs* erupts around us in high definition.

I turn to find the children watching us with part glee, part mortification, and laugh as they launch into a familiar chant of the K-I-S-S-I-N-G rhyme, crooning about sitting in a tree and kissing and what comes after.

I cover my eyes with my hands and groan while Jace tips his head back with a roar of laughter.

This is what falling in love feels like.

CHAPTER 28

JACE

I T'S BEEN A COUPLE days since my stint at Helping Hands and things between Brynn and I are progressing nicely. I quietly rose from bed this morning, refraining from kissing her because I didn't have the heart to wake her. After conditioning, I went straight to class, then met a few of the guys for a late lunch where we hung out for a while. The whole time, however, I thought about Brynn and how I couldn't wait to see her.

I used to watch my friends and their girlfriends with something close to pity. I thought they were stuck, tied down, and forced to answer to someone else. But my eyes have been opened. The way I view relationships is rapidly changing. Now I wonder if this is what Atlas and Graham felt like with Mackenzie and Skylar. I wonder if this feeling I have inside is what I've been missing out on all this time?

It's this need to see her, this line of thought, that's kept me out far longer than necessary today. I'm trying to be cognizant of how much time I spend with her. The last thing I want to do is smother her, seeing as how she has no place to go other than the apartment.

One month ago, I could barely spell relationship and now I'm so far gone over this girl, I'm stressing over not seeing her versus seeing her too much.

I shake my head.

I've gone certifiable; it's the only explanation. But the truth is, I wouldn't have it any other way.

It's almost six p.m. by the time I arrive back at the apartment. I have the entire night free to do whatever I want. A bunch of the guys are going to grab wings and beer later, including Chris, but I'm not feeling it. I'd rather spend my night with Brynn, and as I let myself into the apartment, an unfamiliar surge of anxiety that she might not feel the same, or she might have other plans, shoots through me.

I'll be the sad asshole who stays home sulking just because his girl has plans that don't include him.

I frown when I kick off my shoes and set my keys on the counter, noting the closed bedroom door. Brynn usually leaves it open during the day, so I assume she's changing, sleeping, or otherwise occupied. I hang in the living room for a bit, waiting for her to come out, but when she doesn't, I decide to check on her.

Crossing the room, I knock on the closed door and listen, but I hear nothing.

I try again, calling out, "Hey, Brynn. I was thinking of ordering a pizza, you want in?" Again, nothing. "We could pay to stream that new chick flick that's out in theaters." I frown at the answering silence. "I'll cover the twenty bucks."

When she still doesn't respond, my stomach clenches. I wonder if she's pissed at me for something. Maybe she's come to her senses and wants nothing to do with me. "I'll even spring for ice cream."

I hear a low groan come from the other side of the door, and my frown deepens. Slowly pushing it open, I peek my head inside to see Brynn lying in my bed, covers drawn to her chin. "Brynn?" I step further inside and cross the room for a closer look. Her cheeks are flushed, a slight sheen to her skin.

I reach out to feel her forehead when she moans and rolls onto her back, swatting at my hand half-heartedly as her glassy eyes meet mine. "Go," she rasps. "I'll get you sick."

Concern knots my brow. "You're burning up. How do you feel?"

I half expect her to push my hand away again and tell me to leave, say she's fine. I'm so used to years of hostile interactions between us, there are moments this new dynamic still catches me by surprise.

Bryn grunts. "Awful," she mutters, trying to snuggle further into the blankets. "And cold, so cold."

"Shit. Did you go to class today?" I ask, knowing that if she didn't, I should definitely be worried. Brynn's not one to shirk her responsibilities.

She shakes her head. Or at least I think that's what she's doing, but the movement is barely perceptible.

"You definitely have a fever, and I don't have a thermometer." I curse under my breath, annoyed I'm not more prepared. "How long have you been like this? You seemed fine when I left." Though if I'm being honest, she'd been asleep, so I have no way of knowing for sure. She'd been so peaceful I didn't want to wake her, but now I'm pissed I didn't give her that kiss. Maybe I would've known.

"My throat was a little sore when I woke, but I just thought it was allergies . . ." she says, trailing off. "Until I tried to stand and realized I had body aches, too. I laid back down, thinking I'd sleep a little longer, and the next time I got up, I was miserable." A shiver punctuates her words.

I stand there, staring down at her while contemplating what to do.

We should probably check her temperature, so we know if it's something we need to worry about, but I also don't want to leave her to run to the drugstore until I know she's okay. "I'll be right back."

She hums in acknowledgment as I head out of the room toward the bathroom. I turn on the shower, adjusting the temperature until it's tepid. Hopefully, she's not too sick to stand under the cool spray without assistance because as much as I'd love to see Brynn naked, I'd rather do it when it's amicable and her brain is firing on all pistons, not when she's burning up with fever.

Moving to the bathroom closet, I find my shaving kit and remove the bottle of ibuprofen I keep there, uncapping it and shaking two into the palm of my hand before I grab her a glass of water from the kitchen. A few minutes later, I reenter my bedroom and help her sit up. "For the fever and aches," I say, handing her the pills, and watch as she swallows them down with a grimace I assume is a byproduct of her sore throat.

Before she can snuggle back into the bed, I grip the edge of the blanket and fling it off. "Hey!" she yells, her protests feeble as she grapples to cover herself back up.

"I know you feel cold, but that's the fever, and I'd like to get it down." I slide both of my arms underneath her, one cradling her legs and the other her back. "Come on," I say as I scoop her up.

"Jace, no," she groans. "You're going to get sick."

My heart pinches. *She's worried about me.*

"It's fine," I say. "I'm not worried about it."

"You should be," she mumbles. "I'm dyyyyying!"

I chuckle, unable to help myself because sick Brynn is fucking adorable. "You're not dying, and I hardly ever get sick. Trust me." It's true. I have the immune system of a racehorse. "A cool shower will help get your fever down until the medicine starts to work."

Her eyes meet mine as I step into the small bathroom and her brows pull together in concern. "How cold?"

My lips twitch. "It's room temperature. So, you won't freeze, but it'll probably feel colder than it is since you're feverish. We can't make it warmer, though, or it won't help."

She nods as I set her on her feet. "Do you need help getting undressed, or . . .?"

"*Pah!*" She manages. "You wish."

I laugh, relieved she's well enough to joke around. "A man can dream."

She groans, and I set her on her feet. "Get going." She points, her gaze hooded, cheeks flushed with fever.

"I'll be right outside if you need me."

"Fat chance, Taggart," she murmurs as I close the door. I hear the clinking sound of the shower curtain rings as she draws it open then closed.

I swallow as I sink down to the floor, too worried about her to leave until I know she's finished, dressed, and tucked back into bed.

Man, I'm a simp.

I settle in and sling my arms over my bent knees, trying to keep my thoughts from focusing on the fact that Brynn is naked just behind that door. Only a total creep fantasizes about someone when they're miserable and sick.

Instead, I train my thoughts to focus on what I can do to help. I need a thermometer just to make sure her fever doesn't get worse. Maybe some cold and flu meds. Tea and honey for her throat. Lozenges. Chicken noodle soup. What else?

Fuck. I rake a hand through my hair.

My parents never did this shit for me when I was a kid. If they were even around at all when I got sick, they stayed as far away as possible, claiming they couldn't afford to miss work. It was only Harriet, our housekeeper, that ever showed any semblance of concern. But she wasn't always around, either. There were plenty of times I suffered in silence.

Still, I force my memories to the times she *was* there for me and vaguely recall several instances when I magically found the fridge stocked with homemade soup and the pantry full of crusty bread for toast. Cough drops and medicine suddenly appeared. Menthol ointment, vitamin C chews, and elderberry syrup found their way onto my bedside table. Those times, she stopped by the next day, acting like she left something at the house. Once I was older, she no longer needed to pretend because by then, I realized she was the only one checking up on me.

"How long do I need to stay in here?" Brynn calls out, her voice strained from what I imagine is a swollen throat.

I slide my phone from my pocket and check the time, surprised to find more than ten minutes have passed while I've been lost in thought. "You're probably good to come out."

The water turns off and the shower curtain rattles again. A few minutes later, the bathroom door swings open, and I'm not prepared for what I see: Brynn is standing before me in nothing but a towel, skin and hair damp from the shower.

Every muscle in my body freezes. A water droplet falls from her hair to her chest, rolling down her skin and my gaze follows its path. I swallow as a fireball forms at the base of my spine.

Rubbing a hand over the back of my neck, I ignore the fist of desire clenching in my stomach.

"Eyes up here, Taggart."

Caught staring, my gaze jerks to hers, and I clear my throat. "Um, I'll, uh . . ." I point to the ground as my mouth goes dry. "I'll just wait here while you get dressed."

She passes me with little more than a smirk, which is how I know she must really feel like garbage. In her absence, I close my eyes and pinch the bridge of my nose, trying to calm the fuck down.

When the door creaks open a minute later, I take it as an invitation to check on her, but I don't trust myself not to make a fool of myself, considering all the blood in my body has rushed south and has yet to leave its post.

Instead, I head for the front door and swipe my keys off the hook as I call out, "I'm headed to the store. I'll be back."

After I unload everything I've purchased, I take the carton of chicken noodle soup and pour Brynn a bowl of it. I bought the kind you find with the prepared foods, not the canned stuff, which tastes like crap. Fat noodles, huge chunks of chicken, and carrots swim in the golden broth as I pop it in the microwave. While it heats, I fill a glass with orange juice, and search the kitchen for something I can use as a makeshift tray. Finding a cookie sheet, I shrug and place her drink on it, along with some crackers and a spoon. The lozenges I bought follow, and once the microwave beeps, I add the bowl of soup and slip the thermometer into my pocket.

I carry everything to my bedroom, taking care to be as quiet as possible as I sit the tray on my nightstand next to where she's curled up into a ball, her face slack with sleep, mouth slightly parted.

The sight of her pinches at my chest. This version of Brynn, the one that's sick and vulnerable, is so different from the fiery, take-no-prisoners girl I know. It makes me wonder how many other versions of her I've yet to discover, and if I'll be lucky enough to get the chance.

I sink down on the edge of the bed, gently brushing a lock of hair from her face, glad to see her skin has cooled some. She's no longer sweating, but her cheeks are still slightly flushed, and after a couple minutes, she stirs and blinks at me. "Hey," she says, pushing herself up into a seated position. "What time is it?"

"A little before nine."

She nods. "I think the meds helped with the fever, but I still feel terrible. My throat hurts so bad I can barely swallow."

"Maybe this will help," I say, turning for the tray. I pick it up, motioning for her to lean back against the headboard while I set it on her lap.

Her head bows as she stares down at the contents, and she glances back up at me, her eyes round in surprise. "Are you gonna eat?"

"Already did," I lie. "Don't worry about me."

She nods and lifts her spoon, taking a tentative bite before she smiles. "This is good. Thanks."

"Sure thing." I reach out, rubbing her shoulders and her neck, moving to the muscles in her back, and she moans in response. "Eat your soup, and I'll keep rubbing," I say, motioning toward her food.

She nods, and dips her spoon back in the bowl, eating quietly while I massage her aching muscles. Once she's done, I rise to my feet, but she reaches out and grabs my hand before I can get very far. "Where are you going?" she asks.

"To let you rest, but I'll be back to check on you. Do you need anything else?"

"No, this is great. Thanks, Jace."

I hesitate for a moment, my gaze drifting over her small frame tucked away beneath the blankets and feel a pang in my chest, wishing I could stay. But she's sick and doesn't feel well. She needs her rest, not me keeping her awake. "Let me know if you need anything else."

It's pitch black when I wake to someone grabbing my arm and shaking it. "Jace," a hoarse voice croaks. I open my eyes and glance around, my vision blurry with sleep as I take a minute to clear the fog from my brain. "Jace," the voice says again at the same time I focus on her.

I sit bolt upright, noting the crease in her brow. Even in the dim lighting, I can see the flush in her cheeks has returned but the rest of her has drained of color. "What is it? What's wrong?"

Without saying anything, Brynn flicks on the lamp beside the couch. I wince from the sudden light burning my retinas when she lifts the hem of her T-shirt.

Any other time, I'd be fucking ecstatic at the prospect of Brynn flashing me, but as the cotton rises, it reveals a spray of bright red blotches covering her normally smooth skin.

"What the hell is *this*?" she cries, her voice froggy from her sore throat.

"Um . . ." I try not to panic as I assess the situation, but it doesn't look good.

Does she have the fucking measles? The mumps? Hell, if I know.

Carefully, so as not to further freak her out, I lower the soft cotton and glance up at her. "Maybe we should take you to urgent care."

She nods, and the fact that she agrees with me so readily tells me just how shitty she feels.

Five minutes later, we're cruising downtown to the closest med express. According to Google, there's one of those pharmacies with an urgent care clinic only five miles from campus.

We arrive quickly to find the waiting room relatively empty. I help Brynn while she walks on wooden legs into the clinic, then lowers herself into a chair. Her skin is hot to the touch and when I tell her I'll be right back, she mumbles something unintelligible.

With worry gnawing in my gut, I take the clipboard from the receptionist and fill out the intake form the best I can, asking her the odd question while she leans against my shoulder as if sitting is too much of a chore.

After the nurse calls Brynn back, I sit and wait. My shoulder is damp with sweat from where she laid her head and nerves tangle in my chest. It's probably just a weird virus, something she picked up at Helping Hands. I'm sure she'll be fine with a little rest and TLC. This is just a precaution.

The door swings open sometime later and Brynn ambles out, shoulders slumped. Her gaze finds mine and she holds up a white pharmacy bag. "Strep throat."

I sigh, relieved. "Seriously?"

She nods. "Who freaking gets strep throat in July?"

"And the rash?"

"Scarlatina."

I wrinkle my nose as we start for the door. "Isn't that—"

"Scarlet fever? Yeah."

I laugh, and she scolds me with a look.

"Do you think you got it at—"

"Helping Hands? Most definitely." She stops in front of me and scowls. "The bad news is you'll probably get it next."

"Nah. I never get it," I say as I guide her toward the exit.

"What do you mean you never get it?"

I shrug. "The flu, colds, sinus infections, sure. But strep throat? Never. I had my tonsils removed when I was eight, and I swear it's the reason I've never gotten it since."

Brynn grunts. "Lucky."

By the time we step outside, the sun has risen. I open my truck door for her and wait as she slides inside before I close it and get in the driver's seat.

My gaze lingers over her face—the soft spray of freckles over her nose, the gentle curve of her jaw, her plump, pink lips—and I swallow. Even sick, she's the most beautiful thing I've ever seen. "Well, at least the good news is you'll probably start to feel better in twenty-four to forty-eight hours once the antibiotics kick in, and at least you won't get worse in the meantime."

She hums in agreement and her head falls back against the headrest, her eyes fluttered closed.

Once we're back at the apartment, I help her inside and into bed. Despite her protests, I heat a small bowl of soup for her, so she doesn't get a stomachache with her meds, and afterward, I bring her some ibuprofen and a cup of hot tea with honey for her throat.

"This is weird," she says, after a moment.

"What?"

She shakes her head. "You. This." She waves to the empty bowl of soup and her cup of tea. "Were you a bedside nurse in your previous life, or were your parents just extra when you got sick?"

I laugh and reach out, smoothing a strand of hair away from her face. Not because it was in her eyes, but because I *needed* to touch her. "It definitely wasn't my parents, but sometimes, Harriet used to help me when I was under the weather. She'd check up on me and made sure I had everything I needed. I think, since my parents didn't pay any attention to me, she worried a little more than necessary." I shrug. "Then, once I got much older, I guess I learned to take care of myself." When Brynn frowns, I glance away. "I'm sorry. That sounds . . ."

Sad? Lonely?

I swallow. I don't finish the sentence because any adjective I can think of sounds too damn pathetic.

She reaches out and squeezes my hand. She must sense my desire to drop it because she sets her tea on the nightstand and lies back in bed. In the days prior to her getting sick, we'd been sleeping together, but I don't know what the protocol is under these circumstances. It's not like I have much experience to draw from. She's the longest relationship I've had, if you can even call it that, and we haven't exactly discussed labels. With her sick and miserable, I assume she wants her space, so I start to rise like I did last night.

"Wait. You're leaving?" she asks.

I glance down at her, grinning at how childlike she looks: pink-cheeked and glassy-eyed, tucked into bed. "I just thought you might want to get some rest."

"Do you have something you need to do?"

I shake my head.

"Then, stay." She reaches out to me, and my heart leaps inside my chest.

I nod and take her hand, entwining our fingers as I sink back down onto the bed and slide underneath the covers.

"You really don't think you'll get sick?" she asks, staring over at me, a crease of worry between her brow.

I reach out and smooth it with a finger. "No. Haven't had strep since I was really young." Then I shift her onto my chest. Her head sits perfectly in the nook between my face and collarbone, and I inhale, breathing in her coconut scent while I run my fingers through her hair and over her scalp.

A small moan rumbles in her chest, letting me know she approves. The sound hits me like a punch to the gut, and I force myself to breathe.

"Tell me about getting your tonsils out. Why'd they have to remove them? Did it hurt?" she asks.

"I was about eight and got sick, some sort of virus, but my tonsils became infected, and when the tonsillitis didn't respond to treatment, they decided it was best to remove them." I continue to play with her hair, thinking about it. "It hurt pretty bad but wasn't anything unbearable. I got to eat a lot of ice cream, which was basically every eight-year-old's dream."

"I remember the time Teagan broke his arm. I was so jealous of all the attention he got."

I hum a noncommittal response. My parents are not the Nicholses.

"What?" She shifts onto my shoulder, craning her neck to look at me.

"Nothing. It's just . . . my parents weren't even there."

She frowns. "What do you mean they weren't there?"

I shrug, indicating it's no big deal. Like their absence in my life didn't leave scars, but something tells me she can see right through it. "The week before, they had left for a business trip. I was sick, but the tonsillitis had really only just become an issue. I had medication already. I'm sure in their mind, they thought it was okay to leave. Harriet stayed with me while they were gone, like she did when I was young. A week later, when it became really bad and we found out I needed surgery, we called them, but they asked if it was an emergency. My father had yet to close his business deal, and my mother didn't want to fly home alone."

"That's terrible," Brynn says quietly. "They should've been with you."

I swallow, and my heart clenches at the memory. "I think Harriet wanted to demand they come back, but I begged her not to. I knew what my mother would be like if she left before she was ready, and I'd rather have no one at all than have to deal with her sulking."

"So, you had the surgery without them?"

I nod. "Harriet was there, and she was enough. She took care of me until I healed up."

Brynn's quiet for a minute, and I wonder if she pities me.

"Has it always been like that with your parents?" she asks. "Them not being there?"

I think about lying. Sugarcoating the truth is easier, but something stops the generic response from slipping past my lips. I don't want to lie with Brynn, no matter how pathetic the truth makes me feel. "Yeah," I murmur. "I think most of my childhood consisted of them gone. Harriet was supposed to be a chef and housekeeper, but she was a nanny 75 percent of the time until I turned thirteen, and my parents deemed me old enough to stay on my own."

I don't know why my parents never stuck around. Sometimes I just think they're selfish. Other times, I wonder if they even know how to love.

"That's why you spent so much time at our house," she murmurs.

I say nothing, letting my silence speak for me as I play with the long strands of her hair.

Brynn shifts, her thigh brushing mine, sending a bolt of desire through my core. Her hot breath fans over my chest, her breasts pressing into my side, and I imagine kissing her plump lips.

The girl feels like she got hit by a freight train, and you're fantasizing about her lips. Asshole.

A low sound vibrates in her chest before she barks out a laugh, and I smile. "Something funny, Cupcake?"

"I was just thinking."

"About?"

"This is the hardest you've ever had to work for sex." She splutters again, laughing even harder. "It's certainly the longest." Her hand rises to her throat. "Oh, my gosh, laughing hurts!" She groans.

I chuckle, unsure of what to make of her teasing before I reach out and tilt her chin with my fingers until our eyes meet. "Laugh all you want, but did it ever occur to you that maybe sex isn't the only thing I want?"

CHAPTER 29

BRYNN

I PACE ACROSS THE floor. If I have to wait much longer for Jace to get back from practice, I might wear a hole in the rug. After several days of rest and medicine, I finally feel like myself again, and I don't intend to waste another minute. I'm ready. Impatient. I even changed into something nice and did my hair, relieved all my aches and pains are gone.

The apartment is quiet, and after having spent so much time holed up in Jace's bedroom, I'm going stir-crazy.

When I woke this morning feeling whole again, I wanted to cry tears of joy. The first thought in my head was of Jace.

I think of how sweet he was when I was sick. I'm not sure I've ever felt so cared for in my life.

I pause at the sound of the key in the lock, wondering if Chris will be with him. More often than not he isn't around, and I'm hoping today isn't an exception.

Please don't be with him.

The door swings open and I pause, watching as Jace steps inside and drops his gym bag to the ground, then glances up at me with a smile. "Hey," he says, his voice warm.

I crane my neck. "Is Chris with you?"

He shakes his head. "He headed home after practice."

I bite my lip trying to hide my smile as I step forward, closing the space between us. Reaching up, I say nothing as I take his face in my hands and press my mouth to his.

He sucks in a breath, hesitating only a moment before his hands find the small of my back and he draws me in. My chest meets his, his lips patient against my own. It feels like a lifetime since I last had his mouth on mine, so when he draws back, I nearly cry at the distance. I know what I want, and I'm not stopping until I get it.

"You seem better today," he says, eyes twinkling.

"I woke up with no body aches, and no sore throat." I smile, unable to hide my enthusiasm. "Which means . . ." I walk my fingers up his chest to his neck. "I thought we could . . ."

He laughs and reaches out, grabbing my roaming fingers and kissing each one. "Brynn, we don't have to." I frown as he adds, "I mean, I want to. Fuck, I want to more than anything, but don't you want it to be . . . I don't know . . ." He rakes a hand through his hair while I clasp my hands around his neck, enjoying the sight of him fumbling for words. He's so rarely speechless, and it might be the cutest freaking thing I've ever seen. "Special? Or . . . something. I just don't want you to think you have to do anything you're not ready for just because—"

I press my fingers to his lips. "I want you."

His Adam's apple bobs, and I watch the movement before I cover it with my mouth, slightly nipping the soft skin with my teeth.

Jace groans. "Brynn . . ."

"I want you," I repeat, unashamed as I meet his gaze.

I'm not sure I've ever wanted anything more in my life. The last few days unwind in my mind like a ball of yarn: Jace taking care of me, bringing me soup, cough drops, and tea. Jace fussing over me and tucking me into bed. Taking my temperature and forcing me into a cool shower. His strong hands kneading my sore muscles. Long fingers raking through my hair, lulling me to sleep. The worry carved into the crease of his forehead. *Jace. Jace. Jace.* He's already infiltrated my head, but now he's in my heart, too. He's in every waking thought. Every breath I take. And now I want him inside me, too.

I slide my hands underneath his shirt, taking in the smooth, hot skin beneath my fingers. The muscles of his abdomen clench as I explore, my breath hot on his skin as I press a kiss to his collarbone.

He grunts, and I feel his resolve slip in that single sound. "Brynn, I'll wait for you," he says, his voice a whisper as he places his hands on my shoulders, as if it can stop my perusal of his body.

I shake my head and the movement causes my lips to skate over the top of his chest. I know he's worried I'm rushing into this. Maybe he thinks I feel pressured, considering his reputation. But I don't. Never once have I ever felt like Jace has asked something of me I don't want to give.

I pull back, meeting his fiery blue eyes, hooded with lust. My gaze flickers from his face and the restraint I see there to his chest, hugged by the soft cotton of his T-shirt, and then to his athletic shorts. I smirk as I reach out, curling my fingers into the waistband of his shorts.

"I want you, and unless you tell me otherwise, I'm going to have you, Taggart." I push them down, revealing black boxer briefs, then take several steps back, allowing me the chance to soak him in. I bite my lip, then back myself toward the bedroom. "I'll give you five seconds to refuse me."

"What about Teagan? We haven't—"

"Five, four—"

He exhales a rush of breath and frustration, his expression tortured as I continue to count. "Three, two—"

A growl, and then, "Fuck it."

He flies toward me, slamming my back into the wall beside the bedroom door.

I yelp in surprise as he presses his body to mine. I can feel his arousal against my leg as his mouth finds my neck, my jaw, skating toward my lips. "I've wanted you for so long," he says, his breath heavy against my skin.

"Since we first kissed?" I ask with a breathy sigh.

"Longer." His large hand slips beneath my shirt, covering my breast, and I moan while his words sink inside me like a promise.

Longer.

He's wanted me longer than the night I moved in here. Longer than I ever realized.

I pull away from his mouth for a moment, staring into his eyes as I try and catch my breath. "How much longer?" I ask, breathing heavily.

He grins, nipping at my lip. "How long is too long without making it creepy?"

"High school?"

He licks his lips, his gaze solely focused on my mouth. "Definitely throughout high school."

"But—"

"Every time you sassed me, I wanted to teach you a lesson."

"*Oh.*"

"You have no idea what you've been doing to me all this time, Cupcake."

I take another moment to absorb his words, marveling at the fact this beautiful man has wanted me for years, and all the while I was clueless.

Slowly, and with his eyes on me, I peel off my shirt and drop it on the ground, followed by my jeans before he pushes me into the bedroom. We stumble and fall to the bed, a tangled knot of limbs and seeking hands. I roll over him, shoving him to his back and take a moment to cup his face in my hands, staring down at him, before I slowly lower my head and brush my lips over his. My fingers seek the hem of his shirt and I tug. He leans up, sliding it off while the muscles of his abdomen coil and clench in sharp definition.

His hands clutch my hips, drawing me to him while my thoughts scatter. His mouth presses hard aching kisses against my own as his hands move and shift, tracing the soft curves of my body like he's trying to study them, like he's playing a symphony over my skin.

His fingers skim over my back until they meet the clasp of my bra, and he removes it before he rolls me over and I'm lying on the mattress. Lips skim down my neck to the dip of my collarbone, until I feel the hot gust of breath over my breasts. His hands cup me perfectly, followed by his hot mouth.

My breathing falls apart, lost in sensation.

Part of me can't believe this is real. That Jace is here with me. That the person I'm falling for, the one I fit perfectly with has been right in front of me all along.

I arch my back, pulling him to me and I brush my lips over his, slanting my mouth. His tongue darts out then retreats, and he nips my lip, tongue flicking over it, sucking on it.

A quiet groan rumbles in my chest, but he absorbs it with his mouth.

This kiss, it's enough to make me lose my mind.

My nails dig into his back as he removes the remaining barriers between us. Gripping the lace below my belly button, he slides it off.

Heat fists low in my belly, and time blurs. The world around me fades into nothing. It's just him and me. Our mouths and hands. Breath and beating hearts. Each of us exploring and tasting and *feeling*.

His mouth never leaves mine as I hear the opening of his nightstand drawer, then the crinkling of foil.

I move my mouth to his neck, nipping the skin below his jawline as he readies himself for me. When he's finished, he lowers himself onto me and takes my mouth once more.

I cling to him as he rocks into me, finally taking me fully.

A gasp escapes my lips, and I breathe his name. Sensation follows, building inside me. We're all hands and trembling sighs, skin and touch, and shaking limbs. Until all that's left is the glorious heat swelling and expanding inside of me as the love I feel for this man takes a hold in my chest. This person I thought I hated.

And when I let go, the last vestiges of my walls crumble, and he joins me. But instead of crashing, I fall on a crescendo, followed by a soft wave washing me to shore while he cradles me in his arms. His kisses turn soft and sweet, an ode to everything we just shared, and I realize there's no turning back now. Whatever doubts I might've had about us vanish, and all that's left behind is the complete and utter certainty his arms are exactly where I'm meant to be.

CHAPTER 30

BRYNN

I LIE ENVELOPED IN Jace's arms, my body languid, limbs sore, and lips swollen. I'm tracing little circles on his chest when my stomach rumbles in the silence, and he laughs. "I take it you're hungry?"

"Very." I yawn, stretching my arms overhead before I push myself up into a seated position, holding the sheet over my chest, suddenly feeling shy.

Jace's gaze drifts to the cotton, and he slowly slides it down. "Don't hide from me, Cupcake," he whispers as he leans into me and skates a soft kiss across my lips.

"What time is it?" I ask against his mouth.

"Time for me to take you again."

By the time Jace and I tumble out of bed, it's after two o'clock.

I laugh as I watch him pull on his clothes, then reach a hand out to me. "Something funny?"

I shake my head. "Just thinking about how unlikely of a couple we are."

Did I just call us a couple?

I wait to gauge his reaction, but he just smirks, lifting a hand to touch the heat rising to my cheeks. "Not so unlikely." He pecks me on the mouth. "But I do like the label, Cupcake." When he leans back, he winks and turns for the door. "I'll be in the kitchen."

I exhale a shaky breath once he's gone, then close my eyes and flop back in the bed, a giant smile spreading over my face.

Pure bliss. That's what being with Jace feels like.

After a few minutes of replaying the past few hours with perfect precision in my mind, I change and run a brush through my hair before I pad my way to the kitchen in my bare feet.

Jace stands at the stove in nothing but the pair of athletic shorts I removed earlier, and I take a second to praise the Griffins' athletic program while simultaneously marveling at the fact this man is mine.

"I hope omelets are okay." He glances up at me and pours the beaten egg mixture into the skillet where it sizzles.

And he's cooking for me.

"Better stop looking at me, Cupcake, or you won't get to eat."

I bite my lip to hide my smile and idly wonder if dying from happiness is actually a thing.

I make my way to one of the stools at the counter and take a seat as I watch him, the muscles flexing in his arms as he works. Once he's done, he plates our omelets together with some toast, then sits beside me and we dig in.

"This is amazing," I say, between bites.

"It's one of my specialties, but don't get too excited, I don't have many," he jokes, but after a minute, Jace drops his fork and pushes his half-eaten omelet away from him.

I frown. "You're not hungry?"

"What are we gonna tell Teagan?" he blurts.

"Well, I don't recommend telling him about the last few hours." I chuckle, but I see he's serious, so I drop my smile. "You're that worried about what he'll think?"

He nods, a muscle flickering in his jaw. "He wanted me to protect you, to watch after you and I . . ." He shoves a hand roughly through his hair. "Fuck. I'm not sure this is what he had in mind." He laughs dryly.

"I'll explain it to him." I reach out and take his hand. Now that I know more about his parents and how little of a support system he had growing up, I fully grasp his fears and concerns more than ever. Losing Teagan or my family would be like losing his own. "I'll tell him how it just sort of happened. He'll understand."

He glances down at our intertwined hands. "And if he doesn't?"

I lean toward him and kiss him. "Then we'll make him."

CHAPTER 31

BRYNN

I HURRY TO THE *basement below the school gym and enter the locker room with the note from my secret admirer clutched in my hands. Light from the hallway spills inside, illuminating the metal lockers for brief seconds before snicking shut and plunging me into darkness.*

The dance is nearly halfway over. The bass from the music in the gym fills the darkened space, matching the rapid beat of my heart.

Maybe I'm a romantic or just foolish, I'm not sure which, but when I started getting anonymous notes from a secret admirer nearly three weeks ago, I felt flattered. Some of them were cute rhymes or poems, but most of them were simply an ode to all the things they liked about me: the sound of my laugh, my lips, hair, eyes, or the way I carry myself in the halls. Each one was a mini declaration. Each one sent a shockwave straight to my heart.

So when I received the note today at school, asking me to meet him in the locker rooms during the dance at half past ten, I couldn't resist.

Finally, I would get to meet him and take his hand in mine. Maybe even kiss his lips and share a dance with him.

I wonder who he is, if I sit beside him in class. Maybe I talk to him every day. Or maybe he's never even mustered the courage to say hello. He could be a sophomore like me, or an upperclassman. I have no idea, but the suspense is killing me.

I'm nearly vibrating with excitement by the time I carefully cross the locker room floor, my heels echoing against the hard tile.

I can't see anything, and I have no idea where the light switch is. For the first time tonight, I wish I hadn't left my phone in the car, but I didn't want to worry about looking after it all night.

I can barely see my hand in front of my face as I spread my arms out, feeling my way, until I meet the cold, hard metal surface of the lockers and decide to turn back for the door. There has to be a light switch somewhere, and I'm guessing that's where I'll find it.

I feel my way, but quickly realize at some point I've turned around, as my hands meet the cool porcelain of what feels like a sink.

Shit.

I hear the creak of a door behind me, so I turn my head, listening carefully as it echoes shut. Maybe I can follow the sound to the front of the locker room?

The snick of a lock follows, and my head lifts at the same time my stomach plummets.

That must be him . . .

I swallow, my pulse accelerating as I call out, "Hello?" The sound of my voice ricochets off the walls as I wait for him to answer.

Nothing.

Fear creeps down my spine as I call out, "Can you turn the light on? I can't—"

A rough hand clamps over my mouth while the other presses something hard and cold against my throat.

"If you make a sound, I'll slit your throat," a low, quiet voice skates over my skin. I try to place it, but the shock of fear is making it hard to think.

I take shallow breaths, almost afraid to breathe, to move, as the hand clamped over my mouth slowly releases me while the other one stays in place, holding the hard object I assume is a knife against my windpipe.

If you make a sound, I'll slit your throat.

I swallow, cringing at the hot breath in my ear and the sour scent of booze.

The telltale sound of a zipper pierces the quiet, and I can feel him grappling with his pants. The knife tightens. Hips grind into me from behind and I whimper.

His free hand reappears, groping my breasts over top of my dress while a tear slides down my cheek.

My body begins to shake as I squeeze my eyes shut, letting him feel me up.

Thoughts ping-pong in my brain.

Do I fight?

Do I run?

If you make a sound, I'll slit your throat.

I sob and I can feel the sharp edge of the blade as he squeezes my breast so hard I have to bite my lip to stop from crying out. It's a subtle warning to be quiet, one I heed before he slides the groping hand down my side to my leg and to the hem of my dress.

I softly whimper as he roughly yanks the hem of my dress up around my waist.

He planned this, *I think*. To lure me.

He never liked you.

Stupid, stupid girl.

My heart is a racehorse inside my chest, pounding so hard I think it might break through my ribs.

He yanks my underwear down, his breath, stale with alcohol skitters across my ear, and when his fingers find me, I recoil at his touch, but there's nowhere to go.

My mind races as his hand disappears until he removes the one in front of my throat and places it on my back instead, shoving me over the sink in one hard, fluid motion.

My mouth hits against the metal faucet and my eyes water and burn from the sharp stab of pain. The metallic taste of blood fills my mouth as I grip the sides of the sink, bent over, thoughts spiraling.

His hips are still pressed firmly against me, pinning me in place where I feel him now, bare on my backside as I realize what's about to happen, what he's about to do.

I hear the crinkle of foil behind me, and panic claws at my chest, a beast ready to be let free.

The hand holding the knife has dropped to my abdomen. It's still there, but it's loose as he struggles behind me.

With a grunt, he moves his hips ever so slightly; I rear my elbow back as hard as I can, aiming for where I feel his breath against me, hoping like hell I don't miss.

The blow to my elbow brings fresh tears to my eyes. It cracks against something hard, and he cries out. Something clatters to the ground, and I pray it's the knife.

Regardless, I know I only have precious seconds, as I spin around and start to run.

A hand clamps down on my arm, but I shove at him, punching and kicking and screaming. Something catches on my strap, and it rips. This time, when his hand finds my mouth, I sink my teeth into his fingers.

His blood-curdling scream pierces the quiet, and he yanks his hand away at the same time I release him and run.

The heels of my shoes clack on the hard floor, but I don't dare take the time to remove them as I feel around the room.

I sob, cursing myself for making a sound as I hear footsteps shuffle behind me.

Searching the wall, I hurry, my fingers trailing over the cold metal surface of the locker room, then the wall, then . . . a door handle.

I feel for the lock, finding it just as the footsteps grow louder behind me.

I flick it open as I scream and burst outside into—

"Brynn. Brynn, wake up!" the familiar voice cuts into my consciousness, pulling me from sleep. "You're having a bad dream."

My eyes fly open, and I wake with a start to find Jace wrapped around me.

Moonlight filters through the window of his bedroom, his features twisted in concern.

I try to catch my breath, and for a moment, I wonder if I'm feverish again before I realize my skin is slick with perspiration because I was dreaming, having a nightmare. *The* nightmare.

I haven't dreamed about that night in a long time. Maybe I'm due. But I wish it could've happened when I was alone and not wrapped up in Jace's arms.

I sit up in bed, and as if sensing my need, Jace hands me a cool glass of water.

My hands tremble as I bring it to my lips and down it in seconds. When I hand it back to him, my heart races as I try to calm down from the fear rattling around in my brain.

"What the hell was that?" he asks.

"I just need a minute." I close my eyes, inhaling through my nose as I push on the edges of the memories.

After a few minutes, I open them again. I have every intention of telling him it was just a bad dream, nothing more. But the way he's staring at me tells me he knows there's more, and I wonder if he can read my thoughts when he says, "That wasn't just a dream, was it?"

Or maybe he just knows me too well.

I look into his eyes, a lie on the tip of my tongue. It would be all too easy to shrug it off, to tell him it was nothing. That I have night tremors. They started when I was fifteen.

But for some reason, I can't bring myself to do it.

"I have something to tell you," I say, my voice thick. "Something only Teagan knows. Something *bad*." My voice quivers on this last word.

He nods, taking my hand in his, and his touch is so gentle, my face crumples. Tears fall from my eyes, unbidden and so quickly I have no idea how they got there. Fear and shame wash over me, almost as strong as the day in the locker room when I experienced them firsthand. It's almost enough to keep me quiet. Until I stare into Jace's kind eyes, filled with worry, and realize that I love him.

I'm not sure when or how I fell, but at some point, I stopped keeping track and holding back. Loving someone means taking a giant leap of faith that you won't get hurt and hoping those feelings will be returned, so I inhale a shaky breath and freefall.

"It started a few weeks before Sadie Hawkins sophomore year . . ."

It's been three weeks since Jace and I consummated our relationship. And two weeks since I told him my deepest, darkest secret. Afterward, he held me, whispering words of reassurance in my ear.

You're not alone.

I'm sorry I never knew.

I wish I had.

But I'm here for you now.

If you ever need anything . . .

If you want to talk . . .

God, Brynn, you're so strong.

You're the hero of your story.

Incredible . . .

Brave . . .

But I don't ever want you to shoulder this alone.

And as it turns out, his comments that night outside the locker room weren't for me. He'd made zero assumptions about my appearance and whereabouts. Instead, I turned my fear and shame from that night into paranoia and incorrectly assumed he was talking to me, when in reality, he was really talking to Graham, messing with him over his crush on Mackenzie.

To think all this time, I hated him . . .

I glance in the closet one last time, and once I'm satisfied I've packed everything, I turn to the dresser and open the top drawer. It's hard to believe the summer semester is already over. I can remember moving in here like it was yesterday.

"I can't believe I spent my last night here," I say as I grab a handful of underwear and put them in my bag.

"Excuse me. It definitely was *not* your last night." Jace sits, propped up in bed by pillows. He's shirtless and has one arm tucked behind his head, completely at ease.

"I might be convinced to have the occasional sleepover," I tease.

"Occasional, huh?" he asks, bolting upright, yanking my arm, and pulling me onto the bed.

I yelp in surprise, then giggle as he tickles my sides, but I manage to roll out from under him and back to the dresser, pointing a finger at him. "Behave!"

He grimaces as if the thought leaves a bad taste in his mouth. "You never know, you might get another deranged roommate and need to stay here again."

"Are you hoping for that?" I laugh.

"I mean . . ."

I lunge forward and pinch his chest as he barks out a laugh. "Of course not. I hope you have an amazing roommate, Cupcake," he says, smoothing a hand over my hair. "You deserve nothing but the best."

"Oh, yeah?"

"Yeah." He places a finger under my chin and tips my face toward his as he grazes a trail from my mouth to my jaw.

"I need to finish packing," I say, then push away from him, leaving him to pout.

"Why is Teagan picking you up, anyway?" he asks.

"Because we hate each other, remember?"

Jace grunts, and I can't help but think he's so freaking cute when he's sulking.

I toss my underwear back in the drawer and drop down to the bed, crawling on my hands and knees toward him as my gaze rakes over his bare chest. "And since we agreed to wait until after football season to tell him, we have to keep acting like mortal enemies."

He cups my ass with his hands. "Fuck. It's going to be hard to keep my hands off you while we're home."

"You'll manage," I say with a grin.

"What if I don't?" He buries his face in my neck, breathing me in. I swear I'll never get used to this man wanting me this much. "I might spontaneously combust from the restraint. It's a thing, look it up."

I snort. "We'll make sure to get some moments alone."

He lifts his head, and our eyes lock. "Promise?"

"Promise," I whisper against his lips before I brush a soft kiss over his mouth. "Now, I need to pack. Stop distracting me." I pull away, and he groans again as he flops back on the bed.

I roll my eyes. *So dramatic.* Though I secretly love it.

I place the last of my underwear in my suitcase while Jace watches me with eagle eyes. "Is your mom still supposed to be there when you get in?" I ask.

"That's the plan." He sinks a hand into his hair. "I'm still shocked she agreed to delay the start of her trip so she can see me. It's gonna be weird, the two of us actually spending time together."

I flash him a smile. A little over a week ago, I encouraged him to tell his parents how he felt about them being gone when he returned home, and to ask if one of them could hang around for his arrival at the end of summer, but I never really expected him to do it. I was so proud when he did, and even happier at the positive outcome. Though she seemed shocked by the request, his mother agreed to delay leaving with his father by a couple days, so she could at least have a day or two with Jace before flying out to meet him in Denmark.

I glance over at him in the following silence, noting the way he's worrying his lower lip with his teeth, and my chest squeezes. "Hey, it's gonna be great," I say, hoping I'm right.

"Yeah, yeah, I know," he replies as if trying to convince himself.

"And then afterward, you're gonna come hang at our house for a couple days, right?"

He nods. "As long as your parents won't mind."

"Are you kidding me? My parents love you. Sometimes I think my mom loves you even more than me."

He points to himself. "I mean, can you blame them?"

I roll my eyes. "Teagan will love having the extra time to spend with you, too."

Jace winces. "But don't you feel guilty keeping this from him?" He rubs the back of the neck. "I hate it. We're brothers. We don't hide things from each other. I mean, shit, I used to tell those guys everything. The stuff we've shared and gone through . . ."

My shoulders slump. "I know. I don't love it, but we decided it's easier this way, right?"

He nods, his mouth a firm line. "I know he's going to be pissed at first, and we only get a couple weeks off before we start official workouts for the fall season. I don't want to be the reason his head isn't in the game. But as soon as football is over in the fall, we'll tell him."

I zip up my suitcase and cross the room, sit on the edge of the bed, and I grab his hand. "We'll drive out to Maryland together if you want."

Jace exhales, staring down at our intertwined fingers. "I don't know. I think maybe it needs to just be me. Man-to-man."

"Okay." I nod. "Whatever you want."

He lifts my hand and kisses my palm. "We just have to keep him from finding out in the meantime."

CHAPTER 32

JACE

THE DRIVE HOME GOES surprisingly fast, despite not having Brynn with me. After she left for the dorms to say goodbye to Charlotte and Samantha, where she also planned on waiting for Teagan to pick her up, I headed out. Without her there, it felt kind of depressing, and there was no use in hanging around in an empty apartment when I'd see both her and Teagan soon enough.

The miles pass quickly, and before long, I pull into the long curve of our driveway. I park my truck in front of the huge garage, rather than inside it. Dad keeps his Porsche in there when he's away on trips, and even though our garage is huge, I'd rather not hear about how I parked too close to his second child.

I hop out, staring at the sprawling brick exterior of the home I grew up in. Inside, it's filled with more rooms than we need. All of them are professionally decorated and outfitted with only the best furnishings. Most of the space sits untouched, the furniture as pristine as the day it was purchased. Outside, the lawn is lush and green, the landscaping perfectly manicured. I know without checking, the pool out back is as clear and blue as the sky above me.

Such a waste for a family that's never in it.

I exhale and head for the front of the house, a strange mixture of wariness and hope at spending time with my mom spreading through my body. Part of me is hoping Harriet will be here, though it's not her typical day to work. Still, it would be nice to see her, and I make a mental note not to spend every waking moment at the Nichols' household after my mom leaves so I can catch up with her while I'm home.

For some reason, opening up to Brynn about my parents made me look at Harriet in a whole new light. I always enjoyed having her around, but I hadn't realized until recently how much her presence in my life meant to me.

I walk up the flagstone path and use the pin pad to enter the combination, and when the lock clicks open, I head inside. The same cavernous foyer greets me. A console table with a vase of fresh flowers sits in the middle. To the right, the sprawling staircase winds out of sight like a set of wooden teeth.

My shoes squeak on the floor as I walk through it and head for the kitchen where I'm greeted with dozens of black cabinets, a massive island, and marble countertops. I lean against the island, contemplating what to do with myself while I wait for my mother. If she's on time, I still have another hour until she gets home.

On a whim, I head to the refrigerator and fling the door open, pleased when I see more than a dozen containers of food, each labeled with yesterday's date. A yellow sticky note clings to the outside of one of them, and when I pluck it off, I read:

> *You look like you lost weight! Better eat. Besides, you probably need a break from all that cafeteria food I know you've been consuming.*
>
> *Enjoy.*
>
> *Harriet*

With a laugh, I pull out the first container to find my favorite chicken burritos. I know how much Harriet loves to feed me, and I love to eat, so it works out.

After I heat up some food and eat until I'm stuffed, I decide to head outside to the pool. It's beautiful out, sunny and hot; the perfect day for a swim and a good way to waste the rest of the time until my mom gets here.

I open the French doors and pad my way out to the stained concrete surrounding the pool. I set my cell phone down on one of the little tables beside the lounge chairs and remove my T-shirt, opting to swim in my athletic shorts rather than take the time to change into swim trunks. The water is cool and silky over my skin as I dive in and begin to swim some laps.

My brain races as I glide through the water. I think about Brynn and what she's doing at this very moment. I imagine she's on her way home with Teagan and think about how awkward it will be talking about me as if nothing's changed between us. I wonder how hard it will be for us to play it cool in front of her family. Part of me is glad to have a couple days to prepare. Keeping my hands off her is going to take a lot of restraint. Acting too friendly might be enough reason alone to arouse suspicion. Falling back into our old roles won't be easy, but I can't stand the thought of simply avoiding her these next two weeks, so I'm left with little choice but to put my acting shoes on and pray for the best.

After I'm sufficiently exhausted and my muscles tired, I push up out of the pool and head to the pool house, taking a towel from the stack Harriet keeps there and wrapping it around my waist. I wander back to the table where my phone is and check the time. It's half past one, which means my mother's late.

I frown but try not to let it get to me. She's never been punctual, so I'm not sure why I expect her to be now.

Lying back in one of the lounge chairs, I decide to wait for her outside while I dry off. But sometime later I startle awake by the sound of a lawn mower next door, and realize I fell asleep. I check the time again and see almost another hour has passed, so I rise from the chair and head inside.

Maybe she got here, saw me sleeping, and didn't want to wake me?

I find no sign of her downstairs, so I take my bags up to my room, then quickly shower the chlorine from my skin and change. By the time I'm finished, she's still not here, and she's nearly three hours late.

A sinking in the pit of my stomach tells me she's not coming, but I don't want to believe it. I make a million rationalizations for why she's not here yet, for why she doesn't care. She hit traffic, ran into a friend which held her up. Maybe she had an emergency that delayed her getting home after driving Dad to the airport. She might have had an appointment that ran late. Maybe she stopped for groceries. Maybe I got the time wrong, and she's not late at all. But deep down, I know they're just excuses, and when my phone rings thirty minutes later and I see Mom's name on the screen, I know without a doubt why she's calling.

I steel myself as I answer, my spine stiff. "Mom, you're late."

I hear her answering huff on the other line. "Is that any way to greet your mother?" A staticky sound falls over the phone followed by the muffled sound of her voice as she speaks to someone in the background. Then she says to me, "I'm sorry, dear. I was just calling to see if you got in okay."

I clench and fight the urge to scream. "Mom, you're supposed to be here."

"Don't get prickly with me, Jace. You know how busy we are."

"You're not coming," I state, my throat tight.

Silence fills the line, and for a moment, I think I lost her until she clears her throat. "No. I'm sorry, but you know how much I hate flying alone, and the idea of renting a car by myself to meet your father in a foreign country is unpalatable. I just can't handle traveling by myself, and being a woman, it's unsafe, really. Just the other day, I was watching the news, and there was this story about a young woman who was . . ."

I stop listening. Nothing she says matters anyway. It's just the same old excuses, the same reasons for not being present, when in reality, it's because neither of my parents give a damn.

They don't care that it's been months since I've been home, and that after these two weeks, I probably won't be able to visit until the holidays. Then again, why should it matter? They'll probably take a Christmas trip, anyway.

"Sure, Mom," I say, interrupting her mid-sentence. "It's fine. I can fend for myself."

I always do.

Unable to listen to any more of her excuses, I hang up while she's still talking. It's something I never would've done before, too afraid to upset her, but if she doesn't care, why should I?

The first thing I do once the line goes dead is type out a text to Brynn.

ME: She's not coming.

BRYNN: Are you sure?

ME: Positive. Just got off the phone with her.

I wait, but she doesn't type anything else, so I sigh and stare out the window, wondering what to do with my time. The Nicholses aren't expecting me for another two days, and the last thing I want to do is impose on the time they have to spend with their children.

I should probably text the guys. See if anyone else is home yet and up for hanging out. After all, I haven't talked to them as much in the last few weeks, probably because it's hard to talk to the guys I'm used to sharing everything with while hiding the best thing that's ever happened to me from them.

With a sigh, I open my contacts when my phone starts to ring, and Brynn's name lights up the screen. Butterflies awaken inside my chest and the lump of emotion returns to my throat as I answer, pressing the phone to my ear. "Hello?"

"I'm sorry," she says, immediately.

A shot of warmth skates through my veins. "It's okay."

"No, it's really not, and you have every right to be pissed."

My throat tightens further, and I have to clear it to speak. "Are you guys home yet?"

"We just pulled in and I snuck up to my room with my bags, so I could call you."

I sigh and close my eyes. "I miss you."

"I miss you, too. Come here. You have no reason to stay there now, and I hate the thought of you in that big house all alone."

I laugh, but it falls flat. "This is my house, remember? I've been alone in it for most of my life."

"Jace, don't. Even if your parents don't show it, you have a million other people that love you. You know that, right?"

My eyes sting, forcing me to blink. What the fuck is wrong with me?

"You're not getting sappy on me are you, Cupcake?"

"Maybe you've changed me. It's your fault for kissing me on the couch that night."

"So you admit you liked it even though you stormed off in righteous indignation," I say, hearing the smile in my voice.

"Of course I did." I can practically hear her rolling her eyes through the line. "And then you had to go and be all sweet and sexy and . . . well, you only have yourself to blame for me going mushy on you."

My heart squeezes. "I'll take a mushy Brynn as long as I still get the feisty one."

"You can have any side of me you want."

I arch a brow and laugh. "Is that a promise?"

"Depends. At least come for dinner tonight. My parents love you, so you know they won't mind."

I groan, knowing she won't let up until I accept. "I know they won't *mind*, but they'd probably like some time with just you and Teagan before I come barging in. Your sisters probably want to hang with you, too."

I've been inserting myself into their family for years, so I'm not sure why the idea of doing so now feels like an intrusion, but it does.

Maybe because you're banging Brynn and keeping it from them?

"It's not like that, and you know it," Brynn says.

I pinch the bridge of my nose, unsure.

"Besides, *I* want you here. Doesn't that count for something? Come for me if not for yourself. *Please*?"

I sigh and bring a hand up to the tight spot in my chest because I can't resist a pleading Brynn. "Okay. I'll come for dinner and then we'll see." I hang up after promising I'll be over in an hour and exhale a lungful of air.

Ready or not, it's time to face Teagan. I only hope I can look him in the eye, knowing I'm lying straight to his face.

CHAPTER 33

JACE

T HE MINUTE I PULL into the Nichols' driveway, my phone pings.

I chuckle under my breath, then step out of my car with a groan.

Pretending this girl doesn't completely own me in every way is going to be the death of me.

I head toward the side of the house where I usually enter without knocking, but I find myself pausing by the door, struck with a stab of awkwardness.

Just because Brynn and I are hiding our relationship doesn't mean I need to feel weird around the Nicholses now.

Shoving it aside, I enter to the scent of whatever Nikki is cooking, and kick off my shoes on the worn rug in the mudroom. The Nichols' home is smaller than mine, and infinitely homier, with framed family photos gracing nearly every wall, fluffy mismatched pillows on the couches in the living room, soft throw blankets, and scrapes on the wooden floors, probably a result of lots of rough and tumbling when we were kids. If Nikki is at home, there's guaranteed to be a candle burning on the chunky coffee table, and more often than not, music's playing when some sort of sporting event isn't on the television. Homemade cookies or baked treats are almost always pushed on you the moment you walk through the door. It's all of these things and more that I love so much about being here, and as I move past the washer and dryer and walk through the big barn slider door into the kitchen, it dawns on me just how much I've missed it.

Brynn's wide smile is the first thing I see when I enter the brightly lit kitchen and I match it with one of my own before my gaze shifts to find Teagan, one brow raised as he glances between us. "Hey, man, I thought you said you weren't coming?" He heads for me and claps me on the back.

"What's up, man?" I tilt my chin. "It's been a while," I say, trying to tell my racing heart to calm the fuck down. I didn't even think about the fact Teagan wasn't expecting me before I rushed over here. Normally, I would've texted him first. "Uh, yeah." I shrug, trying to act natural. "You know my folks."

"Ah, Elizabeth and Donald strike again, huh? Where they off to this time? Belize? Santorini? The Galapagos?"

"Teagan," Brynn scolds.

My gaze darts to her at the same time Teagan's brow creases, and butterflies swarm my chest. Defending me is not something old Brynn would do.

"Worse," I say with a roll of the eyes, then worry I'm trying too hard. "Denmark. Like they haven't been there before."

Teagan grunts.

"You know you're always welcome here," Nikki says as she leaves her perch at the stove to place a warm hand on my arm. "I'm just finishing up here, but there are fresh rolls and honey butter to snack on in the meantime, if you're hungry."

"You always did know the way to a man's heart." I wink at her, and she laughs.

"Why do you think I married her?" Joe Nichols calls out from somewhere down the hall.

"I see some things never change." Nikki flaps a kitchen towel at me. "You're just as big of a flirt as you've always been."

"Ew, Mom. You're the one flirting," Brynn says as she proceeds to fake gag.

"What can I say? Your mom has impeccable taste," I say.

Teagan snorts and heads for the fridge while Brynn makes a show of scoffing.

Nikki chuckles, then turns back to the stove while Brynn flashes me a thumbs up before Teagan turns back around.

"Want something to drink?" Teagan asks from the depths of the fridge.

"Sure. I'll get it," I say as I stand beside him and pull two glasses from the cupboard, then proceed to pull a Coke and lemon out of the fridge. I pour two glasses and freeze mid-lemon-squeeze when I realize my mistake.

Swallowing, I feel the heat of Teagan's gaze boring into the side of my head.

"Thanks," Brynn says, rudely swiping a glass out from under me, then turning to Teagan. "I've trained him well. It only took a few dozen times of busting his balls for him to find some manners." She flashes me a meaningful look, and I'd kiss her for saving my ass if I knew it wouldn't be the nail in the coffin. "You should've seen how long it took me to get him and his roommate to leave the toilet seat down." She shakes her head. "*Animals. . .*"

Nikki laughs while I shrug guiltily, but Teagan only seems slightly mollified by her response. The stiff set of his shoulders remains even when his frown dissipates.

"Right," he says, through slightly narrowed eyes.

I tense under his gaze moments before screaming erupts down the hallway, followed by the pounding of feet so loud, it sounds like a stampede.

Trista and Sabel come crashing toward me and wrap me up in a hug, their short arms around my waist. "Jace, will you have a tea party with us?" Sabel asks.

"Please?" Trista says, clasping her hands in prayer.

"It depends. What kind of tea are we drinking?"

Sabel whispers, "Trista snuck a Mountain Dew from the little fridge in the garage."

"I heard that," Nikki calls out. "And we're eating in five minutes."

Sabel's cheeks redden as she tilts her head, waiting for my answer.

"Tell you what. Since we're eating soon, why don't we wait until after dinner? Then we'll have more time."

Sabel purses her lips as if she's considering my suggestion. "Sounds like a deal. Come on, Trista, let's go pour the tea!" With a squeal, they turn and head for the stairs that lead to their shared bedroom. I know when they drag me there later, they'll have a full table ready for me, complete with plastic teacups and pilfered soda and snacks.

"By the way, I hope you kids are up for it because I'm planning a big barbecue for next week," Nikki informs us. "Teagan's already let the boys know, but we have family and neighbors coming, too."

"Noted," Brynn says.

"Don't sound so excited." Nikki laughs. "You know, if you have anyone special who you met back at school, you're more than welcome to invite them."

"Mom." Brynn glares.

"What?" she shrugs. "You didn't meet any nice boys over the summer?"

I wait until Teagan turns his attention to Brynn, then offer her a devilish smirk and mouth, *"Did you?"*

She purses her lips to hide a smile. "Well, the first guy I talked to ended up being a real jerk, so after that I kind of swore off trying to get to know anyone new." Brynn steps forward and grabs a sweet roll from the basket on the island.

"Oh." I don't miss the disappointed edge of Nikki's tone. "So, no one else caught your eye? I could've sworn when I spoke to you these last few weeks you sounded, I don't know, happier. Or maybe brighter is a better word?" Nikki shakes her head, then turns back to the pan on the stove and adds some seasoning. "I even told your father I'd bet money on the fact that you met someone."

"Nope." Brynn shakes her head and slathers her roll in honey butter and crams a bite in her mouth. "No one."

I roll my lips in an effort to hide my smile.

Across from us, Teagan crosses his arms over his chest and leans back against the refrigerator. "Nah. Brynn would've told me if she was seeing someone, right?" he asks, though his tone tells me he's not so sure.

Brynn swallows. "Totally."

Her eyes flicker to mine, and I clear my throat. "I'm pretty sure she's telling the truth," I say, hoping to sell the lie without sounding like I'm pushing. "I mean, she spent a lot of time at the apartment these last few weeks. I don't see how she could've been dating someone."

"How much time?" Teagan's woolly gaze shifts to mine.

Shit.

"Uh . . ." How much time is normal, and how much is too much? My brain fires on all pistons, but it's as though all my common sense has ground to a halt.

"May I remind you, it's you who suggested I move into the apartment. Why wouldn't I spend lots of time there?" Brynn chimes in.

Teagan shrugs, his expression sheepish. "You're right." He scratches his head, and I try to ignore the stab of guilt that follows.

"Hey, she did go on a blind triple date with her friends a few weeks back," I say, throwing it out there in both a brilliant stroke of genius to get him off our trail and to mollify my guilt.

Both the truth and a diversion. *You're welcome.*

"Oh, how did that go?" Nikki asks, heading to the cupboard for plates.

"Well, I hate to kiss and tell, but . . ." she says and my gaze darts to hers. I frown. "I might have received the hottest kiss of my life that night."

Teagan grimaces. "TMI."

Nikki's eyes sparkle. "Well, that sounds promising."

Brynn clasps her hands together and gives a coy little shrug. "Yeah, you never know. Might be something." She glances up at me from underneath thick lashes, and my body lights up like a fucking Christmas tree.

Luckily for us, Nikki pulls the attention away from us before Teagan catches the brief, heated exchange. "What about you, Jace? Any special ladies?"

When did Nikki become so nosy? I never noticed before.

"Oh, I don't know . . ." I hedge at the same time Teagan comes up beside me and claps me on the shoulder with a scoff.

"He's trying to be polite, Mom. Jace doesn't do relationships, so if there was a special girl it would be fleeting."

My gaze drills holes in the side of his smug face as he brushes past and heads toward his mother to grab the stack of plates from her hands.

"Thanks, dear," she says as she moves to the fridge. "I swear I had another bottle of dressing in here. Brynn, sweetie, can you grab one from the pantry?"

"Sure thing." Brynn shoots me a meaningful look as she backs away and turns.

I risk a glance at Teagan who sets the last plate down before he heads to the utensil drawer to grab the silverware, while I try to come up with a reason to join Brynn in the pantry.

My gaze scans the table, the island, and shifts to the kitchen counter where I zero in on the wire napkin holder. "Oh, hey, You're out of napkins." I cross the room to the empty wire basket and lift it up, waving it around like, *See, evidence!* "I'll go grab some."

Without waiting to see if anyone even acknowledges my exit, I turn and make a beeline for the walk-in pantry. It's just around the corner, behind the kitchen, and adjoins the mudroom. The second I step inside, Brynn wastes no time and throws her arms around my neck, drawing me in for a kiss.

"We probably have one minute before Teagan's done setting the table and our absence draws attention," I say against her lips.

Behind me, she quietly shuts the pantry door, and the automatic light sensor clicks off.

I reach out, cupping her face in my hands as she presses her body flush with mine. "Do you have any idea how hard it is not being able to kiss you when I want?"

"I don't know," she says, her voice husky. "You might need to show me."

With a groan, I lower my mouth to hers and push her back against the wooden shelves. The kiss is urgent, neither of us taking our time because we know we only have precious seconds, minutes if we're lucky.

My hands slide up her sides, dipping beneath the hem of her shirt as I angle my head further and part her mouth with my own, and the world beyond fades.

I forget about my mother breaking her promise.

I forget the sense of loneliness while I walked around my empty house.

I forget about Teagan just outside, or Nikki preparing for dinner, or Joe and the girls hovering somewhere nearby.

I forget about everything except me and Brynn and her magic mouth.

Her hands tighten around the back of my neck as she sinks deeper into the kiss. A groan rumbles in the back of her throat, encouraging as I nip at her lower lip.

"Where the heck did they go?" Teagan calls out, sounding like he's only feet away.

I spin Brynn around so I'm standing directly behind her, and quickly swipe the bottle of dressing off the shelf, pretending to be reaching for it up above when Teagan flings the door open.

"Found it!" I say victoriously as I lower my hand and show her the dressing. Turning, I glance over at my shoulder. "Oh. Hey, man. Brynn couldn't find the dressing even though it was right in front of her face."

I roll my eyes for good measure, but I'm not sure he's buying it.

Teagan stares at us through narrowed slits, his gaze bouncing between us. "Why was the door closed?"

"It was?" Brynn and I ask at the same exact time.

We glance at each other, and I snort out a laugh while her cheeks burn a deep shade of red.

"You're acting weird," Teagan points out.

"I am?" I ask, trying to keep a straight face. *Don't show your cards, Taggart.*

Teagan scowls at us one last time before he turns on his heel and heads for the kitchen, calling out, "Dinner's ready."

Dinner goes smoothly, without any more blunders or close calls. Teagan and Brynn carry the conversation, talking about their classes and what awaits them in the fall. Mostly, I stick to silence whenever possible because it seems like the safest bet at this point, even when football becomes the topic of conversation.

By the time I push my plate back, I'm already tired of the charade and dying to find a way to get Brynn alone.

"Wanna shoot some hoops like old times?" Teagan asks, and when I glance at him, I can't help but feel like this is a test.

I shrug, a casual lilt to my voice as I answer. "Winner gets double dessert?"

"You're on." He grins. "Dessert is turtle brownies."

I groan. Nikki's turtle brownies are my favorite.

"Sure, just leave the women to clean up." Brynn scoffs.

I should make some smartass comment about a woman's place being in the kitchen; it's what I would've done before to get under her skin. But I stay mute, aware of Teagan's assessing gaze. I'm petrified to make a mistake.

I can't lose him. I glance around the table at the Nicholses, and think of my own home, empty and quiet. *I can't lose this.*

We rise from the table with a promise to the girls I'll only be a little bit longer. I follow closely behind as Teagan heads for the mudroom, my gaze lingering on Brynn as we pass.

We toe on our shoes, and Teagan grabs a ball from the garage as we head outside into the sunshine. The hot afternoon has cooled into a pleasant evening with a soft breeze. It's gorgeous out, the kind of night Teagan and I would normally spend hours messing around on their driveway court before taking it to the backyard with a football, or heading to Crow's Creek. But it's our first night home, which holds the implication we'll spend the night in. I'm hoping that also means I can bail and head to bed early. Turning in early means a reprieve from the guilt jangling inside my head like loose change.

Teagan dribbles the basketball toward the hoop. I remember the day we helped Mr. Nichols put it up, digging a hole for the metal post and pouring the concrete. We bugged him mercilessly for two days until he finally deemed it dry and safe to play.

A soft breeze ruffles my hair as Teagan turns to face me, still dribbling. He stares at me for a moment like he has something to say, casually crossing the ball between his legs in a figure eight, and tips his chin up. "You and Brynn seem to be getting along better?"

My heart pounds in time with the ball, but I shrug. "We were forced to live together for six weeks. It was bound to happen."

"Was it, though?" He narrows his eyes and passes the ball for me to check, whipping it to me with more force than necessary.

Sweat pricks the back of my neck. Did he see more than I thought when he opened the pantry door?

"Weren't you the one who suggested I bury the hatchet?"

His mouth twists. "Sure. But when you showed up unannounced today, Brynn didn't even bat an eye. Buried hatchet or not, the Brynn I know would've had something to say about that. I just find it . . . weird, that's all."

I nod slowly, trying to come up with some kind of excuse or explanation for why Brynn's hatred of me has cooled so drastically, but I come up short. My mind is blank. "Huh," I say, tossing the ball back to him. Apparently, I'm playing stupid. "I didn't notice."

Teagan dribbles, his eyes sharp. We start to play, and it might be my imagination, but the one-on-one game seems a little more intense than usual, a little more competitive.

Sweat beads my back, and my T-shirt clings to my chest as I check him, arms waving in the air, chest forcing him off his target. He backs up and fakes right while I go left, taking one to the hoop, then fist a hand in the air with a cry of victory.

I take my time. The rough surface of the ball meeting my palm. We face off, sneakers squeaking, pivoting, and turning before I overpower him and make a tough shot from the side corner.

Twenty minutes later, we're both panting and out of breath. It's a tied score, and since the next basket takes us to ten, whoever sinks one wins.

Teagan moves the ball to the top of the court. Meeting my eyes, he tries to fake me out, but I catch the movement in his waist and block him. The ball pounds on the pavement, and he tries again. I dart right, nearly swiping the ball. He desperately tries to get around me, but he can't, and when he goes for a three-point shot, I jump and catch the ball mid-air.

Teagan curses and I feel him at my back, wrenching my arm. For some reason it feels like we're fighting for more than dessert. But I want that damn brownie. I want Brynn.

Teagan manages to get in front of me and he darts at the ball. I cross hands, putting my hip into it and push him off. I find a rhythm, dribbling to the top of the court and down the center. Eventually, he'll let up and I'll find my opening. I can wait. I have patience for days.

"You wanna hear something crazy?" Teagan says, his breath labored.

"Trying to distract me?" I fake pump right, but he delivers an elbow to my ribs. The wind whooshes from my lungs, but somehow, I manage to hang onto the ball.

"For a moment in there"—Teagan tilts his head toward the house, and I use his temporary distraction as my chance to drive in for a layup—"I thought maybe there was something going on between you and Brynn."

My steps falter and I bumble the ball in my hands, making a terrible shot as I nearly fall on my ass. Stumbling, I right myself before my face eats the concrete, but not before Teagan rebounds the ball and dribbles it to the top of the court, then takes the shot, and sinks it.

I grunt as I straighten. I'm out of breath and my heart is pounding. But not from the game.

Teagan saunters closer, his eyes on mine as he comes to a stop in front of me and claps a hand on my back. "But then I thought, nah. The Jace I know, the one who's my best friend, forever a Rebel and my teammate, he would never do that to me."

forever a Rebel and my teammate, he would never do that to me."

CHAPTER 34

JACE

I LIE IN BED, staring at the ceiling of the Nichols' guest bedroom. When I was younger and used to sleep over, I always crashed on Teagan's floor. As we got older, and at Nikki's urging, I started sleeping in here instead. It's around that time the length of my stays increased from a day to several, sometimes even a week. And they never seemed to mind. Quite the opposite, actually. They made me feel like they *wanted* me here, which is more than I can say for my folks at home. It's not like I talked much about my parents' lack of involvement in my life. In fact, I guarded it like a secret, but I always got the feeling they knew. And this is how I repay them . . . by taking something that isn't mine, something I have no right to.

Brynn is too good for me. She's kind and sweet and smart. She's witty and fierce. One of the most resilient and beautiful creatures I've ever met. Anyone who can't see that Brynn is the total package is a fucking moron. It's no surprise she comes from a family that's every bit as amazing as she is. She's everything I'm not, and I don't need someone to tell me I don't deserve her to know it. Yet I took her anyway.

My stomach twists and I squeeze my eyes closed, trying to imagine what the Nicholses will think when they find out about us. Am I insane to imagine there's even a remote chance they might be happy for us? It's one thing to welcome me into their home as their son's friend. It's a whole other thing to accept me as their daughter's boyfriend.

And Teagan . . .

Is there any way on this planet it won't completely destroy my relationship with Teagan?

I blink my eyes open, breathing through the heaviness in my chest.

So much is at stake. Which is why Brynn and I have to be careful, stick to the plan. We'll come clean in the fall, after football season. With any luck, by then, Teagan will see a change in Brynn. He'll see she's thriving at school and is happier than ever, because I'll be sure as fuck to do everything in my power to make her happy. He'll have to accept us.

Sure, he might be angry at first, livid even. But he'll come around when he sees how good we are together. And the Nicholses will follow suit. Nikki has already said a million times she thinks of me as another son. That has to count for something, right?

I tell myself it'll be fine. It has to be. There is no other option. I only wish I didn't have to try so hard to convince myself.

A soft creaking sound draws my attention. My ears perk and I whip my head in the direction of the door to see a dark figure looming in the shadows.

For a moment, I think it's Teagan. He knows, and he's come to end me. When they flick the lock on the door, it only confirms this theory.

With my pulse pounding like a freight train barreling through my chest, I watch helplessly as they turn and step into the moonlight streaming from the window. An angel emerges; Brynn smiles, and my heart leaps into my throat as she creeps closer and climbs onto the bed, straddling me above the covers. She's wearing a canary-yellow camisole sleep set trimmed in white lace and she looks so good. There's a moment before I can even get enough breath to come to my senses, because Brynn sneaking in here is asking for trouble.

"What are you doing here?" I hiss, glancing at the now closed door as if to make sure no one saw her come in here.

She glances down at her hands, and I realize she's holding something. "I brought you a brownie," she says, offering me the cellophane-wrapped dessert. "Teagan's such a meanie. I can't believe he really wouldn't let you have one, but I know how much you love them and didn't want you to miss out."

My heart wants to melt, but it's too busy fighting for survival, afraid that at any moment, Teagan or her parents will come barreling into this room and bust us.

"Thank you," I say, taking it from her and placing it on the nightstand. "Later, when I'm not deathly afraid of getting caught and murdered in my sleep, I'm going to savor every bite."

Brynn chuckles and leans down to brush her lips over the edge of my jaw. "You're cute when you're jumpy."

Her hands wander to my shirtless chest and I grasp them in mine before they can head further south. "And you're frightening when you're brazen."

"Relax," she whispers. "It's almost one a.m. Everyone is asleep, and the door is locked, remember? No one can get in unless we let them in."

"We're not asleep," I point out before my second brain gets any ideas. "And it's called a key."

Brynn chuckles and presses into me as she stretches to reach my mouth. "You're also cute when you're nervous."

A half whimper, half groan escapes my chest.

"I missed you," she whispers against my lips before angling her head, slanting her mouth over mine while her fingers sink into my hair.

I resist for a solid thirty seconds before I can't take it anymore and I reciprocate. My hands find her waist, sliding up her back when she rocks against me, and I fight to remember why this is a bad idea.

"We shouldn't . . ."

"We should," she counters.

"But Teagan . . ."

She presses a finger to my mouth. "If you mention my brother's name again while I'm turned on and straddling you in bed, I might end you."

I nod, breathless, because she has a point. "Fair enough."

And I'm a weak, weak man because when she sinks back onto me and starts trailing her mouth down my neck to my chest, all my restraint goes out the window.

Flipping her over, I take her mouth with mine, showing her how much I care, showing her exactly how I feel about her as my hands slide down her torso beneath the waistband of her shorts. When she moans, I stifle it with my mouth.

I know I should stop. Restraint is my friend. This is too risky.

But when it comes to Brynn Nichols, I'm lost.

So rather than ask for permission, I'll beg for forgiveness.

BRYNN

I take a sip of my coffee and chase it with a bite of blueberry muffin, then groan. I forgot how good these were. Funny how you can be away from something and not think twice about it, but once you have it again, you wonder how you ever went without. I haven't had one of these muffins since the day before I left for summer semester at AU, but now I've reminded myself how absolutely amazing they are, and I'm not sure I can go all fall without one.

Or maybe I'm just super hungry. Maybe it was the middle of the night workout that spurred my appetite.

A smile snakes across my face at the thought.

"What's with you today?"

My head jerks at the sound of Teagan's voice. For a moment, I forgot about him, and I nearly choke on a blueberry.

Coughing, I feel my cheeks burn as I take a sip of my coffee, then meet his eyes. "Nothing. Sorry. Just forgot how much I loved these." I hold the muffin up as evidence.

It's not a lie.

Teagan grunts and takes a huge bite of his scone, eyeing me skeptically. "Still, something's with you. You seem . . ." He chews a minute longer waving a hand in the air as if trying to come up with the right word. "Different."

Shit.

I want to lie. Deflection is definitely the route to go, but Teagan knows me better than anyone. We're twins and the whole telepathy thing between us has always been strong. One way or the other, he's going to know something's up with me, and if I don't at least give him something, he'll go looking.

We don't want him looking.

"Well, actually . . . when I told Mom there weren't any boys at school, I wasn't 100 percent honest with her."

Teagan's eyes widen, and he reaches up to scratch the golden scruff over his jaw, as if needing a moment to absorb the thought of me liking a boy. "So, is it serious? Are you just dating? Hooking up?" He winces as if the latter causes him physical pain.

"I think it's serious. I mean, it's still pretty new obviously, so I don't want to get ahead of myself, but . . ." I pause a moment, trying to think of how I can describe it without showing my hand. ". . . it feels like we've known each other forever."

Teagan shakes his head and leans back in his seat. "I don't get it. Last we spoke, you swore off boys because of that douchebag—"

"Stanley."

"Whatever." He rolls his eyes. "How can you be serious about someone so quickly?"

I shrug. "It just sort of happened. I don't know. I don't want to say too much because it's new. That's also part of the reason I didn't mention it to Mom. You know how badly she wants me to find someone, and I don't want her getting excited just for me to let her down."

"You know she just wants you happy."

"Of course," I say, nodding. "But you know what I mean."

"Yeah, I do, but I don't want you to get hurt. You need to be careful."

I bite my lip. Suddenly, the melting whipped cream in my latte is fascinating. "I will, but I don't think you need to worry. He won't hurt me."

When he doesn't say anything right away, I risk a glance at him to catch his sour expression. "Who is he?"

"Huh?" I blink up at him as if I hadn't heard the question.

"Who is he?" he says, slower this time. "Is he another frat boy?" Teagan rolls his eyes. "I really hope not."

"No, he's not a frat boy," I say, hesitantly.

"Why didn't Jace tell me about him?"

Guilt shimmies under my skin like a splinter, and I grind my teeth against the pain. "Jace isn't my keeper, Teagan."

"Whatever. So, who—"

"Listen, can we just . . . let this drop for now?" I ask, my heart in my throat. "*Please.* It's new and he and I are just figuring things out. I don't even know where this is headed long term, but I promise he's a good guy, and I'm happy. Like, really happy, T. Happier than I've been in a long time."

His gaze searches mine, looking for any evidence contrary to what I'm saying. And when he doesn't find any, he nods, his mouth a tight line as he says, "Okay, Brynn. We'll do this your way for now. But if he hurts you, or you need something, I better be the first to know."

CHAPTER 35

JACE

BEFORE BRYNN CREPT OUT of my room at dawn, we decided it would be best to keep our distance this morning. We both need a break from the charade, especially since our acting skills are weak at best, and Brynn is overdue to spend some alone time with Teagan. Meanwhile, I need advice.

I have no idea how this conversation is gonna go, but I'm hoping an outside perspective from someone who knows all three of us will give me some direction. Mostly, I just want to make sure I'm doing the right thing by waiting to tell Teagan, and if anyone knows what it means to hold a stable relationship out of the five of us it's Knox.

His girl might've broken things off with him this summer, but they'd been together for three years, which is an eternity when you're only eighteen.

I exhale, trying to calm my nerves as I wait in one of the red vinyl booths at Mel's Diner. Lifting my cup of coffee, I take a sip when the bell on the door chimes, and I glance up to see Knox filling the doorway.

I offer him a little wave, and he heads my way. Standing, I slap him on the back and give him the once-over. "The summer looks like it's been good to you. What's up, man?"

He settles into the booth, taking the seat across from me. "Not much. Good to see you again. You went radio silent these last couple of weeks."

I nod, raking a hand through my hair. "Yeah, sorry. End of semester was crazy with finals and conditioning wrapping up. How are things down south?"

"Eh, as can be expected I guess," Knox says as he motions for the waitress to bring him a cup of coffee. "Got your text about Crow's Creek tonight. Is the whole gang gonna be there?"

"Of course."

"Damn. It'll be nice seeing everyone and catching up. Group chats just aren't the same."

"Agreed." I take a sip of my coffee, hating how awkward I feel with this secret weighing on my chest. It's like a ticking timebomb waiting to detonate. Still, I find myself stalling. I wait until the waitress delivers Knox's coffee and takes our orders before even considering broaching the subject of Brynn, and even then, I do so with barely restrained nerves.

"So, I have to be honest, man. I asked you to meet me for more than breakfast and catching up." I toy with the handle of my mug and the fist in my chest tightens.

Knox arches a brow, raising his own mug to his lips with one beefy arm. He takes a tentative sip, then says, "If you came to ask me to marry you, the answer is no. I don't swing that way."

I snort. "You know blondes are my type."

"Ah! So you came to ask for Teagan's hand in marriage. In that case, I give you my blessing."

I bark out a laugh. It feels good to shoot the shit with a member of our old crew, but then my smile fades as I realize I stand to jeopardize everything by having a relationship with Brynn if Teagan won't accept us. Will they take sides if this thing implodes?

I sober at the thought. "Whatever I say stays between us, right?" I ask, flicking a glance up to him.

Knox tips his chin, taking my mercurial mood in stride. "Of course. Talk to me, bro. What's going on?"

I drag a hand over my face, unsure of where to start. "Shit. I don't how to say this . . ."

Knox leans closer, whispering, "Did you get in trouble with a chick? Maybe take things too far when she was drunk or . . ."

I flinch and straighten. "What? Fuck no."

Is that what he thinks of me?

Is that what they all think of me?

My pulse pounds in my temples. I know I have a reputation, but I thought my friends knew me better than that. My encounters with women have never been anything short of consensual.

"Okay," he drawls like he doesn't believe me, and I have to admit, it's not giving me a whole lot of fucking confidence about where the direction of this conversation is heading.

"I'm just gonna come right out and say it since whatever you're thinking is clearly worse." I inhale, steeling myself for his reaction, then blurt, "Brynn and I are seeing each other."

Knox stares at me for a moment before he bursts out laughing. "Good one," he says, bringing his mug to his lips.

The blood drains from my face, and when I don't so much as crack a smile, he sobers.

"You're serious."

I nod.

His eyes widen before he whistles and sets his mug down. "How the hell did that happen?"

"I don't know. I mean, I think I've always had feelings for her, but I thought she hated me. I never imagined that might change. But then one thing led to another and . . ." I shrug.

"Are you just fucking or actually dating?"

I curse under my breath. "Seriously?"

"What?" He shrugs. "I think it's a fair question, all things considered."

In other words, considering the fact I'm notorious for not seeing a chick more than once.

"I care about her, man. Like really care about her. And I'm pretty sure she feels the same."

"Oh, *shit*," Knox bellows. "You're falling for her, aren't you?"

I glare at him, saying nothing, which only makes him tip his head back in hysterics.

Maybe this was a mistake.

"I'm glad you think this is funny, dude."

"Teagan's gonna kill you," he says between gasps for air.

"You think I don't know that?" I hiss. "That's why we're here." I wave between us with a jerk of the hand. "And I was *hoping* for some advice."

Knox sobers and shakes his head, his lips pinched. "Are you absolutely sure about her, man? I mean, there's no chance this is gonna fizzle out in a few weeks?"

I swallow, toying with my silverware. "Not on my end, no."

Knox blows out a breath as he stares at me. "Obviously you gotta tell him, man-to-man. He'll never respect you if you don't."

"That was my thought, too. We were gonna wait till after the fall season, you know, just so he's not distracted or worrying about her, but I was at their place yesterday and I think he's suspicious something's up. It got me wondering if maybe we shouldn't wait. If maybe we should come clean now."

"He's gonna be pissed either way. If you wait, he might be angrier that you lied for so long, but there's also the chance you might not have to tell him at all if things don't work out."

I grimace. As much as I hate hearing it, it's not like Brynn and I haven't said the same thing, but I hate the thought we might not work. "Right. That's what Brynn and I thought, too."

"And if you tell him before everyone goes back to school and he's not over it, then it'll fuck with your season *and* his."

I cross my arms over my chest. It sure as shit would mess with my game if my best friend wasn't talking to me. Not to mention the turmoil that kind of tension would cause for Brynn, so I know it would fuck with his, too. "Yeah, I agree. So, you think we're right for waiting?"

Knox nods. "Definitely."

"Then why does it feel like I have a fucking bowling ball sitting on my chest?"

Knox scoffs, avoiding my gaze, and I wonder if he's placating me. Maybe he thinks I'm a shitty friend. "Man, any time you have a secret this big which you're keeping from your brothers, it's bound to hurt."

The waitress delivers our food as his words settle in my gut like nails.

Seemingly unfazed, Knox picks up his fork and starts to dig in. "Either way, tonight is gonna be interesting. Damn bro, I'd hate to be in your shoes."

BRYNN

I haven't seen Jace since I left him in bed this morning, and if this is what withdrawal from my favorite human feels like, I hate it.

Even spending time with Teagan today, who up until this point used to be my favorite person, didn't ease the feeling.

After breakfast, Jace texted me and let me know he'd meet me at the party tonight, which was fine by me. If last night taught us anything, it was that pretending to be something we're not is harder than either of us thought it would be, so I'm in no rush to repeat the show.

I check my reflection in the mirror for the hundredth time, assessing my outfit. I'm wearing a pair of ripped cutoff jean shorts and a cropped top. Both show more skin than I'm used to, but I like how casual yet sexy they are. My first thought is what Jace will think, which is how I know I'm a goner.

Stepping out of my room and into the hall, I bump into Teagan. "You sure you're cool with going tonight?" he asks, and I can practically hear his skepticism.

"Of course. It'll be nice to see some familiar faces."

He stares at me for a beat as if assessing my answer before his gaze flickers down my outfit and he frowns. "And that's what you're wearing?" he blurts out.

"Yep." I glance down and spread my arms out. "Why? What's wrong with it?"

Teagan scratches his jaw, his gaze homing in on the sliver of skin exposed by the hem of my shirt. "Nothing, it's just, don't you think it's a little . . . revealing? Sometimes it gets chilly at the creek at night. Maybe you should grab a flannel or something to cover up with?"

I level him with a glare. "There's gonna be a bonfire and it was ninety today. I think I'll be fine."

Teagan grumbles something under his breath as he follows me down the stairs. "All the guys are gonna be staring at you."

"So let them." I turn to him on the landing, a challenge in my eyes.

His brows rise. "Wow."

"What?"

"Nothing. It's just, not too long ago . . ."

I would've covered up, afraid the way I looked might invite trouble.

"I know." I shrug like it's nothing. "I guess I'm finally comfortable in my own skin again. Just be glad, okay?"

He searches my gaze, then nods. "If you're sure, but if you want to leave at any time, let me know."

"I will, but you don't have to worry."

Once we arrive at Crow's Creek and Teagan parks, we crest the hill to the sound of laughter. Voices drift toward us, and I'm shocked to see more than two dozen bodies ambling about, drinking from plastic cups, and talking by the fire.

Leaning into Teagan, I whisper, "I thought it was just gonna be the guys and maybe a couple others?"

He scans the crowd. "People must've gotten wind that we were having something tonight." He glances down at me. "You good?"

I nod, feeling only slightly intimidated as I scan the faces of the partygoers, zeroing in on the one I want to see the most. Jace stands next to a cooler, beer in hand as he talks to Graham, and when he tips his head back, I can hear his laughter from here.

"I'm gonna grab a drink," I say, figuring it's as good an excuse as any to approach, when a tall blonde I recognize as Penny Cooper from high school cuts in front of me and sidles up beside him before I even have a chance to make my presence known.

I pause, irritation pricking at my skin as I watch her lean into him, her dress riding up her thighs as she whispers something into his ear. My stomach sinks, but I remind myself he has no idea I'm here, and he can hardly push her away from him. We're supposed to hate each other, and for all they know, Jace is every bit the player he was in high school.

Still, I can't help feeling unsettled. He and Penny had a couple of flings in high school, and though I know it was nothing more than that, I can't expect girls not to talk to him. He's easily the hottest guy here, and the couple of months spent at AU have only honed his already muscular physique. Girls are bound to notice, and it makes sense Penny might assume they could have another go. If I get jealous every time a girl approaches him, I'll go crazy. At the end of the day, until I can claim him, all I can do is remember that no matter how awful it feels to see her flirting with him, he's mine; that's all that matters.

Mustering my courage, I push my shoulders back and close the distance between us, positioning myself between Jace and the cooler. "Hey, guys." I force a smile and pray it doesn't look as plastic as it feels.

"Brynn?" Graham gasps. "Bro, am I seeing things?" He glances behind me, and I realize Teagan's followed me. He shakes his head. "I haven't seen you at one of these in years." He offers me a side hug, then claps Teagan's arm. "Did this guy drag you out?"

"Something like that." I feel the pull toward Jace like an invisible string, but I force my gaze steady.

"Aw, it didn't take too much prodding," Teagan says, grabbing a beer from the cooler at our feet.

Unable to take it any longer, my line of vision shifts and my eyes lock on Jace whose heated gaze takes a slow perusal of my body before returning to mine, and I feel my cheeks flush.

We're still staring at each other when Atlas sidles up beside Jace and slings an arm over his shoulder. "Brynn, maybe you can settle the bet we have going?"

Reluctantly, I give Atlas my attention; I'm not sure undressing each other with our eyes will help us fly under the radar. "Um, sure?" I say, uncertain.

"Seriously, dude," Jace says, his tone exasperated, which tells me he knows what Atlas is about to say.

But Atlas just smirks. "When we all left for the summer, the guys put a poll on how many chicks Jace would hook up with."

"Atlas!" Mackenzie, his girlfriend, scolds.

"What? It was their idea," he says, motioning toward the rest of the guys.

In my peripheral, I see Jace grab at the back of his neck while Penny giggles beside him.

"Oh?" I say, trying to keep my tone light even though I'm dying a little inside.

"Obviously, you don't have a full body count, but since you were forced to live together, we figure . . . you have to have some idea . . . ?"

"You lived together?" Penny pipes up.

Jace turns to her, his features tight with discomfort. "Uh, yeah. It's a long story."

It takes every ounce of effort I have to keep a straight face because the guys already know the story behind our living arrangement, which makes me wonder why he doesn't want to tell it to *her*. Is he worried she'll think we're together?

I jerk my head away from her to see Knox, Teagan, Atlas, and Graham all staring at me, waiting. "Um, are you asking if I know how many girls he slept with?"

Jace's brow furrows, and my head begins to throb.

Am I supposed to lie to keep up the charade? Feign ignorance? Tell the truth? After all, they want a body count, not names.

"I'm not really sure." I fidget. "I mean, there was one girl he brought back to the apartment, but she didn't stay long . . ."

"No way there was only one," Knox says, turning to Jace, who shoots him a sharp look.

Teagan snorts. "Apparently, he doesn't last long. Maybe word has spread."

They're joking, I know they are. This is what guys do. But I can't help but feel my hackles rise, and apparently, I'm not the only one offended by the teasing.

"I don't know about that." Penny slides a hand up Jace's chest and bats her eyes at him. "I can vouch for him. He can definitely last."

The guys snicker while Jace clears his throat and stares at the ground; I wonder if he's wishing for it to swallow him like I am.

"Okay, so who else?" Teagan presses. "No way she was the only chick. Talking with a girl on campus counts, because once he sets his sights on a chick, it's game over."

I shift and glance at my brother, but my gaze finds its way right back to Jace again, particularly to the place where Penny's hand still rests on his chest.

Anger blooms inside my chest, but I shove it down. "There weren't any others," I blurt, shocked by how much I want to tell them the truth, to stake my claim. "And, actually, he didn't even sleep with the other girl. He sent her home before it could get that far."

Penny drops her hand—thank heavens—while the others stare at me as if they didn't hear me correctly.

"Say what, now?" Graham asks.

"That would mean his body count is zero," Teagan says.

Silence swallows the space between us before they look to Jace for an explanation, and he shrugs. "I wasn't feeling it."

"You weren't feeling it," Graham repeats like he spoke in a foreign language.

Teagan frowns. "Since when does Jace Taggart pass up—"

"Who are you and what have you done with our friend, Jace?" Knox asks, settling a hand on his shoulder.

Jace shoots each of them a dark look before he downs his beer and moves to the cooler for another, putting him infinitely closer to me. I only wish it was because he couldn't bear the distance between us and not because he needs another drink. But at least it puts him further from Penny.

He cracks open the beer and tips it back, his Adam's apple bobbing as he shotguns all of it in a single go, then tosses it at his feet and grabs another. "Maybe I've changed," Jace says with a shrug.

He pops the top, this time only taking a sip as his eyes meet mine over the rim.

"You, change?" Teagan snorts. "Yeah, okay, buddy."

"If you're looking for something more serious, I'm game." Penny shrugs, and I want to scream, *WHY ARE YOU STILL HERE*?

Jace shoots her a withering look which seems to do the job as she shrinks back, turning to talk to a group of people a couple of feet away.

"Shit. Who guessed the least?" Knox asks, as if it's just occurred to him he might not have won the bet.

Atlas raises a fist in triumph as Mackenzie sidles up beside him. "I had four."

"Four?" Teagan blinks. "Shit, man. That's low."

Atlas shrugs. "I figured he'd be too focused on football and policing Brynn."

Jace narrows his eyes. "Four was the lowest fucking number?"

Everyone else just shrugs guiltily while Teagan laughs, and it occurs to me he's being kind of a dick. It makes me want to tell him. It makes me want to let him know Jace is amazing in and out of bed. But I don't. I keep my mouth shut because I promised Jace I would. And because I can't tell if I'm right to be angry, or if it's my defensiveness talking.

"Shoot. Remember that time at junior prom where Jace went missing, and we went looking for him?" Knox asks Graham, jabbing him in the ribs.

"And we found him in the bed of his truck with his date *and* Millie Peterson?" Graham chimes in.

"Speaking of Millie"—Teagan tips his beer toward the other side of the bonfire—"she's here tonight."

"And she's watching you as we speak," Graham adds.

"Oh, shit," Atlas says while the others laugh.

My stomach roils. I haven't even touched the beer in my hand, and I think I'm going to be sick.

Unable to stop myself, I look across the bonfire until I find her. Sure enough, Millie is here, and she looks more beautiful than ever with the firelight playing over her rose gold locks. She's wearing a short romper that showcases her long, toned legs.

When I turn back around, Jace's eyes are boring into me, but I don't meet them, afraid I'll drown if I do.

I fall quiet, and thankfully, the subject changes. Eventually, our little group moves to the fire and we all take a seat. I sip on my drink, trading in my untouched beer for a Coke, which isn't nearly as satisfying without the lemon, while the guys talk about their glory days and catch up on what they missed over the summer. Atlas holds Mackenzie in his arms while Graham cuddles an adorable brunette I recognize as Skylar, the girl he started dating this past Christmas. The girls, bless them, try to draw me into a conversation of our own, but I'm not fully present and am having trouble following along. Though if they notice, they don't say anything.

Teagan sits beside me. Knowing how protective he is, I'm sure it's not by chance, and I wonder with a stab of irritation if he'll forever play sentinel, running off any guy who so much as looks in my direction.

But none of these things are what hold my attention.

Instead, I'm drawn to Jace, several seats down. He's on what has to be his fifth beer, and though he's not drunk yet, it's obvious to me he's drinking to cope with the pressure of keeping us a secret. I'm not sure how I feel about that. I do, however, know how I feel about the girl beside him, sitting so close she's nearly on his lap.

It's been more than thirty minutes since Millie sat down beside him, and my patience is wearing thin. My skin itches with my restraint. I'm not sure how much longer I can sit by and watch all the single girls here stare at my man. And I definitely don't know how much longer I can watch Millie talk to him like they're the only two in a room.

Rising from my spot on the grass, I tell Teagan I need to go to the bathroom and head down the slope of the hill toward the cabin where I plan to wallow like a toddler who didn't get a cookie before bed. I only get midway down when a hand captures my wrist.

I halt and turn, expecting it to be Teagan wanting to escort me in the dark, but find Jace instead. "Hey," he says, his voice soft.

I glance behind us. We're mostly obscured from view, thanks to the grade of the slope, but it wouldn't take much for someone to see us.

Jace must catch the direction of my thoughts because he takes me by the arm and guides me a few hundred feet further down, near a couple of parked cars, before he yanks me behind an old oak tree.

His scent surrounds me as he leans in. "Cupcake, what's wrong?"

I exhale, biting my lip as I stare at the ground and my thoughts scatter.

What's wrong?

Everything.

Nothing.

He pinches my chin, causing my gaze to turn until it meets his eyes. "Talk to me."

I open my mouth, but I feel entirely ridiculous. What can I say? That I'm jealous? Insecure? Depressed at the thought of hiding us? Scared that he's not ready for this—for us—because he's always been known for casual hook ups and nothing more, while I have zero experience in comparison?

Instead, I say, "I thought Penny was bad, but I want to rip Millie's perfect hair out by the roots."

Jace barks out a laugh and presses his forehead to mine. "You're cute when you're jealous, but you know you have nothing to worry about, right? This is just temporary. We talked about this. There's only one girl at this party who's caught my eye, and she's right here."

His words are a salve to my open wounds. "You sure?"

"Positive," he whispers, then tucks a lock of hair behind my ear. "You're the only one I want." He pulls back as if reading something on my face I'm not willing to say. "Does it bother you? All the stuff the guys were saying about me and . . . well, you know . . . ?"

I'd be lying if I said it didn't, and I don't want to lie to Jace.

"I mean, maybe a little?" I cling to him, gripping the soft material of his shirt in the dark. "What if you decide I'm not what you want? Or that you'd rather go back to something casual?"

"Never gonna happen."

I sigh, sinking into his arms as I tip my head and accept the warm press of his lips before he jerks away, his gaze darting somewhere in the distance.

My ears perk up, and I turn, searching for what drew his attention when I hear it.

"... a little weird Jace hasn't hooked up with a single chick?" The sound of Teagan's voice drifts to us on the breeze, and I feel Jace stiffen.

A few yards off, I zero in on Graham, who's reaching into the bed of Jace's pickup with Teagan at his side. "What are you saying?" he asks, handing Teagan a case of beer.

Teagan grunts and takes it. "You don't think ... I mean ..."

Even from here, I can see the widening of Graham's eyes in the moonlight. "Oh, shit, dude. You think Jace is hooking up with Brynn?"

Teagan shrugs. "It's crossed my mind."

Graham runs a hand down his face. "No, dude. No way. He wouldn't."

"I don't know. They were both acting kind of weird yesterday at the house."

"Would he do that, though?"

Teagan snorts. "I wouldn't think so. Then again, we both know how Jace is."

I risk a glance at Jace to see how he's taking this, and note the hard set of his jaw.

"Okay. But if he is, then what?" Graham prods.

A moment of silence stretches between them while my heart hammers against Jace's chest.

"I don't know, man," Teagan says after some time. "If he is, he sure as shit doesn't care about me and our friendship, I can tell you that much."

"Do you think you could move past it?"

Teagan shakes his head and leans against the truck. "I don't know."

"Dude, that would be so messed up. Could you imagine? What the hell would we do? It'd be like having two divorced parents." He chuckles. "Would you have to share custody?"

Teagan snorts. "Shit no. If Jace is screwing my sister, I get custody."

Jace grunts, pale even in the shadows as he leans against the tree. He looks like all the wind has been knocked from his lungs. Both Teagan and Graham must hear it because their heads whip in our direction.

Panic claws up my spine as they take a step closer, peering into the shadows. Without thinking, I step away from the tree into the moonlight and they assess my emerging figure through narrowed eyes.

"Sorry," I say, trying to sound upbeat as I saunter toward them and hook a thumb behind me. "I just went behind the tree since the cabin was locked. Walk me back up?"

CHAPTER 36

JACE

MY THOUGHTS ARE A cancerous mass in my head as I walk to the Nichols' house from my place. Originally, I planned on spending the night at home, and I still intend to go back, but not before I talk to Brynn first. So after Atlas and Mackenzie dropped me off, I waited twenty minutes to start for the Nichols' residence, cursing myself for having one too many beers. If I could drive, and my truck wasn't still at Crow's Creek, I'd be there already.

Tonight did not go how I hoped, though in hindsight, I wonder how I thought this would go. Did I really think we'd be able to spend the break together, all while hiding what's really going on between us?

I rake a hand through my hair as I finally come to her street. I'm losing my freaking mind, along with control of the situation, and the worst part is I have no idea how to rein it back in.

After we almost got busted and Brynn saved my ass, I went back to the bonfire and kept my distance. Which meant both Millie and Penny took turns trying to garner my interest, and like the asshole I am, I went along with, allowing them to hang on me and laugh and flirt because I was scared to death anything else would arouse Teagan's suspicions.

I can only hope Brynn gets it. Surely, she understands how much my friendship with Teagan—with all the guys—means to me. She heard it with her own ears. Teagan isn't going to take our relationship in stride, and it's going to force the guys to choose sides. Based on tonight, I know whose side they're on.

And if this is how they feel, I can't imagine how her parents will feel.

I can't lose them. They're like family, the only people who give two shits about me.

This is why we need to be extra cautious, maybe even spend more time apart over break than we originally anticipated. Only sneaking away when we're absolutely sure we won't get caught. Over time, I'll make Teagan understand. Over time, he'll see I'm a changed man, no longer bouncing from woman to woman. He'll see I've settled down, that I'm ready for a commitment, something serious. And when I tell him about my feelings for Brynn, he won't be as angry. Because he won't be able to deny I'm better for it.

I still want Brynn in my life. Nothing has changed. My feelings for her are every bit as real and strong as they were before the party, so I hope she understands my suggestion to cool it just until we get back to school.

As I near her house, I can see the glow of lamplight through her window. I pull out my phone and shoot her a quick text.

ME: Hey, you up? I was hoping we could talk. I didn't get to say goodnight.

BRYNN: Sure, I'm here.

ME: Okay. Unlock your window, and I'll come up.

I duck behind the old maple tree in their yard at the side of the house, then climb the thick limbs until I reach her window. It's a bit of a leap, but luckily I'm tall, so the three-foot gap between the outstretched limb and her house is nothing and I jump onto the shingled roof.

Leaning down, I slide the window open and easily slip inside to find Brynn unpacking her suitcase and hanging clothes in her closet. I take the flurry of nervous energy flowing between us as a bad sign and wait until she spins around to assess her mood.

Her brow pinches as she clutches one of the sundresses I love so much in her hands and clears her throat. "I didn't expect you to come here."

I frown at this. Did she really think I would end the night without at least talking to her?

"I needed to see you," I say by way of explanation, but when she says nothing in return, I sink my hands into my pockets and lean back against the wall. "Tonight didn't go as planned."

She turns back to the closet and begins to hang the sundress, her movements short and sharp as she says, "I'm surprised you didn't go home with Millie."

My stomach sinks. "You're kidding, right?"

When she says nothing and reaches back into her suitcase for another garment, I close the distance and grab her hands. "Brynn, look at me." She bites her lips before her violet eyes lift to mine. "You know the only reason I even talked to her or Penny was to get Teagan off our trail."

She sighs and glances at the floor. "I guess . . . I don't know. That, and the things the guys were saying . . . I guess they got in my head a little? Especially when you ignored me the rest of the night."

I place my finger under her chin and lift her head. "It fucking killed me to stay away from you. Every second I'm apart from you is a waste. But we've had one too many close calls with Teagan and . . ." I exhale and shake my head. "Tonight, when we overheard him with Graham, it woke me the fuck up. If I ever had any doubt before about whether he'd accept us, I know he won't now. At least not yet. And the prospect of losing him and pitting the rest of the guys against me is a hard pill to swallow. Throw in the rest of your family hating me and it's not something I wanna think about."

"But we have to tell him eventually, Jace. We can't hide this forever."

"I know. But with time—"

"What if time doesn't help?"

Shit. She already thinks the worst. "It will. I've given this a lot of thought."

Her brows rise, and I sense I've said the wrong thing, so I try again. "Think about how much more convincing it will be if we tell Teagan once we've been together for six months. Right now, it's just weeks, so he'll think the worst. But if we prove to him before he even learns about us that this is the real deal, that I'm not just playing around, and I'm serious, he'll be forced to take us seriously, too."

Her shoulders slump, but she doesn't contradict me, which I take as a good sign.

"So, maybe, just while we're home, we cool it. No more sneaking around. No more hiding. I'll hang with Teagan and the guys, and then once we're back at school, we can pick up where we left off."

Her eyes widen, emotion flashing through them like a thunderclap. "And what if I don't want to be your dirty little secret? Because that's how this is starting to feel."

Icy fingers grip my chest as I grapple with a way to make this right. I step forward and draw her into my arms, but she's stiff, unyielding. "No, Brynn. Don't you ever fucking say that." I lean back again, holding her by the arms as I look into her eyes. "Do you hear me? This isn't about you."

Her lips press together, and if the moisture in her eyes is any indication, she's holding back her tears.

"I told Knox," I blurt. "This morning, at breakfast."

She tips her head. "You did?"

I nod, eager to make her see how much I care.

"And what did he say?"

I laugh, but there's no humor in it. "Well, he was surprised, that's for damn sure." I release her arms and sink my hands into my pockets. "And he didn't exactly give me a warm and fuzzy feeling about coming clean to Teagan, but he seemed to think it was smart to wait, just in case . . ." I trail off, not wanting to say the words because I have every intention of hanging onto Brynn with everything I have, and I don't want her to think otherwise.

But she's smart enough to read between the lines, and she scoffs. "In case we don't even make it through the fall?"

I say nothing, because what can I say? And why is she angry about this when we talked about it weeks ago and agreed? We said we needed time to see where this might lead before telling him, and what I'm proposing now isn't all that different from the original plan.

"Brynn, you know that's not . . . I have every intention of being with you at the end of fall semester."

She turns and fumbles with her suitcase, zipping it closed and trying to lift it onto the shelf in her closet. As she struggles, I take it from her hands, and hoist it above my head onto the wooden shelf, but as I do so, something crashes to the ground.

I shove the suitcase further back on the shelf as my gaze falls to the source of the sound, and I see Brynn scrambling to collect the wooden jewelry box along with its contents.

I frown as I bend to help her. "Sorry, I didn't know there was something still in . . ." I trail off as I pick up the familiar leather cuff, turning it over to reveal the metal plate with the inscription "Bub," and my insides turn to stone.

I glance over at Brynn to see her watching, the color draining from her cheeks, her knuckles white as they clutch the now busted box and a slip of crumpled paper in her other hand.

I swallow as I finger the leather in my hand, trying to make sense of why she has it, let alone why she keeps it tucked away like a buried treasure, but I come up blank. So, I ask, "Why do you have Knox's bracelet?"

CHAPTER 37

BRYNN

Why do you have Knox's bracelet?

The words ricochet inside my skull like a bullet.

I blink over at Jace, my stomach tight as I glance between him and the leather cuff, certain I heard him wrong. It's been a long night. I'm tired and emotional, and my mind is playing tricks on me.

"What did you say?" I ask.

He twirls the bracelet in his hands, his gaze homing in on the inscription I've wondered about more times than I can count. "This bracelet. Knox called it a cuff, but he got it sophomore year from his mom. She always called him Bub." His lips quirk at the memory.

"You're sure?" I ask, and something about the way I say it must alert him to a bigger issue because his smile fades.

He nods slowly, as if trying to put together a puzzle he doesn't yet have all the pieces to. "I remember it so well because we gave him so much shit for it. When he stopped wearing it, we just assumed it was because he was tired of us making fun of him for it."

My throat swells. I can't speak. Can't breathe. Can't fucking hear through the rush of blood pumping in my ears.

All I can do is stare at the crisp leather with the metal plate, mind spinning as I try and comprehend the reality of the situation.

The bracelet belongs to Knox.

Knox was the one who wrote me the note asking to meet him in the locker room.

Knox was the secret admirer.

Knox was the one to trap me and threaten me with a knife.

Knox was the one who touched me and groped me in the dark.

Who tried to . . .

I bring a trembling hand up to my mouth in an effort to stifle the moan bubbling to the surface. Or maybe it's vomit; I'm not sure.

It's too much.

I can't process this, especially with Jace staring at me like I'm a crazy person.

Knox is one of Jace's best friends. He's one of my *brother's* best friends.

Their crew is ride or die.

They'd do anything for him.

They trust him with their life.

Jace just sat here two seconds ago and told me he couldn't lose any of them. I have no idea what's going through his head, but I also know I can't address his concerns when I'm at war so violently with my own.

I straighten. Woozy on my feet, I stumble slightly and Jace braces me with a steadying hand. "Brynn? What's wrong? Talk to me."

It's the second time he's said that to me tonight, and I can't help but think I'm not worth the trouble. Maybe that's why he wants to pretend we're not together.

I shake my head.

I need to be alone.

I need him out of here so I can process.

I press one hand to my stomach and the other to my mouth, afraid I might be sick. "I don't feel so well," I mumble through the churning in my gut.

"You think you might throw up?"

I nod. "I need you to go."

"Was it the beer? I didn't see you drink anything. I'll stay and help. I'll—"

"No." I shake my head violently. "We can't risk you getting caught here."

"Like I give a shit about that right now, Brynn. You need me. Let me help you."

I hold my hand up, shaking my head as I walk backward toward the hallway. "Go. Please." I barely get the words out before my stomach pitches and I dry heave into my hand.

"Brynn—" Jace reaches.

"Go!"

The concern in his blue eyes remains, and I can't take it. I can't take him looking at me with so much compassion when I have no idea how he'd feel or who he'd side with if he knew the truth. "I'm serious," I add, my tone sharp. "I don't want you here right now."

The second the words leave my mouth, I turn for the bathroom, ignoring his crumpling expression as I close the door behind me and fall apart.

CHAPTER 38

BRYNN

I'M STARING OUT THE living room window, waiting until Teagan jogs down the sidewalk and out of sight, before I text Jace back.

Bypassing the string of worried texts from last night, I take a deep breath and start a new one.

I go back to staring outside, this time at nothing, and am unsurprised when he texts back almost immediately. It's early, but if he's like me, he got very little sleep.

I close my eyes as my mind races with everything I need to say and do when he gets here. After my sleepless night, I'm still unsure I've come to terms with the fact that the boy who assaulted me three years ago was Knox. The betrayal sinks deep, slicing through my heart like the flick of a switchblade, and if it hurts this much for me to know it was him, I can't imagine what it'll do to both Jace and Teagan. The five of them may have started as friends and teammates, but they've become so much more over the years. They're like a band of brothers. They've been through a lot together, especially in the last year, and I know how scared Jace is at the prospect of losing Teagan and possibly the others to our secret. He loves them. All of them, including Knox.

A few weeks ago, I poured my heart out to Jace and I couldn't have asked for a better response. I'd been validated and comforted. I felt cherished and strong. Regardless, he won't believe me when I tell him. How can I expect him to believe it when I barely believe it myself?

Believing is too hard, too painful. So, he'll confront Knox and ask him. Of this I have no doubt, and then it'll be his word against my own, and I'm not sure I'll be able to take it when Jace chooses his over mine.

When he doesn't believe me, then what? The pain of that will be so much worse than the pain of losing him now, on my own terms.

Maybe we were headed in that direction, anyway. At least that's what I tell myself.

It's not hard to believe after last night. I saw how Penny and Millie fawned all over him. Half the girls at the party had been eyeing him like a piece of candy. Even his own friends were shocked to hear he wasn't playing the field at AU. And the fact that he wanted to cool it while we're home and hide it from everyone doesn't bode well.

Jace Taggart is not the kind of guy to go to college and suddenly get serious about a girl. He avoids commitment like the plague, and right now, things are new and fresh and so of course, he thinks this will work. But what happens when he gets tired of me? What happens when he gets bored? I have no reason to believe he's capable of staying for the long haul.

It's a miracle we've even lasted this long, and it's only a matter of time before he trades me in for someone new and breaks my heart.

The doorbell rings, startling me from my thoughts, and when I glance out the window, I realize it's Jace.

He never rings the doorbell or knocks. This is his home almost as much as it is mine. For years, he's just waltzed right in like he owns the place, like he's part of the family. So, the fact he's knocking now tells me he knows something's not right.

Before I can lose my nerve, I swing the door open and step aside so he can come in.

He's wearing a blue baseball cap, an AU T-shirt, and shorts. He looks so handsome and effortlessly sexy it makes my heart ache.

Waving him in, I make my way to the sofa on wooden legs and sink into the worn cushions while he takes the seat across from me.

I clear my throat, struggling to find my voice when he breaks the silence first.

"Shit, Brynn, you're scaring me." He scrubs a hand over his face and a dry laugh escapes his lips. "Hell, the whole way here I had to talk myself down. Tell myself you weren't asking me to come here just to break up with me."

He meets my eyes, and I know what he's doing. He's looking for something—anything—that tells him he's wrong. But he won't find it.

"Jace . . ." My voice cracks, and I curse myself for showing emotion when I need to hold it together.

A hiss of air escapes his lips as he flops back against the chair. "That's what this is, isn't it? That's why you asked me here. You're ending us."

I swallow. "I've given it a lot of thought," I say, parroting what he said last night, "and I think it's for the best. Neither of us has any idea how Teagan will react when he finds out we've been sneaking around behind his back, and I know how much you value your friendship. Not to mention everyone else—"

"I value you more," he says. "And I can make this work. If this is about last night, all I wanted was to wait until we got back to school. I *know* I can make Teagan understand."

"But don't you see? Maybe it shouldn't be this hard. We shouldn't have to run around and hide. If this is right, then we shouldn't have to try to convince people that what we have is real."

"No, that's not true," he says, shaking his head, his tone frantic. "And it's not like that."

"But it is."

He stares at me for a moment, both of us locked into position, unyielding and unwilling to bend.

"Then tell him," I say, my voice thick. "Tell Teagan about us right now when he gets back from his run." I wave my arm toward the door. "If I'm number one, and it's not like that, then you'll tell him, consequences be damned."

"It's not that simple," he says, his gaze wild.

"It is, actually." I stand, allowing righteous anger to fill my veins because it's the only way to get through this, the only way to push him away.

Jace rises and takes a step toward me, grabbing my arm and pleading. "Please," he says with a slight tremble to his voice. "All I'm asking is for a little time for all our sakes. It's not about being ashamed or afraid of commitment or putting you first."

"It's over."

"It's not." He shakes his head, then says, "Fine. If that's what you need, I'll tell him right now."

"And what happens if you're right and he severs your friendship? Then you'll resent me? No." I make a slashing motion with my arms. "Either way, we're screwed. You'll wind up hating me in the end."

Jace blanches. "What do you want me to say?"

When I don't answer, he rakes his hands through his hair, bracing his hands on his head. "So, in one breath, you want me to tell everyone about us and stop hiding, but in the next, you're telling tell me it won't matter anyway. Basically, I'm fucked, and you just don't want to be with me."

I say nothing, clenching my jaw so hard, my teeth ache. It's better to take the blame, to let him think I'm done. When I say nothing, he fists his hands out in front of him.

"We were good until that stupid fucking party. I knew this would happen. I knew in the end, you'd decide I'm not what you want."

"It's not the party," I say, hating how personal he's taking this. But what did I expect? Breakups are always personal. They always hurt.

"Oh, yeah, then what is it? Enlighten me."

I stare at him for a beat, feeling my resolve weaken, knowing I can't let it. "I guess I just want . . ." I swallow, hating the hope I see glittering in his eyes. "I want a guy who's so proud to be with me, he doesn't care who knows it. A man who won't allow other women to flirt and hang on him even for a second because he can't stand the touch of someone else, and because he knows it would hurt me. I want a man who doesn't need his best friend's permission to date me."

I know my words cut deep when he sucks in a breath, looking as though he's been sucker punched. My words feel heavy on my tongue, knowing it was both of our choice to keep our relationship a secret from Teagan. I'm every bit as culpable, but still, I *need* to push him away.

He stumbles forward, his voice wobbling as he says, "Don't do this, Brynn. Don't give up on us. Maybe I screwed up, okay? But all you had to do was tell me how you were feeling. You have no idea how much I care about you. How much—"

"What. The. Actual. Fuck."

I whip around to the sound of the gravelly voice behind us and suck in a breath. "Teagan…" I start, but he doesn't so much as look in my direction. Instead, he's laser focused on Jace, who is as white as the walls behind him.

Raising his hands, Jace takes a step forward, as if he can placate Teagan like a wild dog, with slow movements and a soft tone. "Teagan, I can explain."

"You fuck her?"

"Teagan!" My stomach clenches as I turn to my brother and place a hand on his arm, but he shrugs me off.

"Answer the question," he snaps.

"That's none of you—"

"Yes," Jace says, his tone hard.

I turn my gaze to him, mouth agape as I watch him straighten. He squares his shoulders and resolve hardens the blue of his eyes.

"You son of a bitch." Teagan charges toward him, yanking him by the collar of his shirt, and I yell for him to stop.

Jace says nothing; he doesn't even put up a fight as Teagan shoves him back while my useless cries bounce off the walls. "Teagan, you're better than this," I say, grappling at his arms, hoping to diffuse the situation. Teagan's not a violent person. Nor is he confrontational, but I've never seen him so angry.

Jace stumbles but quickly rights himself as he moves around a piece of furniture, ducking when Teagan takes a feeble swing. Raising his hands in front of himself, he murmurs, "I care about her, man. She's not—"

"Just another one of your girls?" Teagan fumes. His hands clench as they face off, and then he snaps and charges him like he's a linebacker, and not the tight-end position he usually plays. "You lying sack of shit!"

His head and shoulder barrel into Jace's stomach. A hiss of air escapes Jace's lungs when he makes contact, and they crash into the end table. The lamp shatters as it falls to the ground while they wrestle for purchase beside it.

Teagan gains the upper hand, rolling on top of Jace and pulling his arm back, his fist ready to strike when the sound of my mother's voice makes him freeze. "What the hell is going on in here?"

I turn to her. Tears stream down my face, unchecked as they roll underneath my chin.

My mother's gaze quickly flickers to me, then back, her mouth a tight line as she takes in the scene before her.

Teagan lowers his arm, settling for bunching Jace's shirt in his hand as he leans down to speak to him. "How could you do this to me?" Teagan seethes. "You were supposed to be my best friend."

"I am."

Teagan shakes his head, releases his shirt, and stands. "You were."

Jace's nostrils flare and his gaze flickers to me, then to my mother beside me before his head falls back against the ground with a thud. "It just happened. I couldn't *not* fall for her."

Teagan laughs, the bitter sound sending chills up my spine. "You know when I asked you to keep an eye on her for me, this isn't what I had in mind."

"I know."

"I trusted you," Teagan says with so much venom in his voice, it curls my toes. "I trusted you like a brother."

Silence stretches. Only the sound of their breathing and the pounding of my heart fills the room. Until my mother steps forward and places a hand on Teagan's arm. "Jace, honey," she says, "I think maybe you should go home."

CHAPTER 39

BRYNN

T HE PORCH SWING CREAKS as I sink down onto the wooden slats. Outside, insects buzz and the air smells of freshly mowed lawn. Inside, the house is quiet with the vague stench of loneliness. Mom ran to the grocery store with the girls to buy food for the party next weekend, and Dad's working.

I've barely spoken to anyone since yesterday morning when Mom walked in on the fight between Jace and Teagan. I'm sure she had no problem puzzling together everything that's happened, especially with Teagan skulking about. He was probably thrilled to fill in the gaps. I wouldn't know because the minute Jace left, I spent the rest of the day locked in my bedroom where I promptly blamed myself for everything.

It's only been twenty-four hours since I broke Jace's heart, crushing mine along with it, and I miss him like I'd miss a leg or an arm.

I can still feel his desperation as he tried to convince me we could make things work. I can picture with perfect clarity the defeat and resignation in his eyes when he spoke to Teagan. But the worst . . . probably the worst moment was when my mother asked him to leave. I'm not sure I've ever seen utter devastation come to life before until that moment.

Everything he was so afraid of came to fruition, and I can't help but feel like it's all my fault.

The noisy squawk of the screen door pierces the quiet, and I crane my neck behind me, glancing back to see Teagan. Rising to my feet, I turn for the door. I came out here for fresh air, not a lecture. Whatever he has to say, I'm not interested in.

"Can you please just sit and talk to me?" His hazel eyes find mine, pleading as he shoves his hands in the pockets of his khaki shorts. "*Please.*"

I stare at him for a long moment, debating what I want to do. I can't possibly feel any shittier than I already do, and I can't avoid him forever. So I sit back down and wait for him to take the floor, refusing to be the first one to speak. If he has something to say, I'm sure as hell not going to make it easier on him.

He inhales behind me before walking toward the swing and sinks down beside me.

My throat tightens, the urge to cry pricking at the back of my eyes. No matter how much I want to stay mad at him—and I *am* mad—Teagan is my best friend, the one person in my life I can always count on.

"Can I just ask why?" he finally says.

"Why what?" I ask, though I know what he means.

"Why him?" He clears his throat. "How did it happen?"

I glance over at him, my mouth a thin line. "Do you really want to know?"

Teagan grunts and pinches the bridge of his nose, looking more distraught than I've seen him in a long time. I almost feel sorry for him. *Almost.*

"Just . . . spare me the gory details, but yeah, I wanna know."

I shake my head, wondering where to begin because in truth, this war between me and Jace started a long time ago, and I'm not sure when my feelings started. Pinpointing the exact moment I felt something more for him feels a little murky.

"One minute we were hating each other and the next . . ." My gaze shifts out into the yard. Below the porch a butterfly floats around the purple tufts of Mom's lavender. "He's different than I thought he was. There's so much more to him than meets the eye. People don't give him enough credit."

Teagan snorts, and I turn my narrowed gaze on him.

"Including you," I say, watching that sink in. "He's your best friend, you know. Or at least he was, until you acted like an idiot yesterday." Teagan's eyes darken and the muscle in his jaw flickers, but I keep going. "There has to be *some* reason you kept him around all these years. He's been your best friend for a long time. Was it only because he's a fun time and good with a football? Because if there's nothing more to him or your friendship, then maybe I've misread you. Maybe I've been wrong about you, too."

"Of course not," he snaps. "There are plenty of reasons why we're friends, but that's not the point."

"How is it not the point?"

He opens his mouth, but nothing comes out.

"You want to know what I think?" I arch a brow.

"No, but I have a feeling you're gonna tell me anyway." He sighs and leans forward, his elbows braced on his knees.

"I think you know what an amazing person he is. And I think you realize the reason he's bounced from girl to girl is because his parents are never around. He doesn't know what love feels like, let alone what it looks like. All they've ever taught him is that he's not enough, and people who love you, leave." Teagan bows his head, his throat working, but I don't let up. "Jace has wounds, but you look past them because he's your friend. You love him anyway, and he's been nothing but loyal to you from day one. He's been there for you, your whole crew. For years, he's held your little group together like glue. When you want a good time or a laugh, you call Jace. If you need help, you call Jace, because you know he'll be there. You want to lift someone up? Jace. He's funny and smart and considerate. But for some reason, you think he's not good enough for me. Why?" I demand.

His mouth opens, and he straightens on the swing, but it takes him a moment to speak. "He doesn't do relationships. The reasons why don't really matter because he's never been serious about a girl in his life, and you deserve better than someone who bounces from bed to bed."

A ball of anger fists in my spine. "But isn't that for me to decide? And who says when he finds the right one, that won't change?"

"It's Jace." He lets out a dry laugh and turns to me, meeting my eyes. "Hell, you saw how he was acting the other night. If he cares so much about you, why was he letting those chicks hang all over him? Is that the kind of guy you want?"

"He was scared."

Teagan snorts.

"He didn't want to lose you, T," I snap, feeling my composure slip. "When he overheard you talking to Graham and saying he'd be dead to you if we were hooking up, he freaked out. And, okay, maybe he overcompensated a bit, but it turns out he had every reason to worry." Teagan pales. "You didn't know that, did you?"

I wait, but when he says nothing, I continue, "We talked about it before we came home, and we both agreed to keep us a secret until after football season." Teagan's face twists like he doesn't want to believe it. "He's been nothing but petrified of your reaction to us being together since the start, so much so he was willing to risk what we have in order to keep you from throwing a tantrum."

"He could've come to me like a man first and asked if—"

"I don't need your permission, Teagan!" I shove at his shoulder. "I'm my own person, and I can decide who I want to date."

His throat bobs. "Fine. Maybe you're right. But if I recall, it sounded a whole lot like I walked in on you breaking up with him. At least that's what it sounded like, so why the hell are you defending him?"

"Because . . ." I trail off, my throat so tight I can't push the words past.

Because I'm scared.

Afraid he won't believe me.

That he'll choose Knox over me.

"There's more to it than that," I say because I can't tell Teagan. Not yet. "But it hurts that after all this time you can't trust my judgment. After everything I've been through, it's offensive you think I don't have a mind of my own, or can't think for myself and make my own decisions."

"It's not that—"

"I trusted the wrong person in high school. I took one look at those anonymous love letters with hearts in my eyes and fell right into his trap." *Knox's trap.* "But I've learned from that mistake. I'm not as naive as I once was. I don't go into anything without my eyes wide open."

I knew what I was getting into with Jace. I just didn't plan on Knox ruining it. But in the end, I had to protect my heart.

Teagan runs his hands through his thick blond waves and growls. "You're right, okay? Maybe I should've trusted you, but what the hell was I supposed to think?" He waves an arm in the air. "A couple months ago when you left, he was a player and you completely loathed him, and then you come back, and everything's changed. It's a lot to wrap my head around. It would've been nice if you just told me from the start."

I inhale. He has a point. We should've been upfront from the beginning, but I have no doubt Teagan would've interfered in the same way he's doing now. "Maybe we should have, but you wouldn't have felt any different then as you do now. You still would've been angry and told him to stay the hell away from me."

His mouth pinches. "Maybe. But you said so yourself, he doesn't know how to love. What makes you think that can change?"

I exhale, thinking about how good we were together, thinking about how he took care of me when I was sick. How he held me in the dark after my nightmare and listened to my story. How he made me feel protected and cherished and strong.

"I don't know if there's a way to describe love that'll make sense to someone who's never felt it. It's this feeling of being full, like you're bursting with warmth and light. You're weightless and everything is brighter than it once was. Suddenly, the world's problems seem small . . ."

I expect Teagan to scoff or make a joke, but he doesn't. Instead, he stares intently at the side of my face, brows drawn while I talk.

"I told him." I swallow, and when I turn to him, tears glisten in my eyes. "I told him what happened."

Teagan sucks in a breath. "You told him about Sadie Hawkins?"

I nod, knowing this admission is more powerful than anything I could have said.

"Shit." Teagan exhales a shaky breath and runs a hand over the back of his neck. "And he was good about it?" Another nod. Because that moment was too intimate, too special to share in detail. "If you care about him so much, then why break up with him?"

All I can do is shrug, because I can't tell him about Knox. Not yet. I'm not ready, though after yesterday, I have more confidence Teagan will believe me if I do.

"When it comes down to it, Jace cared for me, I have no doubt about that. But at the end of the day, he'll always put you guys first. He's too afraid to lose his friends."

Lie. You're a coward who can't bear to tell him the truth because you're scared he won't believe you.

"That's it? I'd get it if you were pissed at him for the way he acted at that party, but are you really gonna hold it against him for not telling me? Sounds like you both agreed to keep this a secret, so there has to be more to it. Either that, or you're just scared."

I swallow, because Teagan's words hit home. "Maybe I am scared."

"Did you ever think to give him a choice?"

"What do you mean?" I ask, numb.

"Did you ask him to choose? Because if you didn't, how do you know he wouldn't have chosen you?"

JACE

I sit outside on a lounge chair by the pool, staring at the bright blue water. I contemplate jumping in, but don't have the energy. Or maybe it's this stabbing headache. The sunglasses shielding my eyes from the morning sun do little to keep the pain in my head at bay, although half a bottle of vodka in one evening will do that to a person.

After I left the Nichols' house yesterday, I drove around town, half out of my mind. It took everything inside of me not to turn the vehicle around and head back to her. But then I remembered the look on Nikki's face when she told me to go home and the anger percolating in Teagan's eyes, and I knew returning wasn't an option.

Eventually, I made my way back here where I found Harriet waiting for me. She instantly knew something was wrong, but didn't push. Instead, she did what she always does and fed me until I couldn't move. Afterward, she asked me about school and my summer while I lied through my teeth, pretending everything was fine and my world hadn't come crashing down around my ankles earlier that morning. By the time she left, I was so exhausted from acting like I wasn't dying inside, I hit the liquor bar and didn't quit until I passed out on the couch sometime later.

Now, I'm nursing a brutal hangover, but I can't even find it in me to care because I'm so fucking depressed, I want to drown myself in another bottle.

My thoughts churn over the turn of events these past few days, wondering where the hell I went wrong. I should have avoided Millie and Penny, told them to get lost when they flirted with me. I should've told the guys I found someone special, even if I couldn't say who. I should've done more to show Brynn I cared and that I'd put her first.

I should've come clean from the start.

In hindsight, lying to Teagan was the dumbest thing I could've done.

I should've been upfront with him instead of waiting until fall. I can sit here and pretend I didn't want to ruin his football season, but it was selfish. I'd been so blinded by fear he wouldn't be able to accept me in Brynn's life that I let it cloud my judgment. At the end of the day, I should've let the chips fall, and he could either deal with the fact that I'm in love with his sister or not. Either way, I'd still win because I'd have Brynn.

Instead, I'm left with nothing.

Teagan might never forgive me, the Nicholses no doubt hate me, and Brynn dumped my ass for being such a coward. She thinks I chose my friends over her, but what she doesn't know is, if I had any inkling she'd see it that way and end things between us, I would've chosen her from the start. Although, maybe even then, it wouldn't have been enough for her. Maybe *I'm* not enough.

I glance around the empty backyard, to the quiet pool. I'm certainly not enough for my parents to stick around. Never have been.

The fact of the matter is, I've spent my whole life playing second fiddle to Dad's career and their relationship. I've always been left behind, forgotten, and it's made me question if I'm even worth it. Maybe Brynn dumping me is just further proof that I'm not.

Before yesterday, my biggest fear was being alone. Now I realize how wrong I was.

Because my biggest fear is not being enough for the people in my life to want to stick around. A bitter laugh bubbles in the back of my throat at just how fucking pathetic I sound.

Unable to take anymore, I rise from the chair and head back into the house, making a beeline for the bar. I've promised myself one more day of getting wasted and forgetting my problems before I deal with them. But I only get a couple feet inside before my doorbell rings, and I groan.

I can't think of one person who wants to see me right now, except maybe Atlas, Graham, or Knox—that's if Teagan hasn't trashed my name already. Regardless, I'm not in the mood for company.

I pause at the wet bar, my hands fisting a bottle of liquor with a name I can't pronounce. I think it's French. I don't know. It looks expensive, and it probably is—one of my father's imports—but as long as it does the job, I don't give a shit what it is. It all tastes like ass anyway.

The doorbell rings again, and I tip my head back with a sigh before I yell, "Coming!" and make my way toward the front of the house and swing open the door.

I suck in a breath at the sight of Nikki Nichols, gaping at her as my cheeks flush with shame. "Hey, Mrs. Nichols."

She arches a brow blonde brow. "Mrs. Nichols? You haven't called me that since the sixth grade."

My hands begin to sweat as I hold onto the door, glancing outside for signs of Teagan. Maybe he's waiting in the bushes to jump me.

"He's not with me," she says, reading my mind. "Can I come in?"

I step back, embarrassed I forgot my manners and hating how awkward I feel. "Sorry," I mumble as she glances around the cavernous foyer before I wave her on. "The living room's over here," I say, turning and heading down the hall to our right. I take a seat in one of the stiff sofas while I assess my home with fresh eyes. In comparison to the Nichols' household, it's cold and dark and uninviting, devoid of everything I love so much about it there. The walls are filled with expensive artwork rather than old drawings from when I was a child. There are no photographs from family vacations or scuff marks on the floors. No toys littering the ground. Everything is in its place and pristine, unused. Their house is lived in and filled with love while mine looks and feels more like a museum.

As if reading my thoughts, Nikki glances around her. "You have this big old place all to yourself?"

I clear my throat and nod, and when Nikki returns my gaze, her blue eyes soften. "Teagan told me what happened."

I drop my gaze to the floor, unsure I want to hear what she thinks of me. "I'm sorry."

"For what exactly? For falling for my daughter?"

My gaze flickers back to her, and I frown. "Well, no, but for . . . not being honest about it, I guess."

"But you have fallen for her, haven't you, Jace?" She reaches out and places a hand over mine as I shrug guiltily. "I should be thanking you."

My brows rise. I'm not sure I heard her right. "Excuse me, but what?"

She smiles and there's so much affection in it, my heart clenches in my chest. "There was a time when Joe and I were so worried about her. One minute we had this vibrant, funny, energetic teenage girl and the next, she was replaced with someone we didn't recognize. She was sullen, cynical, and withdrawn. We went round and round with her, asking if something happened, asking how we could help. Eventually, we got to the point where we feared pushing might be hurting more than it was helping, so we stopped. After a while, she got a little better and we saw a glimmer of her old self, so we let it go entirely. But she never really returned to being the carefree version of Brynn she was before."

She shakes her head, emotion swirling in the soft blue of her eyes, and I have to force myself to glance away, afraid she'll see in my expression that I know. That Brynn told me about the night that changed her.

"That is, until this week." My head lifts. "This week, she was happier than I've seen her in a long time. The brooding, cynical girl was gone, and in her place stood the bright young lady I thought we'd lost. I suspected a boy might be the reason, which is why I asked her about it." She shrugs, holding her hands out, palms up. "Mom's intuition. Looks like I was right."

I shake my head. "I don't know about all that."

"I do." Nikki tips her head and squeezes my arm. "I'm not saying there aren't other factors that caused the change, but you were definitely a huge part of that."

I swallow, my previous guilt returning with a vengeance. "I'm sorry we didn't tell you."

"Eh," she shrugs and waves a hand as if it's nothing, "I can understand why you didn't. Teagan can be . . . overprotective." She grins. "But he'll get over it. In fact, I suspect he's already getting over it right now."

"I don't know . . ." I want to believe her, but the look in Teagan's eyes is seared into my memory.

"Well, I do." She slaps her hands on her legs as if the conversation is over and her word is final.

I wish it were that easy.

"I also want you to know that you're welcome in our home any time, even if you're not dating my daughter or friends with my son."

Doubt creeps into my head and my heart, but she must see whatever expression plays over my face because she adds, "I only asked you to leave yesterday because you both needed to cool off." She cocks her head and grimaces. "*And* because you two broke my favorite lamp." She points at me. "Teagan's paying for that. As for Brynn, I don't know what all happened between you two, but I can tell you that most things can be fixed. You just have to want them bad enough."

Her words are a balm to my wounded heart. "I want her more than anything."

Nikki grins. "So, what are you waiting for?"

"I don't think she—"

Nikki reaches out and clasps my face in her hand, forcing me to look at her. "Maybe it's time you realize you're worthy of love and what that means. Just because you make a mistake doesn't mean you can't be forgiven."

CHAPTER 40

JACE

Once Nikki leaves, I sink back down onto the couch as my mind wanders.

Could it really be that simple? If I pursue Brynn and refuse to let her push me away, will she come around? Will Teagan?

Something tells me there's more to Brynn taking a step back from us. After Crow's Creek, she might've been upset about how everything went down, but not enough to push me away. It wasn't until . . .

The jewelry box.

The second it fell and split open, she went into panic mode.

I replay the moment in my mind, recalling how she seemed shocked to discover the leather bracelet belonged to Knox. But why the hell did she have it if she didn't know who it belonged to?

Another memory from weeks ago, fights its way through my subconscious. The night I drove Brynn home from her triple date, when she got all weird on me. Chris had been asking why she hated me so much, which I came to find out later was the result of a misunderstanding the night of her attack. She thought my snarky remark was directed toward her and not Graham. I'd seen her shoving the same wooden box back into her bag, then.

A chill creeps down my spine.

Something tells me the contents of the jewelry box have to do with the night she was assaulted. It's the only thing that makes sense.

But if that's true, then Knox's bracelet must have something to do with it.

I couldn't see his face, it was too dark . . .

I tried to flee, pushing and clawing, when something snagged on the strap of my dress and ripped it . . .

I swallow. Could it have been the leather cuff? It would explain why she didn't know whose it was. But that means . . .

I stand and hurry down the hallway for the kitchen, wincing as my head throbs harder with every step. My cell phone sits on the massive island where I left it, and I swipe it up, opening my text messages.

I take a deep breath as I find Knox in my contacts. I run a hand over my mouth as I stare down at his name, remembering what he said at breakfast the other morning. *Did you get in trouble with a chick? Maybe take things too far when she was drunk or .*

. . Man, any time you have a secret this big which you're keeping from your brothers, it's bound to hurt.

My stomach roils as I type out a text and hit send before I lose my nerve, hoping I'm just paranoid.

> **ME**: Hey, man, just sitting here reminiscing about old times. Remember that leather cuff your mom gave you for Christmas sophomore year? The one we bullied your ass about? Whatever happened to that?

My heart pounds in my throat as I clutch the phone in my hand, my knuckles turning white as I wait. I'm almost certain I'm wrong. I'm simply overreacting, high on emotions or hungover—maybe both—and my imagination is running wild.

My stomach clenches when text bubbles dance across the screen, indicating he's typing.

> **KNOX**: LOL of course I remember. You guys insisted on calling it a bracelet, made fun of my ass so bad I stopped wearing it.

> **ME**: You still have it?

Maybe I'm being obvious, but I don't have two shits to give.

I groan, bowing my head as I think about my next response. I can't exactly call him out on it until I talk to Brynn. It's a huge accusation to make—a crazy one—without confirming my suspicions first, and it's entirely possible I'm jumping to conclusions, but my gut tells me I'm right.

My head spins as I try to make sense of how someone I thought I knew so well could do something so sick.

I close my eyes, thinking back to that night, but my memory is fuzzy. For me, it was just another lame high school dance—a chance to drink, hook up, and have fun with my friends. Funny how the same moment in time can be inconsequential to one person while being pivotal for another.

I vaguely recall Knox going stag, but I can't be sure. Shortly after the dance, he asked Carrie out and they'd been an item ever since. Now I wonder if that was calculated. Maybe in his post-assault paranoia, he thought suddenly having a girlfriend would be a good diversion.

Fuck, I feel like a crazy person.

Am I really accusing him of this?

I need to talk to Brynn. It's the only way to know for sure, but it would certainly explain why she suddenly pushed me away. It's not like my behavior that night helped matters. I gave her a reason not to trust me. And so, when I shocked her by telling her the cuff belonged to Knox, all her old fears and insecurities rose to the surface.

She didn't think I'd believe her.

CHAPTER 41

BRYNN

THE SCENT OF GRILLED meat fills the air as I step out onto the back porch behind my mother. Smoke curls out of the grill where my father is flipping burgers, the sizzling sound mingling with the conversations floating around me and the soft music trickling through the outdoor speakers. Somewhere in the background, a dog barks and children scream. It's a normal summer afternoon, the kind I love. But I stand on the concrete, numbly staring out at the familiar faces clustered around the folding tables in the backyard. I begged off the first hour of the barbeque, using my freshly broken heart as an excuse to be antisocial until my mother practically dragged me out of bed, threw a sundress at me, and told me to get dressed.

Now I groan as I squint into the sun.

Teagan raises a hand, motioning for me to join him and the boys, and though several girls sit with them, they're coupled up, and I'm not in the mood to be reminded that I can no longer claim that title.

A burly figure sinks down beside Teagan, and my stomach wrenches. I'm also not in the mood to go anywhere near Knox if I can help it.

It's my fault he's here. I should've told Teagan. I'm not sure what I'm waiting for, but I just couldn't seem to choke the words out any time I tried.

Our eyes lock across the wide expanse of yard, and maybe I'm imagining things, but I swear I see nerves flicker in the dark depths of his eyes.

Turning, I quickly dart for the back door, my stomach in my throat as my mother catches my arm and turns me right back around again.

I focus on breathing as I cross the backyard, sinking down into a chair beside my little sisters at the furthest table while I try to calm my racing heart. The only way I'm getting back inside is if I tell my mother everything, and I'd rather not spoil her party, so instead, I try my best to get through the meal.

I keep my gaze trained only on the table in front of me, offering my mother a tight smile as she takes the seat across from me and pushes a plate of food at me like I'm a child. I want to barf at the thought of eating, but I know she's worried and won't let up until I do, so I take a few bites.

Teagan's laughter floats toward me, but I avoid gazing in his direction to see what's so funny. As far as I'm concerned, their little table doesn't exist. Although he makes them pretty hard to ignore when he appears a minute later and begs me to join them. When I refuse, I know he takes it personally. He thinks I'm still angry with him, and maybe I am, but it's as if all those walls right after the incident have risen again. I feel more alone now than I have in a long time. I'm on an island by myself, the waves of my secrets swiftly eroding my shores. Only this time, it's not because I'm afraid of *what* happened; I'm afraid of *who*.

When I can't stand another minute longer, I push my plate away and rise at the same time the music from the stereo turns off, blasting us into silence.

My mom startles and starts to rise just as a new song clicks on and she settles back down. "Ain't No Mountain High Enough" blasts through the backyard, a startling contrast to the pop music playing previously.

I rise from my seat and turn to head for the house when Jace steps out of the French doors and onto the patio.

I freeze. The breath catches in my lungs at the sight of him. He's dressed casually, his dark hair perfectly messy from running his hands through it, and even from here, his blue eyes find mine, piercing straight through me.

I have no idea what he's doing here. For a moment, I think maybe he and Teagan have made amends, and maybe my brother asked him to come. But a quick glance in my brother's direction and the crease in his brow tells me that's not the case.

I expect him to close the gap, to come closer and ask me if we can talk. But instead, he stands there, his eyes on me the whole time until I finally I ask in a quiet voice that barely rises above the music, "What are you doing here?"

The corner of his mouth quirks in one of his breathtaking smirks as he says, "I'll skip the part where I ask if you're available for bar mitzvahs or birthday parties because that won't make sense, and go right to the part where I tell you I've forgotten something back home."

I frown, confused.

He waves a hand toward me and says, "This is the part where you ask what it was I forgot, and then I say, I realize I forgot to kiss you."

"What the hell?" someone says from behind, but Jace's gaze never wavers from mine as he takes another step closer while my mind tries to catch up.

"Then we'll skip the whole awkward part where you invite me inside and uh"—he clears his throat, glancing at my mother—"and head right to the ending, which is the best part, really. Only there's one thing Darcy didn't get right," he says, and it clicks, what he's doing.

The music.

Everything he's saying.

He's recreating the end of *Bridget Jones's Diary* for me.

I cover my mouth with my hands, afraid to laugh, afraid to allow my heart to soar like it wants to.

"That ending was perfect," I say. "What did Darcy possibly get wrong?"

Jace steps even closer, until he can reach out and touch me. "He forgot to tell her he loves her. Because I love you, Cupcake. I have for a while."

A burst of startled laughter comes from behind me. Probably from one of his friends thinking this is some kind of joke. I'm too busy reminding myself to breathe as I stare up at Jace to care.

Because he loves me. Jace Taggart freaking loves me.

And I love him back.

The staggering realization sweeps through, nearly knocking me off my feet. "Can you say that again?" I ask. "Just one more time to be sure I heard you right?"

Laughter rumbles around me.

"Wait. He's serious?" a voice says. "Is this for real?"

"I *said*, I love you." The muscle in Jace's jaw flexes as he reaches out, taking my fingers in his hands. "I don't care who knows it or hears it, and I certainly don't give a damn about anyone's approval but yours. I should've owned it from the start because you're the best thing that's ever happened to me. Because I love you, and I'd rather have you and nothing else at all, than everything without you."

My lips part only to allow a soft cry to escape while my heart splinters. I want to reach up and wrap my arms around his neck, stretch onto my toes and kiss him, but something holds me back. And I know what it is. "Jace, I . . ." My voice cracks and my chest swells with emotion, taking up too much space for words.

"Had you given me the choice, had it been between you or telling everyone, I would've chosen you," he says, his voice low.

"I just got scared, but I promise from here on out, every time I'll choose you. If I could go back and change it—"

Unable to take it any longer, I reach up and slide my hands onto the nape of his neck as I pull him to me, pressing my mouth against his.

Applause erupts around us, starting as a whisper and turning into a dull roar. Until he pulls back and grins down at me with a twinkle in his eye.

"Don't you have something to say to me?" He arches a brow, and I frown as the applause dies down and the familiar notes of "Ain't No Mountain High Enough" hit a crescendo, and I laugh.

"Maybe I need to kiss you better." He frowns before he parts my lips with his one more time and the people around us fade away until all that's left is us and this perfect moment he created, teasing and tasting and leaving me breathless.

A grin skates over my mouth, turning into a full-blown smile. I pull back and say, "Wait a minute . . . nice guys don't kiss like that."

He fists a hand beside me, whispering in my ear for only me. "Oh, yes, they fucking do."

I laugh before he can kiss me again, but I can see in his eyes that he wants to. "How did you remember that?"

"I remember everything about you, Cupcake, remember?"

My fingers play with the hair on the nape of his neck, and I know that even though I'm scared, I love him, and it's unfair of me to doubt him, to make his decisions for him. I owe it to myself and to him to see this through, to give him a chance. "I love you, Jace," I say before we're bombarded. "I love you so damn much my heart hurts."

He exhales, melting into me with what I think is relief as he presses his forehead to mine. "Thank God."

People come at us from all sides. Graham shoves him in the shoulder, eyes wide. "Dude. Teagan mentioned this possibility, but . . . well, I have no idea how the hell this happened, but congrats, man."

"You two are adorable," Mackenzie chimes in, giving me a little squeeze.

"Dude." Atlas glances between Jace and Teagan. "I can't believe you fucking kissed her like that and you're still alive. Is this okay, man?" he asks, his gaze resting on my brother.

Teagan's woolly gaze falls on Jace, and everyone falls silent as we wait for his response. "I was wrong," Teagan says, sticking a hand out for Jace to shake. "You're family, and I should've given you the benefit of the doubt."

Jace accepts his hand, his throat bobbing as he says, "Thanks, man, and I'm sorry, too. I should've told you."

Teagan shakes his head. "You're like a brother to me, and I know that if I can trust anyone with her, it's you. Hell, that's why I asked you to watch out for her. I hope we're still cool."

A soft smile curls the corners of Jace's lips. "We're cool. I probably would've done the same in your shoes."

A dozen other people rise to their feet and approach us, all of them asking us about our relationship, when we started dating, and how.

I guess when you barely date through all of high school, then leave for college only to return two months later to a guy publicly professing his love for you, it leads to a lot of curiosity. I'm about to hit my limit when Jace's gaze finds mine above the crowd and he nods toward the house, mouthing, "Let's talk."

I extricate myself from the conversations around me as politely as I can, then quietly slip into the house beside Jace.

JACE

I try not to rush Brynn as she closes the door behind me, but it's taking all my restraint not to blurt out the question on my mind, the one thing running circles through all my thoughts.

Was it Knox?

Instead, I enter her room and cross the floor, my muscles as restless as my thoughts while I pace in front of her bed.

Brynn said she loves me.

My heart swells at the memory.

She fucking loves me, and at the end of the day, that's all that matters.

"Jace, there's something I need to tell you."

"Okay," I drawl, ceasing my pacing and shoving my hands in my pockets to hide my clenched fists.

"When I broke up with you, it wasn't because I thought you were putting your friends first and me last. Not really. I was scared. I pushed you away because . . ."

Here we go.

My heart pounds like a drum. "Because . . .?"

Her throat bobs, and my gaze homes in on the delicate skin at her throat. The insatiable desire to kill anyone who hurts her floods my veins.

"You wouldn't believe me if I told you."

My gaze flickers back to hers. "Try me."

Her mouth flattens, and I can see the storm of indecision in her eyes; I can tell it's weighing on her by the dark moons beneath them and the pinched set of her brow. Holding onto this secret is killing her.

Moving closer, I take her hands in mine and dip my head so we're at eye level. "Did you mean it when you said you loved me, Cupcake? Because I meant it." When she nods, I add, "Then trust me. Trust *us.* Whatever it is, you can tell me."

I could ask her right now. I could outright tell her my suspicions and all she would have to do is confirm them, but I *need* her to take this leap of faith. I need her to trust that I'll cradle her heart in my hands and protect it.

"I didn't know until the other night, when you were in my room and we were talking about the bonfire and how poorly it all went. You helped me with my suitcase and the little wooden jewelry box fell . . ." Her words trail off, but I nod for her to continue. "The bracelet, you said it was Knox's and asked why I had it . . ."

I close my eyes, waiting for the blow I know is coming.

"It was Knox, Jace." Her voice trips over the words, trembling like a leaf in the wind, fragile and lost. "The cuff caught on the strap of my dress when I was fighting him off that night. I never knew whose it was until now."

A soft moan escapes the back of my throat; my worst fears confirmed.

I want to run outside and see the fear in his eyes as I approach. Rip his throat out with my bare hands. Bloody his face with my fists.

How could he do this?

I've known him for years. Put everything out there on the field, with him by my side. We went to school dances, parties, family gatherings. We even got matching Rebels tattoos.

He let Graham lean on him after Kenzie's car crash, attended her mother's funeral.

He visited Atlas and Graham in the hospital after their accidents this past year.

He's not just a friend. He's a teammate, a brother.

But all this time he's been the devil in disguise . . .

A sob escapes the back of Brynn's throat, reminding me of what's most important. She's all that matters. Making sure she's okay, and that she knows I believe her. So, I fight the urge to take care of Knox and take care of her instead.

My arms come around her, and the dam on her emotions breaks. The floodgates open as her tears soak into my shirt while I rub her arms, her back, trying my best to comfort her. I whisper that everything's going to be okay over and over in her ear, feeling fucking useless because there's nothing else I can say or do to make her pain go away.

Eventually, her breathing evens out and her tears subside. She pulls away by the tiniest of fractions, and stares up at me through wet eyes. "I was so afraid you wouldn't believe me," she says, her voice scratchy from crying. "I thought you'd take his word over mine."

"Never." I shake my head, brushing the hair from her eyes.

"I'm so sorry," she whispers.

"Don't ever apologize for this." I swipe my thumbs beneath her eyes, wiping away the soft mascara smudges, before I place a gentle kiss over her head. "You okay?" I ask her.

She nods and glances up at me. "But I *am* sorry I doubted you."

"What did I say about apologizing?" I drag my hands down her arms. "I can't imagine how you felt when you realized . . ." I trail off, my throat constricting as anger shoots through me, bright and sharp like a shooting star.

"What are you gonna do?" she asks, looking up at me from underneath the fringe of her lashes.

I exhale a ragged breath because what I want to do and what I should do are probably two very different things. "I don't know."

She searches my expression as my jaw tightens. I have no idea what she sees on my face, but I can't imagine I'm succeeding at hiding the fury running through my veins.

"Can we go to your place for a while?" she asks.

The question surprises me, and I wonder briefly if she's worried about what I might do to Knox when she adds, "I want to go somewhere so we can be alone. Somewhere we won't get interrupted. I just need time with you."

I nod, relief blooming inside my chest. For a moment, I was afraid she was going to ask me to let this go, and I'm not sure I'm capable of pretending that I don't know one of my best friends is a monster. "Of course. Whatever you need," I say because I would give this girl the fucking world if I could.

She sniffs and takes a step back. "Let me just clean up really quick." When she tips her head toward the bathroom, I force a smile.

"Take your time. Meet you downstairs?"

I watch as she nods and heads for the bathroom, waiting until she closes the door to leave the room.

I take the stairs two at a time with one destination in mind.

For Knox's sake, he better pray he's gone when I get there because if not, I don't trust myself to stop until he's no longer breathing.

My feet hit the landing, echoing in the walls around me, joining the sound of voices trickling to me from the living room. I round the corner, passing Teagan who's standing in the entryway. They must've slipped inside when Brynn and I retreated to her room.

"Hey, where's—" Teagan starts, but I don't give him time to finish before I zero in on Knox, propped on the arm of a chair in the Nichols' living room.

I head straight for him, giving him no time to react as I cock my arm and pop him in the mouth. The blow is so hard he falls from the chair onto the floor.

I idly recognize the sound of someone screaming as I hover above him while he covers his face like the fucking coward he is.

"Are you insane?" Graham calls out, grabbing at my arms while I pin Knox to the ground with a hand around his throat.

"I know what you fucking did," I grind out, staring into the ice of his blue eyes. "And you're going to fucking pay for it."

I watch as Knox's face turns red. His cheeks puff. But all I see is the red haze of rage.

I could kill him and die a happy man, of this I'm sure.

"What the hell is going on?" Teagan comes up behind me and yanks at my arm while I fight him off.

"Get the hell off me," I hiss as Graham helps. "Let me at him!"

Together, they manage to pin my arms behind my back. I thrash and pull and yank against their hold on me, bucking like a wild animal. My teeth gnash together, my face hot with pure, unadulterated hatred. "You're a fucking monster!"

The darks of Knox's eyes dilate as he drags in a breath, a hand at his throat as he scrambles to stand up. "What the hell, man?"

A spurt of dark laughter bubbles from my lips.

I stop fighting Teagan and Graham, so they let up, but Atlas shifts to hover in the space between us, and I'm vaguely aware of Mackenzie and Skylar cowering in the corner.

"Knox, what's he talking about?" Teagan asks, his gaze shifting between us.

"Yeah, Knox, tell him." I jerk my head, my lips curling in disgust.

"You're fucking crazy," Knox spits out, wiping the blood off his busted lip, and I charge him again. I get another right hook in, catching the side of his face and grazing his jaw as Atlas hooks his arms under mine, and hauls me away again.

"Let me fucking go!" I scream.

This time when Teagan talks, he addresses his attention to me. "What did he do? What's going on?"

I stare at him for a moment, debating my choices. It's not my story to tell, but I also kind of blew Brynn's cover by losing my shit.

I have no idea what to do, but when I hear footsteps behind me, I turn to see Brynn.

She hovers at the entrance to the living room, her wide eyes taking in her surroundings. Knox's bloody lip and Atlas pinning my hands behind my back are dead giveaways. And when she meets my gaze, all of the fear, anger, and shame she's ever felt about her assault moves through the violet of her eyes like a riptide, threatening to suck her under.

Maybe I should regret my actions. Maybe I should never have touched Knox, but I can't find it in me to feel remorse. He deserves to pay for what he's done, and the only thing I'd do differently next time is wait until no one else was in the room.

But if she's ever wanted closure on what happened to her, now is the time. This is her chance, surrounded by people who love her. People who will protect her.

"Brynn . . ." I rasp out, my voice a plea. My eyes conveying what she already knows, that she needs to tell them.

She inhales a sharp breath, then turns to Teagan and says, "It was Knox."

Teagan's brow furrows, unable to connect the dots. His mouth parts, trying to comprehend what she's telling him, but she beats him to the punchline.

"Teagan, it was Knox who assaulted me sophomore year."

All the blood drains from Teagan's face.

Pity replaces the anger in my stomach as I watch him slowly comprehend what she's told him.

"What's she talking about?" Teagan glances at Knox, his voice barely above a whisper.

Knox snorts. "How the fuck should I know? She's as crazy as he is." He jerks his head toward me. "You deserve each other."

"I'll fucking kill you," I say, trying once more to get to him, but Atlas' arms are like steel traps, holding me down.

Atlas grunts with the exertion. "Just wait a fucking minute," he grinds out.

Teagan steps forward, and I stop struggling with Atlas to see what he'll do. "Was it you?" he asks, his tone oddly detached.

"Hell, no," Knox yells, his nostrils flaring.

Brynn steps forward, her steps slow and deliberate as she walks by me, brushing past Teagan, and coming to a stop only a foot in front of Knox, lifting her chin. Holding her fist out, she uncurls her fingers like the fronds of a fern slowly unwinding, to reveal the leather cuff nestled into the meat of her palm. "I think this belongs to you."

A hush falls over the room.

I can feel the questions swirling around us from our friends. I can hear the breath in my lungs, and the beating of my heart.

Knox swallows, and it's then that I see it. The split second of worry flickering in his eyes, the guilt that he's been found out. But it's replaced as quickly as it appeared, by a hardened look that shows no remorse. The muscle in his jaw ticks as he stares wordlessly at the bracelet. "So?"

"It snagged on my dress when you put your hands on me." Tears glisten in her eyes. "The bracelet caught on my strap and tore it." She tips her head. "Do you remember? Because I do. I remember everything from that night."

A deafening roar comes from beside me like a charging bull at the same time Teagan flies at Knox. His fist connects with his chin. But he's wild with anger, and Knox delivers one back before he growls at us to control him.

Across from me, Graham folds his arms over his chest. And behind me, Atlas' arms fall. A subtle acknowledgment of whose side they're on. Teagan lands another blow to Knox's face, this time popping him in the nose. He stumbles back, and Teagan's on him again, lifting him by his shirt as his fist thuds on the side of his face. The rest of us watch on, equal parts shocked, angry, and regretful.

"Enough!" Brynn calls from behind at the same time Knox falls back against the entertainment unit, knocking the television from the stand where it falls to the floor with a crash.

"I don't know what to fucking do. Do we stop them?" Atlas asks.

I shake my head, watching Knox with a sick kind of fascination as Teagan lands another blow, then reaches out and grabs his throat.

"Jace!" Brynn comes to my side, gripping my arm in her hands, her eyes wide with alarm. "You have to stop them. He's gonna kill him."

I stand there entranced by my need for vengeance as I stare into her eyes, torn between being the better man and wanting him to pay. But I can see this is upsetting her, and that's the last thing I want, so I nod and step forward just as Knox makes a feeble attempt to defend himself and they fall to the ground.

I cross the room in two long strides and Atlas and Graham help me pry them apart. "It's over," I grind out. "Stop."

Atlas and I each handle Teagan, and I hiss when a fist meant for Knox connects with my lip. In the meantime, Graham shoves Knox toward the door as Teagan points at him. "You better never show your fucking face again, or I'll finish this, you hear me?"

"She went to that locker room willingly," Knox says, both an admission and what I imagine he hopes is a defense while his gaze darts around the room, hoping to find someone on his side.

My pupils flare and I take a step forward, ready to kill him myself when Brynn touches my arm. "Jace . . ."

Beside me Teagan, clenches his jaw and wrestles in Atlas' arms like a rabid dog, and I turn to him, gripping his face in my hands. "Let it rest now," I say, meeting his fiery gaze. "It's over. Brynn wants it to be over."

His nostrils flare, his chest heaving as he shakes his head at the same time the slamming of the door draws our attention to the front door. Outside the large windows we see Knox jog down the Nichols' yard toward his car.

Teagan darts to the door, but I hold onto him like a lifeline. "Let him go."

"What the hell . . .?"

I close my eyes as Mrs. Nichols' voice echoes through the room. When I blink them open, Teagan's face is ashen as his gaze swings toward the sound.

Nikki stares at the mess around us. "Not again. Teagan . . ." Her gaze bounces between us, and I hang my head.

I have no idea how we're going to explain this one, and I'm not looking forward to trying, but to my surprise, Brynn steps forward and grabs her mother's arm. "Mom, I have something I need to tell you guys." When her voice breaks on the words, the bloom of anger fades from her mother's cheeks, and she nods.

"Okay. Let me go get your father."

As soon as she leaves the room, Teagan turns toward our friends. "You guys should probably go."

We watch as they quickly right the furniture, then head for the door and say their goodbyes, with Mackenzie pulling Brynn in close as she murmurs, "Call me any time, you hear?"

Brynn nods, and the rest of them leave one by one. They probably have more questions than answers, but an explanation will have to wait for another time; Brynn has to deal with more pressing things.

Nikki and Joe rush into the room not more than a minute later, and I turn to leave, giving Brynn's hand a squeeze as do. But, she pulls me back.

"Stay."

CHAPTER 42

BRYNN

J ACE AND TEAGAN FLANK me on the couch and my parents sit across from us in stunned silence. Mom glances at me through watery eyes, her cheeks wet from crying while I explained everything. My father hands her a tissue, his face pinched. I wonder if he's thinking about dragging Knox back to the house to finish what Jace and Teagan started.

Mom reaches out and takes my free hand while Jace holds onto the other. "I wish you'd told us. You know we would've helped you. We could've been there. I suspected something happened, but never in a million years—" Her words choke on a sob.

"Mom," I squeeze her hand. "It's not your fault you weren't there for me. I should've told you. I wish I would have now, but . . ." I swallow, searching for the right words to explain myself so I can put her at ease. "Afterward, I was scared and . . . ashamed about a lot of things. I put myself in a really bad situation that could've ended a whole lot worse, for one. And I guess I thought if I shoved it down, it might go away. Then, when I told Teagan, it was enough to get me by, so I just dealt with it the only way I could. I'm sorry."

She glances at my father, her eyes frantically searching his face. "What do we do now?"

My stomach clenches with the question because all I want is for this nightmare to be over. I faced Knox. I got closure, and even if I wanted him to pay, I'm not foolish enough to think there might be any viable legal recourse we can take. Even if they found Knox guilty, he was a minor at the time. He'd get a slap on the wrist for an assault charge. It's certainly not worth dragging my story into the local media and reliving the whole nightmare over again.

My dad sighs, his hands fisting on his lap. "Maybe we should ask Brynn what she wants?"

I straighten, glancing at the two boys beside me. The warm hazel of Teagan's gaze burns through me, waiting, while the languid blue of Jace's anchors me. Both give me the strength I need. "I want to enjoy the last week of break, then go back to school in the fall with my boyfriend," I say as Jace squeezes my hand. "I'd like to live my life without this hanging over my head for once, and I finally feel like I can do that."

I inhale a ragged breath. "It's over," I say, realizing for the first time it's true. "For so long, I kept holding onto what happened as some sort of reminder not to drop my guard, to be careful, and to learn from my mistakes while rebuilding my life. But I'm done doing that. I've rebuilt my life already. I've stopped being angry and scared all the time, and now I just want to *live*. I want to put this in the past where it belongs. I don't want to rake his name through the mud only to suffer alongside him."

Mom's forehead creases. I can tell she wants more, but I also know even if we pursue anything, she won't get it.

Beside me, Teagan wraps an arm around my shoulders. "Knox lost his friends and his dignity today," he tells me, shrugging his shoulders. "Let's leave it at that."

Mom drags in a breath before both she and my father rise to their feet and cross the rug to draw me in for a hug. I stand there for what feels like an eternity, letting them hold me, knowing they need it more than I do. I've had years to cope with the resulting trauma from that night while they've only had minutes.

"Well, now that the party is over and everyone went home, can we all have supper together?" Mom asks, wiping at her still-damp cheeks. "I'll order in."

I bite my lip and glance up at Jace. Though I wanted to be alone with him, I know my parents need to be near me right now, so they can see me protected and laughing and happy. And it's the least I can do after keeping this secret. "Jace?" I ask.

"Of course." His eyes soften before he glances up at my parents. "But if we watch a movie after, and I know we will, I'm picking."

"Uh, not so fast," I say, chiming in. "We need something uplifting, not an action flick where half the cast dies or they're running for their lives."

"Um, you just lived a chick flick," he says, motioning to the French doors that lead to the backyard. "What more could you want? A little action and violence sound amazing right now."

"I'm with Jace," Teagan chimes in.

"I'll third that," Dad says.

My mouth drops open, and I glance between the three of them. "So this is how it's gonna be now? You guys all ganging up on me?"

Teagan shrugs. "You, Mom, and the girls used to have the numbers, but it's equal ground now."

"Um, there's still four of us girls and three guys."

"But Sabel and Trista don't count 'cos they'll be in bed," Jace argues.

"I can't believe this," I say as Jace wraps his arms around me. "You're supposed to side with me."

Behind us Teagan groans. "Guys, seriously. No PDA. The sappy little scene in the backyard was enough to last a lifetime. Give a guy a break, will ya?"

I laugh, catching Mom's smile as she beams over at us with fresh tears in her eyes, glancing between her children.

I know that smile, and I know the sparkle in her eyes.

Just like I know she's right.

I'm damn lucky to have both of them.

JACE

We sit around a table at Roasted like old times, clutching cups of coffee in our hands. Only, instead of shooting the breeze and catching up, our conversation takes on a more ominous tone, and where there used to be five of us, there are only four.

"Wow." Graham stares into the abyss as everything Teagan and I just told them sinks in.

Though they gathered the gist of what happened at the Nichols' residence, we knew they wanted answers, so with Brynn's approval, Teagan and I asked Graham and Atlas to join us for coffee. It's the first time we've seen them since the barbeque, and even though I wish our time spent together didn't have to be so heavy, I couldn't have asked for better friends.

"Fuck. You think you know someone . . ." Atlas trails off and we all nod in agreement.

Lifting his head, Graham asks, "You guys okay?"

Teagan and I glance at each other. "Yeah, we're good," I say.

"And Brynn, she's . . . coping?"

"Brynn's strong." Of that, I'm sure.

"Luckily, she has this guy here, too," Teagan says, slapping a hand over my shoulder.

"Fuck, who would've thought you two would become an item?" Graham asks, and we all laugh, needing the levity.

"Not me." I smirk.

"Not Brynn, either. That's some real hate-to-love shit right there," Atlas says, and we burst out laughing again.

"What can I say?" I shrug, turning to Teagan. "Your sister's irresistible."

Teagan groans. "You're such a fucking sap now."

"Yeah, wasn't it you just a little over two months ago telling us, and I quote, 'If I *ever* get this whipped over a woman, someone please put me out of my misery'?" Graham snickers.

"Should we do you in now or later?" Atlas asks, deadpan.

"Hey, I'm not whipped." *Yet.*

Teagan arches a brow. "Okay, dude."

"I'm not," I protest a little too hard.

"You should see these two together. They're so mushy it makes me sick," Teagan says.

"Based on his little *Bridget Jones's Diary* display in the backyard the other day, we're inclined to believe you," Graham says, and I flip him the bird.

"Hey, they don't call it a fucking grand gesture for nothing."

Teagan laughs. "Whatever. I just can't wait until you two and all your PDA are back in Michigan, so I don't have to see it anymore."

"Jealous?" I smirk. "After all, you're the only single dope left."

"Ah, may I remind you, before Brynn, these guys were the dopey ones," he says, waving a hand toward Atlas and Graham who watch on with equally amused expressions. "And now, *I'm* the dope?"

I shrug. "You said it, not me."

Teagan snorts. "Yeah, well, just remember what Brynn's like when she's pissed. Because your first fight is coming, and then follows the inevitable groveling."

I frown. "Didn't we just have our first fight?"

"No," Atlas and Graham say at the same time.

"Whatever. A fight just means make-up sex."

"True." Atlas nods.

"He has a point," Graham adds.

I turn my smug smile to Teagan who groans and plugs his ears. "TMI. I do *not* want to think about you and my sister. Not now. Not ever. Got it?"

I shrug. "I'll try, but I can't promise anything. Your sister's fucking hot."

"Dude, seriously?" Teagan throws his hands up.

"This is gonna be fun." Graham leans back in his seat with a grin and takes a sip of coffee.

"I concur." Atlas rubs his chin, eyeing us. "I like this new dynamic."

"We'll get a lot of mileage out of it."

Teagan and I groan, and our eyes meet for a brief moment before I shake my head and smile, thinking about how lucky I am. Maybe Teagan is right. I am a fucking sap, because I have the perfect girl *and* my friends. And I'm not sure I could ask for more.

CHAPTER 43

JACE

I LIFT THE LAST of Brynn's things onto the bed of my truck, then go in search of her. I maneuver over the cobbled side-walk, through the front door, and take the steps to her bedroom two at a time, only to find her hovering in front of her closet. I lean my hip against the doorframe, taking her in from head to toe. The pink dress she's wearing is shorter than the ones I'm used to. Over the last few months, I've noticed her style of dress isn't quite so modest, which I take as both a good thing and a bad thing. Good, because she's owning the fact that showing a little more skin doesn't give someone the right to lay their hands on her. Bad, because I get pissed every time another guy checks her out. School this semester is going to be brutal.

"You ready?" I ask.

"Yeah." She turns, and my breath catches at the wooden box in her hands. Lifting her gaze to mine, she nods for me to follow as she enters the adjoining bathroom to her room and slides the wastebasket out from beside the sink. Opening the lid of the jewelry box, she lifts the leather cuff out and stares at it one last time before she chucks it into the can. The wooden box with the note follows, and then she removes the trash bag and ties it, handing it to me as she says, "Do you want the honors of taking the trash out?"

"Me?" I point to my chest, and she nods. "You sure?"

I don't know all the reasons she's held onto this for so long, but I want to make sure she's ready to part with it.

Her answering smile puts me at ease. "I think it's about time, don't you?"

I don't say anything. Instead, I lean forward and press a brief kiss over her mouth because this girl . . . she gets me every fucking time. I'm so damn proud.

I grab her hand in mine, holding the bag with the other as we descend the stairs together, exiting the house via the garage, pausing at the giant trash can waiting to relieve us of the garbage in my hands.

"My mom and dad said goodbye and they love you, by the way." Brynn grins. "They were bummed they couldn't be here this morning to see us off. Also, Mom *might* have loaded me up with about five dozen cookies for you and Chris."

I grin. "Too bad Chris will never see a single crumb. Fall season means our nutrition needs to be at the top of our game."

Brynn laughs. "You're cruel."

We step outside, underneath an overcast sky gray with clouds, and amble down the driveway to find Teagan waiting for us, legs crossed as he leans against my truck.

He lifts a chin. "You got everything?"

I glance over at Brynn and her nose scrunches a little as she smiles. "Yep. I think we're ready." I squeeze her hand. "You leaving for school today, too?" I ask, glancing back up at Teagan.

Teagan shakes his head. "I decided to wait until tomorrow to head out. I still have some shit to pack."

"Well, drive safely because the next time we see each other, it'll probably be on the field kicking your ass." I clap him on the back, and he snorts.

"More like wiping my ass when I make you eat the turf."

I tip my head back and laugh while Brynn shakes her head. "Can't you just cheer each other on?"

"Have a killer season, man," I say, dabbing him up.

"You know it." Teagan brings me in for a one-armed hug and claps me on the back. "Watch after her for me, yeah?"

I lean back and look him in the eyes, serious as I nod. "Of course, I will."

Teagan nods and turns to Brynn, wrapping her up in a giant bear hug and lifting her off her feet with a growl. When he sets her back down, he ruffles her hair as she swats his hand away. "Take care lil' sis."

"Four minutes!" she screams.

"Those were a long ass four minutes." He points. "Just ask Mom."

Brynn snorts.

"And just because I ship you two now," he says, pointing between us, "doesn't mean I won't kill you if you hurt her." He pauses at me, and I raise my hands.

"Noted. But you don't have to worry," I say, wrapping an arm around Brynn's waist and drawing her in. "She's safe with me."

"All right, get going, you two." Teagan waves toward the truck. "I can sense a kiss coming any minute, and I've seen enough of that in the last week to last a lifetime."

I bark out a laugh as I round the truck and help Brynn inside.

"Text me when you get there," Teagan adds.

"Okay, Dad." I smirk as Teagan gives me the middle finger, and I climb inside.

The engine rumbles to life when I turn the key, and I glance over at Brynn. "Ready?"

"Ready," she smiles, and we offer Teagan one last wave as we pull out of sight.

I park my truck outside the dorms, and I can't help but think back to that early day in June when Brynn found me leaning against her mother's car. She was so pissed; I could see the steam coming from her ears.

I grin as I help her down from the truck.

"What are you smiling about?"

I shake my head and place a soft kiss on her lips, grinning like a fool, still getting used to the idea I can kiss her whenever I want and she won't deck me. I'm kind of loving it. "Nothing. Just how much I love you."

"Liar."

I laugh as I grab two of her suitcases and we head inside.

She got her new roommate assignment a week ago, and I think I'm more nervous than she is to see what she's like.

Elizabeth Brian, a totally normal name.

I know Brynn has Charlotte and Samantha, but I pray this chick is cool and they hit it off because she deserves this, and then some.

We pause in front of her room, and she knocks, but when no one answers, she glances at me. She takes a deep breath and unlocks the door, then steps inside to find it empty. "I'm the first one here," she says, and I'm both relieved and nervous.

After I carry in the rest of her stuff, we unpack her things and settle her side of the room just how she wants it. We're almost finished when we hear a knock on the door and I freeze.

Brynn meets my eyes, a flicker of nerves moving through the sparkling violet of her own before she calls out, "It's open."

A second later, a tall brunette with a single streak of purple in the front of her hair peeks her head in. I hold my breath as she takes a step inside pulling a rolling suitcase behind her, followed by two middle-aged people who I assume are her parents. "Hi," she waves a hand, flashing us a tentative smile. "I'm Elizabeth, your new roommate." She takes a step closer to Brynn, holding her hand out. "I assume you're Brynn Nichols?"

Brynn's pouty lips split into a wide smile. "That's me." Then she turns to me. "And this is my boyfriend, Jace. He's a wide receiver for the Griffins."

My attention turns to her with a grin, surprised that her comment almost sounded like bragging. I've never known Brynn to be boastful, but for some reason, it feels good when it's regarding me.

"Oh. Wow. Hi." Elizabeth cocks her head, assessing. "Do you have any friends?"

The three of us laugh before Elizabeth turns to the two figures behind her hovering in the doorway, and she waves them in. "These are my parents. Pam and Daniel."

Her mother waves. "It's so nice to meet you. Where are you all from?"

Elizabeth rolls her eyes. "Sorry in advance for the millions of questions they're about to bombard you with, but they were super worried I'd be stuck with a psychopath for a roommate. That would be the *worst*, but clearly, you're normal."

Brynn laughs lightly. "Yeah, I know exactly what you mean. That *would* be the worst."

Nearly an hour later, Brynn walks me outside to my truck to say goodbye, at least for now, and to give Elizabeth a little privacy with her parents.

I back her up against the driver's side door and lean into her with one arm propped above her head. "Are you sure I can't convince you to come back to my place?" I run my free hand down the side of her bare arm, and she shivers. "Chris won't be back until tonight."

I can see the war in her eyes before she shakes her head. "As much as I would love that, I feel like I should hang with Elizabeth and get to know her a bit, you know?"

I groan. "Fine. Get a new roommate, and I get the shaft. I see how it is."

Her answering laughter fills the emptiness in my chest. "Poor Jace."

I stick my lip out in a pout. "I know. I'm practically neglected."

Her gaze flicks to my mouth. "I guess I'll just have to make it up to you."

"Mmm. That sounds promising." I dip my head and brush my lips over her mouth, sinking into it as her hands move into my hair, threading through it as a moan rumbles in the depths of her chest.

Her lips are soft and persistent, and I yearn for more while her coconut scent sinks into my bones.

By the time I pull back, the rapid rise and fall of her chest presses against my own, and I want her even more than before.

"You know, I can share. You could just live with me during the week and with Elizabeth on the weekends."

She bites a lip, fighting a smile. "Like shared custody?"

"Precisely. But in our scenario, I'm the good parent, the favorite."

"Ooh. Should I call you Daddy?"

Heat fists in my belly as I growl and nip her lower lip. "You can't say shit like that unless you want me to throw you over my shoulder and take you back to my place."

"Is that a threat?" she asks, her voice a breathy rasp in her throat.

"Damn right it is."

I lower my mouth to hers once more, kissing her until her hands grip my waist and we both come undone. I'm about to lift her up and wrap her legs around me when someone passes by us and whistles.

Pulling away, I chuckle as I lean my forehead against the cool glass beside her head and take a deep breath. "Brynn Nichols, you're going to be the death of me."

"I think you've said that once before."

I lean back and meet her eyes. "It's true."

She grins as she gives me a chaste peck on the lips, while I groan because I know where this leads. *Nowhere.* "Do I have to leave?"

"I really think you should," she says, biting back her smile for the millionth time.

I'm glad she thinks it's funny how much I want her.

"What happened to shared custody?"

She lifts her gaze to the sky as if deep in thought. "Tomorrow's your day."

I groan as I take a step back and rake a hand through my hair. I can't think clearly when she's this close. I have half a mind to make her a genuine offer to live with me, and I would if I actually thought she'd accept. That's how serious I am about her. But I know how much having the full college experience and making girl friends means to her, so I don't.

"You'll call if you need anything?"

She nods, and when I take another step back, she steps up onto the sidewalk.

"Tell Charlotte and Samantha I said hello."

"Will do."

I point. "And tell Elizabeth this isn't over. If she even fucks up once, I'll see her in court."

Brynn laughs and rolls her eyes, then blows me a kiss, and I feel my heart fucking balloon in my chest. "Love you, Cupcake." I wink.

Crimson blooms in her cheeks. "Love you back."

EPILOGUE

BRYNN

A BURST OF CHILLY autumn air whips through the stadium, stealing my breath. The score is tied with less than a minute on the clock. My nerves are shot. I'm not sure how much I can take as I watch the guys take the field after a timeout.

I stand in the section meant for family and friends of the Griffins, wedged between my parents. My father proudly wears a Wildcats jersey to support our brother, which has earned him quite a few dirty looks from Griffin fans until I boldly shouted, "That's my brother" when Teagan caught an interception only ten minutes into the game. Now the fans around us have begrudgingly accepted we're straddling the fence. Though if I'm being honest, as proud as I am of my brother, my feet are firmly planted on Griffin ground.

Number 87, Jace's number, is emblazoned on my cheek in glittery blue paint. I'm wearing his oversized jersey with a pair of leggings and a scarf to ward off the cold.

My breath fogs out in front of me as I glance over at my mother, her hands clasped in prayer. I wonder who she's praying for, since she's wearing a jersey she handstitched, one-half Griffins, one-half Wildcats. But that's Mom, loving us all equally and not wanting to choose sides.

I watch as Jace lines up in his spot at the end of the line, and my heart does a little flip inside my chest. Watching him in uniform doing his thing is probably the sexiest thing on the face of the planet, and I have to fight my mind from drifting to places I don't want it to go with my parents beside me.

Later.

The center snaps the ball to the quarterback, and I suck in a breath, watching as Jace manages to get around the man covering him. His feet fly across the turf. He waits until he's hit his target, only feet from the end zone before he turns, arms outstretched, as Damon launches the ball in a perfect spiral.

Time slows, and I hold my breath as a defender reaches for it, nearly grabbing Jace's arm in what surely would've been a pass interference call if it weren't for Jace, quick on his feet, taking one giant step forward to meet the ball. He catches it, cradling it in his arms as he turns, weaving just out of reach, and takes a running leap into the end zone headfirst, scoring the winning touchdown.

I lift my arms in the air as screams erupt all around us.

A glance at the clock tells me there are only twenty-four seconds left in the game. Enough time for the field goal and extra point. The Griffins win.

Jace spikes the ball on the ground and turns as his teammates make a beeline straight for him. I recognize Chris by the number on his back as he smacks Jace's helmet, then grabs his face mask and yells something excitedly, then retreats. Damon is next, followed by the others. I watch them celebrate, my heart growing by the second, before he turns to the stands, finding me first before forming a heart with his gloved hands. He places it in front of his chest then points at me, and I catch my breath.

Behind his helmet, I know he's wearing one of his sexy smirks, and even from a distance, I can picture his smoldering blue eyes, and melt.

He turns to his teammates and joins in with the celebrations when out of nowhere, a player in a Wildcat jersey jogs across the field. It only takes a few minutes for me to realize it's Teagan.

They slap hands and exchange words for a moment before Jace draws him in for one of those one-armed bro hugs guys do. Once they part, they walk side by side off the field, and I'm not sure what they're doing until they continue toward us in the stands.

I descend the bleachers with my parents beside me, leaning over the railing as Jace yanks his helmet off, revealing a mass of sweat-damp hair. He jogs the rest of the way to meet me with Teagan trailing behind him, headed for my parents.

"Nice jersey, Cupcake," Jace lifts his chin and stops in front of me, his breath fogging the space between us.

I smile, leaning down to take his face in my hands, staring into the eyes of the man I love. "I thought you'd like it."

He hums under his breath as I lean closer, my mouth hovering just above his. "More than you know."

I shift at the last minute, my cheek grazing his as my lips brush the shell of his ear. "Maybe I'll let you take it off me later."

"Promise?"

"Promise," I whisper, then turn my head and kiss him.

Free Illustration!!

Join my newsletter list and get an adorable digital download illustration of Jace and Brynn together in his campus apartment! Use it as a background on your computer or screen saver. Print and frame it. Or just keep it to look and swoon at.

By joining, you'll also be the first to hear about new releases, sneak peeks, cover reveals, giveaways, and more!

Go to **graciegraham.com** and subscribe!

About Gracie

Gracie is a contemporary young adult author who loves romance and writing fictional characters. When she's not busy telling lies for a living, she's likely wrangling her three kids, cooking subpar meals, and procrastinating. Feel free to reach out to her on social media! She loves talking to readers and chatting books!

Search for her on these platforms:

Gracie's Gang (FB Group)

Facebook Page

TikTok

Instagram

Pinterest